Cathryn Hein is a best-selling rural romance and romantic adventure author. A South Australian country girl by birth, she loves nothing more than a rugged rural hero who's as good with his heart as he is with his hands, which is probably why she writes them! Her romances are warm and emotional, and feature themes that don't flinch from the tougher side of life but are often happily tempered by the antics of naughty animals. Her aim is to make you smile, sigh, and perhaps sniffle a little, but most of all feel wonderful.

With three generations of jockeys in the family it's little wonder Cathryn was born horse mad. After scoring her first horse at age 10, upon whom she bestowed the eternally romantic name of Mysty, Cathryn spent the remainder of her teenage years in equine bliss riding pony club and hunt club, and competing in eventing, dressage and showjumping until university beckoned.

Armed with a shiny Bachelor of Applied Science (Agriculture) from Roseworthy College she moved to Melbourne and later Newcastle, working in the agricultural and turf seeds industry. Her partner's posting to France took Cathryn overseas for three years in Provence where she finally gave in to her life-long desire to write.

Cathryn's novels include the rural romances *April's Rainbow*, *Summer and the Groomsman*, *The Falls*, *Rocking Horse Hill*, *Heartland*, *Heart of the Valley* and *Promises*, and the romantic adventure *The French Prize*. From debut release she has been a multiple finalist in the Australian Romance Readers Awards and the 2014 awards also saw her in contention for Favourite Australian Romance Author.

Cathryn currently lives at the base of the Blue Mountains in New South Wales with her partner of many years, Jim. When she's not writing, she plays golf (ineptly), cooks (well), and in football season barracks (rowdily) for her beloved Sydney Swans AFL team.

cathrynhein.com

T0363188

Wayward Heart

Cathryn Hein

mira

First Published 2017
Second Australian Paperback Edition 2017
ISBN 978 1 489 23743 9

WAYWARD HEART
© 2017 by Cathryn Hein
Australian Copyright 2017
New Zealand Copyright 2017

Published by
Harlequin Mira
An imprint of Harlequin Enterprises (Australia) Pty Ltd.
Level 13, 201 Elizabeth Street
SYDNEY NSW 2000
AUSTRALIA

® and TM are trademarks of Harlequin Enterprises Limited or its corporate
affiliates. Trademarks indicated with ® are registered in Australia, New Zealand and
in other countries.

Cataloguing-in-Publication details are available from the National Library of
Australia www.librariesaustralia.nla.gov.au

Printed and bound in Australia by McPherson's Printing Group

For Jim

CHAPTER

1

It was spring but outside the wind was vicious at Admella Beach. It bit and cut, carved lines in the dunes, and created seaweed, sponge and cuttlebone tumbleweeds. Jasmine Thomas's timber house groaned against the onslaught, while the fire in the lounge danced and cast strange shadows. A she-devil's fire.

An appropriate fire.

Jas fingered the note again, the second poison-pen missive she'd received this past month. Her eyes scanned the text one last time, then she screwed the note into a ball and threw it onto the flames. They fed, nibbles at first, then flared bright and devouring until the note was no more.

She hugged her arms to her chest and watched the coals glow. It had to be a local. The notes were hand-delivered, and by someone familiar with her routine. The weather was fickle in the south, the front door of her ageing weatherboard cottage unprotected. If the letters had been left early in the day there was too much risk of them getting blown away or soaked with rain. Both notes had been dry, not a hint of dampness, tucked under Jasmine's welcoming doormat but poking out far enough to be unmissable.

How ironic that after almost four years of heartbreak and self-reproach, of secrecy and furtiveness, of Mike's toxic version of love, the moment she'd freed herself someone had discovered her secret. And taken it upon their outraged selves to act upon it.

Jas supposed it could be worse. She could wake to slashed tyres, arrive home to broken windows. Have people cross the street to avoid her. But there'd been none of that. The tiny fishing village of Port Andrews had carried on as normal. Locals called hello. Elaine at the fish and chip shop still grinned and gossiped. Fishermen and beachcombers waved when Jasmine cantered her darling grey show horse Ox along Admella Beach, the sweeping bay beyond her back doorstep. Work at the building society in Levenham—a 26-kilometre commute north—bumbled along, the staff the same as usual, customers unchanged. Her secret had seemed safe.

She should have known such a thing could never be safe.

Jas sighed and kneeled to poke at the fire, readying it for another log. Sleep would be hard to come by tonight. Again. She thought life would become easier with the burden of their affair lifted, but she still ached for Mike. He was an arsehole but in the times when she wasn't hating herself he'd made her feel amazing. Amazing, alive and truly loved.

No doubt his wife Tania had once felt the same. Perhaps she still did. Jas hoped so. Destroying her own heart was one thing, destroying an innocent woman's—a woman with a family—was something else.

Jas rose and wandered into the kitchen. Though it was almost dark, the window pulled like a magnet, latching on to something inside her. Uncertainty about what lay outside. Fear that someone could be secretly watching. She loathed that feeling. This was her home. She'd worked hard for it. No one had the right to make her feel wrong inside its walls. Yet with two letters they had.

Jas looked anyway. The last of the sun was dissolving in a puddle of apricot and indigo. Her crushed limestone drive, now grey with wear and wind erosion, snaked faintly towards the road. The gate stood open, jammed into place with grass that had long tangled and clumped itself around the rails. After the first letter she'd considered closing the gate but dismissed the idea as ridiculous paranoia. Now the urge to sprint out into the howling dusk and force it shut was huge.

She folded her arms again as her throat began to thicken and ache, and tears prickled. It took several minutes to breathe the tears away. Jasmine's nature had always been positive and fun. She had bounced through life as springy as the dark curls that surrounded her face. Misery had never been her way. She certainly wasn't going to give in to it now, no matter how much her heart bled, or how sorry for herself she felt.

And she sure as hell wouldn't give in to some vicious poison-pen sneak.

Jas straightened her shoulders, flipped the bird at the window and the world outside, and without a backward glance, set about preparing dinner.

She was on the couch in front of the telly, half dozing off a belly full of pasta, when the knock came. At first she thought it was another of the house's ceaseless creaks and bangs. The wind was still up, a frigid southerly gusting at near gale strength. Jas had long acclimatised herself to the noise. In the winter when storms raked the coast, the timbers protested like arthritic old women, groaning and moaning and startling her with an occasional shudder. The sea, only a dune away, added a background roar.

The knock came again: a sharp, urgent rap that shot a bullet of fear down her spine and made her sit upright.

Jasmine's two-bedroom house was situated half a kilometre from the edge of Port Andrews, set back off the road on a narrow five-acre block. It was small, perhaps unappealing to some, but Jas was single and it suited her needs, and she had come to appreciate its cosy intimacy. But not now. Now her beloved house seemed too isolated, the walls too weak. The outside too close.

Swallowing, nerves ratcheted up, Jas crept towards the window edge and lifted a tiny sliver of curtain. A dark figure stood near the front doormat. A man with his hands dug into his pockets and his shoulders hunched against the cold. No car stood in the drive but she wasn't surprised. Mike knew better than to leave his distinctive vehicle in view. He had more to lose from discovery than she did, after all.

Jas let the curtain fall back and rested her hand against the ache in her chest, contemplating whether to answer or not. A week ago he'd turned up drunk and crying, promising a world he would never give. Terrified at the thought of him driving, she'd let him stay. It had been a mistake, one she'd vowed never to make again.

His urgent knock became a pound, followed by a yell of her name.

'Come on, Jas. Let me in.'

She closed her eyes and leaned against the wall. He didn't sound drunk this time, but that needling Antarctic wind would sober anyone in a hurry. And her traitorous heart was filling with longing and loneliness.

'Jas, please!'

She scrubbed her palm up and down her forehead, wracked with indecision. This had to end. She had to make a break for her own sanity and for the sake of his marriage.

The hammering stopped. She dropped her hand and held her breath, waiting for the sound of a car door, for the rumble of an engine, anything to signal he was leaving, but it was hard to isolate specific sounds against the whistle of the wind and groans of the timber. Breathing hard, she snatched up the television remote and poked the Off button but it was still difficult to make out what was nature and what could be Mike.

Jas stood in the centre of the room with her hands together and licked her lips. Still no engine noise. Perhaps he'd parked further away and walked? He'd done it before, in the summer, when the days were lazy and long and there was more chance of his car being spotted. The council had carved several parking bays for surfers along the coast but an unauthorised one, created by locals and screened with boobialla, lay closer to her house and ran from the road to Admella Beach along the eastern edge of Ox's paddock.

She waited a few seconds more before crossing back to the window. With her back to the wall and her head turned sideways, she slowly fingered back another edge of curtain.

A palm slapped against the window. Jas shrieked and stumbled backwards into the lamp table. She went down, right hip and elbow banging the wooden floor painfully.

'Jas, let me in. I'm not drunk, I promise.'

Eyes smarting against the pain, Jas rolled onto her bum and rubbed at her bruises. 'Go away!' Then softer, 'Just leave me alone.'

'Jas, I love you. I'll find a way for us.'

But pain had hardened Jasmine's heart. They were just words. Words he'd said many times. More lies in a life that was already bloated with them.

Jas gave her hip a last rub and using the edge of the sofa, eased gingerly to her feet. She stared at the prostrate table. The lamp was between its legs, the belly of its handpainted china base cracked apart, fittings and wires rudely exposed. She'd found it at a second-hand shop and paid little for it, but that wasn't the point. Matched with a bright new shade, the lamp had added colour as well as light to the room. Jas adored it. That someone as unworthy as Mike had caused its destruction made her jaw tighten.

Limping, she set about tidying the mess, not caring what Mike did. He could freeze outside for all she cared.

Jas was conveying the broken lamp parts to the fluorescent brightness of the kitchen when she heard a different kind of noise, one that made her hackles rise.

'Oh, no you don't.' She spilled the lamp remains onto the bench and sprinted back down the hall.

But she was too late. With a final rattle, the back door swung open and smacked against the wall as a blast of ice and sea-tainted air snatched it out of Mike's hands.

She dived for it, bellowing as she did, 'Get out! Get out! Get out!'

His palms were up—the pleading, reasonable man. 'Jas.'

'No.' She shouldered all her weight against the door and pushed. The wind gave a muscular gust, but momentum and grit created enough force to jam his foot hard.

He yelled but didn't remove it. 'Jesus, Jas. Steady on.'

She kept pushing, fury at the invasion driving her. This was her house, her sanctuary. He didn't belong here. He never had, and never would.

'What are you doing?'

Her eyes narrowed. 'Get your foot out of my house.'

'Come on, Jas, you're being unreasonable. It's freezing out here. I just want to talk.'

His patronising tone only infuriated her more. How many times had he used that on her, exploited her weakness, convinced her that he was the one who could solve all their problems as long as she listened, as long as she did it his way?

Too many.

She kicked at his foot, wishing she wearing something weightier than ugg boots. 'We've nothing to say to each other. Not tonight, not tomorrow, not ever.'

Mike suffered the kicks, his focus on her face. Jas recognised the expression and wanted to laugh.

He blinked rapidly, his mouth fighting a downward curve. 'Don't do this. Not to us.' A tear formed and was splashed sideways by the wind.

A month ago, perhaps even a week, she would have succumbed. Not tonight. Not after the letters, not after the lamp, and definitely not after his attempted break-in.

'Save your tears for your wife. They don't work on me anymore.' With a last fury-filled lunge, Jas flung herself as hard as she could against the door.

This time he couldn't sustain his hold. With a bellow of pain, Mike yanked his foot away. The door slammed. Jasmine snapped down the lock and pressed her back to the timber. She scanned across the hall to the laundry for something to wedge against it and remembered the rubber door stoppers she used in summer to keep the house open and let a breeze through.

The door shuddered against Mike's fist. 'You don't mean this!'

'Oh,' muttered Jas to herself as she hurried into the laundry, 'I sure do.'

With the rear secured she strode for the front. When that stopper was jammed tight she stood back, folded her arms and tuned into the night.

The wind and sea continued to roar. Her heartbeat clogged her ears. Every sound kept her on edge. Jas began to tremble slightly as the fear he might not leave, that he might turn dangerous, crept over her. She slid backwards from the entrance, seeking the kitchen and the safety of its potential weaponry and her mobile phone. Listening.

Finally, with the sweat growing clammy on her skin, she heard a car door slam. Seconds later, a powerful engine revved. Jas ducked towards the window, taking care to stay side on and out of view. Lights swept up the drive as a car crept slowly from the rear of the house and gathered speed. Moonlight splashed the roof of Mike's dark BMW sedan, highlighting its rapid path to the road. In a skid of tyres the car swung out onto the bitumen and accelerated. Tail lights glowed and disappeared like winking eyes until all that was left was howling wind and darkness.

And a heart torn between relief and misery.

CHAPTER

2

Digby Wallace-Jones hunched his shoulders against the cold and continued to walk. It was all he seemed to do these days. Walk, drink too much. Not speak. Sometimes, when he looked to the south and saw the hated slopes of Rocking Horse Hill, tears would fall. For Felicity. For himself and the void she'd left.

He missed her like he would miss his heart if it was cut out. Without Flick life was beatless, bloodless. Nothing flowed in his veins except anger and loss, and the pain of his leftover, never-to-be-reciprocated love. Even the nightmares, with their looming, hyper-magnified visions of her perfect face, were a kind of blessing. He could touch her in those dreams. Say things. Alter time. Save her.

But there would be no saving her. Right now he didn't want to save himself either.

Footfall after footfall, he trudged on through the stripped leaves and twigs that strewed the footpaths of Levenham. Exercise was good, the counsellor advised, but all it did was give Digby more time alone in his head with its caverns of loss and anger.

People stared. When he bothered to look up he could see them peering through car windows as they passed. If he ventured near the main street the scrutiny would grow worse, prickling his back and making his scalp itch. Everyone in Levenham knew who he was and everyone thought they knew his loss, but they didn't. No one could ever comprehend his suffering.

His grandmother had tried to explain that she understood. She too had lost—a husband, a lover, a friend. Digby was not unique, and while that knowledge would never make it easier, he needed to realise the truth of her experience. Time would heal. Life would bring new opportunities for love. He simply had to be patient.

But for Digby time only meant hell, sitting in his apartment above the old converted stables at the Wallace family's majestic 1890s mansion, Camrick, knowing that with every second Flick moved further away from him. Time was lying alone in a bed that had once been warm and scented with her, thinking of something she'd like and turning to tell her, only to find a void. Time was finding yet more ways to avoid his family, friends and colleagues and their fearful expressions. Time was too much of nothing.

The footpath swung right and opened onto the large park that extended behind the town's library and council chambers. The oaks were in full leaf, casting shadows that danced with the breeze. It was calmer today. The storm that had raged through two nights before had faded. A few branches had come down. Digby inspected the broken limb of a tree as he passed, the professional in him instinctively calculating the damage and treatment, when the truth was he didn't care. He'd yet to return to work at the Department of Primary Industries, where he'd been employed as a horticultural scientist and district adviser since leaving university.

He doubted he ever would. The inquest had killed any chance of that.

He'd been starting to recover. Not much, but the ragged rawness of his sorrow had lost its painful edges. A kind of dullness had settled in. Then the inquest into Felicity's death arrived like a bulldozer, and the crumbly, fragile walls he'd been trying to build around his grief and horror were smashed to the ground. Everything came back. The roar of Rocking Horse Hill as its old quarry collapsed, the clench of panic and terror. The hysterical barks of Em's dog as Josh tried to drag Em back from the edge. The sickening vision of Felicity's grip slowly slipping from his sister's.

Then the screams and bellows as the hillside gave way in an avalanche of rock and dirt and mud, carrying Digby and the cherished new world he'd found, so filled with love, with it.

A man appeared at the edge of the park with a small dog on a leash. Digby turned immediately away and kept moving, hands thrust into his pockets. The urge to run from the risk of contact was huge, yet Digby also knew he couldn't keep this self-imposed isolation up forever. But there was no one he could trust. Not his mother, or grandmother, and absolutely not his sister Em.

A few late lunchtime walkers were out. It was past one-thirty and most workers had returned to their desks. Levenham wasn't large— around 15,000 people—but it acted as a service city for the region's agricultural, forestry and fisheries industries. Tourism was on the rise too, now that local vineyards were winning accolades and investing in cellar-door facilities. There was a time when Digby was proud to say he'd played a small part in that success, but no more.

A bench sat empty in the shadows of one of the oaks. He settled down with his perpetually cold hands still plunged into his pockets to stare at nothing. Perhaps his lack of interest in anything local was a sign it was time to move on. The Wallaces had been the weave in

Levenham's fabric for generations, the region's abundance fuelling a growth in wealth that his ancestors had used to help build a town they could be proud of. Their foundation stones, embedded like rocky fingerprints, were everywhere, from churches to fountains and civic buildings. His sister ran a business here. His mother and grandmother still played their part on committees and volunteer groups. In time, as heir to the family fortune, it was expected that he would too.

Digby let out a shuddery breath. A year had passed since Felicity's death and yet nothing had changed within him. He still hurt, still missed her. Still tripped over every tiny reminder of their time together like a blind man in the dark. Maybe it was time to leave, escape the pressure. Find somewhere far away, with a landscape flat to the horizon in every direction. A place without any reminders of Rocking Horse Hill.

He blinked against the heat building in his eyes, blindsided by the thought. He couldn't leave. She was here, the last traces of her. All he had.

'Digby?'

He glanced up then rapidly looked aside, using his upper arm to rub his eyes.

Jas must have known what she'd seen but was kind enough not to say anything. Instead she sat down beside him, opened a plastic lunch box and began rummaging inside.

'If it's any consolation, I'm having a pretty ordinary day too.'

It wasn't, but it was good of her to say. Digby forced what he hoped resembled a smile and resumed staring over the lawn.

'I have a ham and cheese sandwich I can share, if you're interested.' She dug a little more and pulled out a muesli bar, angling it towards him. 'Or there's this.'

'Thanks, but I'm not hungry.'

She sighed. 'I wish I wasn't, but if I don't eat I'll never make it through the rest of the afternoon.'

Jas took a bite of the sandwich and chewed for a while. Digby hoped she wouldn't bring up Em. He wasn't in the right frame of mind to talk about his sister. And he sure as hell didn't want to talk about her wedding, no matter how much Digby owed her fiancé Josh. It was bad enough that Digby was best man. Only loyalty and gratitude to Josh for saving his life at the quarry had made Digby agree to it, and not a day went by when he didn't wish he'd said no. Hearing them say their vows in the same church where he and Flick had planned to marry, watching their happiness, would take strength Digby wasn't sure he possessed.

'Can I ask you something?'

Digby eyed her, then looked away, shrugging.

'If I wanted to put a lock on my gate, what would be the best way to do it?'

Digby swung back. 'Why would you want to lock your gate?'

This time it was Jasmine's turn to avoid his gaze and shrug. 'Just a question.'

He kept up his study. Jasmine was his sister's best friend. She'd been a fixture at Camrick and the Wallace property at Rocking Horse Hill since he was a boy, invited to all but the most intimate of family events. He knew her. Jasmine was fun, warm and welcoming. Locking her gate? That didn't fit.

What also didn't fit was the fatigue showing on her pretty face. Her normally healthy pink skin was pale, making the bruised circles under her eyes appear even darker, and her shoulders had a defeated sag. Jasmine had always been proudly large-chested and never shied from showing her assets off, plus years of riding show horses had given her a straight-backed posture. Today her body was so hunched it was as if she were in hiding, or protecting herself.

Digby felt a stir of worry. 'What's up, Jas?'

'Nothing. Nothing at all.' But she refused to look at him.

He observed her for a few moments longer and let it go. What did he care about her secrets? He had enough of his own to worry about. He leaned forward as though to press himself to his feet, and felt a hand on his arm.

'Stay? A bit longer?' She waved her half-eaten sandwich. 'At least until I've finished this?'

Digby frowned at the need in her tone and nodded, but there was tension now. The tension of his unspoken questions and the puzzle of what she was hiding.

'What sort of latch is it?' he asked after a while.

'Hook and eye. I was thinking just a padlock over the hook would do.'

'Probably. You could also fit a bike chain, running from the gate around the strainer post.'

She chewed on that. 'That might be easiest. One of those ones with a combination lock so I don't have to worry about a key.'

'Won't stop anyone climbing the fence though.'

'No,' she said softly, staring at the lunchbox rested on her lap, 'it won't. But it might be enough.'

'Enough for what?' When she didn't answer he prodded again. 'Jas?'

She glanced at her watch. 'Oh, look at the time.' She took a last bite of her sandwich, dumped the rest into the box and closed the lid. She stood, the smile fixed on him clearly faked. 'Thanks for your company.'

Digby felt a weird urge to laugh. His company? He'd barely strung two sentences together.

He rose to stand with her. 'You sure you're all right?'

'Yeah, I'm fine.' Her wide blue gaze fell on his. Blue eyes. A knot formed in his chest as he remembered Felicity's face. 'The more important question is, are you?'

'I'll be all right.'

She pressed her palm against his upper arm. 'I hope so.'

With a last smile she left him, hurrying across the lawn towards the main street and the building society where she worked, leaving Digby frowning in her wake.

CHAPTER
3

Digby flicked off the car radio. The last thing he wanted tonight was an announcer's cheer. What he did want Digby had no idea, but it wasn't that upbeat inflection or yet another bloody love song. He hated love. He hated everything.

Levenham's fringes gave way to highway. The speed limit increased to 110 kilometres an hour. He eased his foot down. The lights of his Mercedes scorched the darkness with blazing tunnels of white. He liked the car's power, the panther speed of its response. Perhaps if he'd bought a Merc instead of that useless Jeep he'd have made it to Rocking Horse Hill in time to prevent Felicity's panicked flight to the quarry. Seconds had mattered that night. And he'd been late.

He sped westward, aware he'd have to turn south soon to avoid any glimpse of the district's other ancient volcanic cone. There were so many of the things, scattered like acne across the plains of western Victoria and into this lower corner of South Australia. Since the accident Digby couldn't stand the sight of them. Once harmless hills were now symbols of the earth's treachery and triggers of pain. He knew his feelings were irrational. The hills weren't alive. They possessed no conscience. They just were. Still he charged them with blame.

The night was clear and a three-quarter moon cast the rural terrain in an eerie, spectral glow. The kilometres ate away, gobbled by his leaden foot and the car's supremacy over the land. To the left on a rise, a crop of silvery wind turbines stood in formation like alien creatures about to attack. Digby slowed as his turnoff appeared.

The road was narrow and isolated, but fully sealed and in reasonable condition. Familiar with the route and confident it was unlikely to be patrolled, Digby lowered every window then pressed his foot down dangerously hard. His grip tightened as the car surged. Fence lines and the occasional shed flew past. Wind blasted across him, buffeting the car's interior. The land blurred as he lost himself in the sensation of speed and noise and his imaginary race towards her.

It wasn't enough. It was never enough to drown the echoes in his head.

He slowed, panting, tears pricking his eyes, and remembering his promise to Josh he braked to a stop. For a long while he sat in the car in the centre of the road and breathed until his urge to howl at the earth and the moon like a rabid animal abated. Finally he wound up all the windows and continued his drive to nowhere.

Tonight had been yet another disaster. Tuesday evening family dinners at Camrick were a longstanding tradition that had gradually slid away after Felicity's arrival. Now his mother was desperate to revive them. Em and Josh were to be married. Children would come along. They had to return to being the family they had once been, and that included Digby. The pressure on him to comply had been enormous, and getting worse.

Very different to the early days when everyone tip-toed warily around him, took care in what they said, respected the force of his grief. Even Granny B had remained deferential, and she had no love for Felicity. That front remained united even as the months passed, shadowed by the looming inquest, an event they all feared. But the inquest was long over, Felicity's life and death had been analysed, commented upon and concluded, until she'd become another file in the state's archives, gathering dust.

Closure. That's what they apparently had now. Stupid, ignorant platitude. Others might have closure, all Digby had was death. But no one saw it like that. Instead people began to regard him with confusion, pity, even a touch of scorn. She'd been gone a year. Why couldn't he move on like a normal person?

Granny B had been the first to lose patience. Not that she'd snapped or been short, but her usual hauteur had gradually leaked back into her manner. Even disguised, he could read her old-school disapproval: Digby was a Wallace and should show more backbone. His mother had gently suggested more counselling. Her partner Samuel attempted a paternalistic, 'You can talk to me, son' approach. His mates had been sympathetic before tiring of his apathy and misery. Digby responded by clamming up and isolating himself even further. Now he was being dragged forcibly out.

And what a mess it had created.

Adrienne should have known what it would do to him. She should have served dinner in the kitchen. He could have coped with that. Maybe. Instead they'd all sat in the grand formal dining room, with his family staring nervously at one another around the table while Digby sweated and glanced at the door, his mind overwhelmed with memories.

Images, sounds, feelings. The past resurrected in all its beauty and horror, and so much of it centred in that room. The tick of the cherry-wood mantel clock as he'd waited, excited beyond belief for Felicity's first arrival. Standing at the dining-room door with his arm around her, presenting his shy new fiancée to his family with a chest so ballooned with pride and love he wanted to burst.

Her past had never mattered to him. Felicity was Digby's future and that was all that he cared about. Others cared though, his grandmother in particular. From first meeting she turned suspicious, believing Felicity a gold-digger like Digby's old girlfriend Cait, and when Granny B learned of Flick's attempted manslaughter conviction there was no hiding her disapproval and family tensions ran high.

Digby had protected Flick as best he could. They didn't understand what she'd been through, how much compassion she deserved. Her life had had been hell, controlled by her drug-dealing, violent family then an even more violent partner. The stabbing had been self-defence, even if the courts didn't see it that cleanly, and she'd served her sentence.

Buoyed by his love, Flick had tried to fit in but her attempts were given sinister intent by his family. The rift grew until one fateful night in the dining room Granny B accused Felicity of being a cuckoo in the nest, trying to steal not only favour but Rocking Horse Hill from Em. Felicity took revenge by locking Granny B out on her balcony on a freezing night, with no one to hear her calls for help.

Digby had truly believed Felicity's lies, that it wasn't her, but it was. He hadn't wanted to believe it even when Em, who'd been on her side, voiced doubts. He'd had to ask Felicity though—where she'd been, why she hadn't heard Granny B's cries for help—and they'd argued over it. The bewilderment and pain she'd shown at his questioning would live with him forever.

It was Em who had unravelled the truth, when Felicity failed to keep her lies consistent. Furious and vengeful, Em promised

Felicity that not only would she be exposed, but she would lose Digby's precious, protective love, and it was that which caused Flick's fragile mind to finally crack. Lost and terrified of returning to jail, she'd driven to Rocking Horse Hill to plead her case again with Em and somehow during the confrontation his sister was hurt. Panicked further by Josh and Digby's arrival, Felicity sprinted to the property's abandoned quarry, unaware that heavy rain had destabilised the area. The ground fell away and despite all efforts to save her, Felicity was crushed when the entire wall collapsed.

She'd been wrong. Digby would have still loved her. He would have forgiven. But, thanks to his sister, he'd never been given the chance.

Digby had been so adrift in the past he'd barely noticed his mother placing his soup in front of him—a steaming bowl of lobster consommé with tiny crayfish meatballs that Adrienne must have spent hours making. Digby had stared at it, willing himself to find the strength to eat. He lifted his spoon and dipped it into the soup. His hands trembled as he brought the spoon to his mouth, the consommé making plopping sounds as it slipped back into the bowl. He hovered, breathing shakily, aware they were all pretending not to watch.

His mother said his name. Granny B gave up feigning disinterest and regarded him openly, top lip curled. Josh and Em exchanged a worried look. The walls began to bend and crowd in on him. Digby's head swelled loud with recriminations. His shaking intensified. She should have been here as his wife, sharing his life and love. Not dead. Not lost to him.

The spoon fell into the bowl with a splash and a harsh clatter. He jerked upright, napkin dropping to the floor, and wiped his greasy hands on his jeans, eyes only for the door and escape. 'I have to go.'

Samuel half rose from his seat as Digby reeled out. He glimpsed Josh signalling for Samuel to sit, then he was in the hall and all his energy was channelled into making it outside into air he could breathe.

Far enough away from Camrick's walls for the claustrophobia to ease, Digby halted on the gravel drive and tried to swallow away his despair. Stones crunched as Josh crossed to join him. Thank God for Josh. If Samuel had tried to play father figure again Digby might have punched him.

He glanced at his friend's face and down at his feet as shame for his weakness filled him. 'I can't do it, Josh. I tried but ...' He shook his head, wanting to cry.

'I know. One day you will though.'

There didn't seem much else to say that hadn't been said a thousand times before, and so together they stared southward at the night, the silence accepted between them. Digby wondered if Josh was remembering too. They might not show, but Josh had scars of his own.

Josh turned to study Digby's face. 'You right?'

'Yes.' Outside in the cool air he felt better, calmer, less haunted.

Josh continued to observe him. Finally he nodded, but his next words spoke a warning. 'I love your sister and I love your family. Don't do anything stupid. They've been through enough. We all have.'

It didn't take a rocket scientist to know what Josh meant, but one thing Digby knew, for all his grief and loss and darkness, that wasn't him. He met Josh's gaze with strength. 'I won't.' He breathed in. 'I promise you.'

Josh nodded and tilted his head back to survey the starry sky, his relief palpable. Then he squeezed Digby's shoulder. 'Take it easy, okay?'

'I will. I might go for a drive.' He waved vaguely towards the stables and his apartment above the five-car garage. 'I don't want to ...' He sucked in a breath.

'Yeah.' Josh looked up at the line of windows. 'Yeah,' he repeated, the word loaded with understanding. Then he gave a small smile of reassurance. 'Do what you have to do. I'll let them know.'

Digby kept the Mercedes at a safe speed. There were not enough words in the universe to thank Josh for what he'd done for Felicity, or for him. It was Josh who, risking his own life, had dragged Digby to safety from the quarry ruins then raced back in a futile attempt to dig Felicity from the disintegrating rock face. His friendship felt like the only crutch Digby had left in this life, and he refused to let him down.

The road began to snake as it wound south-eastward. The number of buildings alongside increased as the land switched from cattle and sheep grazing to dairy farming. A few centre-pivot and lateral irrigation systems spread skinny, gleaming metal arms across the paddocks. The ground turned rockier as limestone outcrops broke the soil surface, the tips ghost-grey in the moonlight.

At the coast road Digby turned left. He wound down his window and let the sound and scent of the Southern Ocean fill the car. Behind him, perched on a high promontory, Port Andrews's lighthouse flashed streaks of man-made lightning through the night. Wave crests flared white then fizzled away where off-shore breakers crashed against the dangerous reefs that lurked further out to sea, and had embedded so much tragedy into the area's maritime history.

He slowed to fifty for the town. The harbour's rocky breakwater stretched out to sea, keeping the moored boats of the fishing fleet safe within its embrace. A stand of Norfolk Island pines blocked his view of the jetty and beach. Further on, the trees ended and lawns and playgrounds gave way to grassy dunes and the sweeping pearlescent sand of Admella Beach.

The turnoff to Levenham came and went. One day Digby might brave that route again, but not tonight. One glimpse of Rocking Horse Hill hauling its menacing bulk skyward through the darkness and any solace he'd earned for himself over the last half hour or so would vanish.

The hill wasn't the only thing that kept him travelling eastward. The sight of Admella Beach rekindled his curiosity about Jas and her strange behaviour in the park the previous week. The coast road would take him straight past her gate. He had a sudden desire to see if it was locked.

Half a kilometre past the town's outskirts, where the land gave way to more dairy farms and wide drains dumped water from the reclaimed wetlands into the sea, Digby spotted Jas's small white weatherboard house. Although the windows were lit, the house appeared isolated and lonely. There was nothing growing here except dense boobialla, beach spinifex grass and a few squat trees, trunks made crooked by endless gusts and canopies truncated by sandblasting winds.

Her gate was open. Digby slowed, but didn't indicate. She'd be happy inside her little house, watching telly or reading, or whatever Jas did in her evening hours. His arrival, the waft of sadness that surrounded him these days, would only spoil her contentment.

The entrance slid past. He accelerated, his heart thudding with anxiety. Despite the evening's events he felt a pull of need for connection with someone: human contact, even if the only exchange was silence. It was a thought as disquieting as it was compelling. He wasn't used to that need and it frightened him.

It took another 25 kilometres for Digby to realise he wanted to turn around—25 kilometres and a hundred sweaty hand-twists around the steering wheel. Even then, as he found a place to make a U-turn, he wasn't certain he'd have the guts to actually pass through the gate. He did it though, bumping down Jasmine's eroded drive fifteen minutes later with his headlights flashing against the walls of her cottage, his breathing rapid.

He turned off the engine and studied the house. A curtain jerked open a fraction and was quickly released. No turning back now; she'd seen him. Yet Digby's fingers remained tense and stuck on the car's door handle.

He squeezed his eyes shut and tried to urge himself on. He could do this. It was nothing. A quick hello to see how she was, ask why she needed to lock her gate. Where the defeat in her body had come from. A few minutes. He didn't even have to go inside. Do it all on the doorstep then walk away and drive some more until he was tired enough to return home and confront the emptiness of his rooms without wanting to break down.

Digby opened his eyes. Jasmine's motionless form was outlined behind the kitchen window. For a few moments longer they watched one another from behind their glass shields, until the stupidity of it had Digby finally opening the door and walking to her front step. The air was redolent with the smell of ozone and vibrated with the tide's constant rumble.

With no doorbell that he could see, Digby rapped on the screen door's aluminium frame.

It seemed to take a strange amount of time for Jas to move from the kitchen, as if she was as hesitant and wary as he was. Locks turned and the door crept ajar, prevented from opening fully by a thick brassy chain. Jasmine's face and body were in shadow as she hovered a good pace away from the narrow cleft of space.

Flooded with uncertainty and incapable of a hello, Digby grimaced what he hoped would pass for a greeting and stared sideways back towards the village.

'Digby?' She sounded astonished. Light vanished as the door closed, followed by a rattle as the chain was unfastened. Then the door was slung wide and Jas was fumbling a key into the screen-door lock.

The security had him frowning. He'd been to Jasmine's numerous times for summer barbecues and birthdays; once as an extra for a dinner party when another guest pulled out. He couldn't recall door chains or security screens. And key-locking a security door while she was inside was dangerous. What if there was a fire?

He stepped back as the screen swung outward.

Jasmine's expression softened as she regarded him. 'Bad night, huh?'

He nodded.

'Want to come in?'

Digby glanced at his car, at the road, at the barren landscape of her garden.

'Just for a while,' she went on. 'I can boil the kettle. Make tea or coffee. I think I have some hot chocolate somewhere.'

Digby began to blink, his focus on the wall past her head. He could feel the moisture building on his eyelashes and hated himself for it. Hot chocolate. How could he have forgotten that? Felicity had loved it and he'd always made sure to buy her containers of the best Belgian flakes, spoiling her. And himself. Kissing her after she'd drunk it was like tasting heaven.

'Wine then,' said Jas, lightly touching his arm. 'Come on. I could do with a glass myself.'

She held the door open, smiling encouragement. For a heartbeat Digby hesitated, then he took in her kind smile and felt the neediness rise again.

'Thanks.'

She led him to the brightly lit kitchen. It was small and hadn't been modernised, but Jas had filled it with colour. Pink retro canisters were lined up along the bench, their contents spelled out in angled white modernist font. She'd placed stickers on the painted cupboard doors—flowers and butterflies, vibrant happy things. The fridge was covered in magnets holding photos of her family, of Jas on her parents' farm as a little girl, along with postcard-sized images of 50s-style film posters and fun advertising in over-the-top acid colour. A pot of pink cyclamen sat in one corner, flowers nodding at the end of their stems as though half asleep.

'Tonight didn't work, did it?' Jas said, opening a cupboard door and reaching for a bottle of red wine. 'I take it Adrienne insisted on having dinner in the dining room.'

At his quizzical look, she explained. 'Em told me. She didn't like the idea either and thought something casual in the kitchen would be better. God knows your mum's kitchen is big enough, but apparently Adrienne has this bee in her bonnet about making everything normal again.'

Digby found his voice. 'It'll never be normal.'

Not without her.

Jasmine's blue eyes turned sympathetic. 'No. I guess not.' Turning her back, she reached up to another cupboard and took down two pink-stemmed wineglasses. She generously filled both glasses, handed one to Digby and raised the other in a toast.

'If life can't be normal, let's at least hope it can be better.'

They clinked glasses and sipped, Digby wondering what wasn't normal about Jasmine's life. She had a job, friends, a home. Maybe she wanted a husband and kids? Seeing her best friend in love and soon to be married was bound to arouse longing.

Jas ushered him into the lounge. A well-tended fire was burning merrily, and the light was dimmer in here, subdued by a stained-glass shade over the single main bulb. A paperback lay discarded on her flowery three-seater sofa. She cleared it away to a side table and indicated for him to sit.

Digby looked from the seat to her, to his wineglass and finally the door. He wanted to leave. He wanted to stay.

His voice emerged husky and cracked. 'I don't know why I'm here.'

'Doesn't matter. I'm just glad you are.' When he still didn't move, she smiled. 'Just sit. You don't have to talk.' The smile turned wry. 'I'm not exactly in a chatty mood myself.'

Digby hesitated a little longer before he obeyed, cradling the bowl of his wineglass between his hands and staring at the gently sloshing liquid.

Jas took position at the other end of the couch, elbow rested on the arm, feet tucked beneath her. The fire crackled warmth.

'No padlock on your gate,' he said after a while.

'Not yet.'

Her tone caught his attention. 'But there will be?'

'Maybe.' She took a sip of wine and set her glass down next to the paperback. She picked the book up, flicked a page back and forth and put it down again.

Digby's brows furrowed. 'You shouldn't read in the dark.'

'I know, but my lamp got broken.'

'How?'

Her gaze drifted off to the fire. 'Long story.'

He swished his wine. 'I have nothing else to do.'

'Digby, trust me, you don't want to hear this tale of woe.'

He probably didn't but that didn't mean he wasn't curious. There was something not right about Jas and he wanted to know what. 'Can't be any worse than mine.'

Digby's dry tone had them regarding one another in surprise. While not exactly jokey the words were certainly lighter than his usual miserable hollowness. Slowly they shared a smile, and with it the atmosphere lifted.

Jasmine began to ease off the sofa. 'Nothing could be worse than yours, Dig, but I think I'll hang on to this tale a bit longer. No offense,' she said over her shoulder as she crossed to the television stand. 'We'll watch a video instead.' She crouched and rolled out a drawer. DVDs were crammed inside. She flicked for a while and drew one out. '*Doctor Who*, "The Beast Below". Best episode ever. You'll enjoy it.'

He did. He more than enjoyed it. The touching ending even made his eyes moisten. Jas was outright crying, fat tears sliding over her cheeks. When she caught him looking she laughed.

'Does it to me every time.' She sniffed loudly and wiped her eyes on her sleeves.

The credits slid up the screen. Now that it was over they'd have to talk, or he'd have to leave. Digby felt his uncertainty return. He'd found a peculiar kind of comfort here but it was easy to feel that way when engrossed in a gripping television show. Without the action, music and drama, it was just him, Jas and the rustling, crackling fire. And all the things not said.

'I should go,' said Digby, rising and retrieving his wineglass from the side table. Not giving Jas a chance to stop him, he carried it into the kitchen and placed it in the sink. When he looked back she had her shoulder rested against the doorframe, her head tilted.

'You're welcome any time, Dig. I want you to know that.'

The simple sentiment moved him too much to answer. Swallowing, he looked back at his glass. Wine residue stained the base. He picked it up and rinsed it carefully before placing it on the rack to drain. Not much, but a little return of kindness.

She didn't follow him out to the car but stayed on the front step, watching. A year ago he wouldn't have hesitated to kiss her cheek in thanks. These days he found that kind of contact too hard. Instead he'd looked at her, hands thrust into his pockets, and nodded before striding out to the car.

Jas would forgive him, he was sure of it. Sometimes words were too much, too big, to squeeze past the gravel wall of his throat.

He drove back the way he'd come, the memory of her patient return smile lingering until the highway lights marking the outskirts of Levenham drew the sorrow back up from his soul, and Felicity took over his world once more.

CHAPTER
4

Emily's historic bluestone house at the base of Rocking Horse Hill was as warm and deliciously scented as always. Jas stood at the enormous floor to ceiling windows of the lounge and soaked in the slowly fading view while Em created her usual magic in the kitchen.

Sunset dappled the hill's slopes. Warm shades of orange and yellow fought darker greens and browns for dominance as the rays lengthened and the light changed. Where trees had been planted, long shadows stretched fine fingers towards the cone's rocky tip. To the right, the exposed rock of the quarry scar sparkled as though innocent.

Strange how something so majestic could have ruined so many lives. No wonder Digby refused to set foot on the place. Looking at that scar was like staring at an open grave.

A shudder passed through her. Turning her back on the hill, Jas idled over to where Em's collie Muffy was sprawled by the slow combustion fire. Her fluffy black and tan tail flapped as Jas crouched to tickle her downy ears.

'She's getting lazy,' she said as Muffy soaked up the attention.

'She's getting old,' replied Em. 'I don't know for how much longer I'll have her.'

Jas rose and crossed to the kitchen bench. 'She's a tough old thing. She'll be around a while yet.'

'I hope so.'

Em resumed mixing batter. She'd promised Jas her favourite whiskey-poached pear and chocolate pudding for dessert, but a last-minute crisis at PaperPassion, Em's shop in Levenham, had made her late home and she was still preparing. Not that Jas minded. Since Josh had moved in it felt like ages since they'd had the chance to talk alone. Tonight he was at basketball training.

'Josh wants to get another dog now, but I don't know. I don't want Muffy thinking we don't love her, and a puppy might be too exhausting.'

'Might also give her another lease on life.' Jas snuck a finger into the side of the bowl and scooped some mixture out. She sucked on her finger and rolled her eyes back into her head at the intense chocolate hit.

Em smacked her hand, laughing. 'No cheating.'

'I can't help it. I swear that stuff tastes just as good raw.'

'You won't fit your dinner in if you keep this up.'

Jas had already had several taste-tests. Eating at Rocking Horse Hill was like dining at the best of restaurants. The only place better was Camrick, where Em's mum held a narrow culinary edge.

'No worries about that.' She patted her belly. 'Plenty of room.'

It was good to be hungry. Lately Jasmine's normally robust appetite had been nonexistent. Anxiety had quashed it. Even now in the safety of Em's kitchen her mind was half on what she might find at home.

Em poured the batter into a greased tin and handed the bowl and spatula to Jas with a smile. She leaned on her elbows and observed as Jas made short work of the velvety sweet remnants.

'Any more visits from Mike?'

Bitterness filled Jasmine's mouth. Not wanting Em to catch the confusion of want and dismay burning her face she carried the bowl to the sink and turned on the hot water, her appetite destroyed. She stared out the kitchen window at Em's orchard and the line of cypress trees beyond. 'I saw him at lunchtime, when I was in the park.'

Em moved to join her at the sink and reached across to turn off the tap. She studied Jas for a moment. The heat in Jas's face worsened as she realised Em wasn't about to let her wriggle out of the details.

'And?'

'And he tried to come over.' Her mouth twisted as she met Em's gaze. 'I ran away.' She took a quaky breath. 'I'm such a coward.'

Em stroked her hair, concern softening her gaze. She could be as imperious and aloof as her glamorous grandmother when the mood took her, but inside she was the most compassionate and loyal of friends. 'You are not.'

Jas shook her head. She was. She should have let Mike approach, showed him her disdain, her empowerment; showed him that along with her love for him, his control over her was dead.

Except that was a lie. Like Frankenstein's monster, this one still breathed.

For all her talk, all her fury, all the promises she'd made to herself, the urge to go to him had been almost as strong as the need to flee. The realisation had affected Jas for the remainder of the afternoon and she'd been shorter than usual with her staff. She'd caught their sideways looks but there'd been a lot of those lately. Fear that one of them knew, that they might be behind the harassment, had her quailing.

She swallowed and breathed deep. 'I had another message.'

'Oh, Jas.' The words were pure distress. 'What did it say this time?'

'It didn't say anything. It was dog shit, pushed through the mesh of the screen door.'

'You have to report it.'

Her hands knotted together. If only it were that simple. 'I can't.'

Em took her shoulders and turned Jas to face her. Worry creased her lovely face. 'You have to.'

'And tell them what? That for the last four years I've been having it off with our opposition's married boss? Like that wouldn't get around town like wildfire.' She eased out of Em's grip and walked back to the other side of the bench. She loved her friend, but she also needed a barrier between Em's desire to protect her and the impossible reality of her predicament. 'Anyway, it's not threatening, just messy.'

And sickening for its symbolism.

Maybe she deserved it. In that intense, heady period when Mike held her in thrall, Jas had been enraptured, her emotional entanglement so tight she'd betrayed even her own sense of right and wrong. Consequences belonged in another time and place. She'd been capable of anything as long as it meant another second with Mike.

But she was not that woman any more. She was not. No matter what her heartbreak.

'I don't like this, Jas. Someone's deliberately trespassing on your property when you're not home and trying to scare you.'

'I don't like it either but it's only notes and dog crap.' She shrugged, trying to be brave. 'Whoever it is has to be watching, which means they'll soon see that Mike's out of my life and stop.'

The worry didn't fade from Em's face. 'But you said he hadn't been around. Why attack again?'

'A final message? The last word? A warning not to do it again?' Jas tilted her palms. 'Who knows. People are petty and weird.' Her hands fell. 'It'll sort itself out.'

'And if it doesn't?'

'Em ...'

'I know, I know.' Em opened the fridge and took a bottle of white wine from the door. 'But it's hard not to worry after what happened with Digby. Like you say, people can be weird. And dangerous.' They both knew she meant Felicity.

'How is he?'

It had been two days since Digby's surprise arrival at Admella Beach and in the moments when Jas wasn't distracted by work, Mike, or the craven antics of her trespasser, she'd wondered whether she should call or text, just to see how he was. Perhaps reiterate that he was always welcome, that she harboured no expectations, not even conversation if he didn't feel up to it.

Em blinked as she poured them drinks. 'Tuesday night was awful. I told Mum to serve dinner in the kitchen but she wouldn't listen.' She rested the bottle down, hand gripped around its neck, her face clouding with memory. 'You should have seen him, Jas. He couldn't stop shaking. And he kept staring at the door as if he expected her ghost to walk in.' Em's knuckles whitened as her fist tightened. 'Josh promised he was fine, that he just needs time. But he doesn't look fine, he looks haunted.' Anguish twisted her mouth. 'We're so afraid for him.'

Jas was about to tell Em not to be, that Digby had been rattled but okay by the time he'd left her place on Tuesday night, but she stopped herself. For some reason, revealing his visit felt like a betrayal. The way he'd looked at her on the doorstep—unable to speak but his gaze brimming with gratitude—had been a moment so intimate it felt too personal to share. The situation with Mike was very different, but there'd already been enough betrayal in Jasmine's life. She couldn't do it to someone who was hurting even more profoundly than she was.

Jas peeled Em's fingers away from the bottle and returned it to the fridge. 'He'll be all right, Em. Just give him space to heal. Josh is watching out.'

'I know he is, but Josh can't be with him all the time.' Em stared out the window. The sun was almost set now and the slopes were murky with shadow. Against the darkening sky, the cone's rocky edge appeared craggy and dangerous, as though the volcano was snapping bites out of the heavens with broken teeth. 'If anything happens to him it'll be my fault.'

'Don't you dare think that. Digby will be fine and what happened to Felicity was never your fault.'

'I drove her to it, Jas. If I'd have been more understanding ...' She swallowed as her voice cracked. 'I know what she did to Gran was wrong but she was so damaged. And our lack of acceptance only made it worse.'

What Em said was true, Felicity had been damaged. More acutely than any of them realised. Her childhood had been appalling, adulthood not much better, but that didn't excuse what she'd done to the Wallace-Joneses. From her very arrival the girl had worked to cleave their close-knit family apart. It wasn't enough she had Digby, she wanted everything Em had too, including Rocking Horse Hill. Em had been left in a terrible state over whether her brother, who ultimately owned the property, would force her out of her beloved home.

Under normal circumstances he wouldn't have dreamed of it. Even as a boy Digby had been creeped out by the way the crater loomed over the farm but, as Jas well knew, love could make people behave oddly. Felicity might have been messed up, but that didn't mean she didn't know how to take advantage and Digby, with his intense feelings for her, was easy to manipulate. A year on and the family was still trying to heal from the mess she'd left behind, Digby most of all.

'It wasn't your fault,' Jas repeated. 'She ran because she was afraid of what she'd done, not because of anything you said or did. No one knew the quarry was that unstable. No one. You're getting married soon. You don't want to start life with Josh with this hanging over you.'

Em let out a sigh. 'I know you're right. It's just that while I can reason intellectually that her death wasn't my fault, inside ...' She patted her chest. 'It hurts that Digby blames me still.'

'He'll come around. Just give him time.'

Em's kitchen timer called her to action and Jas couldn't help feeling relieved. They'd been friends forever and she didn't like keeping things from Em, especially when they related to her own brother. It wasn't fair in the face of her loyalty. Even when Teagan, the third member of their close circle, had condemned Jasmine's affair with Mike, Em had remained sympathetic. As Em once said, hearts were strange creations and sometimes far more powerful than heads. A human vulnerability Jas and Digby knew all too well.

Despite Jasmine's tough words, on her arrival home that night she made sure to secure the gate behind her. The previous Saturday she'd hauled out the whipper-snipper and cleared away the thick grass that had taken root around the rails and strainer posts. As the machine vibrated her arms, she'd told herself it was just a precaution. The gate wouldn't need to be closed and it certainly wouldn't need padlocking. Yet in the wake of the latest assault, creating at least the illusion of security seemed prudent. This was only for her peace of mind, like the newly fitted front door chain. A safeguard to ease her disturbed sleep.

When the chain was on its hook she stood at the gate and gazed towards Port Andrews. The breeze was mild and sea-scented, the lights along the foreshore and breakwater glowed prettily. Out to sea the lighthouse danced its beam over the reefs. It was a scene that would normally feel comforting, but not tonight. Tonight her stomach was knotted with the fear that someone here, someone she knew, hated her. Jas might not be a true local but she'd lived in the area long enough to feel part of the community. To think someone within that small group had come to despise her enough to intrude onto her property and feed dog crap through her screen door was nauseating.

And it wasn't fair. Not now. Not after she'd given Mike his marching orders and broken her own heart doing it.

The breeze caught the moisture in her eyes, turning it cold. Jas sniffed and turned away. Closing the gate wasn't much in the way of defiance, but perhaps it would send a return message that she wasn't to be messed with either.

She drove the car into the garage and locked it, then dumped her handbag and lunch box on the back verandah and trudged over to Ox's paddock. He was waiting by the fence, his grey coat protected from tail to ears by a heavy rug. He released a deep rumbling whicker at her approach and Jas felt her eyes sting again. No matter what, this was one sweetheart whose love she could guarantee.

She kissed his long regal nose and pressed her face against his silky cheek. 'Foxy Oxy, what am I doing?'

His ears twitched and his breath was warm, and he stood solid and stoic as she poured her heart out in a babble of confusion and misery and despair, while the sea sang its soothing song and the moon rose higher, blessing them both.

Jas looked up at the sound of a slowing vehicle. This time of year there was little traffic along the coast road. She frowned as the headlights dipped and swung towards the house. Planting a quick kiss on Oxy's muzzle she darted back to the garage, keeping to the sheltering shadow of its rainwater tank.

The car was idling at the gate entrance with its door open. A figure stood by the strainer post, head bowed, unmoving. He remained that way for a few seconds longer before suddenly pivoting to survey the road back to Port Andrews.

Jas squinted, trying to make out who it was. The car was dark, sleek and low, like Mike's BMW, the figure around his height with a similarly long, lean build. Her heart began to thud hard and loud as she pleaded silently for it not to be Mike.

The man turned back, reached for the gate latch and stopped. He retreated a step and rubbed the back of his neck. Jas frowned, observing this strange behaviour with deepening confusion as he swung back to the car and opened the door. Once again he didn't follow through, stopping with one hand on the car roof and the other on the door.

What felt like minutes passed. Jas waited, torn between wanting to run for the relative safety of the house and watching the stranger.

Something in her gut told her this wasn't Mike. This person was nervous and wary. Mike's confidence was so high he never hesitated over anything. He was never wrong, never out of place. Never the one to step down. An unmovable king on a false throne.

The man rubbed his dark hair and with purposeful strides crossed back to the gate, unhooked the latch and pushed it open. As he passed back in front of the headlights, Jas caught the outline of his face and in a single breath the fist of anxiety that had gripped her so fiercely released.

She left the shadows and went to fetch her belongings off the back verandah step. By the time she'd made it to the front of the house, Digby had pulled up at the end of the drive. She waved and headed up the steps to the door, expecting him to follow. Despite scrubbing with soap and water, the smell of crap lingered. She'd have to unhook the screen and blast it with the power washer. Another chore for the weekend.

Jas had unlocked both doors and opened them when she realised Digby hadn't moved. She stood against the screen, tilting her head in a way she hoped was welcoming. Finally, the car door opened.

She said nothing as he approached, afraid it might be the wrong thing. The skin around his pale hazel eyes was crinkled with fatigue and he looked sadder than ever.

'Hi,' he said, both fists rammed deep into the front pockets of his jeans.

'Hi.' Jas smiled. '*Doctor Who* and a drink?'

His head bowed and his brow furrowed in a way that suggested suppressed tears and shame. Jas knew all about that, but it seemed more awful to observe it in a man, especially one as blessed by the genetic gods as Digby. It didn't seem right to spoil that beautifully handsome face with grief.

All Digby had done was love with the fullest of hearts.

'Come on. You can sort my fire out while I'm getting the drinks.'

This time she chose 'Voyage of the Damned', a Christmas special made even more memorable thanks to the casting of Kylie Minogue as the Doctor's potential love interest. As always, Jasmine's face was wet with sentimental tears by its conclusion.

'I love that episode,' she said, reaching for a tissue and blowing her nose rowdily.

'Yeah,' he said, sounding surprised. 'It was good.'

She began tidying the remotes and stopped. It had to be late, after ten-thirty at least, but she didn't want Digby thinking she was shooing him out into the night.

He noticed though. 'I should let you get to bed.'

When Digby made no move to rise, Jas busied herself ejecting the DVD and putting it away.

'Your gate was shut,' he said as she was sliding the drawer closed. She stayed crouched on her haunches. 'Yes.'

'Why?'

'No reason. Just security.'

He picked up his empty wineglass and regarded it. The fire gave a snap that jolted Jas but Digby seemed too consumed with thought to notice.

Digby looked up and held her gaze. 'What's up, Jas?'

'It's nothing, Dig. Don't worry about it.'

'I don't like—' He stopped, his mouth tight as though holding something in. For several seconds he stayed that way, then he let out a breath and rose, lifting the glass to her in a half-toast. 'Thanks.'

'You're welcome, Digby. Any time.'

At the door he lingered, hands once more thrust into his pockets and brow deeply furrowed. His words, when they came, were stilted with uncertainty. 'If you're in some sort of trouble ...'

'I'm not.'

He opened his mouth as if to protest and thought better of it. He bent to kiss her cheek, the touch so brief and light it was like the whisper of a falling feather, then he was striding to his car as if escape couldn't come quick enough.

When Jas arrived home Friday evening, she found a reeking pile of dead slimy rock cod smothering her front step. Jammed into the mouth of the topmost fish was another note. Though her eyes were watering and her body screamed for her to run, she bent and tugged the paper free.

The words 'whore' and 'marriage wrecker' were dismissible for their unoriginality. What had her throat closing over and her lungs squeezing painfully was the final shouted salutation.

GET OUT.

That night, she padlocked the gate.

CHAPTER
5

Jas felt like she was shrivelling, crawling in on herself like a scrabbling, frightened animal. Every thought was full of suspicion and fear. Prickles kept rising on her neckline whenever her back was turned to Port Andrews, as if she could sense her harasser watching her from the village, but whenever she jerked round there was nothing except blue and white shacks, Norfolk Island pines and a sleepy village street.

The front step still stank of rotten fish. She'd spent a disgusting hour and a half the evening before dumping cod carcasses into a bucket and trekking over the dunes, spade handle clenched in her fist, to bury the fish below the high water mark. At least crabs and other sea scavengers would gain something from their deaths. All Jas had gained was fear.

Saturday had dawned crisp and clear. The air was warm with positivity that Jas tried to draw strength from, but worry and lack of sleep kept her sapped, her movements sluggish. After removing the screen door and setting it flat on some limestone blocks, she sprayed the front step, door and walls of her house with heavy-duty car wash, before using the power scrubber attachment of her high-pressure cleaner to remove every last trace of faeces and fish from the house and screen door. Then, gripping the pressure gun like an AK-47, Jas blasted everything clean, muttering action-movie lines as she pretended she was mowing down enemies.

The exercise proved cathartic and it was with a lighter step that she walked up the road to the gate, removed the new combination-lock bike chain she'd purchased on the way home the night before, and swung the gate open. Em was bringing her horse Lod down after lunch for a ride along Admella Beach. Leaving the gate shut and locked would only lead to more interrogation and nagging, and it seemed unnecessary, perhaps even weak, to keep it closed while she was home. Her harasser preferred the cowardice of covertness.

It was the perfect day for a ride. Spring was finally bounding joyfully across the landscape, bringing with it the scent of anticipation, and the hypnotic cadence of Oxy's gait combined with the rhythmic, back-and-forth flush of tide would be good for thinking. Now she was rid of Mike and his curdled love, Jas needed to consider the future. At last she had the freedom to plan her life. The expectation that any day he would leave Tania and come to her was gone. He was never going to abandon his marriage and Jas had been an idiot to believe he ever would. Plus what guarantee did she have that he wouldn't do the same to her as he'd done to his wife? Unlike Digby, whose love for and loyalty to Felicity had never wavered in life or death, Mike had no comprehension of either virtue. All the man cared about was himself.

She twirled the chain a few times and squinted towards the village. Whoever it was spoiling her idyll was targeting the wrong person. He was the one who cheated and lied, not Jas. It wasn't her who was married when the affair began. It wasn't even Jas who'd made the first move. And she sure as hell wasn't the one who'd lied about being single. A lie he'd maintained until his suspicious behaviour proved otherwise.

Jas had wanted to break it off the moment she found out about Tania, but Mike had insisted his marriage was a sham, that he didn't love his wife and was only staying for the kids. That if Jas could hang in there, believe in him and the unique passion igniting them, they'd be together. What a fool. Any movie, any book, any magazine article about infidelity revealed what a hackneyed tactic that was. Yet she'd chosen to believe him, against the advice of Em and Teagan, and the truth in her own soul.

That human frailty called love had a hell of a lot to answer for.

Twirling the chain one last time, Jas trudged back to the house.

Em's company and the soothing, familiar sounds and sights of Admella Beach eased Jasmine's anxiety. The ride, Em's friendship, the pure dome of sky and wrinkled glass sea, felt normal, unsullied by Mike or her harasser's corruption. She chatted to Em as they rode, about nothing in particular: Jasmine's Melbourne-based brother Richard, how her parents, who owned a grazing property north of Levenham, were faring, local news, a touch of national politics, mutual friends, wedding preparations. As they talked, the horses swivelled their ears, occasionally skittering and dancing at the fizzing tide and wash of seaweed. Joyous, like their mistresses, to be out in the sun on this glorious stretch of beach.

This time of year, Em, Teagan and Jas would typically be at a show, competing in saddle horse and other equestrian events. The spring season ran from September until early December, with the two-day Levenham show in the middle. But Teagan was now settled in New South Wales with her new love Lucas, and without her the season had lost some of its charm. And with Em's wedding only five weeks away, and preparations and parties taking up a lot of their time, this year they'd decided to restrict competition to a few select shows only. Jas couldn't help lamenting the change. For all Teagan and Jasmine's disagreements, with Em as peacemaker they'd formed a solid trio and had enjoyed their days together, competing and sharing laughs and end-of-long-day fatigue and satisfaction. This change made her feel like they were all finally growing up, moving into the next phase of their lives. All except Jas.

She let Oxy have his head but Lod, who was as competitive as his mistress, always seemed to keep a nose in front. Jas didn't mind. It was the rush of air past her ears and the sheer thrill of the gallop that filled her with delight, along with the emancipating sense of tossing all her troubles to the wind.

Seagulls swept skywards in squawking flocks and settled again behind them. The horses' hooves made wet slaps against the sea-washed sand. In the gully between two reefs a couple of dedicated anglers bobbed in their dinghy, eyeing them as they raced. Every now and then the brightly coloured floats of a crayfish pot would pock the sea surface, like lost Christmas baubles. Jas sucked in the pleasure of the day, filling her soul with its purity. Fortifying her strength.

This was what mattered. Friendship. Happiness. The multicoloured magnificence and peace of the place she'd made home.

'Fish and chips?' said Em when they'd reined the horses back to a walk and turned for the return leg. She inhaled deeply, as though already smelling dinner. Sea air and a ride always made them hungry. 'I haven't had that in ages.'

'Neither have I.' Jas patted her soft belly. Unlike Em, who stayed elegantly slim without effort, Jas had a predisposition towards chubbiness and had to watch her waistline. 'There's a good reason for that.'

Em gave her a considered glance. 'One fatty indulgence won't hurt and you've lost weight this last month.'

'Only because I've stopped misery eating.' Although that wasn't quite the truth. Since the advent of the poison-pen letters she'd been too anxious to appreciate food.

'You and Digby make a good pair. He's looking thinner too.'

Wary of the subject, Jas looked out to sea. The tide was turning. Soon the hoof prints they'd left on the sand would be washed into oblivion.

'Mum's trying dinner again on Tuesday.'

Jas experienced a surge of sympathy for Digby. Adrienne's anguish over her fractured family was understandable given the closeness they once enjoyed, but forcing family unity on Digby when his head and heart were still full of loss and guilt wouldn't heal the rift.

'In the kitchen this time, I hope.'

'Yes. Mum's finally agreed that keeping it casual will work better for everyone. She's even making ...' Em flashed a grin as she drew out the suspense, '... spaghetti bolognaise.'

'No!'

'True. It'll be homemade pasta, of course, and a slow-simmered ragout of hand-minced pork and veal, but basically spag bol.'

'Wow.' Jas blinked even more at the thought. Adrienne making spag bol was as alien as Em looking scruffy, or her grandmother wearing chain-store clothing. 'I would never have imagined she had it in her.'

'I think she's reached the point where she's willing to try anything. Mum's desperate for everything to be okay by the wedding.'

'You must be too.'

Em's mouth turned down, the pain of her brother's lack of forgiveness and ongoing despair unmistakable. 'I just want to see Digby happy again.'

Jas reached across to cover her hand with her own. 'We all want that.'

Em twisted her fingers to squeeze hers back, a grateful smile linking them. And with the strength of that bond, that fixing of friendship, Jas wished more than ever for peace for Digby's heart. For Em's sake and for all the Wallace-Jones family. But most of all for the troubled man she was beginning to admire deeply for his steadfast love.

The fish and chip shop was bustling with locals and visitors when Jas arrived to fetch an early dinner. Driving away from the house she'd felt fine, happy to run to the village, but the moment Jas stepped into the shop her feelings changed. Every nod, every glance had her returning to the awful fear she'd woken with that morning. Any one of the people crowding the shop could be her enemy, possessing knowledge that would see her reputation in tatters.

'Hey, hey, Jazzygirl,' called Elaine Woodburn from behind her counter. Her round, cheerful face was shiny with sweat and the grease of dozens of meals. 'What can I do you for?'

Jas pushed her way past a couple of bare-chested surfers, their colourful wetties unzipped and pulled low to their lean hips. The day might have been gorgeous but the Southern Ocean's temperature was not. 'Two serves of fish and chips thanks, Elaine.'

'Butterfish or whiting?' It might have been a while since Jasmine's last visit but Elaine knew her customers. Often locals would come in, setting Elaine to work with a simple nod.

Knowing it was Em's preference, Jas chose whiting and paid. Then she retreated to the far end of the shop, near the soft drink fridge, and flicked through a two-day-old *Levenham Leader* newspaper that had been left on one of the tables. But Jasmine's mind barely registered the headlines. Her gaze kept skittering across the shop, assessing and suspicious.

'I see you've been getting a few visitors,' yelled Elaine as she tossed onions for someone's burger. Her daughter Hannah was busy cutting up a roast chicken in front of the bain-marie.

'What do you mean?'

Elaine flipped over a mince patty, before shuffling to pull a basket of chips from a bubbling vat of oil. Leaving it to drain, she finished assembling the burger. 'Flash car there this week.'

'So?'

Hannah's shears halted mid snip. Elaine threw a quick frown before flipping the burger onto a sheet of greaseproof paper. A few heads turned Jasmine's way. She swallowed, aware she was making an idiot of herself but so charged with anxiety she couldn't stop. She stalked back to the counter, the space clearing as people stepped warily aside.

Jasmine's eyes felt like knife slits. 'Have you been watching me?'

Elaine's brow furrowed deeper as she wrapped the chips in paper. 'Derek noticed when he went past. Didn't mean anything by it.' Her voice was quiet, her sideways glance speculative. 'Something up, Jazzygirl?'

Jas fingered a point above her left eyebrow. The skin felt hot, clammy. Of course Derek Woodburn would have noticed a strange car. He drove past her house four or five times a day when travelling between farms, and Elaine was too busy running the shop for creeping around. 'Sorry. Tough week.'

'You sure? You're not looking too flash there, if you don't mind me saying.'

Jas rubbed her forehead harder, trying to relieve the painful throb that had started there. 'I'm okay. Just a headache.'

Hannah slid a box containing a half chicken down the counter, eyeing Jas. Elaine called the surfers over to collect their meal before addressing Jas again. 'Feed of fish'll do you good.'

Jas wasn't so sure about that. The strong smell of oil and frying batter was turning her stomach. Twitching an apologetic smile, she moved to the window and stared out, hugging herself and hating the poison her harasser had injected into her life. This disquieted person wasn't her and yet here she was—scared, suspicious and unhappy, when she should be bouncing with joy at her new-found freedom.

There was something else that kept nagging too, a pulled thread in her mind she couldn't source. It wasn't until Jas was driving back to the house that it occurred to her. Derek could only have noticed Digby's car, not Mike's. Mike's last visit was ten days ago and he'd hidden his car behind the house, out of sight of the road. Digby had parked out front in full view, and it was after each of his visits that the harassment had escalated from harmless poison-pen letters to a whole other level.

Whoever it was had confused Digby with Mike.

In the darkness of the garage, with the fish and chips turning soggy beside her, Jas sat in the car, buried her face in her hands, and breathed hard into her hands. What a mess. What a god-awful, screwed-up mess.

To stop the harassment she would have to ask Digby not to call around for a while, or request that he hide his car from view when he did, and she couldn't do either. The explanation would be humiliating enough, but that paled into insignificance in the face of removing the solace he seemed to take from his visits. If he had any inkling of the problem he was causing he'd stop coming. It wasn't much, she knew. *Doctor Who* and a glass of wine was hardly therapy, but it was something, and she would rather scrub her front door and step a thousand times than snatch that tiny bit of peace away from him.

Determined, she fetched up the takeaway bag, composed her expression, and went to join her friend. Digby's haven, should he want it, would always be open. She'd sure as hell make certain of it.

Except on Sunday morning, when Jasmine returned from a contemplative walk along Admella Beach, she found an exquisite bouquet of perfect red roses propped against the back verandah step. She stared at it for a long, long time before reaching down to pluck the accompanying note from its small envelope.

Sorry was written in Mike's distinctive bold handwriting, followed by *I love you*.

Longing caressed her heart and, for a moment as she reread the words, teased its way past her resolve, but her head knew the words would never be true. Not today, not tomorrow, not ever. It was time to be strong.

Grim-faced and with her jaw jutted, Jas ripped the card into tiny confetti shreds and released them to float on the wind. The roses she flung into the compost, scarlet buds smashing apart like small broken hearts. With a straight stride, she walked to her front gate, swung it shut and wrapped the bike chain in place.

CHAPTER

6

Digby scratched the back of his neck as he regarded the rubber-coated bike chain shackling the steel frame of Jasmine's front gate to the strainer post. He stared up at the house. In the lounge, a soft glow filtered from behind closed curtains, while the kitchen blazed with the eerie blue-whiteness of fluorescent light.

He considered the chain again, not liking what it symbolised, wondering if the 'Keep Out' message was meant for him.

Perhaps it was. He was hardly great company, yet he couldn't bring himself to believe that. Jas had promised he was welcome and he was certain the words had been said with sincerity. The chain was for someone else. The more he looked at it the more he wanted to know who.

Digby walked back to the car and rummaged in the glove box for his mobile. These days he rarely bothered with it, and it was with mild surprise that he found it held enough charge for a few calls. He swiped through his contacts, hunting for Jasmine's phone number, and stalled as he landed on Felicity's name. Her smile beamed at him in the darkness, an electronic ghost.

A choked sound erupted from his throat. The Townsend of her surname seemed to mock him, like a sneer from the universe, chanting 'sucked in, loser'. She should have been Felicity Wallace-Jones, his wife.

His world.

The urge to howl took hold, but it wouldn't help. Like speeding in the Mercedes while praying for a wormhole to whisk him back in time for the chance to reclaim the few precious seconds he needed to save her. She was gone, buried in the cold soil of the Wallace family plot, before her time. The love that should have been and now never would be, slowly decomposing with her.

He breathed past the panic and pain and eyed the bottle of wine lying on the passenger seat. He'd managed dinner tonight, even volunteering to raid Camrick's vast cellar—a legacy of his wine snob Uncle James—for a decent red. They needed a bottle to share with their meal, plus it allowed him a moment's respite from his mother and sister's worried appraisal. The cellar was cool, with a comforting smell of dust and stone, of endurance and strength, and he found himself lingering, not for escape but for peace and the hope that he, too, would survive this agony with fortitude.

As he checked racks and considered vintages, the idea of a thank-you gift for Jas slid into his mind. All eyes went to the extra bottle he carried up and left at one end of the kitchen bench. No one asked and Digby didn't elaborate, but he felt their concern. He was mostly past that now—the drinking himself into oblivion in his apartment above the stables, away from the prying eyes of his family. Only occasionally did the agony become so bad that the only way to wipe it out was via a bottle.

In the past, the sharp shock of seeing Flick's face on his phone would have triggered an episode but already his torment was receding to a dull ache. He didn't need another void. What he needed was to solve the puzzle of the lock on Jasmine's gate.

He took a last shuddery breath and unlocked the screen again, careful to keep his eyes unfocused until Felicity's face and name had once more slid away.

The first call went unanswered. He leaned on the car bonnet and considered the house, then dialled again. Nothing moved behind the curtains, no silhouettes shifted in the bright kitchen light. Digby pursed his mouth as his unease increased. He thought about jumping the fence and jogging down to bang on her door, but the worry she might not want to see him, or anyone, lingered.

Anchored by his disquiet, he searched his phone for her mobile number.

'Digby, hi. How did tonight go?'

'Okay.' He paused, fidgeting. 'I'm at your gate.'

'Oh. Right. Yes. Mmm. Sorry about that. The combination's 4297. Come on in.'

She sounded rattled and unhappy but the invitation was there. Digby took it.

The front door was open when he reached it, Jas standing aside in the shadowed hall, smiling but with a pinched look about her. She was wearing jeans and a pink jumper with the sleeves pushed up, and hiking boots. Her dark curly hair was messy, as if windblown. Though she darted a smile his way, her focus kept skittering beyond him to the grey stretch of her driveway. Digby had the impression of a woman who either expected trouble or had recently experienced it.

As soon as he was inside, she closed the door and slid the chain across, covering the action with a bright, 'Drink and *Doctor Who?*'

He lifted the bottle. 'I brought some red. A gift.' With a sudden surge of shyness he thrust it forward while he gazed elsewhere. 'You know, as thanks.'

She stroked a hand down his upper arm. 'You didn't have to.'

'I wanted to.'

'You're a sweetheart. Thank you.' Tilting her head, she indicated the kitchen. 'Come on, then.'

Digby followed, studying her as she fetched glasses. She'd sounded welcoming, yet every movement seemed stiff and self-conscious, and it was nothing like the gentle pleasure of his previous visits.

'I can go, if you don't want me here.'

She stopped, her expression appalled. 'No! No, don't think that, please. I like having you call in. It's nice.' She smiled and this time it felt genuine. 'I'm just a bit distracted. Work.' She shrugged. 'You know how it is.'

He did. Or rather, he used to. Work seemed long ago now. He glanced around the room while Jas rummaged for a corkscrew. His late uncle James would be horrified they weren't decanting the wine or letting it breathe, but Digby didn't care. The faster they had their drinks and were settled, the sooner he could find out what was going on.

He frowned as he noticed her phone. 'No wonder you didn't hear the phone. The power cord's slipped out.' He reached to plug it back in.

'Don't!' Jasmine grabbed his wrist, shaking her head with shallow jerky movements. 'Please don't.'

Digby eased away, alarm and anger churning. The grip on his arm was like a claw. Someone was hurting her. He felt icy with the need to hurt whoever it was back. 'What's going on, Jas?'

As if suddenly aware of how much she was revealing, Jas released him and waved airily, the action as fake as her smile. 'Oh, it's just a few crank calls. Kids probably. I figured it was easier to unplug it. They'll get sick of the game eventually.'

'Crank calls and a lock on your gate. Doesn't sound like a game to me.'

She stilled, her eyes dropping to the floor, her tone barely more than a whisper. 'Don't, Digby. Just leave it. Please. It's not—' She breathed in hard and lifted her pleading gaze to his. 'I can handle it.'

'Handle what?'

But she shook her head again.

Fear made him harsh. 'Handle what, Jas?'

'It's nothing, honestly. I made a mistake and it's taking a bit of sorting out, that's all. It'll be fine. I'll be fine.'

She returned to pouring the wine. Digby rubbed the back of his neck and studied her. Whatever Jas claimed, she clearly wasn't fine. Her eyes were hollow and worry kept her normally full mouth small. Protectiveness simmered inside him. He'd always been a bit weak, a bit soft. Privilege and wealth had made life too easy, but loving and losing Felicity had changed him. Digby knew what anger was now, what unfairness was. Courage that had once been unreachable for him had been found thanks to Felicity, and it still burned. He wasn't afraid to use it either. What was there to fear for himself? He'd already lost everything that mattered.

Except Jas mattered too. He didn't know why, she just did. Which was why he wasn't going to stand by and let some bastard harm her.

'Does Em know you're in trouble?'

She slid a glass his way, not looking at him. 'I'm not in trouble.'

'Yeah, that's why you're chaining your gate. Well? Does she?'

'Mostly.' Clearly wanting to end the conversation, she held up her glass. 'To friendship.'

Digby hesitated then clinked his glass against hers. 'To friendship.'

They sipped, regarding one another over the rims. Jasmine's eyes widened as the wine's full flavour hit her. She lowered the glass and, swirling the contents, peered into it, mouth parted with awe. 'God, that's amazing.'

'2001 Pyrenees Shiraz. One of the great vintages, or so Uncle James used to say.'

'And you're wasting it on me?'

'It's not a waste. Not on you.'

She laughed and poked a finger his way, the old Jas bubbling through. 'That bit of flattery will earn you "Planet of the Dead". This one's fun. Total kick-arse heroine.' She began moving to the lounge, still talking. 'I wished they'd made Lady Christina the Doctor's new companion, she would have been cool.'

Digby took a last glance around the kitchen, settling his grim gaze on the unplugged phone. She'd sidestepped and he'd let her, but that wouldn't last. Whatever had her so rattled, he would discover the source and remove it. All he needed was to strategise.

Jasmine's prediction that he'd enjoy 'Planet of the Dead' was accurate. Lady Christina was sassy, clever and brave, and more than a bit cute. The episode romped along, veering between drama and humour, and featuring all-consuming metallic stingrays and creatures with heads like flies. It should have been the perfect show to take his mind off things, except it wasn't. Digby couldn't help sliding worried glances at Jas. Even curled up on the corner of the couch, the tension she was trying so hard to hide remained. Every now and then, she'd lift her eyes from the television and tilt her head, as though listening. Or perhaps remembering.

'Planet of the Dead' was nearing its climax when Jasmine suddenly slid her legs off the couch and jerked up straight, then reached for the remote and snapped the sound off.

'What is it?'

'Car.'

Digby checked his watch. It was after ten. 'Bit late for a visitor.'

'Yes.' She rose and moved towards the hall on stilted legs. Digby jumped up to follow but Jas stopped and held up her hand. 'No, you stay. I won't be long.' She looked back at the hall, her shoulders lifting and falling as she breathed deeply. With another few steps she was out of sight.

Digby headed to the window. He tugged at the side of a curtain and peered out. A long dark sedan was parked near his Mercedes. A man stood in front, hands on his hips as he regarded Digby's vehicle. Moonlight shone over his cropped hair and the shoulders of what appeared to be a well-tailored suit jacket. He was about Digby's height but a little more solid, like Digby used to be before grief sapped the life from him.

The door chain rattled and the man swung his head around and swayed. The front light flashed on, illuminating him further. He took an unsteady step towards the house, arms held out from his side as though posing a question.

'Shit,' said Digby quietly as he recognised Jasmine's visitor, and worse, the stagger of a man who was dangerously drunk.

Mike Boland, the supposed gun financial planner the state bank had sent from Adelaide when Gabriel Arthurs retired. He'd been allocated the Wallace family accounts. Granny B had disliked him on first encounter, but she was a raging snob suspicious of everyone whose ancestry she couldn't immediately trace back five generations. Perhaps her instinct had been right.

Digby let the curtain drop and strode out.

Jasmine was huddled behind the screen door, holding the main door tucked tight behind her. She was hissing in an attempt to keep Digby from hearing.

'What are you doing here?'

'You didn't call me. I left you flowers.'

'I threw them in the rubbish. We're over, remember?'

Mike's voice was choked and whiny. 'No. We can't be.'

'We are. Go home. I don't want you.'

Heavy footsteps sounded on the timber step. Digby moved in closer.

'Don't! I don't want you here. Ever!'

'Jas, please.'

'Go away!'

Digby had heard enough. He pulled the door open and stood behind Jas. 'You heard her. Leave.'

Mike paused and squinted, his face turning savage. 'Who the fuck're you?'

'Digby, don't,' said Jas. 'This is my business, not yours.'

That didn't mean Digby was going to stand by and let this piece of shit harass her. Nudging Jas gently aside, Digby unlocked the screen door and stepped out.

'Who the fuck am I? Digby Wallace-Jones. We've met, as I'm sure you remember.'

Recognition followed by horror slackened Mike's jaw. Then just as quickly his posture changed, becoming straighter, but drunkenness glittered in his eyes. 'Digby. Mate. Sorry.' He lifted a hand towards Jas, secure behind Digby. 'I need to see Jas about a matter.' He nodded as though pleased with the explanation. 'Work.'

'Work, you say? Interesting, given you're employed by rival banks.'

'It's to do with the Association of Financial Advisers,' said Jas, stepping out from behind him. 'Isn't that right, Mike?'

'Yeah. Yeah, that's right.'

But Digby's resolve was granite hard. 'I see. And this important matter could only be discussed late on a Tuesday night at Jasmine's home?'

'You're right. Of course. Inappropriate.' Mike waved towards his car. 'I'll go.'

'You're drunk,' said Digby. 'You're not driving anywhere.'

Mike stepped backwards, almost missing the step. 'I can drive.'

Digby regarded Jas over his shoulder. 'Do you know where he lives?'

She swallowed and nodded. 'Ebony Street.'

Digby pulled his keys from his pocket and held them out to Jas. 'I'll drive him back to Levenham. You follow in my car.' When she didn't accept he sighed. The situation was shit but there wasn't any other way around it. 'He can't drive and he can't stay here.' His gaze bored into her. 'Unless you want him to.'

'No.' Her voice was barely a whisper.

Digby curled her fingers around the keys. 'Then this is the way it has to be.' Digby pointed at Mike and flicked his finger sideways. 'You, get in the passenger seat.'

Mike's expression turned mutinous, all attempt at chumminess evaporating under the force of Digby's command. 'Who do you think you are, ordering me around?'

Digby regarded him coldly. He understood the situation now and fury was building like a fire inside him. 'The man who could get you sacked. Now get in the car before I shove you in.'

Mike obeyed, but not before spearing Jas with a bitter glance. For a moment Digby feared she might not be able to hold it together. Her eyes were huge and limpid, her mouth trembling. He wanted to offer some sort of comfort but he didn't trust Mike not to attempt a runner. The man's darting gaze told Digby he was contemplating it.

'I wouldn't,' he warned as he followed Mike to the car.

This time Digby was on the receiving end of one of Mike's razor looks but it had no power to cut. Digby's scars were so thick they'd formed an armour, and Mike's alcoholic anger had nothing on Digby's wrath.

With Mike strapped in, Digby strode to the driver's side. Jas was on the porch, huddled with shame. He paused, regarding her sympathetically. 'It'll be all right.'

Inhaling a shuddery breath, she nodded.

Digby focused on the road while Mike worked his hands open and closed atop his thighs and stared with drunken intensity at his rival. 'So you're seeing Jas?'

Digby didn't answer. The man deserved nothing except a punch in the face.

Mike's jaw jutted. The air inside the car turned viscous with his churning thoughts and huffing beer-stained breath. Though a thousand questions crammed his own mind, Digby continued to ignore him. A man who could lie to his wife couldn't be trusted to tell the truth anyway. Digby wasn't certain Jas could be either, but what would she gain from denial? That she'd been having an affair with this piece of shit was obvious.

He wished it wasn't true.

His hands were fists on the wheel and Digby experienced that familiar surging need to jam the accelerator to the floor and hurl the car through the black night and into another realm. A place where love meant something. Where fidelity mattered.

As if aware further comment would only damage his cause, Mike managed to keep silent for the entire journey to Levenham but when the country road crossed into town he began to shift and tense. Levenham's streetlights flashed Mike's head with sickly orange and yellow, as though exposing his infected core. As Ebony Street came closer, Mike sat up, hand on the dash and eyes fixed on Digby's face.

'My wife ...'

'Now you think of her?' Digby's lip curled.

He indicated and turned into the street, but instead of driving on, Digby immediately pulled to the kerb. Mike could walk the rest of the way. The scumbag's wife and kids were innocent, plus Digby wasn't about to land Jas in the middle of a domestic dispute.

The man stared at him. 'Thanks.'

'I haven't done this for you.'

Mike gave a 'fair-enough' nod. 'Look, I know you won't believe me but I love my wife.'

'Nice way of showing it.' Digby unbuckled his seatbelt and pushed the door open. He wasn't a violent man but the way his emotions were erupting, one more second in Mike's company and he'd be liable to break his nose.

'But I love Jasmine too.'

Digby snorted and climbed out. What would this shit know about love? Love was a universe in which nothing else existed but the person you'd given your heart to. There wasn't space for two.

Headlights appeared at the end of the street—Jas in his Mercedes. Mike remained seated. Digby went to slam the door but stopped as a glacier of cold rage crawled through him. Hands braced on the door and roof, he stooped to look inside.

'If you visit, touch, or even think of speaking to Jas again, I'll move every Wallace account out of your hands. And I'll make sure the bank knows who's responsible. You understand?'

Slowly, Mike nodded.

Message delivered, Digby walked off, leaving the door open to the cool swirl of night.

CHAPTER

7

Digby reached across to squeeze Jasmine's hand. For the half second he could take it from the road she held his gaze, then she turned to stare back out the side window, left fist curled against her mouth.

Digby didn't know what to say, how to broach the subject. Whether it was even any of his business. Now he'd warned Mike off she was safe. It was over. What other role did he have?

He drove at a steady pace. It was late and the road was empty but he had no compulsion to speed. If anything he wanted the journey to last. The chance to work out some sort of comfort for Jasmine. Perhaps solace for himself, too. Another shard had been hacked from his faith in humanity, and it had left him sore.

It wasn't until the headlights hit the sign for Bradley Road that he realised he'd driven the main thoroughfare connecting Levenham and Port Andrews, and shaved the closest he'd been to Rocking Horse Hill since that terrible night. Not once, but twice. Apart from a lurch in his stomach upon seeing the sign, he'd survived.

No emotional collapse, no uncontrollable surge of hatred and fury at what lay at the end of that road. Just the dull throb of loss and impossible want that was such a part of him now. Perhaps immersion therapy had something going for it after all.

He glanced again at Jas and tried to work out how he felt. He was disappointed at her choice, but mostly he was unsure and worried about what this would mean for their fragile friendship. Her steady ease had helped him breathe this past week, and stopped him drowning in himself. Losing that would leave him floundering once more.

'I didn't know he was married.' She spoke to the window, her breath leaving a faint blush on its surface. 'The building society offered select staff the chance to study financial planning. I thought it'd be a good way to get ahead, create a better career for myself, so I put my hand up and was accepted. The initial training included two weeks in Adelaide with a private college. Mike was one of the practitioners they brought in to teach us ethics.' She laughed, the sound bitter. 'Of all the people to teach ethics.'

Digby's fists tightened on the wheel.

'When he told me he was being moved to Levenham I thought my life, my future, was made. Instead it became my undoing. Finding out he was married, that he had kids, what an idiot I'd been ...' Jas was quiet for a while, her head bowed as if the memory had exhausted her. 'You believe in love at first sight.'

It was a statement, not a question. It was no secret how hard and fast Digby had fallen for Felicity. They'd crashed trolleys in a supermarket, and in an instant of shy apologies and smiles he'd known that she would be his heaven and earth and everything in between. Two weeks later they were engaged.

'That's what happened to me,' Jas continued. 'I thought it happened to him too but that was a lie.' Her fingers twisted together with anguish. 'Everything was a lie, and I had no idea until it was too late.'

'You could have broken it off.'

She made a choked noise and turned to face him, anger and regret raising her voice. 'Like you could have broken it off with Felicity? I loved him, Digby. I couldn't stop. It was wrong and I knew it and it shattered me into pieces every day, and then he'd come and put me back together again. He had me so fooled, so tangled and screwed up, I let him treat me like this for nearly *four years*! Then after the quarry accident, when all the press was hanging around and I had more important people than him to think about, I finally found the guts to end it. Four months I lasted. How proud I was, and how stupid, thinking I was free, when all it took was for him to catch me one night when I was feeling weak and lonely, and I was gone again.'

'I'm sorry.'

'Why should you be sorry?' She touched her forehead. 'Shit!'

Digby let the silence weave round them. There was little he could think of to add. Mike hadn't deserved her love but Digby was sure she already knew that, and disliked herself for it. What he wanted to say was that he didn't blame her. He knew what love like that did, how it consumed, but forgiveness wasn't his to grant. This wasn't his personal train wreck. He wasn't the one betrayed.

Except he was, a little. And he didn't like the realisation that he was claiming hurt from her mistakes.

Jas resumed staring out the window as Digby drove on, using the subtle vibration and hum of the car to drift into the safety of numb thought.

Jas had locked the gate behind her when she'd left to follow them. He watched her exit the car and trudge to deal lethargically with the chain and wished again he had some way to comfort her.

Hunched against the cool, she seemed diminished. The woman he'd known since boyhood was outgoing and vibrant, and nothing like this. The world needed her back. He needed her back.

She let the gate swing open and instead of returning to the passenger seat, crossed to the driver's side and indicated for Digby to wind down his window.

'I'm all right now. You can go.'

'No.'

She frowned at the force of the word, her mouth buckled in one corner.

Aware he might have come on too strong, Digby tried to lighten things with a joke. 'Uncle James would roll over in his grave if he knew we'd left glasses of '01 Pyrenees Shiraz half drunk. And we haven't finished "Planet of the Dead". You can't leave me not knowing what happens to Lady Christina.'

Her front teeth dug into her bottom lip and her face took on the crumpled look of someone desperately trying not to cry.

'Don't send me away, Jas. I'm here. I want to help.' He reached out to stroke a stray curl of breeze-blown hair from her face. 'Lean on me.'

She really did cry then, turning from the car to buckle forward, hugging herself as though letting go would see her insides tumble out. Digby threw open the car door and rushed to gather her against him, shushing softly as she bawled and hiccupped into his chest.

'It's okay,' he soothed, stroking her silky hair and kissing her temple. 'He's gone. It's over.'

She didn't push him away as he expected. Instead she cushioned against him, grasping at his clothes, his solidity, weeping and shivering until there weren't any tears left.

Finally, swiping at her lowered eyes, she pulled away, shoulders hunched with embarrassment. '*God.*'

'It doesn't matter.'

Tears still leaked but she managed a wobbly smile. 'That was the last thing I wanted you to see.'

He shrugged. 'I've been worse.' It was true. In the early days, when his grief was at its most raw, there were times when he'd cried the way a toddler does, without restraint or care. Always alone, usually burying his face in his pillow to muffle the noise, or stopped on some isolated road in the district, far from habitation. He wasn't proud of how he'd come undone, the unmanliness of it, but he was also aware that without that release the grief might have built and built until it exploded into something stupid. Jas was no different. Except in her case she had someone to help its passing. 'You needed it.'

'I did.' The breath she took was long and juddery. 'But that doesn't make it any less mortifying. Oh,' she said, eyeing his jumper and wincing, 'that's bad.'

Digby looked down. The fine wool of his jumper glistened with tears and perhaps more. He dug into his pocket and pulled out a hanky: after grief became his constant companion, he'd learned to carry one.

He wiped himself down without fuss, pocketed the hanky again and smiled. 'Can we finish that drink now?'

The fire had burned down but the house remained cosy. Digby reset logs while Jas went off to wash her face, returning after several minutes with the shiraz.

'I figured we could do with a top up.'

With their glasses refilled, Digby settled into his corner of the couch. Jas picked up the remote and skipped the DVD back several minutes to catch them up, and when she was finished it seemed the most natural thing to open his arm and nod to the empty stretch of space next to him. For a few seconds Jas stared, then she lowered herself into the crook of his arm and tucked in.

'Planet of the Dead' ran for another fifteen minutes but Digby could barely remember any of it. All he was aware of was Jasmine's warm body, the way she fitted comfortably against his side, even the scent of her. He let his arm hang while the credits ran, palm cupping the point of her shoulder, hoping she'd stay, but when she moved to sit straight he immediately let go. It was one thing to share a bit of comfort, another to let it linger.

She flipped over to a music channel and turned down the sound. The room filled with the fire's crackle and pop and their suddenly self-conscious breathing. Digby took a last sip of wine. Jasmine's was still half full. Propped at an angle as she was against him, it had been hard for her to drink without spillage.

She took a gulp now and swallowed. 'Digby ...'

'You don't have to explain anything.'

She studied his face. 'You don't condemn me?'

He set his glass on the side table and leaned forward with his palms pressed together. 'I'll admit I don't like it, but condemn you? No. You fell in love and couldn't fall out. It shouldn't have happened but it did. None of us are perfect, Jas. We all make mistakes. He just happened to be yours.'

'You sound like Em. She didn't like it either, kept telling me to end it, that it would never work out, but she never blamed me for the way I felt or my inability to stop it.'

Digby didn't want to talk about Em. His feelings towards her were still confused. Because of Em he'd doubted the woman he loved, and that doubt had driven her to Rocking Horse Hill. It didn't matter that Em's accusations against Felicity were true, Digby was meant to be her champion and he'd failed. And now she was dead, and he was left so lonely and hurt there were days when he believed he'd never recover.

He parted his hands. 'It doesn't matter now. It's over.'

'Yeah, except it's not. It's still here.' She rubbed her knuckles against her chest. 'That love. Like Frankenstein's monster.'

He understood. Even though Felicity was gone, his love remained strong. The only difference was that he knew how pointless it was. Jas probably knew too, but where life existed, so did hope.

'It'll take time, believe me.' He made a self-deprecating noise, like a half laugh. 'I'm an expert.'

'You still love her?'

'Yeah.'

Jas reached to take his hand. 'I'm sorry.'

Shaking his head, he looked away at the fire. His throat felt thick, his heart bruised. He wanted to tell Jas what it was like, the endless longing, the grief of a million should-have-beens. How one half of him prayed that one day it might end, while the other half clung to her, refusing to let go.

But tonight wasn't about his lost path to healing. It was about Jasmine's.

He closed his palm over the top of hers, and gently rubbed. 'Will you be okay?'

She nodded.

'I can stay if you need me to.'

'You've done more than enough.' She gave a sad smile. 'I'm only going to cry myself to sleep anyway.'

The words 'I'll hold you' swooped through his mind like a winging bird, causing him to swallow and look aside.

'Thank you, though. For understanding. For not ...' She gazed upwards, hunting for the words. 'For not judging me harshly.'

He toyed with her fingers, aware it was time to leave, not knowing how. Finally, he looked up. 'Call, if you need me. Any time. It doesn't matter.'

'I will.'

He was halfway back to Levenham, when he realised he hadn't said what he wanted to say. Without thinking, he called Jas's mobile number. She answered with a voice that sounded clogged.

'Don't let this ...' He breathed in. 'Don't become like me, Jas. Keep your hope. It'll happen again. Love, I mean. And it'll be good and right, and everything you deserve.'

She was silent for a long while, and he wondered if his words hadn't been the solace he'd wanted them to be. That he'd made things worse rather than better.

Then she spoke. 'It'll happen for you, too.'

But as Digby glanced to the side and saw the moonlit rocky edges of Rocking Horse Hill's crater, and his heart began to crush in on itself with misery and regret and the searing pain of longing, he doubted that would ever be true.

CHAPTER

8

For the first time in almost three years, Jas called in sick. She rose, showered, applied make-up and dressed in her uniform, taking comfort in routine. But the kitchen, with Digby's half-drunk bottle of wine still on the bench, brought her undone.

The humiliation of last night crashed down on her. Fatigue sucked at her bones, making them weak. Breathing caused sharp pains in her chest. Her eyes felt sandblasted, the skin beneath them puffy and bruised. It was no wonder. Crying had left her exhausted but sleep had only come in fragments. Her mind churned with fear of what Mike might do next. At what her harasser would make of his visit. And Digby's.

Nothing, she hoped. But that didn't calm her anxiety.

After phoning in she returned to bed, but finding no respite from her thoughts Jas rose again, slipped on her riding breeches and warm clothes, and headed out into the clean air and the non-judgemental comfort of her darling Ox.

A strong breeze was scudding clouds across the sky, painting the grassy dunes and pasture in sunshine and shade. As though sensing her fragility, Ox behaved with gentlemanly aplomb, not putting a hoof out of step as Jas practised simple dressage moves in the paddock. She relaxed into his rocking gait, using the rhythm to clear her mind. Except her mind wouldn't clear, not totally, and she found herself thinking about Digby and his kindness.

She'd never asked what he and Mike talked about during their drive. Perhaps she should have. Would Digby have said anything to Mike? Jas had no idea. Before Felicity Jas would have bet her house that Digby would have been non-confrontational, but he was a different man now. Harder. Less weakened by uncertainty. A man who didn't care what anyone thought of him. A man who had nothing to lose.

He had almost said as much when he'd called her from the car. *Don't become like me.* She assumed he meant burdened with loss, bitter, incapable of love, but the tenderness he'd shown her proved otherwise. He'd been a revelation, and nothing like the Digby she'd known most of her life.

She smiled and leaned forward to stroke Oxy's smooth neck and whisper to him. 'What do you think, Foxy Oxy? Am I going to become old and bitter?' The horse's charcoal-tipped grey ears swivelled. 'No,' she said, scruffing his mane and smiling fondly at him. 'Not this little black duck.'

Mike wasn't worth it. Mike wasn't worth anything.

With Ox brushed down, re-rugged and fed, Jas wandered back inside, yawning all the way. The outdoors and exercise had combined to fill her with the sleepiness she craved. Her muscles were more relaxed, her head clearer, and renewed resolve had made her strong again. After a quick wash, she shrugged back into her nightie, crawled under the soft sheets of her bed and was asleep within minutes.

It was after two when she woke. Jas stretched and rolled over to her side where the sun was creeping in a golden stripe across the carpet. Dust motes cast cheerful glitters in the air. Outside, she could hear the steady beat of the sea and the *caaa-caaa* of seagulls. A strange feeling flushed over her. A sense almost of renewal, as if she'd been plunged into some sort of heroic test and come out the other side alive. Better. Stronger.

She stretched again and rose. Her body still felt pummelled by fatigue but it was different, more the aches and pains of garden-variety lack of a good night's sleep than bone-deep emotional exhaustion. And she was starving—another good sign. Perhaps a day off was what she'd needed all along. The chance to be selfish and indulgent. Which made her think of the packet of Tim Tams hiding in the cupboard that she hadn't had the stomach for lately. She dressed quickly in a pair of paddock jeans and the tops she'd worn riding, and strode out into the kitchen to make a late lunch.

There was plenty to be done around the house and yard but, having designated today her mental health day, Jas ignored the chores. Instead, she buckled a halter on Ox, clipped on a long lunge lead, and led him down to the beach for a splash around and roll in the sand.

Oxy loved a beach frolic. He shied playfully at the tide, pawed at the water, sniffed at seaweed piles, and pranced and mucked around, making Jas smile with affection. Her sweet old darling was getting on, but he could be coltish when the mood took him.

When he'd finished rolling and making satisfied horsey grunts and groans, and shaken himself off, she led him back through the dune cutting and coastal scrub, keeping a good look ahead for the tiger and brown snakes that liked to sunbathe on the narrow sandy trail. When the boobialla cleared she turned left, and stopped.

A man was sitting on her back porch.

For a brief moment anxiety flared then quickly faded as the man stood and held his right hand out in greeting. Smiling, she waved back and clicked her tongue for Ox to move on.

'Digby,' she said, when she'd cut back through the rear gate and caught up with him near Oxy's paddock. 'I wasn't expecting you, but it's nice all the same.'

'I dropped into your work, to see how you were. They said you'd called in sick. I got worried.' He scanned her face, concerned. 'You all right?'

'Yes, although I wasn't this morning. Not much sleep, woke feeling like crap. Decided to take a mental health day.' She smiled her reassurance. 'It's working too.'

'Good.' He turned to point at the verandah, where a plastic container sat on the top step. 'I brought you some soup. Mum's minestrone. I thought there was some chicken in the freezer but I must have eaten it. Or chucked it out.' His expression turned sheepish, more like the old Digby she'd grown up with. 'She keeps bringing me food that I can't eat. So I either stick it in the freezer or throw it out, then drop back the container.'

'You've been chucking out your mum's cooking? Digby, you do realise that's a criminal act?'

He grinned. 'I know. Whatever you do, don't tell her.'

'I won't. It can be our secret.'

Another to add to their collection, Jas mused as Digby followed her into the paddock. They'd been sharing a few lately.

With Ox brushed down, rugged and let loose, they wandered back to the house. Digby placed the soup in the sink to finish defrosting while Jas put the kettle on to boil. It was after four and, tempting as the thought was, too early for a glass of wine.

'You haven't plugged your phone back in,' said Digby, eyeing the dead machine.

'No.'

Jas glanced at it and grimaced. She couldn't keep hiding, and she had friends, family, people who wanted to contact her as they normally did, via the home phone. Why should they and she miss out because of someone's petty meanness?

She spooned sugar and hung teabags ready for hot water, and went to sort out the phone. No matter what her resolve, her stomach was tight at the thought of what might happen when she turned the power on. To her relief, other than a few flashing lights as the unit centred itself, there was nothing. No sudden invasive ringing followed by that horrible, distorted voice calling her a whore, and worse. Just silence.

The kettle boiled and clicked off, rousing her. She breathed out hard and went to pour the tea.

They took the mugs and a Tupperware container of Tim-Tams outside to sit on the back verandah. Digby didn't seem in the mood for chatter, which suited Jas. She didn't know what to say anyway, and the thought of broaching the subject of last night—and what he might, or might not have said to Mike—made her cheeks hot.

The morning's fluffy clouds had given way to thickening bands of grey. Out to sea the sky was turning indigo, while onshore the breeze that had been so pleasant was gaining strength.

'Storm coming,' said Digby, squinting towards the southern horizon. 'Forecast predicted one.'

'I haven't checked.' She blew on her tea. 'Too busy sleeping and playing with Ox.'

'It's not severe. The bureau's only talking winds up to 35 knots, bit of rain. Sea will be rough though.' He nodded towards her horse. Ox was hanging over the fence, eyes half closed, his bottom lip drooping in that gorgeously dopey way he had. 'He might need an extra rug tonight.'

Mention of the coming night made Jas quiet. She stared into her tea.

'Are you worried about Mike?'

She nodded, eyes fixed.

'Don't. He won't bother you again.' Digby's voice developed a steely edge. 'Not if he knows what's good for him.'

She looked up then. Digby's face was as iron-like as his words. 'I'm so sorry, Dig. I never meant for you to get involved in my mess.'

His expression softened. 'I know, but I'm glad I was here. You're safe now. Free to move on.'

'Yes,' said Jas, studying the darkening horizon, thinking of the future, where it might lead now she could plan. Somewhere positive, she decided. Somewhere positive and fun and happy and unburdened. Even on good days, the feeling of being captive to something more powerful than her will had thrummed behind her smiles and laughter. Few had noticed, and she'd been careful to keep it that way. But now that thick shadow was gone. She was free, and Jas planned to make the most of it.

Tossing the cool remains of her tea over the lawn, she grinned brightly at Digby. 'And about bloody time too.'

Although she asked, he didn't stay for dinner, but it wasn't until later that Jas regretted not pressing harder. By 7 pm the storm had made landfall and she could have done with Digby's gentle company. Not that Jas was afraid of storms, or worried about damage to her house or to Ox. The house had endured wilder weather than this, and Ox had his shelter and thick rugs. But there was something about rugged weather than made her want to snuggle.

On the few nights she and Mike could snatch together—usually when he'd lied to his wife about business trips or meetings—Jas had adored the simple joy of romantic company. Mike's talent for affection, for making her believe that she was the only person he loved and would ever love, for making her feel special, was unbounded. He was also the most attentive and passionate lover she'd ever had, making those who came before seem like bumbling adolescents.

Losing that passion, that sense of specialness and love, had been one of her greatest fears. It seemed impossible to believe that she could find excitement and pleasure of that calibre again. Perhaps it might never be, but surely another might come close. And if that closeness was reached without all the shadows and chains that accompanied Mike's version of love, then that had to be better.

From the yawns Jas was producing it was just as well Digby hadn't stayed. It gave her the excuse for an early night. She had sleep to catch up on, work tomorrow, and on Saturday she had Em's bridal shower. As chief bridesmaid Jas should have hosted it herself, but Granny B had insisted on it being held at Camrick, where there was plenty of space and guests could catch taxis home should they overindulge on champagne.

Meanwhile, the boys would amuse themselves with a round of golf followed by drinks at the Australian Arms Hotel, after which Josh, Digby and Harry Argyle, the other groomsman, along with Samuel, Josh's dad and brothers-in-law, would trek back to Camrick to share war stories from the day with the girls over a barbecue.

As Jas shuffled into her nightie, the thought made her smile. A party weekend spent with people she adored would be just what she needed.

The future was at last hers to forge.

CHAPTER
9

Even wearing a fuchsia plastic Alice band on her head, topped with two sparkly multicoloured unicorns on springs and a square of pink card on which 'Daffy Duck' was inscribed in glittery gold letters, Granny B still managed to act as regal as a queen.

Not that her manner had much effect on Em's bridal shower guests. Not after well over three hours of multiple champagne toasts, canapés, chatter and silly party games. The mood was warm and relaxed, any last remaining barriers broken down by a hard-fought game of Celebrity Head. A game Granny B seemed hell-bent on winning.

With Em safely at PaperPassion dealing with Saturday-morning customers, Jas and Adrienne had spent the morning transforming Camrick's back yard into a garden-party delight while Granny B stomped around inspecting their efforts and generally getting in the way. For a woman suffering chronic open-angle glaucoma in one eye, practically blinding it, her eyesight could be dismayingly sharp.

The relief when Granny B departed to get her hair done had Jas and Adrienne smiling at one another, and sneaking in an early glass of fizz to calm their frazzled nerves.

By the time they were done the lawn was dotted with inviting white cane chairs topped with squashy navy cushions. Blue cantilever umbrellas created pockets of shade. Pots of cobalt blue lobelia—on loan from a local garden centre, thanks to Adrienne's connections—formed vibrant centrepieces on white cloth-draped tables, while tall plantings of cosmos added attractive green-and-white accents. Tubs of ice were filled with bottles of Krug champagne donated by Granny B, the price of which Jas didn't want to contemplate. Heavy crystal champagne flutes stood in perfect ranks, while small china plates from the Wallace family collection—plain white with a blue art deco rim design—waited in stacks for loading with Adrienne's restaurant-quality canapés. Little blue and white parcels of handmade champagne-scented soaps, each labelled with a guest's name, were placed alongside on crisply pressed linen napkins.

Both Jas and Adrienne were desperate for the day to be special and couldn't help fretting that something would go wrong. They needn't have worried. Camrick looked gorgeous, and more than fit for a queen of Granny B's bearing, let alone a bride-to-be. Best of all, their efforts had Em's eyes tearing up in pleasure and gratitude, and she hugged them both in a way that had Jas once again silently thanking every entity she could think of for the gift of Em's friendship.

As Adrienne settled a bright blue Alice band with dancing butterflies on Em's head ready for the Celebrity Head final, Jas snuck a sly glance at the others and felt a rush of contentment. She hadn't been sure how the game would go down but everyone seemed to find it a hoot, in particular after spying Granny B's allotted character. Jasmine's mum Phillipa and Josh's mum Michelle were both grinning. His sisters, Sal and Karen, both of whom had organised babysitters for their brood, were hitting the champagne hard and outright giggling. The remainder of the group, which comprised Em's assorted school, work and horsey friends, and family acquaintances, and who tended to be intimidated by Granny B's dowager duchess act, were trying—mostly unsuccessfully—to hold back their amusement.

Jas exchanged another satisfied smile with Adrienne before turning to Granny B and inviting her to open the game.

'Am I dead?' Granny B asked in a voice more cut than her crystal glass.

'As if anything could kill you,' said Jas.

The others looked at one another, a few whispering. Was Daffy Duck alive or dead? Technically he wasn't human ...

Jas cut them off. 'I think you count as alive, although perhaps not in the normal sense.'

'Ah,' said Granny B, clever eyes twinkling as she raised a pair of finely plucked eyebrows at her granddaughter, above whose head was written the name of former UK Prime Minister Margaret Thatcher. 'Emily?'

Em tapped her chin. 'Am I female?'

'You are,' replied Jas.

'Am I ...' Em narrowed her eyes at Jas, as if her face might reveal a hint. The two had been friends for so long Jas sometimes believed they could read each other's thoughts, but not today. Jas had taken care with her Celebrity Head choices, deliberately selecting people and characters who were either a bit 'out there' or chosen for pure amusement value. 'Am I in the entertainment industry?'

'Definitely not,' snapped Granny B. 'Although I imagine there were many who would have found throwing you to the lions highly entertaining indeed.'

Jas speared Granny B with a watch-it look. She was the moderator here and more than once the mischievous old lady had derailed the competition with her interruptions and asides. Others might be scared of her bite, but Jas had known Granny B long enough to know she much preferred people who stood up to her.

'No, Em, you're not. Granny B?'

She took her time, lifting her champagne flute and taking a sip, every action elegant and proud. While almost everyone had turned up in a summery frock, Granny B was wearing an exquisitely tailored pair of silver sateen trousers matched with a white silk wrap shirt. Her pearl-white hair was set in 30s style crimps, and diamonds the size of fresh peas sparkled in her ears.

'Am I on ...' she made a slight moue, '... television?'

'You are.'

'How ghastly.'

Em rolled her eyes. Adrienne shook her head. A few titters flew from the others. Granny B tossed a subtle wink at Jas who had to look at her notes to stop from laughing herself.

Granny B considered. 'Am I fictional?'

'Yes.'

Jas could almost visualise the clues whizzing through Granny B's brain. Which was incredible, given the champagne she'd consumed, but like all the Wallace women Granny B knew her limits when it came to alcohol. It was part of her cunning. Many a person had been made foolish by underestimating Audrey Wallace's capacity for drink, and her intelligence.

'Am I a cartoon?'

'Yes.'

Nearing triumph, Granny B sat forward. She scanned Jasmine's face as if, like Em, she thought the answer was to be found there. 'Am I Betty Boop?'

The image was too delicious. Laughter erupted. Betty Boop was all big eyes, womanly curves and childlike manner, whereas Granny B was model thin and far too queenly to be ever considered childlike.

'No,' said Jas, controlling her own giggles. 'You're not Betty Boop.'

Granny B sniffed. 'I'll have you know I would have made quite a flapper.'

'I'm sure you would have.' Jas turned to Em, willing her to ask the right question. Granny B had honed her clues much too fast and now appeared poised to take the crown. Em was the bride-to-be. She should win. 'Em?'

'Am I sporty?'

'No.' Jas raised her eyebrows at Granny B, indicating the ball was in her court.

'If I'm not Betty Boop I suppose I must be Mickey Mouse.'

'Brrrrp,' said Jas, imitating a buzzer.

'Really. This game is rigged.'

'Gran!'

Granny B merely harrumphed and took a swig of Krug, before peering over her shoulder at the unmistakable crunch of cars pulling in to Camrick's gravel drive. Male laughter was soon punctuated by doors slamming and footsteps. The boys had arrived.

Josh was the first to saunter into view, handsome in a pair of jeans and casual shirt with the sleeves rolled up, and a grin that wrapped them all in warmth. Tall like his wife to be, he was also broad and muscular with eyes the colour of treacle. He leaned down to kiss Em hello, then eased back to study the card above her head.

'Nice,' he said. 'Although probably more suited to your grandmother.'

'You smell like beer,' Em said without rancour.

'I know. Sexy, huh?'

Josh leaned close to whisper in her ear. A flush spread over her cheeks and her eyes darted as though worried everyone could hear what he said. They didn't need to—the effect his words had on Em revealed enough.

Guests swapped indulgent smiles. This was a couple deeply in love, bathed in sunshine and happiness and the promise of a future that could surely only be perfect because of that love.

For a moment, Jas experienced an intense pang of envy, followed by a surge of fury. All that time wasted on Mike. All that emotion. And for what? A bunch of lies. She should have had what Em had. Proper love. Passion. Friendship.

The fury died as fast as it had surged. Mike was a mistake of the past, a snakeskin she would slough off over time until her new skin emerged, clean and gleaming under the brightness of her future.

Her focus drifted. Digby was lingering at the back of the group of men, slightly apart, almost as if he felt he didn't belong, when the truth was the mansion and its surrounds were his property, inherited from his uncle James. Adrienne and Em had scored cash, shares and trust income, Digby land and the majority of the family's agroforestry holdings. If he wanted he could have had them all tossed out without notice—bar Granny B, who had lifetime tenancy.

He wasn't looking at his sister and Josh, or his family, or any of the party, but at his apartment above the stables. Jas couldn't tell if it was with longing to escape there or if it was with hope that, by some miracle, he might find Felicity at one of the windows, welcoming him home.

Sympathy gripped her heart. She willed Digby to look her way but he was already turning aside to face the street. For a moment he remained hunched in on himself. Worried, Jas began to rise out of her chair but his head lifted and he gathered himself. When he turned around his expression was set with stoic resignation. There was no escape from this. All he could do was endure.

His gaze finally caught Jasmine's. He shrugged, his mouth twisted into a smile that was more a mask for how hard Digby was finding wedding preparations. The poor man had to be torn between wanting the best for Josh and his sister, and the resentment that clung from Em's part in Felicity's accident. Jas smiled back, hoping it conveyed her understanding and the promise of her support.

Finished tormenting his fiancée with whatever tease he'd conjured up, Josh planted a kiss on the tip of her nose, winked at Jas, waved to his mum and sisters then turned to Granny B, his grin breaking wide as he read the sign above her head. 'I hope you're playing fair.'

'Of course not, Joshua,' replied Granny B, not remotely fazed by the insinuation. Like all the Wallaces, she adored her granddaughter's fiancé. 'That would be no fun at all.'

'Just as well. Anything different and I'd wonder what you were up to.'

'Do you mind?' asked Jas, as one of Josh's mates rummaged through an ice tub and plucked up a bottle of Krug. She might not have paid for it but wasting champagne of that quality on a bunch of blokes who'd spent most of the afternoon in a pub was too horrible to contemplate. 'You're interrupting the final.'

Josh held up his palms and backed off. He glanced at Digby for guidance but it was Samuel who indicated the house.

'Let's leave the ladies to it. Plenty of beers inside.'

Though the men departed quickly enough, the mood had changed. Celebrity Head had lost its sting. After several more questions, Em took out the prize but only, Jas suspected, because Granny B let her. The sly old lady had managed to cover an entire pantheon of cartoon characters without getting close to Daffy

Duck, each wrong guess given with a deliberate air of innocence that didn't fool Jas.

'You tanked it,' she accused when the game was over and everyone was back to chatting. Adrienne had ducked inside to alert the boys they were now welcome to return.

'Me?' Granny B splayed a wrinkled but perfectly manicured hand over her chest. 'Don't be ridiculous.'

'You did.' She kissed Granny B heartily on her powdery cheek. 'Thank you.'

'You give me too much credit, Jasmine.' She tilted her head, watching the men as they sauntered out of the house and along the flagstone path. 'Did I notice a connection between you and Digby earlier?' Her gaze slid sideways, taking in every nuance of Jasmine's astonished expression. 'Don't look so shocked. You're well aware of how I look out for this family.'

'I ...' What to say? She and Digby were friends, but how to explain his visits without them sounding like something else?

'Oh, do stop acting so gormless. It's perfectly all right with me if you two have become close. God knows the boy needs someone.' Suddenly the haughty act collapsed. Sorrow deepened the lines around Granny B's mouth and softened her eyes. 'I worry about him, deeply. I fear he's a very troubled man.'

Discomfort at discussing him had Jas shuffling her feet. What she and Digby had shared was private. Not that he'd told her much, but still. 'He just needs time.'

'He's had time. It's over year.'

'And how long did it take you to get over your own husband's death?'

Granny B kept mute.

'Exactly,' said Jas, her point made. 'Everyone has their own way of dealing with grief. Digby's just finding his way through his.' She tempered her tone as Digby appeared at the back door. Granny B was only worried, as everyone was. 'He'll be okay.'

All the other men were holding stubbies or cans of something but Digby's hands remained dug into his pockets. It was strange that Jas had never found Digby's brand of attractiveness particularly appealing before. He'd always been ridiculously handsome but other than an academic appreciation, the way she'd admire anything beautiful, Jas hadn't thought much more about it. All the Wallaces were good looking and as her best friend's brother, a person she'd known from quiet, studious boyhood through hormonal adolescence and beyond, Digby simply didn't register on her libido's radar.

Observing him now, framed and shadowed, he seemed a lonely figure, but there was hardness too. Tragedy had brought carved marble sharpness to the planes of his face and his eyes had a steely quality that never existed before Felicity. It made him distant and, Jas realised to her shock, sexy as hell because of it.

Too late, Jas caught the old lady's scrutiny and knew immediately she'd been sprung. Jas braced herself for a warning off but Granny B merely rummaged in her pocket, plucked out a rose gold lighter and cigar, stuck the latter between her teeth and with a cagey smile of farewell, strode off.

'The garden looks great,' said Digby when he wandered over to Jasmine's side. 'You and Mum did a fantastic job.'

'Thanks. So how was today?'

He lifted a shoulder. 'Up and down. Golf was good, the pub not so much. Bit crowded and loud. Josh enjoyed himself though. Yours?'

'Busy but worth every effort for the look on Em's face when she came home and saw what we'd done.' Jas smiled at the group surrounding Em. Josh had his arm draped across her shoulder and was kissing her temple while his mum and dad beamed with pride at them, and his sisters stood by laughing at whatever joke they'd made, most likely at Josh's expense. They were a close family. For Em, whose parents' relationship and divorce had been acrimonious, their deep affection was something she admired.

Digby glanced at his sister and then quickly away, his jaw rigid. 'Sorry.'

He frowned. 'What for?'

Jas lowered her voice. 'I saw the way you were when you arrived home. I know it's hard, with the wedding and everything.'

'Don't feel sorry for me, Jas. I don't want that.'

She winced. Of course he wouldn't want that. Who would? 'Sorry.'

'You can cut that out too.' And this time, to Jasmine's relief, there was amusement in his voice. 'Wouldn't catch Lady Christina apologising all the time.'

That made her chuckle. 'No, you wouldn't. But I'm not Lady Christina. Unfortunately.'

'I don't know. I reckon you're a bit like her.'

'Are you serious? How?'

She was intrigued to note he avoided her eye as he answered. 'She's tough, I suppose. Resilient, like you are.'

This from a man who had seen her at her bawling, nose-dribbling, hiccupping worst? Jasmine's astonishment was so great her mouth turned even more goldfish-like than when under Granny B's scrutiny.

'Thanks,' she finally managed. 'I'm flattered you think so. Amazed, but still flattered.'

'It's the truth, even if you can't see it.'

They were interrupted by Adrienne and Samuel, both pink-faced with tiredness and probably drink, but happy after their successful afternoons. They chatted about their respective days, how much they thought Em and Josh enjoyed their parties, which activities worked best and those they'd wished they done differently. Digby stayed for a few minutes, nodding politely without contributing, before excusing himself and drifting off. All three pairs of eyes observed his progress across the lawn.

'How was he really?' Adrienne asked Samuel.

'Quiet, but Josh made sure to keep him involved.' He hugged her close. 'Stop fretting. He's fine.'

Adrienne set her gaze on Jas. 'You'll keep an eye on him, won't you? During the wedding and its lead up? Josh will be busy enough, and Em ...' She didn't need to clarify the rift between Digby and his sister. 'He's bound to find it difficult.'

'Of course, but I think Digby's stronger than you give him credit for.'

Adrienne dug her teeth into her lip, brow remaining furrowed. 'I hope you're right.'

'I am.' She touched Adrienne's hand. 'The wedding will go off without a hitch, Em and Josh will have a perfect day, and Digby will fulfil his duty as best man with pride and dignity. Teagan, Harry and I will make sure of it. You have nothing to worry about. Nothing at all.'

But later that evening, as Jas carried her box of party tricks to her car, she looked up at the stable windows and saw Digby silhouetted against the light. He appeared to be holding something—a thin book or perhaps a photo frame, it was difficult to tell. She stopped and watched, trapped between needing to get home to feed Ox and wanting to go to Digby. To offer him the comfort he'd so generously given her.

Suddenly his head turned. He caught her looking, and for several thumping heartbeats it was as though their feelings were reaching out through the cooling air, lacing together like fingers. Then he withdrew from the window and the connection broke, leaving her alone with her confusion.

Jas had turned along the foreshore road at Port Andrews when her phone rang. Digby's name flashed, and though Jas loathed people who used their phone while driving she couldn't stop herself from picking it up.

'Hey,' he said.

'Hey yourself.'

A short silence followed then, 'Jas ...'

'You want to come over?'

'Do you mind?'

'No. I'd like that.'

He breathed out. 'Thanks.'

'Dig?'

'Yeah?'

'Bring wine. I've had one glass of champagne all day and I deserve a drink.'

She hung up, grinning and filled with a fluttery sense of excitement that she should have admonished herself for but couldn't. Digby was her best friend's brother, a man dealing with demons. A man looking only for friendship. He would not be her rebound.

Unless he wanted to be.

CHAPTER
10

Digby wasn't sure what he was doing was smart, all he knew was that he couldn't stand another minute in his stifling apartment where the air seemed tainted with the scent of Felicity and every sound had him jerking around, hoping to catch her ghost.

She wasn't there. She would never be there no matter how much he wished it.

He thought he'd coped with the day fairly well. If nothing else, he owed it to Josh. Spoiling his friend's celebration wasn't the way to repay him for what Josh had done for Felicity. And himself. But that didn't make it easy. Digby had done his best though. Joining in where he could, trying not to be the dampener on everyone's enjoyment.

Digby didn't begrudge Josh his happiness but witnessing it reminded him how much of his own had been ripped from him. By day's end his soul felt dredged, scraped free of grace, and he'd had to retreat to the stables. Except all that achieved was an exacerbation of his loneliness.

And now he was going to foist it on Jas.

He turned left onto the esplanade and followed it out of Port Andrews, then indicated for Jasmine's. Instead of open driveway, the Mercedes's headlights swept the galvanised steel of her front gate. Latched around the strainer was the rubber-coated bike lock. The sight made Digby frown. She'd known he was coming, had seemed pleased about it. Why lock the gate when he was only a few minutes behind?

The creeping sensation that something was very wrong raised the hairs on his neck. He squinted through the darkness. No welcome light shone over the front porch and only the kitchen light appeared to be on. He scanned left and right, checking for another vehicle, for anything abnormal, but the yard seemed as he remembered. Greying crushed limestone road. Not much of a lawn. A few windblown scrubby trees. The edge of her garage behind. Nothing untoward, yet doubt hovered.

Digby hurried with the bike chain's combination, breathing out in relief when the lock fell open. If she'd changed the code he would have jumped the fence and sprinted to her, whether she'd wanted to keep him out or not. People didn't change mood that fast, not without duress.

He drove faster than normal down the road, the car bouncing as he ignored potholes and eroded edges and focused on the house.

It wasn't until his headlights caught the old chaff bags that his fears really climbed. They were nailed vertically at head height either side of both the lounge and kitchen windows. The garden beds that ran along the front of the house had never been tidy but, even in the shadows, the white of broken branches and sappy scent of trampled geraniums were unmistakable, and Digby was damned sure it wasn't Jas who'd done the damage.

Keeping his gaze fixed on the kitchen window, he turned off the engine and stepped out. There was no sign of movement, no sound other than the whistling sea breeze and the constant murmur of the ocean. He hurried to the house, pausing only to lift one of the chaff bags.

A mineral stench assaulted him. He lifted the bag higher, angling it to make the most of the moonlight. Fury clawed Digby's guts. Someone had spray-painted the word 'whore' in ugly, dripping red capitals. The W was gouged and ragged where Jas must have attempted to scour it off. He checked the side next to the lounge. 'SLUT' shouted viciously from the wall.

He leaped up the steps and banged on her door, barging in before she could answer. 'Jas?'

'In here,' she called from the lounge, her voice weary.

She was on her knees in front of the fire, trying to light it with a shaking hand.

'Jas,' he said, crouching next to her and touching her chin to get her to look at him. 'What's going on?'

She opened her trembling mouth to answer and shut it again, stubbornly twisting out of his grip to concentrate back on the fire.

Frustrated, Digby snatched the matches out of her hand. It wasn't cold, in fact the night was mild. A fire shouldn't have been necessary but from the way Jas was shivering she was desperate for warmth. With a flick he lit another match and set the kindling alight. Satisfied it had caught, he tossed the matches aside and rested back on his haunches to study her.

'Do you know who did this?'

She shook her head.

'Someone who knows about you and Mike?'

She stared at the flames. Shadows danced over her face. Her skin had an almost lustrous sheen from the make-up she was wearing, but her mascara now formed charcoal smudges under her eyes. 'Probably.'

There was too much resignation in her voice for this to be new. Digby thought back to the unplugged phone, the bike lock, the way she'd abruptly stiffened when she'd spotted him coming back from the beach with Ox.

'What else has happened?' When she didn't answer he prodded further, his anger at her tormenter and worry for her making him harsh and demanding. 'What else, Jas?'

'Rotting fish, dog shit.' She made a dismissive gesture. 'The usual cowardly crap.'

Digby tried to keep his breathing steady. Dog crap? Rotting fish? And she'd said nothing? Jesus Christ.

'How long has it been going on for?'

'Two, three weeks.' She looked at him. 'I can handle it.'

'Of course you can. That's why you're sitting here shaking like you'll never get warm.'

'I'm not scared, if that's what you're implying. Just ...' She jammed fingers into her brow and slid them back and forth. 'I just hate knowing there's someone out there who despises me so much they'd do this.' Her hand dropped and her mouth thinned with bitterness. 'It's the unfairness of it too, you know? Why I am I the whore? Why not Mike? He's the married one, not me. Why isn't whoever's doing this tormenting him?' Her gaze turned hollow. 'It's always the woman's fault, have you noticed that? Always Eve, never Adam.'

Digby didn't know what to say. Jas was right, of course. Blame almost always fell on the women in these situations, regardless of where true fault lay. Digby wished he'd given in to his urge and punched Mike in the car like he'd wanted to. Not that it would have made a scrap of difference to what Jas was suffering, but knowing he'd done it would make Digby feel a whole lot better now.

The fire had caught and was beginning to crackle in earnest, yet Jas remained shivering. Shock more than likely. Coming home from your best friend's bridal shower to find your house vandalised would rattle anyone. Shrugging off his jacket, Digby draped it gently around her shoulders.

'Stay there,' he said, stroking the silky dark curls at the back of her head. 'I'll be back in a tick.'

A few minutes later he returned, bearing filled wineglasses. He eased down close to Jas and passed one over. It was awkward sitting on the floor but he needed to be close.

'It won't be as good as the last,' he said. 'Everyone was still in the kitchen when I went across to the house. I just grabbed whatever was closest in the cellar and got out before anyone could corner me.'

'Thanks.' She took a small sip and stared back at the fire. The combusting logs seemed to almost pulse with life. 'What a horrible way to end a good day.'

It was, no question, but the unsettling thing for Digby was that being with her right now it didn't feel that way. Sitting alongside Jas, keeping her safe, gave him an odd sense of worth, the likes of which he hadn't felt since Felicity.

'We'll clean it off in the morning. There's turps at home. We'll try that first and if it doesn't work the Mitre 10 should have some graffiti remover. Otherwise it might be a case of sanding it back and repainting.'

'You don't have to help. I can manage.'

'I know, but I'm going to anyway.'

Jas was silent for a while, then she smiled. 'Thanks.'

Digby covered her hand with his own, meaning only to give it a quick squeeze, but the feel of her soft skin against his palm had him holding on. Uncertain, he checked her face. The smile remained in place. So did his hand. The sense of worthiness that his presence was truly valued intensified.

'Did you want me to get you anything to eat?'

'No. I had enough of your mum's cooking today.' A cloud passed over Jasmine's eyes. 'I don't think I could eat even if I was hungry.'

'Understandable. Have you spoken to anyone about what's been happening?'

'Like who? My parents? The police?' She sighed. 'As I said to Em, I'd have to explain about Mike then. Mum and Dad would be devastated. All the excuses I made, the lies … As for the police, knowing how this place works, it'd be the equivalent of making it front-page article on the *Leader*. What could they do anyway? Drive past every now and then?' Her lip curled slightly, dismissing the notion. 'Whoever it is keeps a watch. They know when I'm out and they know how not to be seen.'

That someone had been spying on her deepened Digby's anger. Whatever mistakes Jas had made, she didn't deserve this.

'I can though.'

Her brow furrowed. 'You can what?'

'Drive past, keep an eye out.'

'Right. And if you catch someone in the act?'

He hesitated. What would he do if he caught them? 'I beat them up?'

Jasmine's giggle was the best sound he'd heard since arriving. She leaned against him fondly. 'Tough guy.'

'That's me, Super Digby,' he said, kissing her hair.

She stilled and Digby thought he heard her breath catch. He swallowed. He'd kissed her without thinking. It was spontaneous. The way he used to be with Felicity.

His face burned. 'Jas—'

Head shaking, she lifted her hand and pressed a finger against his lips. 'Don't.' Inhaling deeply, she focused wide eyes on his and this time her voice was barely a whisper. 'Don't.'

He didn't know what she meant. Don't talk? Don't kiss her again? Panic that he'd overstepped hurtled through his veins but as she held his gaze, as he saw her expression sweeten and yield to longing, he began to understand that whatever this moment held, one thing was certain: it mattered.

Digby felt something tick over inside himself, like a cog moving on. It was a strange feeling—not unpleasant but not completely agreeable either. More a sense of cautious hope. Like he was about to embark on an experiment that had a greater chance of failure than success.

Jas placed her glass aside and shifted to rest on her knees, hands on the top of her thighs. Eyes downcast, she took another deep breath before addressing him once more. 'Do you think ...'

He knew what she wanted to ask. Fear and guilt and five hundred other emotions fluttered through him, beating wings against his chest. But one beat harder than all the others.

Desire.

His voice, when it came, sounded as breathless as hers. 'Yeah, I do.'

'Oh.' The corner of her mouth lifted and her nose screwed up cutely. 'I kind of wasn't expecting that.'

'If it's any consolation, neither was I.'

She gave a soft laugh and just as quickly sobered. 'God,' she breathed, closing her eyes. 'This is so weird. You're my best friend's brother. I've never ... you know.'

'Me either.'

'But it feels right though, doesn't it? For us?'

He stroked curled fingers down the side of her face. Her skin was like satin, warm from the fire and flush with her yearning. Eyes hooded, she pressed catlike against the contact, as if it was something exquisite. The start of a moan vibrated inside Digby.

How long since he'd touched someone with that kind of tenderness? How long since he'd found intimacy, since the burn of loneliness had been soothed?

'Yes,' he said as desire bulldozed over his guilt. Right, wrong, he didn't care. He simply wanted.

A heartbeat, two heartbeats, then they were diving together and his lips were on hers. She was luscious, welcoming and wine flavoured. The kiss at first was delicate, exploratory, but as the connection built it deepened. Their mouths opened wider, moved faster. His breathing turned ragged. Hands dug at clothes, seeking skin. Passion became vocal. Lust rocketed through Digby, turning every other thought to ashes. Heat surrounded him. His brain burned with need, the cold ache of his heart forgotten.

Seconds became minutes, then time ran out and all he knew was the pleasure of Jasmine's yielding body and the sound of her excitement and need as they rushed each other headlong and joyous back to life.

CHAPTER

11

Jas stared at the ceiling, a nervous smile playing over her face. Had last night really happened? Body heat from the man next to her revealed it had, as did the throb of fulfilment between her legs. And it had been exciting and comforting and weird and perfect and scary and silly and a million other things all at once.

Biting her lip, she rolled over, tucked her hand under her cheek and gazed at Digby. Creeping dawn painted the room in shades that seemed to grow more radiant and joyful with every second. He was awake, also lying on his side, facing her. Contrary to Jasmine's haze of disbelief, Digby appeared smug and well satisfied.

'Hi,' he said.

For some irrational reason Jas felt suddenly, stupidly, shy. Ridiculous after what they'd done. Last night was like the breaking of a dam. One kiss and the flow of their desire had become unstoppable. She scraped a lock of hair out of her eye. 'Hi.'

A long moment passed as she tried to read his thoughts. From the way he was scrutinising her in return, Digby was doing the same. What to say though? What if he felt last night was a mistake? Jas didn't think so, not from the way he'd first met her gaze, but this was a man whose grief had been so encompassing he'd barely functioned for a year. Jasmine would bet her life savings she was the first woman he'd been with since Felicity. There were bound to be emotional consequences.

'Did we really do that?' she asked.

'We did.'

'Regrets?' Jas winced at the question. Of all the moronic things to ask the morning after, when it was too late. Plus it smacked of insecurity, and the truth was Jas felt pretty damn wonderful about what had happened. Sex with Digby had been a revelation. Nothing like she'd imagined. Not that she'd ever imagined sex with her best friend's brother before, which made the whole situation even more confounding.

Her mind flickered to the brooding, Heathcliff-like image of him standing at the back door at Camrick, the confusing gut-punch of lust at the sight of him. But she suspected her attraction had begun well before then, in the quiet intimacy of his visits, in the shared drama with Mike. In Digby's new-found masculine protectiveness.

Digby didn't seem to mind the question. 'No. You?'

'None.' The certainty of his reply unfurled a warm, teasing feeling inside Jas. 'Well, maybe one.'

He raised an eyebrow.

She wriggled a fraction closer, her heart already breaking into flutters. 'Only that we didn't do it more.'

He chuckled and reached for her, hauling her onto his chest and kissing her. She wriggled against him, savouring the length of Digby's erection against her lower belly.

'Eveready,' she whispered, nuzzling his neck and nibbling on his earlobe.

A hand slipped behind her buttocks and explored downward. 'I could say the same for you.'

'I like sex.'

'No kidding.'

They broke into laughter.

Suddenly, as though cleaved in half, Digby's laughter stopped. He regarded Jas with a kind of puzzled awe. His gaze raked her face, a small line appearing between his brows.

'What?'

'I don't know, it's weird. I keep thinking I shouldn't be laughing.'

The admission tangled around her heart. Jas fingered the nest of lightly curled hairs on his chest. 'Because of Felicity?'

Mouth closed against emotion, he nodded.

'She would have wanted you to laugh, Dig. Felicity loved you. She wouldn't want you to grieve forever.'

'I know.' But as he spoke his eyes shifted from hers to stare at nothing.

She steered Digby's face back towards hers with her finger. 'Don't think about it. That's for later. Think about this instead.'

Jasmine's mouth closed over his, shutting off any protest, shutting out thoughts of *her*. This wasn't about Felicity or his grief or his confusion. This was about now. About them taking all the wrongs in their lives and remodelling them into something good and right.

The kiss was soft at first, teasing and without urgency. Its languidness allowed her to sense the thud of his heart against her chest, catch the increasing huskiness of his breaths, the thickening of his cock against her belly.

The top sheet slipped down Jasmine's back in a sensuous slither, cool morning air making her skin pucker. His fingers traced her spine, gliding lower with each delicious stroke and tightening her goosebumps even further. His hands weren't coarse like a manual labourer's, nor were they office-worker soft like Mike's. There were rough patches, the occasional callous. Digby was a horticulturalist by profession and though he hadn't worked for a year, Jas knew Camrick's elegant gardens were mostly thanks to him. The scrape of roughness from the wear of work, the knowledge those hands had helped plants grow and thrive and bloom, added extra frisson to his touch. It was as though he was nurturing her into life too, her body ripening under his sure caresses.

She gasped as Digby tumbled her over and propped on an elbow, head balanced on one palm. The other rested in the hollow just below the gap between her breasts, thumb caressing tiny circles. The smile was back on his face. In a lazy sweep, he raked his gaze over her chest, eyelids half lowered in a way that made Jasmine's insides leap with excitement. His eyes slid back to hers and a slow, sexy-wicked tilt curled the edge of his mouth. Still watching her, he bowed towards her turgid nipple and tongued it, then eased back a fraction to blow air over the surface.

Everything puckered. From her nipple to her scalp to the skin behind her knees. Jasmine's toes curled, her fingers with them. She managed a choked 'oh' before Digby angled close again and sucked the nub fully into his mouth.

Her gasp became breathless. Tiny bites shot electricity straight into her groin. Digby's free hand cupped her other breast, finger and thumb rolling the straining nipple. Restless energy twitched through Jasmine's legs and lifted her hips in an involuntary gesture of want. She moaned and reached for him. The skin of his cock was taut and satiny, the tip moist.

Not releasing either breast, Digby lifted his head to regard her with wolfish eyes. It was the sexiest look she'd ever witnessed from any lover. As if he wanted to devour her. Aroused beyond measure, Jas eyed him hungrily, only to jerk back when he scraped his teeth firmly over the sensitive peak of her nipple.

'God!'

The smugness in his gaze when she managed to uncross her eyes had her giggling, but her amusement was short-lived. His fingers were trailing lower, the pads of his fingertips leaving tiny pitter-patters over her belly. They meandered left then right, roving everywhere except where she wanted them.

'You're a tease,' she whispered, arching as he tickled the sensitive skin of her inner thigh.

'I'm only making up for what you did to me last night.'

'That wasn't teasing.'

'Sure it wasn't.' He lowered his head back to her breast and tongued a line to her ribs. Stretching his long legs back, he began to shuffle further down the bed, dragging his hot mouth lower.

'I don't want to be teased, Dig.' She tugged on his hair, forcing his head up. 'I want you. Now.'

'You're spoiling my cunning plan.'

'Your cunning-lingus plan, you mean?' At his expression she laughed and tickled his cheek. 'Later, lover.'

'You don't like it?'

'Oh, I like it, believe me, but there's something else I like just as much. Something that involves you, me and ...' she wiggled her eyebrows, '... that impressive appendage of yours.'

'Impressive, huh?'

'Very.'

She tilted her head, curious if Digby had any idea of how intoxicating he was in bed. There was definite pride there but none of the hubris of Mike. Digby's passion was spontaneous, fired by instinct. Mike had been all technique and mechanics. He'd had turning Jas on so fine-tuned she feared any other lover would be commonplace. But it was Digby's humanity, his chuckles about mistakes, the funny fumblings and hesitant experimentation, the pure heart he put into his lovemaking that made him more special than Mike could ever be.

Jas lifted her chin. 'Come here.'

Digby didn't need to be told again. He scrambled back up the bed and was kissing her before she had time to laugh at his eagerness. And this time when he entered her, there was none of the residual worry of last night, none of the nervousness. Simply two people immersing themselves in the thrilling pleasure and intimacy of sex.

Afterward, in the shower, when they'd spent a leisurely time soaping and washing each other clean, and Jas was feeling yet again ridiculously turned on, she leaned against the tiles and eyed him saucily. 'Remember that cunning plan?'

Digby grinned and braced his hands above her head. Water cascaded over his hair and streaked his chest, turning him sleek, defining his muscled leanness. That was another thing she hadn't expected: the deliciousness of his body. Digby wasn't heavily built but he was fit, with broad, straight shoulders, sexily configured biceps, narrow hips and long, toned legs. She liked the way the hair spread finely over his body too, forming a loose T from his chest down his belly to a thicker tangle at his groin. Stubble had formed on his jaw overnight, adding to his rakish air.

He wiggled his eyebrows. 'You mean my cunning-lingus plan?'

Jas teased a finger over his chest. 'That's the one.'

'You really do like sex, don't you?'

'You have no idea,' muttered Jas as he slid his wet mouth over her breasts and crouched to trace his tongue even lower. 'No idea at all.'

'Good thing I do too,' he said, then killed any further conversation by burying his face between her legs.

If it weren't for the hot water running out, Jas would have been content to linger in the steamy cocoon of pleasure that her shower had become. For several seconds she was too lost in the incredible sensation of Digby thrusting long deliberate strokes in and out of her from behind, hands on her breasts, her own gripping the soap dish, to realise that the water splashing her back was becoming uncomfortably cool. Seconds later it was freezing, forcing them, squealing, from the recess. Too randy and close to fulfilment to make the short trip back to the bedroom, Jas rested her hands on the sink, wiggled her backside and gave Digby a come-on over her shoulder. A few heartbeats and he'd obliged, and the sultry air once more vibrated with the soft sounds of their pleasure.

Half an hour later, Jas found herself sitting fully clothed on her kitchen bench, Digby between her knees, toying with the buttons of her shirt as he snatched farewell kisses. The promised trip back to Camrick to pick up turpentine was being delayed by their reluctance to break the moment. It felt adolescent and silly and sunburstingly brilliant.

'I should go,' he murmured for the fifth time.

'Mmm,' replied Jas, nuzzling his neck.

'This isn't fixing your house.'

'I know, but it's fixing me.'

Digby breathed in sharply—and it wasn't because of the tease of her caresses. He eased back to regard her. 'I think it's fixing me too, Jas.' He breathed out, shaking his head in wonder. 'I don't know how. Or why. It's like ...' He looked up, searching the air, or perhaps questioning God or the sky or the world, for an explanation. Perhaps it was Felicity's ghost he was asking. 'I feel different.' He frowned and met Jasmine's gaze, the question still simmering.

'Good different?'

'Yes.'

Wary of crossing a line, she hesitated before speaking. 'Free different?'

'You mean from Felicity?'

The lack of anger in his tone gave her courage. 'No. I meant more free from hurt. Like maybe there's still good things to be had from life.'

He considered for a while. 'Yeah. Maybe it's something like that.' Then he smiled and kissed the tip of her nose. 'You're a pretty good thing.'

'So are you.' She wriggled her bum to slide closer, and draped her arms around his neck. 'A very good thing.'

The kiss that followed lasted for a long time.

'Jas,' said Digby when they finally parted. He took a breath, his expression serious. 'I like you. A lot. But I need you understand—'

'You still love her.'

He pressed his forehead against hers and held eye contact with worried intensity. 'That doesn't mean I don't care about you.'

'I know, Dig.' She smiled, wanting him to understand. Whatever they were doing, it wasn't typical, it mightn't lead anywhere, but in that moment, that juncture of their lives, it was what they both needed. Whatever the past, whatever the future, the relationship they'd developed was good for them now. 'It's okay, I promise. We'll just take this one step at a time.' She tugged on a lock of his hair. 'Stop stressing, okay? We're having great sex. At least I am. And call me insatiable, but I'm more than happy to have more.' She regarded him from under lowered lashes. 'Unless you don't want to?'

'Oh yeah, I want to.' A grin broke. 'That insatiable thing?'

'Mmm?' she said, reaching for the button of his jeans.

'I don't mind that at all. Not ...' His eyes closed as she lowered his zipper. 'One ...' Jasmine's fingers began to stroke. 'Bit.'

Digby was thirty-two years old. Having his mother freak out because he'd spent the night away from home was galling, to say the least.

He'd barely braked in front of the stables and she was rushing towards him. She hovered beside the car door, shifting from foot to foot, wringing her hands as tears pooled in her eyes. Adrienne Wallace-Jones was a woman renowned for her elegance and poise, but this morning she'd unravelled. Her eyes were streaked with smears of mascara, her hair dull and dishevelled. She wore grey trousers and a white cotton shirt that had come untucked on one side. But the greatest sign of her distress were the lines of fear and exhaustion around her trembling mouth. Digby hadn't seen her like this since the inquest, when they'd all suffered private hells of grief and guilt.

'Mum,' he said, pushing the door open.

He hadn't even straightened when she launched, sobbing as she hurled arms around him and buried her face into his chest. Digby blinked and stared across her shoulder to where Samuel stood on the path. Granny B was at the back door, observing the scene with interest.

Digby held his palms out in a question. Samuel's expression was grim, and more than a little disapproving. With that look, Digby's good mood turned to stone. He glanced at his grandmother but she'd crossed into the garden and was flicking a lighter at the tip of one of her disgusting cigars.

'Mum,' he said on a sigh, trying to untangle her from his body.

'We were worried sick!'

'What for?'

'What for?' She shoved his chest. '*What for*? You didn't come home last night, that's what for!'

'No,' he answered coldly, furious now. 'I didn't. Not that it's any of your business.'

Adrienne's mouth opened and closed in shock. Then she burst into noisy sobs, which had Samuel striding across the gravel to envelop her in his arms.

The glower Samuel shot Digby was thick with condemnation. 'You could have phoned.'

The words 'fuck you' formed in Digby's head. The first scrap of happiness he'd found in a year and it was being spoiled by this shit. 'This is my house. I'll come and go as I please.'

Realising he might have pushed a little too hard, Samuel softened his tone. 'Your mother was worried, that's all. No one knew where you were.' He lowered his voice further. 'She nearly called the police.'

'As you can see, I'm fine.' He turned his glacial gaze onto his mum. This wasn't the first time she'd panicked. He'd had the humiliating experience of being picked up by the local police one night when a desperate escape from the apartment turned into a lonely ramble that had lasted hours. He understood that she was worried, but they'd been through this. Digby wasn't depressed—he was grieving and lonely. The difference was significant but she refused to see it. 'You have to stop this. I'm handling things. What I do with my life, where I go, is no one's business but my own.'

'I know but—'

'No buts, Mum.' He held eye contact long enough for her to see that he was serious, then shifted focus to Samuel. The man clearly had more to say but Digby's rigid expression kept him silent.

'Come on, Adrienne,' said Samuel, steering her away. 'Digby wants his space and you need a rest.'

The way he said 'wants his space' shot Digby's hackles up. Samuel made it sound as if Digby was the selfish one for wanting to live his own life. He glared at the other man's back as he led his mother into the house. Samuel liked to play father figure, mostly for Adrienne's sake, Digby suspected, but he didn't need a father. What he needed was a bit of faith and to be left alone to sort himself out.

Granny B, who'd been strolling around the formal front garden dead-heading roses as she smoked, paused to study him. Digby met her gaze and to his astonishment she nodded as if to say 'well done'. Approval from his grandmother? Digby blinked, unsure he'd interpreted correctly. But there was no missing that small smile or the spark of pride glittering in those all-seeing eyes.

Shaking his head in amazement, he strode to the stables, pushed inside, and leaped up the stairs two at a time.

There were thirty-seven missed calls on his mobile. After phoning Jas the night before he'd dumped it on the couch and headed straight out, ignorant of the drama that would cause. Most were from Camrick, while a couple were from Em's home number and another was from Josh's mobile. Digby turned the phone to speaker and listened to the messages as he wandered into his bedroom and hunted for work clothes.

His mother's voice echoed, each message more frantic than the last. Shame tightened his gut. Digby hated upsetting her. He'd already put her through so much, but he also needed his freedom. Em's messages were calm, simply asking him to call Adrienne when he had a minute, to put their mum's mind at ease. He deleted them all with a sigh.

Finally Josh came on the line.

'Hey, Dig. It's Josh. You've probably gathered by now that Adrienne's freaking out. I've told her you're fine but you know what she's like. Anyway, if you get a chance, call her. Otherwise, whatever you're up to, enjoy it and don't worry about anyone else.' There was a pause. 'I trust you, mate.' Then another beat before Josh laughed and said, 'Christ, I hope you're getting laid.' A shout sounded in the background followed by a half-muffled 'What?' from Josh before the call was cut off.

Digby grinned, then he sobered as he realised that he'd probably have to admit to Josh where he'd been.

The thing was, he didn't want to share what had happened between him and Jas. Digby didn't kid himself that Josh could withhold the news from Em, not something involving both her brother and her best friend. Which meant he couldn't tell him. Once word was out he and Jas would be under constant scrutiny and Digby didn't want that. Not for her, not for himself.

Digby deleted the remaining messages without listening to them. Hearing his mother's almost hysterical sobs was getting him down and he didn't want to return to Jas feeling guilty for what they'd done.

Dressed in clean work clothes, Digby contemplated his wardrobe. A leather overnight bag sat in one corner. Would it be presumptuous to take another change of clothes? Probably, but it'd also be smart. He'd be bound to get splashed with turps and Jas wouldn't appreciate him hanging around stinking. And he wanted to hang around. Now he'd had sex he wanted more of it. A whole lot more.

Although it wasn't just sex. It was the connection, being touched. The intimacy of being with another human. One who craved the closeness as much as he did.

It helped that Jas was sensational in bed. He should have realised she would be. Jas did everything with gusto. When she cried it was loud and messy. When she laughed it was hearty. She ate with appetite, drank with enjoyment, kissed with passion and made love with unbound pleasure, delighting in the joy of his body as well as her own. No strings, no manipulation. Simply amazing, enthusiastic, unconstrained sex.

Felicity had loved him deeply—for all they'd endured Digby had never doubted that—but making love with her had been very different to other women he'd been with, and almost the polar opposite to Jas. Sex with Felicity always had a strange intensity, approached with seriousness and a great deal of care on Digby's part. From the beginning Felicity had admitted her difficult upbringing and the ordeals she'd suffered, but he suspected there was much she still kept hidden. Terrible things that had shaped her attitude towards sex. For her, lovemaking seemed to have little to do with her own satisfaction and a lot to do with pleasing him. Or manipulating him.

There were times when Digby had wondered if Felicity even liked sex. No matter how gentle he was, how loving he tried to be, he could sense a detachment within her. On the rare occasion when he'd tried to broach the subject she'd become so upset he'd let it drop, leaving him determined to be even more caring. He didn't mind. Digby would have shot the moon down if it had made her happy. But it meant sex lost a lot of its fun.

Jas, on the other hand, was like a happy puppy, bouncing around with her mesmerising full breasts, luscious womanly curves, saucy looks and occasional dirty talk. The difference, the lack of pressure, was a massive turn on.

Digby couldn't help smiling. Even thinking about it had made him stiffen.

To hell with presumption. He packed the bag.

Jas was in the garage when Digby arrived back, tins of paint and some ratty bristled paintbrushes lined up on the concrete. The way she grinned on seeing him killed any lingering trace of the bad mood brought on by the scene with his mother at Camrick. Jas was sexy, exciting and real. His blood, so long sluggish and viscous with sorrow, surged life once more through his veins.

She sauntered towards him in a pair of well-fitting faded jeans and a purple polo shirt that was either ancient or had shrunk in the wash. The hem skimmed the waistband of her jeans, revealing a tiny sliver of pale skin with each sway of her hips. The neck gaped from the strain over her breasts. Eyes on his, Jas stopped right in front of him and placed her hand over his heart, before standing on tiptoe to kiss him.

A kiss that had him dumping the plastic bags he was carrying to lean her against the rear of her car and shove his hands up her shirt.

'We're never going to get anything done,' she said as he rucked her top up. Her bra was pink, sheer and with a low lacy edge. He tongued her nipple through the fabric. The nub was satisfyingly turgid.

'Do you mind?'

'God, no. Although if you're going to do what I think we'd better at least move out of sight of the road.'

'Not into exhibitionism?'

She flicked the top button of his trousers, released the zipper and stroked his straining trunks in a way that had him closing his eyes and groaning. 'Are you?'

'Right now I couldn't care less.' Despite his words, he dug an arm beneath Jasmine's bum, hauled her up against his hips and shuffled further into the garage's concealing shadows to prop her on the car's bonnet. They weren't completely out of sight but it was close enough. The way he was feeling this wasn't going to last long anyway.

It didn't, but that didn't mean it wasn't as intoxicating as every other time. Jas had come fast and noisily, with shudders, gasping breaths and loud ecstatic cries of 'Oh god, oh god, oh god,' that had driven his own climax to even greater heights.

'Sorry,' she said, panting and laughing.

'For what?'

'Being a bit overexcited.'

'You don't have to apologise for that.'

Pouting her bottom lip, she blew air upwards over her flushed face. There were tiny speckles of sweat under her eyes and over her brow. 'You've made me all hot.'

'You were already hot. That tight shirt ...' Digby made an appreciative noise.

That only made her laugh again. 'So are you, lover boy. All I've been able to think about since you left was sex.'

They'd been so eager that Jas hadn't fully removed her jeans. One leg was on, the other dangling. Her knickers the same.

'I had the same problem,' he said, helping her back into them.

'Really? You took so long I was starting to worry I'd frightened you off.'

Digby lifted her off the car and pulled down her polo shirt before fixing his own clothes. They'd left sweaty streaks and handprints on the bonnet. 'No chance of that.' Zipped and buttoned, he hunted for a rag and polished off the evidence of their exuberance. 'I had a bit of a problem at Camrick.'

'Oh, Dig. What happened?'

'Mum.'

'Ah. So she noticed you didn't come home last night.'

'Yeah.'

Jas crossed her arms and chewed her lip.

'I didn't tell them where I was, if that's what you're worried about.'

'It wouldn't matter if you did.' She sounded confident, except her body language said otherwise.

Digby placed his arms on her shoulders. 'Wouldn't it?'

Jas let out a breath and rubbed fingers across her brow. 'I don't know. I'd like to keep it private, but they're bound to find out. I think your grandmother's already guessed there's something between us. She saw us talking yesterday and got that look. You know, the one where you can see her brain whirring.'

Digby was all too familiar with it. 'She gave me a look this morning too.'

Jas winced at the news. 'Not good.'

'Don't be so sure about that. I have a feeling she approves. Like Josh, she probably thinks getting laid will do me good.'

'Which it is.'

'You bet.' Smiling, he kissed her. 'Come on, let's sort this house. Then you and I can spend the rest of the day in bed if we want.'

'Oh, I want.'

'Nympho.'

'Speak for yourself, Eveready.'

It gave Digby some solace that they shared a moment of playfulness in the face of what was coming. The words sprayed on her walls were cruel and mean-hearted, sentiments far beyond deserving. The red paint was like a slash across their day, and he worried Jas would shrink back into the bleakness of last night. She sobered a little when the sacking was ripped down but then set to work with determination, mouth set in defiance.

Digby had brought turpentine from Camrick and a bottle of graffiti remover that he'd picked up from the hardware shop on his way through. Though the chemicals stripped the worst of the damage to a faded mauve, the words remained clearly legible against the pale paint of the weatherboards.

'I guess I'll have to strip and repaint,' said Jas, regarding the wall with her hands on her hips.

Digby tried to stay positive. 'It's only a small area. With the two of us it won't take long.'

She pressed her shoulder against his. 'Thanks.'

He bent and kissed her hair. 'I didn't say I wouldn't demand payment later.'

The comment caused Jas to roll her eyes. 'And you call me a nympho.'

It took them the rest of the morning and into early afternoon to scrape all the paint away, clean the timber with a wire brush and then jet off any residue with the pressure washer. While the boards dried, they carried sandwiches down to the beach and sat on the dunes watching the breakers and boats. It was a fine day, the sea calm. Recreational fishermen in dinghies dotted the glittering water. A couple took turns using a whippy thrower to toss a tennis ball along the waterline, their chocolate labrador galloping enthusiastically after it. Further down the beach where the swell curled more, surfers in colourful rashies and wetsuits paddled and bobbed.

Seagulls bickered and paraded nearby as they fawned for scraps. Digby tossed a crust and watched the ensuing squabble with amusement.

'We should go for a swim,' said Jas. 'Wash some of this stink off.'

'We just had lunch.'

'A paddle then.'

'How about a long shower instead?'

'Okay.'

He eyed her. 'You're easily pleased.'

'I'm an easy kind of girl.'

Digby laughed. 'Aren't I the lucky one?'

Which was what he was still thinking the following morning when a grumbling Jas finally crawled out of bed to shower for work, leaving him lying on the rumpled sheets, hands behind his head, smiling with oversex and contentment.

'Quit looking so smug and show a bit of sympathy for those of us who have to go to work,' she said, returning to kneel beside him, pink from the shower and smelling of the lemongrass-scented body wash she used. Her bra and bikini knickers were denim-coloured with white lace edges. The cute sight of them made him want to drag her back into bed and take his time peeling them off.

He ran his finger over the rim of her bra. 'Do you always wear sexy underwear?'

'Yes. My work uniform is boring and sexless. These make me feel nice.'

'I won't be able to look at you again without imagining what's underneath now.'

She tickled fingers low over his stomach. 'I get the feeling I might have a similar problem.' Grinning, she bounded up and began dressing properly. 'Good thing anticipation turns me on.'

'Jas, everything turns you on.'

She poked her tongue out.

Digby eased himself out of bed. He could have stayed there, dozing and thinking of Jas, the things they'd done, but he wanted to walk with her and the vandalised walls needed a final coat of paint.

He trailed her out to the garage, hands in his trouser pockets. The wind was up this morning, the smell of ozone strong. Overhead, the sky was clouding. He hoped it wouldn't rain. Digby needed dry weather if he was going to finish fixing the house.

He held the door open for her, watching as Jas settled her handbag and lunch things on the passenger seat and reached for the seatbelt. She was right about her uniform, it wasn't flattering, but knowing what sexiness lurked underneath gave it a certain appeal, like a tease on his imagination. When she was set he closed the door. She rolled down the window with a smile and started the engine. The radio blared morning wake-up rock music. Jas flicked it off and laid her hands on the wheel, staring at the back of the garage wall. Digby could sense her need to ask. He'd felt the same.

She glanced at him and inhaled deeply. 'I know what you said. About Felicity. About us. But I don't want this to be it.'

'I don't either.'

'But it's not ...' She lifted a hand and weaved it through the air. 'You know.'

'Serious?'

'Yes. No. I don't know.' She regarded him worriedly. 'We've had that much sex it has to mean something, doesn't it?'

He shrugged. 'I guess it means we like having sex with each other.'

Amusement danced in her eyes. 'I think that's been well established.'

An apprehensive silence fell between them. If this went beyond the weekend would it mean they were in a relationship? Digby had no idea. Sleeping with his sister's best friend was as new an idea to him as it probably was to Jas. Except he and Jas were friends too. They'd shared things, personal pains. A special bond existed between them. He might not know what it was or what it meant, but he sure as hell didn't want it broken.

'I don't mind having more,' he said carefully. 'If you don't.'

'I don't.' Relief flooded her face. 'Friends with excellent benefits then?'

'I can cope with that.' He lifted an eyebrow. 'So ...'

'I'll see you at seven. I'd make it earlier only I need to take Oxy for a run. The poor darling's feeling neglected.' She put the car into reverse and held up a finger. 'Seven. Unless I call you for a lunchtime quickie. I'm that horny I could burst.'

Jasmine's parting words kept Digby smiling until the painting was complete. He closed up, taking his time and studying the land between her house and the outskirts of Port Andrews. If someone was observing him back, he didn't notice. All he could hope was that whoever was tormenting Jas had noted his presence over the weekend and realised Jas and Mike were over.

Even so, he fixed the bike chain.

With a last inspection, he drove to the florist he used in Levenham where he bought three bouquets. A fancy box of long-lasting pink-hued natives for his mum, followed by a vibrant, multicoloured spray of mixed blooms for Jas. The final was his standing order for pristine white tulips, which earned him a quickly masked glance of pity from the florist.

Digby said nothing. He was immune to peoples' judgement.

It wasn't their opinion that counted.

CHAPTER
13

Jas had been so astonished and delighted by her colourful bouquet when Digby presented it to her Monday night they ended up having sex on the kitchen bench before the flowers made it into water. Earlier that afternoon, his mum had accepted the box of pink native blooms with humble apologies and a teary, squishy hug that also left Digby feeling more than a bit emotional.

The white tulips, however, had been greeted with the usual stony silence. Despite the balmy afternoon, Felicity's headstone remained as it always was: marble cold, as she had become.

For over an hour Digby perched on the hard raised edge of the slab that covered her coffin with the flowers rested on his lap. The Wallace plot in Levenham's cemetery was located in the historic settlers' section, on a mild slope overlooking a larger modern garden cemetery. It faced westward towards the setting sun and was sheltered by a band of elm trees that, when in leaf, blocked any view of the land to the south-east and the cruel slopes of Rocking Horse Hill.

He'd chosen polished white granite for her grave, veined with only the faintest of grains. For purity, for how she'd wanted herself to be. It was also in defiance of the corruption some believed had lurked in her heart. Felicity wasn't perfect. She was damaged and fragile and made mistakes, some of them harmful. But she had loved him with an angel's grace.

Carved gold letters in antique Roman font spelled out her name, with her birth and death dates at the headstone's base. The most important inscription was in the middle: *Beloved fiancée of Digby Wallace-Jones*, followed by the final few lines from Elizabeth Barrett Browning's Sonnet 43 in elegant script.

I love thee with the breath,
Smiles, tears, of all my life; and, if God choose,
I shall but love thee better after death.

Even now the words didn't convey enough.

Em had come to him with the quote, the paper trembling when she'd passed it to him. She'd known Digby partly blamed her for Felicity's death. Em had blamed herself too, and Digby, so angry, so grief-stricken, couldn't find a way to comfort her. Truth was he hadn't wanted to.

He'd thanked her for this though, words of precious love he could never have found himself. And for her insistence he bury Felicity on Wallace land. For battling his mother and grandmother on his behalf when they objected. Without that Felicity would have been another anonymous, overgrown plaque in the main lawn. Lost in death as she'd been so often in life. Here though, she had meaning.

Here, she forced memory. Here, she would never be the thing she'd feared so greatly: nothing.

Though the stone was cold and uncomfortable, Digby stayed on the grave talking to her, sometimes aloud, sometimes silently in his head. He told her about Jas, about his confusion, his uncertainty about what this meant for his life, where it would lead. He told Felicity he missed her, that he loved her, that there was a hollow inside him he thought would never be filled again. A cave in his soul carved out only for her, one in which she'd painted the walls with her smiles and laughter. With her undying, everlasting, beautiful, heartbreaking love.

Finally, when the afternoon began to fade and the wind veered southerly, he'd laid down the tulips. The delicate white cups of the blooms seemed fragile and ephemeral against the permanence of her headstone and the death it represented. It was like laying down his broken self against the immutable laws of nature.

Then he'd gone home to Camrick and retreated to his apartment until it was time to see Jas and lose himself once more in the oblivion of her generous body and laughter.

Tuesday morning, tired yet feeling strangely purged, he'd left Jasmine's and driven to Josh's new workshop in the light industrial precinct to the north of Levenham.

'You're looking pleased with yourself,' said Josh, glancing up from the exquisite bookshelf he was French polishing. Josh had a knack of turning cast-off timber into things of practical artistry, and his furniture was in solid demand. At the other end of the shed Josh's dad Tom, earmuffs firmly on his head and eyes narrowed in concentration, was feeding sheets of wood into a noisy machine. The air was redolent with the scent of polish and fresh-sawn timber. 'So, are you?'

'Am I what?'

'Getting laid, like I hoped.'

'None of your business.' Digby's tone was mild. Anyone else and he might have minded the ribbing, but this was Josh.

'You'll be in for it tonight. Em's been driving me crazy trying to work out who it could be. If she's twisting her knickers over it, you can imagine what your grandmother and mother will be like.'

Dinner at Camrick. Jas had already reminded him this morning, when Digby mentioned seeing her again tonight. He'd wanted to make excuses but Jas wouldn't allow it. An evening off would do them good. She was tired from late nights and early morning sex, and needed to organise the finishing touches of Em's doe's night, the details of which he was definitely not privy to.

The mention had reminded Digby of his own best man obligations. With little else to occupy him, Digby had finalised Josh's buck's night weeks ago. He'd taken great care with the details, wanting the party to be memorable and in keeping with the person he knew Josh to be. It was costing a small fortune but Digby hadn't cared. The day would be a tribute to their friendship and a gift to the man he owed so much.

'Thanks for the warning,' Digby said. 'I'll gird my loins.'

Sudden quiet enveloped the shed. Tom had turned off the machine he'd been using. Spotting Digby, he held up a leather-gloved hand in greeting and Digby saluted back. Pride and contentment played over Josh's face as he watched his dad shift the planed timber to a stack nearby. Josh's dreams had been made real. He was working with his dad like he'd always wanted. He was soon to be married to the woman he'd loved since he was eighteen. He had a family who adored him. Friends. His world was golden with hope and happiness.

Digby experienced a twist of jealousy. He didn't begrudge Josh, not for a second, but his happiness only reinforced the loss of it from Digby's life. He turned away, feigning interest in a pair of bedside tables made from distressed timber. Rubbed-back paint still clung to some of the wood, giving it a shabby but not unattractive appeal. Digby ran his palm over the smoothly sanded surface of the top, inspecting the grain.

'Oregon?'

'Yeah,' said Josh, moving alongside. 'From old beams. I'm not a fan of the look but the client loves it. They've ordered an entire suite, bed and all.' He studied Digby's face. 'Everything all right?'

Digby nodded. He'd come here wanting to talk to Josh, perhaps ask for his advice. Josh had been through a marriage break-up and divorce. It wasn't the same as a death but there had to be some parallels. Marriage meant love, divorce its loss. Digby wanted to know how a man was supposed to repair himself and move on. Josh had done it. Maybe there was hope for him too.

'Sure?'

'Yeah. I'm just ...' He grimaced. 'You know.'

Josh gripped Digby's shoulder and gave it a friendly shake. 'You loved her. That won't change just because you're shagging someone else.'

Digby let out a breath. He understood that, but understanding something didn't make it easier.

'All it means is that you're coming to terms with her not being here. It's part of the process.'

Rolling his lips together hard, Digby tilted his head back and stared at the open cavern of the roof, with its mesh of robust trusses, silvery corrugated iron and industrial light fittings. He blinked at the prickles in his eyes, loathing his lack of control.

The stages of grief, the process, how sick he was of that. The counsellor he'd seen for a while had harped on about it, how what Digby was feeling wasn't unique. Millions, billions, had been there before him. Like that was supposed to help? Digby's pain, his process, was his own. A thing both embraced and dreaded. While he was still feeling, Felicity remained alive in his heart, but the day the pain and anger and loneliness stopped would be the day he'd have to face that she was truly gone. Acceptance, his counsellor called it.

Josh, who'd seen Digby through enough moments like these before, gave his shoulder another squeeze and moved away to let him recover.

It was another minute or so before Digby had his emotions reined in. He cleared his throat. 'Everyone looks set for your buck's do. Only a couple of your footy mates can't make it. Your mate Angus is coming down from Adelaide for the weekend. I said he could stop at Camrick if he wanted but he said he'd grab a hotel room.'

'Great. Everything's organised then?'

'Pretty much. I've booked the minibus to pick us up from Camrick at ten-thirty.'

Josh cast him a hopeful look. 'Any clues on where we're going?'

'Nope. You'll just have to wait for the big day.'

Josh pointed a finger. 'Definitely no strippers though.'

'Not even a lingerie model. As promised.'

'Good.' He puffed out a breath in relief. 'I don't even want to contemplate what Em would do to me if she knew we had strippers.'

'Or me.'

They exchanged a smile, aware they sounded like a couple of wusses but not caring.

Digby left Josh's with his mind a little more at ease. As much as he disliked it, his future brother-in-law was right. Feeling confused about Jas was part of the grief cycle. It was Digby's fear of its completion that was the problem, and one he'd have to come to terms with if he wasn't to spend the rest of his life adrift and lonely.

Dinner in Camrick's kitchen proved, as Josh had warned, a torment of sly looks and sneaky questions. The entire household appeared to know he hadn't slept in his own bed since Saturday night. Digby tried to concentrate on his meal—fried zucchini flowers followed by baked whole rainbow trout from a local fish farm—and hoped his refusal to play along would be indication enough that he had no intention of satisfying their curiosity. For the most part, it worked on his sister and mother. His grandmother, however, was made of sterner stuff.

Granny B dabbed carefully at the edges of her mouth and laid down her napkin. 'I trust you and Jasmine have been comparing notes, Digby.'

The mention of Jasmine's name lifted the hairs on the back of Digby's neck. He blinked and quickly took a mouthful of wine. Jas had cautioned that his grandmother suspected something. He hadn't expected her to come right out with it.

'About what?'

'Your competing duties as best man and maid of honour. What else?' Her expression was innocent but Digby knew better. This was a fishing expedition and Granny B had him hooked. 'You do both have important parties to organise. It would be rather embarrassing if they clashed.'

'We're sorted.'

Innocence took on a shrewd edge. 'So you have collaborated?'

'As far as we've needed to.' Which was the truth when it came to Josh's buck's night and Em's doe's.

Glitter sparkled in the old lady's eyes. 'I'm very glad to hear it.'

Digby braced himself for more but Granny B seemed satisfied and moved on to her pet project: the launch of a wine festival to coincide with Levenham's art week, in which both Adrienne and Granny B were heavily involved. The region's small but up-and-coming wine and grape-growing industry was gaining attention and awards, and deserved it. Granny B's arch enemy, teetotal vegetarian Councillor Herriott, was still blocking the project on the grounds that such an event was paramount to celebrating alcohol, a drug that caused enough problems in the town as it was.

'She knows,' said Digby when he called Jas later from the stables.

'I told you. Doesn't miss a trick, your grandmother.' Jas sighed. 'I'd better talk to Em.'

'If you want, but Gran seems happy to keep it to herself for now. She dropped the subject pretty fast once she had what she wanted.'

'Which can only mean she's up to something.'

'Probably.' He paused. 'I wish I was.'

Jas laughed. 'What? You can't do without it for a night?'

'I can, I just don't want to.'

'I'll make up for it tomorrow night, I promise.'

As it turned out, Digby didn't have to wait that long. Come eleven-thirty the following day, Camrick was deserted. Granny B was lunching with the mayor and wouldn't be home for hours, while Adrienne had a hospital auxiliary meeting and Samuel was playing golf. When he realised he had the property to himself, Digby phoned Jas at work, concealing his identity behind a fake name.

'Remember your idea of a lunchtime quickie?' In the background he could hear the chatter and beeps of the busy building society— Jas must be in the main customer service area. Digby wondered if she was blushing.

'I do.'

'Interested?'

She cleared her throat. Though she was trying to stay cool excitement leaked through to her breathing, shifting it shallow and fast, which only turned Digby on even more. 'It's an attractive idea, although perhaps not viable today.'

'No one's here. They're all out and won't be home for ages.' He dropped his voice. 'I have a cunning plan.'

'Yes. I'm sure I can make that appointment. Twelve it is. Thank you.'

The phone went dead, leaving Digby laughing and fizzing with anticipation.

By ten past twelve she was in his apartment. Ten minutes after that, whatever ghost Felicity had left had been well and truly sent fleeing by the sound of Jasmine's cries. And Digby had notched another small turn in his cycle of grief.

CHAPTER

14

Jas perched tensely on the end of a timber bench in Civic Park, Mike's ring in her pocket. All she had to do was hand it over and walk away. The final scene in an act that should have been over a long time ago. A play that should never have even begun.

She glanced upwards. Scattered showers were forecast but only a few clouds were scudding across the sky, otherwise the day was mild. That didn't stop her pulling her red work cardigan tighter over her chest.

Jas hated feeling this way. For the past week her life had been filled with warmth. Endless rounds of either having sex with Digby or thinking about having sex with Digby, punctuated with long beach rides on Ox and a Saturday-afternoon dress fitting with Em, during which Jasmine's cheeks had burned with the effort of keeping secret what she'd been doing with her best friend's brother.

As was befitting for Levenham's wedding of the year, Em's gown was spectacular. Three generations of Wallace women had joined forces in its design, and the result reflected their impeccable taste. The dress suited Em perfectly, exposing enough smooth skin to be sexy without sacrificing modesty. Satin had been formed into wide pleats that encircled the tips of her shoulders before crossing over her chest to wrap her ribs and slim waist. From there, the skirt fell in a simple A-line design, with not a flounce, bow or lace trim to be seen. Even her veil was fine organza with plain satin edging.

Jas had sighed at the gorgeousness of it, and indulged in a ridiculous daydream that one day she might wear a similarly beautiful dress, and appear as flushed and proud as Em did. Somehow, that daydream had included Digby, which—after Em's nonstop speculation over the identity of her brother's lover—had left Jas even more flustered and disconcerted.

It had also left her realising that the Frankenstein's monster of her love for Mike had been well and truly destroyed. Unlike the previous year, there would be no resurrection.

Another Sunday spent with Digby had hardened Jas further, and sitting in the staff car park behind the building society early Monday morning, she'd punched out a text. She'd left Digby in bed, ruffled and ridiculously handsome, the sheet rucked down around his hips, exposing his lean belly and the swatch of dark hair that nested above his groin. The look had been so hot, his hooded eyes and satisfied smile so smug, she'd taken her phone from her handbag and snapped a photo. He'd objected, but not much, and she'd saved the photo. Jas had a feeling she'd spend most of the day looking at it.

Mike had answered at morning-tea time with a terse 'OK' that had left her wondering for the thousandth time how she'd ever managed to get suckered in by a cheating arsehole like him.

Mondays were a good day to get things done. And this chore was long overdue.

Jasmine checked her watch. He was late. Perhaps he'd chickened out. It wouldn't have surprised her. In which case, she'd post the ring to his work with no return address and no note. If it ended up chucked out that was his bad luck. She'd done her bit.

'Jas.' Mike appeared from behind, darting glances around the park as he stepped in front of the seat where she was sitting. At first his face was grim, then it seemed to sag at the sight of her and his eyes turned bright. If Jas wasn't used to his duplicity she might have been taken in by the show of emotion. 'You look great. Really great. He suits you.'

Jas didn't want to get into a conversation about Digby. She had one thing to accomplish and was determined to see it through. Standing, she drew the ring from her pocket. 'Hold out your hand.'

He scanned the surroundings again, this time carefully, as if fearing hidden cameras or that his wife would come leaping from behind a tree yelling 'Cheat!'. Slowly he did as she asked.

She pressed the ring into the centre of his palm. 'I thought you should have it back.'

He regarded it, puzzled, then his mouth twisted and he laughed in a way that was horrible for its bitter emptiness. 'What am I meant to do with it?'

'I don't know. Sell it. Buy your wife a present with the proceeds. God knows, she deserves it.'

But that only made him laugh even more acidly. 'Sell it? Jas, it's worthless.'

A wave of cold prickles swept over her. 'What?'

'It's worthless. Zirconia.'

Appalled, she could only stare. That ring was the reason she'd taken him back after nearly three months of freedom. It was the promise of a future she'd hungered for, and now he was telling her that for a piece of crap glass she'd given him almost another year?

Another year of selling her self-respect, of the agony of longing, of soaring hope that never had wings to fly.

'You fuck,' she whispered. 'You absolute fuck.'

With nothing left to say and her humiliation burning, Jas whirled and marched straight-backed across the park, her jaw set, her eyes wide. Every scrap of self-will was centred on maintaining dignity in the face of Mike's insult.

'Jas.' He called again, this time louder. 'Jas!'

She walked faster, her stride as long as her fitted skirt would allow, cursing her stupid uniform, cursing herself. Cursing a world that allowed bastards like Mike to thrive and never pay for their cruelties.

Wishing she had Digby's protective arms to fall into.

The remainder of the day stretched like a long dark winter. Jas dealt with customers with atypical distant professionalism that had her staff glancing at her sideways and steering clear. No bubbly greetings, no pauses for gossip. She did her job and clock-watched, hankering for home and a chance to tend to her bruised and hurting soul in private.

But privacy proved elusive, even at Admella Beach. She arrived home to find Digby at the kitchen sink, peeling potatoes. With the amount of time he was spending at the house it had seemed easier to give him his own key, but good manners meant he usually checked to see if he was welcome. Today of all days he'd chosen to turn up early.

She paused at the entrance to the kitchen and soaked in the scene. The room smelled deliciously of roasting meat. Pots of vegetables were set on the stove. A decanter stood on the counter next to a dusty bottle of wine. Soft rock music was streaming from a portable speaker set up on the windowsill.

It was home like she'd dreamed of but had never managed to make real. A fantasy only glimpsed with Mike, on the rare occasions when he'd snuck over for dinner and she'd been able to play happy families for a few cherished hours. To touch a future she was never destined to reach.

'Roast lamb, with all the trimmings,' he said, smiling and pleased with himself. 'To save you having to stress about dinner.' When Jas didn't say anything he eyed her, then turned off the tap and wiped his hands on a tea towel. 'I'll clean up, if that's what you're worried about.' He cleared his throat. 'I thought it'd be a nice surprise.'

Jas closed her eyes. 'Oh, Digby.'

What a fool she'd been. All that time wasted on an arsehole when there were men like this in the world.

'Jas, what's wrong?'

She sniffed and smiled. 'Nothing. Nothing at all.'

Clearly Digby didn't believe her. 'I didn't mean to intrude. You've been at work all day. I just wanted to help.'

'You're not intruding.' She dumped her things, crossed the room and wrapped herself against him, pressing her cheek hard against his chest to hear the beating of his big considerate heart.

He stroked her hair hesitantly and kissed the top of her head. 'Baby, what's wrong?'

At the use of 'baby', she clung even tighter, feeling stupidly fragile. 'Nothing. I'm just not used to someone as nice as you.'

'I'm not that nice.' He bent to fake-whisper. 'It's all a sneaky plan to get you into bed.'

She laughed and sniffed back tears. 'Liar. Since when do you need a bribe to get me into bed? All you have to do is look at me and I'm ready to drag you off.'

'I'm looking at you now.'

Jas eased out of his arms. Despite her declaration, she wasn't in the mood for sex. Not even with Digby. 'Don't you have cooking to take care of?'

'I'd rather take care of you.'

'You already are, special man.' She reached behind his neck and pulled him close. 'So ...' She kissed him lightly. 'Very ...' She kissed him again. 'Well.'

Digby cupped her cheek, his thumb stroking the corner of her mouth as he searched her face. 'I can turn the oven down, make this a slow-cooked lamb roast.'

'A tempting thought, but I really need to look after Oxy.' She kissed him lightly again. 'I'll be back.'

'Jas,' he said, when she was at the door, 'are you really okay?'

The words were softly spoken, husky with uncertainty. She gazed over her shoulder. The sight of his worried look made her chest feel full and thick.

'Yeah,' she said, breathing in. 'I am now.'

The stress and emotion of the day had left Jas drained. Even a short canter on Ox along the beach in the lowering sun, the sea glittering a thousand colours as though sprinkled with polished gems, failed to energise her. For Digby's sake, she ate her perfectly roasted lamb and vegetables with feigned appetite, praising to the hilt his proper gravy and the complementary, beautifully smooth cabernet merlot he'd chosen.

He accepted her praise with the claim that good food was in his Wallace genes, but Jas could tell from the way he kept surreptitiously watching her that he wasn't fooled.

At bedtime, he sat fully dressed on the edge of her bed and beckoned her to him, directing her to stand between his knees. He rested his arms on her waist, his mouth a thin line.

'Something happened today.' He lifted his head to study her face. 'You came home different. Upset. I thought for a bit it was me but it wasn't. It was something else.'

She stroked her hand over his face. His dark hair was shiny under the light, his cheeks rough with day's end stubble. 'It doesn't matter now.'

'It does. I don't want you to be unhappy.'

'I'm not.' She cupped his jaw, intent. 'How can I be when I have you?'

He looked aside. She'd stepped too far. Jas didn't have him. *She* did. Digby had warned her and yet over the past week Jas had been sure that tie was loosening. He smiled more, laughed more, observed Jas with what she thought was contentment. Perhaps it was, but in his heart, Felicity remained queen.

She didn't know why it should matter so much when it hadn't bothered her before, but it did.

'I'd better go brush my teeth,' she said, and was grateful for the moment alone.

They didn't make love. Unspoken mutual agreement kept the intimacy from turning sexual. They touched though, and kissed. Facing one another and gazing, fingers tracing butterfly steps over features, murmuring compliments about strong jaws and delicate ears and long eyelashes. Silly, affectionate and kind things to hide the pressure of unrevealed hearts until it was time to roll over and sleep.

Jas lay spooned against him, staring at the darkness, sleep refusing to descend. She could pick from his breathing that Digby was doing the same, and wondered if he was pondering ways to extract himself from the relationship. Jas had broken the rule set between them from the start, had turned something joyous into something serious. That her admission was accidental, the fault of a fraught day, didn't matter.

She didn't love him, but today had shown she was stepping recklessly close. The challenge now was to find a way to step back.

'Jas?' he whispered, his hand curving over her belly.

'Yes?'

She heard his swallow. 'If you want to stop, that's okay.'

Jas closed her eyes. Here it came, the careful goodbye. 'Is that what you want?'

For a painful length of time the room remained silent. 'No.' His forehead rested against her hair, his breath caressing the back of her neck, his palm hot against her stomach. The air thrummed with tension. 'I need you, Jas.'

She twisted to face him.

He gazed at her with shiny eyes. 'But you have to understand, I can't offer you much in return.'

'You're wrong. So very, very wrong. You offer plenty.'

This time when they kissed, relief and something else, something heartfelt and stretched with yearning, steered their kisses to caresses, before tenderly easing them into that ultimate of intimacies. Connecting in a way that made them not quite whole, but for a heady, breathless moment, fulfilled.

It wasn't love, but the frangible cliff edge. Jas knew it. Saw the danger. Yet she refused to retreat.

Digby needed her. If that meant risking the fall then so be it.

Because a man like him was worth it.

CHAPTER
15

The phone started ringing deep into the night. Digby surged upright but sleep had him fuddled. By the time he realised what the sound was, Jas had already thrown back the sheets and was heading for the kitchen.

He checked her digital alarm clock. 3 am. Phone calls at that hour were never good news. He picked up his polo shirt from the floor and strode up the hall, pulling it on.

Jasmine's panicked 'Hello' was followed by frightening silence. Digby quickened his step. He found her braced on her palms over the bench, head down and breathing hard, the receiver on its back beside her right hand.

'What is it?'

She didn't answer. Digby stepped closer and it was then he registered the voice. Whoever was on the line was still talking. Glancing at her, he picked up the handset and listened.

The voice was warped, the pitch and delivery low and slow, and impossible to tell whether from a man or woman. Such was its distortion, it could have been a computer.

'You're nothing but a whore,' it said. 'That's what you do. Whore yourself on decent men. Corrupting them. Can't get one of—'

'Who is this?' demanded Digby, although he'd already guessed there'd be no answer.

'—your own. So you steal good men from other women.'

'It's a recording,' he said, hanging up.

'Yes.'

Almost immediately the phone rang again. Jas didn't move. Digby pressed answer, listened a few seconds and disconnected.

'She'll keep doing that until you stop answering or the phone's unplugged.'

'It's the same as before?'

She nodded. On cue, the phone started up.

The phone had an old-fashioned ringtone that was excellent for carrying across the house, but after multiple times its shrill jingle quickly grated. Digby searched for the volume control and lowered it to the minimum setting. The handset vibrated against his palm as if in quiet rage at not being heard. 'She must be listening to know when the call hangs up so she can redial.'

'Most likely.' Jas straightened and turned to lean her backside against the bench, arms folded. 'No fun in tormenting someone if you can't see or hear it.'

Neither of them had bothered with the light switch but there was enough moonglow filtering through the window for Digby to note the forced stiffness of her movements and the hard set of her expression. She was trying to be stoic, but her eyes were edged with suffering and her sweet mouth was thin with despair. The knowledge that Jas was hurting made Digby want to punch something.

'How can you be certain it's a she?'

'A man wouldn't bother.'

She was right. This wasn't something a man would do. Men tended to use direct means of confrontation whereas this was more underhand. The call rang out, then started again. Digby unplugged the power, set the phone down and reached for Jas, cradling her against him.

'It'll be okay.'

Her stoicism crumbled. She shook her head, her voice choking. 'I thought it'd stopped, that the spray paint was the last of it. It's been over a week. I thought whoever it was had noticed you here all the time and finally realised it was you, not Mike.' She rubbed her face. 'God!'

'We'll get your number changed. Make it silent.'

She gave a shuddery sigh, her shoulders slumping in defeat. 'I guess I'll have to.'

'Come on.' Digby steered her towards the bedroom. 'Standing here in the cold won't solve anything.'

'What if she does something else?' Jas asked when they were back under the sheets. 'What if she hurts Oxy?'

'She won't. You're her target, not some defenceless animal. Plus Ox is big and whoever this is, is a coward.'

All the same, the idea was worrying.

Neither of them slept well. Jas was restless beside him. Even when she did drop off it was unsteady, punctuated with twitches, small whimpers and moans. Digby tried to comfort her, shushing softly while holding her close to him.

His own thoughts were messy. What was meant to be a surprise evening of good food and wine, of taking care of her, had been strained by her strange mood on arriving home. Then there was the awkward conversation afterwards when she'd laid claim to him, as though what they shared was more than it was. Her disappointment had throbbed along with his shame. Digby was well aware that he was using her to heal himself, but he'd hoped the exchange was fair. She was hurting from Mike; he was trying to come to terms with his grief. Passion was their solace, friendship their warmth after the cold. It wasn't meant to be more than that.

Yet for Jas it seemed to be leading that way. The truth was, if he dug around in his heart hard enough, he could feel a seed of deeper feeling too. A seed that was growing every day.

And it scared the shit out of him.

Digby sent her off to work in the morning with the promise that he'd return once he'd escaped Tuesday-night family dinner. If not for the crank phone calls he would have suggested a night off, time away for them to reassess. However, he might be confused about what was in his heart, but of his protectiveness Digby was certain.

As soon as Jasmine's car was out of sight, he set to work.

It was nearing 11 am when he'd completed the plan he'd forged and honed in the sleepless hours of the dragging night. Satisfied with the set-up, he drove to a surfer car park further up the coast and walked the return route along the beach, checking carefully before crossing the dunes back onto Jasmine's land.

Digby waited in the house until five-thirty, then locked up, walked back along the beach to his car, and drove home to Camrick. The day had been tedious and wearying but worth every yawn, every pace of frustration, every wayward thought, to know she'd arrive home to safety.

Dinner in Camrick's kitchen was as before, a delicious meal made unappetising by his family's digs and probes. Digby's only saving grace was that his mind kept wandering, which meant he missed many of the gibes. He was thinking of what else he could do to protect Jas. A guard dog perhaps. Motion sensors at the gates.

'Digby!'

He started and stared at his grandmother. 'What?'

'I asked if you'd had your suit fitting.'

For a couple of heartbeats he was flummoxed. 'Oh, the wedding.'

'Yes,' said Granny B, voice like honed steel, 'your sister's wedding. The one where you have the honour of acting as best man for Joshua.'

'Don't worry about Dig,' said Josh. 'He's got everything under control. Buck's do this weekend. It's going to be a beauty.'

'Yes,' said Digby, voice slowing as his thoughts drifted again. 'It will be.'

He'd nearly forgotten about Josh's buck's night. Jas would be busy with Em's doe's night too, which meant ample opportunity for her harasser to attack again. Digby could hire some sort of security patrol, although that was likely to draw more attention than Jas would appreciate. Her property might be outside the village boundary but it was on the main coast road and easily observed by passing locals. Plus knowing she'd had to resort to paid protection would only give the culprit satisfaction.

Appetite gone, he placed his knife and fork together and stared at nothing while conversation continued to flow around him. Wedding talk. Reception details. Flowers. Excitement. He blanked it out. Though Digby was becoming a little more inured to it, wedding talk still made his chest hurt.

His mother collected his plate, her soft hand on his shoulder. 'Are you all right, honey?'

'Yeah, Mum. I'm fine.'

She squeezed his shoulder, her gaze sad.

He reached up to cover her hand. 'Stop worrying.'

'I can't help it. It's a mother's job to worry.'

As soon as he was able, Digby made excuses and escaped. Every eye in the kitchen watched him leave, their silence thunderous with curiosity and concern.

Digby was in the car, about to press the ignition, when Josh caught up with him. He wound down the window and braced himself.

'You were pretty distracted tonight,' said Josh.

'Stuff on my mind.'

Josh nodded. He leaned his hand on the roof of the car and glanced around the garage and back at Digby. 'We're right for the weekend though?'

'Yeah, it's all set. Should be good.'

Josh patted the roof as if in farewell but didn't move.

Digby suppressed a sigh. 'Look, I know you're all worried but I'm fine.'

'It's not me, it's Em.'

His gaze hardened. 'It's none of her business.'

'I told her that but she's worried sick you're going to get yourself hurt or something. She's got some rebound idea going on. You know what women are like.'

'Hurt? Jesus, Josh.' If the notion wasn't so infuriating it'd be laughable. No hurt, no agony, could ever compare to what he'd already experienced.

'I know. But do me a favour? Take care. I need my best man.'

Digby let out a breath. 'I am.'

Josh gave the car another pat and stepped aside. Digby started the engine, put the car in reverse and began to back out, Josh casually following.

'Must be a hell of a lay,' remarked his friend when the car was almost out.

Digby took his eye off the reversing camera to look at him. Josh was grinning like an idiot. Happy for him, trusting. The anger that had been fermenting inside Digby calmed.

It was on the tip of his tongue to answer 'She is', but the day was rapidly approaching when his relationship with Jas would no longer be a secret. It was one thing to speculate, another to know, and Digby wasn't about to do the ungentlemanly thing. Instead he gave Josh a cryptic smile and said, 'I'll see you Saturday,' abandoning him to his conjecture.

The phone was unplugged when Digby arrived at Jasmine's.

'She's still at it?'

Jas rubbed her face, wilted with fatigue. 'Yes.'

There were no dishes in the sink, just a mug. He wondered if she'd eaten.

'Did you get a chance to call your phone company?'

'No. I had meetings, and then some idiot did his nut at one of my staff. Some mix-up with a credit card transfer. It took forever to sort out. By the time I'd calmed her and finished with him I'd missed my lunch break. I had enough time for an apple and a couple of cracker biscuits and that was it.' She gave a ragged smile. 'Good for my figure if nothing else.'

'Your figure's fine.' And it was. Digby liked that she was so womanly. In an attempt to lighten her mood, he snuck a fondle of her breasts. 'As long as you don't lose anything off these.'

His efforts were rewarded with a chuckle. 'Fat chance. Those things would survive a desert island.'

Jas was so exhausted she fell asleep almost immediately. Digby held her close, listening to her steady breathing. She wasn't Felicity, but he cared about her more than he ever thought would have been possible. They had friendship, sex. Important things. Yet with Flick only gone a year, to long for more seemed wrong.

That didn't stop a little part of him from hungering.

Though Digby kept vigilant watch, Wednesday held no sign of Jasmine's attacker and he started to fear that he'd been sprung. She could have been watching when he'd fixed the fake cameras to the front and rear eaves. Could have spotted his return from the beach. Maybe she was satisfied with phone harassment. But as this was his only hope of catching her, Digby was determined to endure until the end, however testing the wait.

At 2:55 pm on Thursday he was finally rewarded.

To while away his boredom, Digby had bought a pad of graph paper and dug out an old draftsman's set of pencils and tools from the office at Camrick. Jas wasn't much of a gardener. Her current efforts ran mostly to keeping alive an overthatched buffalo lawn and a few hardy ornamental plants. Digby set himself the challenge of drafting plans to transform it into something special. With its beachside vista and mild micro-climate the space had potential, and Digby had hours in which to think and imagine. If the design proved interesting enough, he might even build it.

He set himself up in the laundry, which had a window overlooking the rear yard and a clear view of the dunes. If Jasmine's harasser was going to appear, it'd be from there, but to ensure he didn't miss anything, Digby raised the sash window just enough to allow outside noise to carry in.

The metallic clang of a chain at the back gate caught his ear before anything else. Setting his pencil down, Digby shifted to the side of the window, ensuring he was out of sight.

From a distance it was tricky to tell much about her. She was wearing an untucked flannelette shirt in an ugly brown check and khaki trousers, and she was taller than Jas, with a rangy body. A fawn bucket hat covered her hair and shadowed her face. If it weren't for the way she moved and the tell-tale swell of her chest, he might have mistaken her for a man—an ambiguity that was likely intentional.

She was dragging a stained hessian sack behind her, every now and then hoisting it up and hurling it forward, the sack collapsing soggily as it impacted with the ground. Whatever was inside was heavy, and caused her to pant. As she reached the clothesline and lifted her gaze to scrutinise her surrounds, Digby caught a wrinkled face and blinked in surprise.

The woman was perhaps in her sixties. Jas had imagined someone younger—a woman around her own or Mick's wife's age, perhaps married, perhaps with children, who would factor Jas as a threat. Not a woman who should know better, who should have the experience of age and the capacity to see that life's stories weren't told in black and white, but in a thousand shades of grey.

Somehow that made it worse.

Digby's heart hardened.

When he was sure the woman's destination was the rear of the house and not the front, he snuck away from the laundry, careful to keep himself quiet and hidden. He paused next to the front door and set his phone to video, then stealthily made his way around the side of the house, his ears tuned to the curious sounds emanating from the rear.

At the corner he stopped to film her in action. She was standing close to the house, on one of the cracked concrete pavers that ran from the rear verandah to the clothes line. Her sleeves were rolled up and she'd donned a pair of pink elbow-length rubber gloves. Beside her the sack lay open. A lift of breeze sent the reek of it in Digby's direction. He zoomed in, his stomach lurching in disgust as he realised the contents. It was some sort of animal guts. From more than one slaughter, judging by the tangle of entrails.

Her eyes were bright with malevolent glee, her mouth tilted in the curdled smile of a woman thrilled with her own daring. Oblivious to his observation, she bent, lifted a string of slimy intestines in one hand and hurled them at the house. They splattered on the walls and across the laundry window, clinging for a second before plopping to the ground, leaving behind streaks of blood and fluid like a gore-filled abstract painting.

Still filming, Digby stepped into view. 'Enjoying yourself?'

She stumbled and yelped but recovered quickly, and lunged for the phone. Digby let her snatch it, watching with controlled calm as she flung it on the concrete and jabbed the heel of her boot into the screen. The phone cracked and snapped under her assault, well and truly dead. Giving the phone a last savage stomp, the woman regarded him with triumph.

'Won't help you,' he said. 'I set the video to upload straight to cloud storage. There's also that.' Digby indicated the fake camera he'd fixed to the eaves, unobtrusive enough for both Jas and the woman to miss but easily recognised once pointed out. 'More than enough to go to the police with.'

Dread contorted her face. She attempted to dash around him but Digby blocked her path. Twice more she tried, Digby foiling her each time, until she gave up and simply stood with her legs apart and glared.

'I know you.' Her sneer strengthened. 'You're that Wallace boy.'

That she recognised him wasn't a surprise. After the tragedy and then the inquest, Digby had had his face plastered all over the media. He'd have been more shocked if she didn't know who he was.

'So I am. And you are?' He tilted his head. 'Not keen on introducing yourself? That's okay. I'm sure you'll be easy to identify from the footage.'

She licked her lips, eyes darting as if searching for escape before settling coldly on him. 'I suppose you think yourself in love?' Her top lip rose, exposing her teeth like an animal. Her words emerged in a snarl. 'You're wasting your energy. She's using you the same way she used him. She's a whore.'

Digby breathed through his nose to steady his temper.

'Bet you didn't know they were together Monday.'

Together? Jas and Mike? The news was like a stab. He blinked at how much it hurt.

Her eyes lit up at Digby's reaction. 'Didn't know that, did you?' She nodded, pleased. 'The little whore can't help herself. Slut like her deserves to be run out of town.'

If she hadn't looked so gleeful at his upset Digby might have maintained his temper, but her malice had him losing it.

'How Jas lives her life is none of your fucking business.' He stepped closer, fists clenched at his side, looming, his fury stinking like the guts she'd flung. 'You have no right. None. No right to be here, no right to judge. You're a vicious, shrivelled-up old woman with nothing better to do but spy and spit hatred.'

To her credit the woman stood her ground. 'I have every right. That man is married to my cousin's daughter. It was a good marriage, a loving marriage. Until *she* came along.' She jabbed a finger towards Jasmine's house. 'That whore seduced a good man away from his adoring wife and family.' Her voice dropped, shaky with rage. 'I know what it's like to have your life destroyed by a woman like that. To be abandoned, to have children left fatherless. I won't stand by and see that slut do it to Tania.'

'Mike Boland a good man? Jesus, get your head out of the sand. He's the one who lied and cheated, not Jas. He lied about his marriage, about his kids. And for what? So he could get his leg over whenever he wanted.'

'She led him to it!'

'No. She didn't. He's a piece of shit.'

She jerked her chin up and down. 'Look at you, defending her. You're as blind as he is.'

Digby gave a bark of laughter. Blind was one thing he wasn't. He'd had enough of arguing with this vicious cow anyway. 'Clean up your mess.'

She crossed her arms. 'Make me.'

Digby shrugged. 'It's either that or I take the footage to the police along with a well-documented list every other act of vandalism you've done. They'll want to know why, of course. Which means I'll have to tell them all about your precious can-do-no-wrong Mike. How long before that bit of gossip gets around town? I might even spread a bit myself, just for the fun of it.' He smiled nastily. 'Trust me, dragging his name through the mud would satisfy me no end.'

'You wouldn't dare.'

'Oh, I'd dare. You know why? Because I don't give a shit about you or Mike or anyone except my family and Jas.' He held her gaze. 'Now clean up your fucking mess.'

The dead sincerity in his tone must have worked. With a last look over her shoulder she began scooping up guts. Digby stood guard, legs apart, arms akimbo. When only a few smaller entrails remained, he went to the shed, retrieved the power washer and scrubbing brush attachment, and connected it to the hose.

'Not a smear left,' he ordered, handing her the wand.

To Digby's relief the walls and windows, not having had a chance to dry out, washed down easily. Any more minutes spent with this woman than necessary was an anathema. He wanted her gone. Permanently.

She turned off the washer and glared at him. 'Satisfied?'

'No.'

'More punishment?'

'No doubt your small mind will take it that way.'

Her jaw worked.

Digby held up a finger. 'One phone call, one single step near this place, one word to Jas, and I will come after you. And I will drag your precious Mike, and his wife and kids, along for the ride.' His finger flicked towards the sack. 'Now take your filth and fuck off.'

It wasn't the best of speeches but it was enough. Digby dogged her to the back fence and out to the top of the dunes where he stopped, tracking her progress along the beach until she disappeared behind a small headland.

After another five minutes' surveillance to be sure she wasn't coming back, he trudged to the house. The sack had left a stain on the concrete that he needed to wash off, the cleaner had to be put away, and there were the remnants of his phone to sweep up.

When Digby was satisfied all trace of the afternoon's drama was erased, he trekked back to his car and drove into Levenham. First stop would be for a new phone, then the florist for Felicity's tulips, followed by the badly needed solace of her cool and constant grave.

CHAPTER
16

Jas woke Saturday morning with excitement and optimism bubbling through her veins. Since Wednesday night there'd been no more phone calls, vandalism or any other torments from her mystery harasser. Although she wasn't quite as confident, Digby seemed assured the trouble was over. His voice on the phone line asking who was calling had frightened whoever it was into backing off. Jas could only pray he was right.

With Josh's buck's party an all-day affair, Digby had driven down for Friday-night dinner but left soon after. In preparation for her own busy Saturday, Jas had gone to bed early and much to her amazement slept through. Worry had been playing havoc with her sleep patterns, leaving her waking tired and even more stressed, but a solid, uninterrupted night's rest had done wonders.

After a long drive from New South Wales, Em and Jasmine's friend Teagan and her handsome fiancé Lucas had arrived in Levenham the day before. Jas had offered them her spare bedroom but Teagan had refused, not wanting to intrude. With two weeks still to go until the wedding, and with Teagan's parents plus her aunt and her aunt's partner due to arrive the week leading up to the big event, she and Lucas had instead rented a serviced farmhouse on one of the winery properties to the west of town. Jasmine couldn't help but feel relieved. She loved her friend, but Teagan's presence would have made seeing Digby difficult, and as much as Jas was trying to steady her wayward emotions the thought of not seeing him left her feeling as angsty as an adolescent.

There was also the risk of Jasmine's harasser starting her antics again, regardless of Digby's assurances. Teagan had never hidden her disapproval of Jasmine's affair with Mike and, unless Em had let on, she'd be unaware it had resumed after the earlier break-up. Discovering it had endured for almost another year would not make for friendly relations. This was Em's special time and Jas didn't want arguments, especially hackneyed ones that should have been buried long ago.

Unlike Josh's buck's party, which was starting in the morning, Em's wouldn't commence until midday, when they were all due to gather for a champagne luncheon in the upstairs private function room of the Australian Arms Hotel. Granny B, who'd insisted on having a say in proceedings, had pulled her purse out and some favours in and engaged an Adelaide-based costume designer, complete with vast wardrobe, along with a stylist, three make-up artists and hairdressers, whose job was to transform them all into '50s-style glamour queens. A cocktail-making class would follow after which they were all to be ferried out to Ryan's winery for dinner and ballroom dancing, with band and instructors all laid on.

It was, Jas hoped, to be perfectly fabulous and perfectly Em.

Jas spent the morning playing with Oxy. The poor old sweetheart had been neglected of late and his forlorn long face hanging over the fence that morning had swelled Jas with guilt. The horse had been her friend and confidante through all the joys and tribulations of her life, and she owed him her attention and affection.

The morning was glorious, the sky a pristine azure dome, the air salt-scented and fresh. Seagulls swirled on gusts, reconnoitring the beach. A flock of native black swans from the wetlands cruised over, intent on a cleansing sea bath. The road was busy with surfers and fishermen ready to catch the tide, and families with children looking forward to a day at the beach. Jas brushed Oxy's dappled grey coat until it shone, trimmed his mane and tail, picked his hooves, cuddled and massaged and chatted nonsense, but a corner of her mind remained on Digby.

Jas wasn't sure if it was her imagination or their own distraction over Josh's and Em's parties, but over the last two nights she thought she'd sensed a slight distancing on Digby's part. It wasn't something she could pin down. They made love the same as always, with freedom, laughter and ardour. Occasionally though, she'd caught a fine frown that was covered with a smile so fast she wasn't sure it had been there at all.

When she'd asked if everything was all right he'd been dismissive, yet the lingering sense of not-quite-rightness had remained.

The afternoon and evening proved hilarious. Granny B was in fine form, quaffing champagne as she strutted around, unlit cigar in hand, ordering people about. Possessing an incredible designer wardrobe herself, and not having put on an ounce of weight since she'd married almost sixty years ago, Granny B had turned up at the Arms in a sexy figure-hugging vintage Schiaparelli evening gown and full-length fur coat, leaving everyone—including the stylist—gobsmacked. If that wasn't enough, she'd flirted outrageously with their mixologist, drunk everyone else under the table, and gleefully flaunted her astonishing stamina by outdancing them as well. If it weren't for an appalled Adrienne forcibly escorting her out the door, Jas was sure Granny B would have taken off home with one of the male dance instructors.

Em was in fits of giggles. Non-drinking Teagan, as keen as Jas for Em to have fun, had been surreptitiously topping up Em's glass whenever she wasn't looking, and the result was a wonderfully relaxed bride-to-be who'd danced the tango and the salsa, and happily joined in a very wobbly cha-cha snake of hysterically laughing women.

'You're brilliant, you know that?' said Em, slinging an arm around Jas and kissing her heartily on the cheek. Despite her champagne consumption, Em remained as stunning as ever in a strapless burgundy satin gown that fitted and flattered her body beautifully. Her hair had been slicked back into a chic bun, exposing her swan-like neck and perfect shoulders.

In a bright blue halter-neck dress that flaunted her generous assets, Jas was feeling equally as wonderful. 'You should thank your grandmother more than me. She organised most of it. Most of my time was spent calming her excesses. Did she tell you she wanted to hire *Puppetry of the Penis*?'

'No, but it doesn't surprise me in the least. I'm thanking my lucky stars she didn't hire the Chippendales.' Em smiled. 'She was in a class of her own tonight.'

'She was. I'm not sure Adrienne is going to forgive her in a hurry either. Or Granny B your mother. I swear she was about to drag that dancer off to the loos for a quickie.'

'Not the loos,' said Teagan. 'That'd be far too common. My bet would have been the counter of the wine-tasting room. She could shag and drink at the same time.'

Em clapped her hands over her ears. 'Please don't mention my grandmother having sex anymore. It's too horrible.'

'Speaking of sex,' said Teagan, 'I wonder how the boys are faring.'

Em's eyes narrowed. 'If I find out Digby hired strippers there'll be trouble.'

'I'm sure Digby organised plenty to keep them occupied without resorting to strippers. Not his thing, anyway.' Jasmine's mouth tilted a little as she realised that claim perhaps wasn't quite true. In the privacy of her bedroom, Digby had proved himself rather partial to her silly stripteases.

When she glanced back at her friends, Em was grinning towards the dance floor where Josh's sister Sally was untidily attempting to perform the paso doble. Teagan, though, was studying Jas thoughtfully. Cheeks burning, Jas quickly looked away again.

It was well after midnight by the time Jas had changed out of her costume, conducted a quick whip around the venue to make sure nothing had been left behind, and helped shuffle the last party-goer into the minibus. Unlike the other guests, who had been picked up by bus and were to be delivered home the same way, Jas had driven. Forcing the driver to make the trip to Admella Beach had seemed selfish, and with her property under assault, Jas hadn't wanted to stay overnight in Levenham anyway.

Bar its usual arthritic creaks and protests, the house was quiet and more than a little lonely when Jas arrived home. Yet as weary as she was, after removing the heavy make-up, brushing the spray out of her hair, and changing into her nightie, she couldn't bring herself to go to bed. Instead, Jas poured herself a glass of the beautifully aged shiraz left over from one of Digby's visits and settled into the lounge with the television and her mobile phone.

A flick through the channels revealed a dozen movies she either had no interest in or had seen before. She tried the entertainment programs to no avail, finally settling on one of the sports channels and World Cup Showjumping. With two Australians competing it was about as diverting as anything else on offer.

It took ten minutes for acute boredom to set in. Although it wasn't really boredom, more restlessness. Jas wanted to know how Digby had fared, if the day had gone as well as he hoped, but it was late and contacting him seemed needy and intrusive.

After several minutes of umming and ahhing over the wisdom of her actions, Jas caved and sent a brief text—simple words, hopefully to make him smile. *Hope you had a great night. We did! Home and tired and need bed. Can't help thinking it'd be much more appealing with you in it.*

She waited, hoping for a reply, but the phone remained silent. With a sigh Jas tossed it on the end of the couch and sipped her wine, staring sulkily at the showjumping. Irritated, she picked up the remote and surfed to one of the easy-listening music channels. Murphy's Law dictated they would be playing one of her favourite love songs, one she'd spent ridiculous hours mooning over Mike with. An inner morbidity had her leaving it there.

The song should have been a lesson in love's disasters, instead it only made her longing for Digby worse.

It was wrong. Not just wrong but a waste of emotion. She wanted him. In her bed, in her life, in her heart.

And the worst of it was he would never want her back the same way.

Jas was enjoying the most delicious dream when she roused enough to realise it wasn't a dream at all. The warm hand on her shoulder was real, not imagined. Her eyes snapped open, adrenaline breaking like a storm as she registered a figure sitting on the edge of her bed. Squealing, she scrambled sideways, arms flailing as she tried to reach for the heavy steel-cased torch she kept on her bedside table.

'Jas, Jas, shh. It's me, Digby.'

'Bloody hell!' She panted for a moment. 'You scared me stupid!'

'I'm sorry. I didn't know the best way to wake you.'

Recovering, Jas sat up and scraped curls of sleep-mussed hair from her eyes and forehead. Although her heart was pounding from shock, there was no denying some of those thudding beats were due to joy at seeing him. 'What are you doing here?'

'I needed to ask you something.'

'And it couldn't wait?'

He looked towards the window. It was hard to read his expression. After the magnificent day, the sky had clouded over and now the moon and stars were dulled, their glow ineffectual. 'Probably.'

She slid closer and placed her hand on his arm. 'What's wrong? Was it the party?'

'No. The party was great.' He was quiet a moment. 'It's you.'

'Me?' Jas wasn't sure she liked the sound of this.

'You met Mike this week.'

So he'd found out. She sighed, ashamed at not telling him, but even more saddened at being questioned. Bleakness settled in her bones. 'It's not what you're imagining.'

'How do you know I'm imagining anything?'

'Your voice.' Upset, she slid down the bed and turned on her side, away from him.

'I just want to know, Jas.'

'Why? What difference would it make? It's not like we have claims on one another.'

He sighed and stretched to lie behind her, arm curling across her belly, breath tickling the hairs at the back of her neck. 'I don't want you hurt.'

'I'm fine.'

'I also need to know if I have to make good on my threat.'

She rolled over to stare at his face. 'What threat?'

'That he was to stay away from you.'

Digby had threatened Mike? The revelation was astonishing. 'Or else what?'

'The specifics don't matter. What matters is who made the contact. Was it him?'

Jasmine didn't know whether to be offended or flattered that Digby had gone in to bat for her. Part of her felt outraged that he believed she needed help to manage Mike, the other part rejoiced that he could care so much.

'Jas?'

'It was me. I asked him to meet me.'

Digby's eyes closed in what she could guess was relief. He pressed his forehead against hers and shook his head. 'God, Jas. Why would you do that? The man's an arsehole.'

'I know. And I'm a fool for ever believing he was anything other than one.'

'So why meet him?'

'I wanted to return a ring. He'd given it to me as a pledge that he was serious, that one day we'd be together. I thought it was valuable and it didn't sit right that I should keep it. I thought maybe he could sell it and buy something nice for Tania with the proceeds.' She sucked on her bottom lip. Even now, the pain that she'd been betrayed so badly, that she'd been so gullible, remained. 'Turns out it wasn't real. Just a cheap bit of zirconia.'

'That must have hurt.'

'Yeah, it did. My own fault. I should have known he never meant it.'

Digby seemed as content as Jas to let silence drift for a while.

'I'm glad you're here,' she whispered.

He brushed knuckles gently over her cheek, eyes shining. 'Me too.'

'Did you get my text?'

'No, I left my phone at home. Anything important?'

'Not really. Just to say hello. Mention how boring bed was without you.'

She could feel his amusement through the darkness. 'Aren't you tired?'

'Exhausted.' Smiling back, she reached for him. 'But after all the naughty things I ate today the exercise will do me good.'

CHAPTER
17

Jas poured a cup of tea and left it to brew, then crossed to the window to stare out at the glum day.

Though she knew she should let it go, Digby's murmur in the night troubled her deeply. It had happened late, after he'd fallen asleep, restless and muttering. He'd rolled over to press his head against her chest and Jas had smiled and stroked his hair. It had been a contented moment when she'd let her imagination soar into what could be, but it had turned jaundiced. A single whispered name revealed there was only room for one woman in Digby's heart.

And it wasn't her.

They had a solid, caring friendship and great sex, but nothing more. Jas had to accept that, and if her sacrifice meant Digby found some peace from his pain, then so be it. Perhaps this would be her penance for Mike. Her gift to set at least someone's world to rights.

It beat the alternative, which was feeling angry at a universe that seemed hell-bent on causing her unhappiness. Jas refused to be anyone's victim, even Fate's.

She finished making her tea and wandered outside, sipping as she went. Digby's car sat behind hers in front of the garage. He'd wanted a walk and Jas wasn't in the mood. The tide was in, a big one, and she never liked it when it swept so far up the beach. It felt creepy. The foaming churned edges of the waves seemed cold and covetous, pushing aggressively towards the dunes as if the sea was hungry.

Jas perched on Oxy's fence and watched him grazing. She should have been cleaning the house or attending to a dozen other chores but they could wait. A moment to breathe, to settle, was what she needed—equilibrium so she could face Digby's return with strength.

Her tea was almost finished when a car sounded in her drive. Jas frowned, before an onslaught of panic had her leaping off the fence. Digby's car was in plain sight. Depending on who the caller was there'd be questions, perhaps worse.

'Please, please,' she whispered, praying for it not to be Em, but the gods weren't listening. Stomach muscles clenched and blood racing, Jas stood rooted at the edge of her back lawn as Em's four-wheel drive slowed to a standstill.

Em alighted, her gaze on Digby's Mercedes. A small, gift-wrapped box was in her hand. Pausing, she regarded the car with a frown. For several heartbeats she appeared more puzzled than anything else, then her mouth dropped in shock. She glanced towards the house before catching sight of Jas. Immediately her expression frosted over.

Several long strides and Em was in front of her. 'So it's you.'

Jas kept her chin up. She would not be ashamed of her relationship with Digby. 'Yes.'

Em turned away, one hand to her forehead as though trying to soothe a deep headache. Suddenly she swung back. 'What the hell were you thinking?'

'Em ...'

'Don't you "Em" me! You know what he's been through. You know how fragile he is. Yet you do this?'

Jasmine cupped her hands forward, pleading. 'Em, please. You have to understand. It's for us both.'

'For you both?' She barked a bitter laugh that had Jas shrinking inside.

'I know I should have told you, explained, but with the wedding and everything it seemed better to—'

'Better? How can this be better? He's a mess, Jas. A mess! How could you possibly think that sleeping with him would help?'

A tear slicked out of Jasmine's right eye. She swiped it away. 'Because it does.'

Em shook her head, and backed off a few steps as if in disgust. 'You'll break his heart.'

Break Digby's heart? What about her heart? Jas couldn't believe Em wouldn't even listen. She couldn't help it, her voice rose with her surging anger. 'What heart? He doesn't have one. *She* stole it!'

Em crossed her arms, her mouth lifted in a sneer. 'And you think fucking him will bring it back?'

Jas blinked in shock. Em never spoke like that. Never.

'He came to me,' said Jas, wiping once more at tears that refused to stop. 'He was lonely and wanted someone to talk to. It was never meant to be more than that.'

'I'm sure.'

'Don't, Em. Don't spoil it just because you don't understand.'

For several strained seconds they locked eyes. Jasmine's gaze pleading, the coldness of her friend's gradually easing as doubt and years of trusting friendship ate at her conviction. But before Jas could say anything further, Em's focus jerked seaward.

Digby was coming over the dunes at a pace.

'Please,' said Jas, whipping back to Em. 'Don't fight over this. It's not worth it.'

But by the time he'd come close enough to catch sight of Jasmine's tears, a fight was exactly what Digby appeared to want. His expression was dark with fury. His eyes narrowed on Em and filled with blame.

Jas threw one last pleading glance at her friend before stepping forward to intercept Digby, determined to protect what little relationship he had with his sister. 'It's okay, Dig. Em's just a bit shocked.'

'Spreading her venom, more like.' He rested his hands on Jasmine's shoulders. 'You okay?'

The kindness in his tone, the futile hope it gave, brought on another involuntary tear bubble. Jas sniffed and nodded. 'Why don't we go inside and talk over a cuppa?'

He didn't answer. Instead he gently stroked the tear away and leaned forward to kiss her forehead. Jas closed her eyes at the tenderness of the gesture. Maybe it would be okay.

Her optimism was misplaced. Releasing his grip, Digby turned to his sister. 'Where do you get off?'

If Em was stunned before, she was even more dismayed by his question. 'What do you mean?'

'Can't help yourself, can you? You always have to spoil things.'

'I'm not trying to spoil anything. I just don't want to see anyone hurt, you or Jas. I've only ever wanted to protect you, you know that.'

Jas tugged at Digby's arm. 'Please, don't. Let's go inside. We'll talk it through.'

'Protect me?' scoffed Digby, ignoring Jas. 'From what? You have no idea about me, what I think, what I feel. Nothing.'

'I know you're grieving for Felicity, but ...' Em stammered to silence as Digby threw his head back and shook it slowly back and forth in disbelief. She glanced at Jas, and for the first time there was no anger, only fear.

'I don't want your protection,' said Digby. 'I don't want anything from you. You ruin everything that's good.'

Em stared at him, speechless. Then with Wallace fortitude, she lifted her chin. 'Believe what you like, but the honest truth is that I've only ever wanted to see you happy. If you're happy with Jas, then I am too, but—'

Digby puffed a noise. 'Always a "but" with you. What? Jas not good enough for me?'

'She's my best friend, Digby. Why would you think I'd say that?'

'Oh, I don't know. How about history? No one's ever been good enough in your eyes. Not Cait, not Felicity, now not Jas.'

Em breathed in deeply and spoke with calm Jas could only admire her for. 'I would love for you and Jas to work out. But you've both been hurt very badly.'

'We know what we're doing, Em,' said Jas. 'It's all right.'

'I worry.'

'I know you do,' Jas replied. 'But I promise we're okay. It's not serious. It's just ...' She glanced at Digby, who stared back, inscrutable. The next word left an ache in her chest but she said it anyway. 'Comfort.' Hurting, she avoided his gaze and concentrated on her friend. 'It's also private.'

'I'm not going to tell everyone, if that's what you're worried about.' Em addressed Digby. 'I assume Josh knows?'

'No.'

'Oh.' She shifted uncomfortably. 'I'd like to discuss it with him, if that's okay?'

'Discuss it?' Digby made another disparaging noise. 'What? You think we're children who need permission?'

'No! I don't know. I ...' Em bit at her top lip. 'We're getting married in two weeks. You're his best man. Jas is my chief bridesmaid. How can I keep this from him?'

'Do what you like,' he said, waving a hand. 'I've stopped caring.'

'Dig.' Jasmine's voice was sad and soft. It hurt her to see Digby and Em fight, and she knew only too well how Em had suffered after Felicity's death, even if Digby didn't.

Digby closed his eyes as if he understood he'd gone too far. 'I'm sorry.'

'Don't be.' Em's eyes were glistening with tears and guilt. 'I know nothing I do or say will change the way you feel about me, and you're right—this is none of my business. I'll leave you to it.' Holding out the gift-wrapped box, she grimaced at Jas. 'For you.'

'What is it?'

'A gift, to say thank you for last night and the bridal shower, and,' her gaze slid towards Digby and quickly away, 'everything else.' When Jas made no move to accept, Em placed the box in her hands and wrapped her own over Jasmine's. 'Take it. Please.'

Jas nodded. 'Everything I've done has been done with pleasure for a friend. I don't need presents, but thank you.'

Em pressed her hands a little firmer and let go, and without another word walked to her car, straight-backed, head up, dark hair whipped behind on the breeze.

Digby and Jas said nothing as Em started the engine and put the car in reverse. She stared out the windscreen at them, half-lifted her hand from the wheel as if to wave and let it drop. Without another glance, she reversed out of sight, Jas watching her the entire time.

When Jas looked back at Digby he'd moved a few steps away, and stood facing the dunes. Jas placed her hand on his back and stepped around his side to look at him. Fatigue etched lines in a face made even more tired-looking by stubble and the whip of sea-spray and wind during his walk.

'I can't deal with her, Jas. I just can't.'

'Why not? You know Felicity's death wasn't her fault. It was a terrible, tragic accident.'

'I know that. But seeing her with you when I topped the dunes ...' He breathed in shakily. 'The way she was standing, the look on her face. It was like Flick all over again.'

'I've known your sister almost all my life. I can handle her.' Besides, Jas wasn't Felicity.

'You shouldn't have to, not when it comes to you and me.' He sighed and rubbed his face. 'What a fuck-up.'

'No, it's not.' Placing the box on the ground, she threaded her arms around him and locked them in the hollow of his back, looking up with a smile. No one would come out of this hurting. No one. Except maybe herself, and Jas was already resigned to that possibility. 'Em will be fine once she gets used to the idea. Josh probably won't care. Your grandmother already suspects and seems to approve, and your mum will be relieved you're with a friend instead of brooding alone somewhere.'

'What about you, Jas? How do you feel about it?'

Jas pulled him closer, reaching up on tiptoe to concentrate on his mouth so she didn't have to keep eye contact. 'Why don't you come to bed with me and find out?'

Later that afternoon after Digby had gone, Jas wandered into her kitchen and picked up Em's gift from where she'd left it on the counter. She used scissors to cut away the raffia bow. Em had a wrapping technique that was like origami and didn't require tape, and the paper opened out into neat folds. The box was made of stiff blue cardboard, and when Jas removed the small envelope she saw the distinctive Swarovski crystal symbol on the lid. The card was handpainted in Em's skilful style and showed two young girls holding hands as they skipped towards a pair of grazing horses: the two of them as little girls, horse-mad, carefree.

Friends.

Jasmine's throat thickened. She swallowed it away and opened the card. The inscription was simple and heartfelt: *To celebrate your new wings and say thank you. I love you, my friend. Fly long and fly bright. Em.*

It took several blinks to clear the prickles from her eyes, hating that they'd argued, that their precious friendship had suffered over nothing. Jas would repair it though, no matter what it took. Curious about the wings reference and the contents of the box, Jas set the card aside, lifted the lid and carefully removed the top layer of foam packaging.

Nestled inside was an exquisitely rendered crystal butterfly, its facets flashing every shade of the rainbow.

Her new wings.

Bright, beautiful and free.

CHAPTER
18

Josh was pacing near the door to the stables when Digby pulled into Camrick. One glance revealed his mood. Mouth set, low brows, fists swinging at his sides. Digby parked in front of the garage door and alighted from the car.

Josh stood a few feet away. Muscles flexed in his arms. 'You and I need to talk.'

'Yeah, we do.' Digby glanced at the big house and back at Josh. Though there was no sign of movement, he'd bet someone was watching. Granny B in the shadows of her balcony, no doubt. She could sniff trouble like a shark scented blood. 'You want to do it here or at the pub?'

'The way I'm feeling the pub probably isn't a good idea.'

Digby shrugged. 'Fair enough. Come upstairs. There are beers in the fridge.'

Josh stalked him up the stairs, his work boots loud on the timber treads. Digby nearly asked what projects he'd been working on but decided against it. Josh wouldn't care for small talk. This was a discussion that had been a long time coming. Though Josh wasn't a pussy-footer like the rest of Digby's family, he'd still been careful and sympathetic. Not anymore. This involved Em.

Digby pulled a couple of Crown Lagers from the fridge and cracked the tops. After handing one to Josh he took a swig from the other and leaned against the kitchen bench. If Josh wanted to turn this into a fight he could. For him, Digby would take it, although he'd rather not have to. Not with the wedding around the corner.

Josh took a mouthful and swallowed. He regarded Digby, clearly choosing his words. 'This thing with Em has to end.'

'Easier said than done.'

'Why?'

'You know why.'

Josh's jaw tightened. 'It wasn't her fault.'

Digby raised an eyebrow.

'All right. So she did something shit. You think she's not sorry? You think it doesn't tear her apart?'

Digby looked away. What Josh said was probably true but that didn't change the fact of what Em had done. If she hadn't told Flick that Digby would never forgive what she'd done to Granny B, Felicity might never have panicked and run to the quarry. He returned his gaze. 'Maybe, but sorry doesn't change anything, does it? Flick died thinking I didn't love her because Em took it on herself to tell her so. No "sorry" is going to make that go away.'

'She knows that. She carries it around every day.' Josh tilted his bottle towards Digby. 'But you need to forgive her. For yourself, if not for her.'

'You been seeing that counsellor, have you? He's big on forgiveness.'

'For fuck's sake, Dig. Get over it.'

'Get over it?' Digby slammed his beer down, the contents foaming up and spilling out the top. 'How can I get over it? She died!'

Josh remained unmoved. 'Yeah, she did, and it's shit and I'm sorry for her and for you. But you lived, Dig. So did I, so did Em, and now we need to get on with it.'

As quickly as it had flared, Digby's temper faded. No one understood, not even Josh. Yes, he wanted to get on with it. He wanted it badly. Life, love, laughter, happiness. All the things he knew existed, that he could have because Felicity taught him he could. But he wanted it all with her. His angel. His love.

And he could never have that because of his sister's jealousy and vengeance.

'You know what I hate the most?' His voice cracked and he swallowed, blinking rapidly. 'I hate that Em has this chance and I don't. I hate that it's going to be her walking down that aisle instead of Flick, stealing all the love and joy Flick should have had.'

Josh's head lowered. 'Jesus, Dig.'

'But you know what else I hate?'

Josh looked up.

'Myself, for feeling this way.' He held Josh's gaze. This was the truth, the horrible honesty that he hadn't revealed to anyone, not even his counsellor. 'It's fucking killing me.'

'So change.'

'I'm trying.' He reached for his beer, saw the foaming head and dumped it in the sink. He hadn't wanted it anyway. 'Jas is helping.'

'Jas?' Confusion suddenly morphed into astonishment. 'You're shagging Jas?'

Digby blinked. 'Em didn't tell you?'

'No.' Josh shook his head in disbelief. 'No, she didn't. She came home upset and when I tried to find out what happened all she'd say was that you and her had an argument.'

'She came to see Jas at Admella Beach. I was there.'

'Oh, yeah. The butterfly.' At Digby's expression he clarified. 'Em bought Jas a crystal butterfly as thanks for everything she'd done.'

So that's what was in the box. Em probably wished she hadn't gone to the expense now. 'She wasn't impressed by the news. Had a go at Jas.'

'Which is when you had a go back.'

'Pretty much.'

'Shit.' Josh took a slug of beer, worry lining his brow. 'Not good news for the wedding.'

'No.'

Josh contemplated a while. 'All right. I'll talk to Em, you talk to Jas. Those two are more important than me and you. Em and I could get married in a registry office tomorrow and I'd be happy but this is Em's big day. And our families'. It's up to us to put all the other shit aside and make it right.' He downed the last of his beer and placed the bottle on the sink. 'I'd better go.' He strode to the stairwell, eager to get home to Em.

'Josh?'

He paused, one hand on the rail, and regarded Digby over his shoulder.

'Are we good?'

'We are, but that doesn't let you off the hook with Em. You need to sort your problem.'

Digby was aware of that but as he'd said, easier said than done. 'I'll do what I can. Just don't expect miracles.'

Josh looked as though he was going to comment further, but instead nodded. 'All right.' He took a couple of steps, changed his mind and backed up. 'You and Jas, is it serious?'

'No.' Except the denial sounded wrong. 'Maybe. I don't know.' Digby shrugged. 'I like her. A lot. But ...'

But what? So she wasn't Felicity. No woman would be, and it was her difference he liked. So why the but?

Josh answered for him. 'Too soon?'

'I guess.' Although he wasn't certain it was that either, not entirely. Something niggled though. A little irritation in the back of his mind he couldn't quite reach to scratch. Not about Jas, but about himself. He let it go and moved across to the stairwell. 'Whatever it is I'd prefer to keep it between me and Jas. For now, anyway.'

'Smart idea. Everyone has enough to worry about with the wedding, without throwing that into the mix. I'll keep it under my hat. So will Em. Right. Gotta go. I'll see you Friday for the spa.' Finally he grinned, the good-humoured Josh everyone loved. 'Should be interesting. Harry's terrified, the big girl.'

'We'll have to scare him even more then.'

'We will.' He tapped the rail. 'Look after yourself, Dig. I need my best man.'

When Josh had gone Digby retreated to the lounge to stand at the window with his hands in his pockets. Dusk cast stringy shadows over the gravel drive and coated the park opposite in khaki and grey. He glanced across at the house. His grandmother was standing at the corner of her upstairs balcony, tumbler in one hand, cigar in the other, blowing smoke balloons into the clean air. She raised her glass towards Digby as if in salute. He didn't acknowledge it. The sight of her on the balcony had brought an ache to his chest.

He stepped back out of sight and plucked up Felicity's photograph, his favourite, where she smiled out at him like a heaven-sent angel. An angel with luminous skin, white-gold hair and eyes the colour of the summer sky. A woman who should have done no wrong, yet did.

Digby closed his eyes as the vision of their final moments at Rocking Horse Hill played in his head. Em's panicked warnings for him not to come any closer to the collapsing quarry. The smell of peat and broken plants as dirt broke away beneath him. Stretching for Flick, pleading with her to take his hand. The powerful suck of the earth. His promise to always be there for her. Em's sobs as her grip began to falter.

Felicity's mud and tear-stained face turning to his, calm with resignation. The whispered 'I love you'. His own in return.

Then the terrifying realisation of what she had planned.

He couldn't remember after that. Josh said Digby had lunged for her, even though to do so was suicide. Digby thought he recalled his own roars but Josh said he couldn't hear anything above the landslide and Em's screams.

In his dreams Digby reached her, had her within his protective hold, only for her to be wrenched away by a force impossible to fight. Truth was he was likely unconscious after his dive and missed her all together. He hated that thought, like he hated that their last words weren't enough, that she didn't believe him. Yet her own love for him had remained strong against that betrayal.

Christ, he'd never forgive himself for that. How the hell was he meant to forgive Em?

Digby opened his eyes. 'I'm sorry, Flick. So sorry.'

Giving her face one last caress, he put the frame down to look out the window once more. Past the drive, over the parkland and trees, past Rocking Horse Hill, was Admella Beach and Jas. Two women who couldn't be more different in looks and personality.

One he loved. The other ... He let out a long sigh and rubbed at his hair. The niggling thought was back and this time he was certain the problem was him. A fault in his psyche preventing what he felt for Jas from developing into something more.

He didn't love Jas, not the way he had Felicity, but she mattered. She made him forget his grief and helped him smile. She'd even helped him to feel again, what it was like to be touched, appreciated, nurtured. What it was like to protect someone. Plus he wanted her like crazy. She was playful, adventurous and sexy as all hell.

And what was Digby in return? Damaged, bitter and jealous. Too weak to do anything but dread the wedding of the man he loved like a brother and the sister he couldn't yet forgive.

Whatever his screwed-up feelings for Jas, if he was going to make it through the next two weeks he'd need her more than ever.

CHAPTER
19

Em's final dress fitting was a warm-hearted affair, with champagne and giggles and oohs and ahs. The Wallace women had chosen well and the German-born dressmaker—or couturier, as Granny B grandly referred to her—was not only an expert seamstress but also knew how to make a bridal party feel special.

Antje ran her business from a custom-built studio at the back of her house. Half of the studio was dedicated to her craft, with a polished timber floor, sewing machines and overlockers of mind-boggling complexity, cutting boards, custom storage units and dressmakers' mannequins. The other side was fitted with lush carpet, lounges and angled mirrors for consultations and fittings. A large sliding glass door bathed the area in light.

Jasmine's dress had been finished the week before and hung on a rack ready to be taken for pressing with the other gowns, which meant she could relax with a glass of fizz and a broad smile while Teagan and Em took their turns being fitted. Having had her bridesmaid's dress made via emailed measurements, Teagan's required a few tweaks. Em's, on the other hand, required only hemming and a small tuck at the waist. Even incomplete, it was stunning. As was she, protected by the unwavering armour of Josh's love.

Jas had phoned Em on Sunday, immediately after opening her gift. Apologies and tears had followed, and it was proof of the strength of their lifelong friendship that a single phone call could put them back to rights. Even so, Jas had been careful to back it up Monday with a lunchtime call into PaperPassion. She and Em had eaten their sandwiches together behind the counter, sipped cups of tea, and shared the chocolate éclair that Jas had grabbed from a bakery along the way.

Em was desperately curious about Jasmine's relationship with Digby but did her best not to pry. Torn between respect for Digby's privacy and her friendship with Em, Jas erred on the side of caution and revealed little, while remaining steadfast that the relationship was healthy for them both.

'He laughs, Em,' Jas had said. 'Not often, but more and more all the time.'

Em had frowned. 'So he's over Felicity? He must be if you and he are ... you know.'

'No. No he's not.' Jas had had to swallow at the roughness that admission left in her throat. 'He misses her terribly. I doubt he'll ever stop.' Knowing there was more underlying the question than Digby's feelings for his late fiancée, Jas had regarded Em with sympathy. 'He'll forgive you, Em. In time. Once he's finished grieving for her.'

'But if he's with you, that means he's moving on, doesn't it?'

'It's not as simple as that. Our relationship is more a comfort thing. A way to halt the loneliness that comes with loss.' Jas took a last bite of éclair, feigning composure when inside she felt dragged with sadness.

Em couldn't seem to get her head around the idea, which was understandable. Other than a highly regrettable instance in her youth, Em had never been into casual relationships. She picked at crumbs, sorting them into little piles on her plate. 'So there's no future with you and Dig?'

'Who knows? The thing is, neither of us are thinking about that. We're taking each day as it comes. Which is why we're not advertising what's going on. People will only form expectations when that's not the point.'

'But what is the point?'

'Like I said, comfort.' And great sex. A thought that at last gave rise to a smile.

'Oh, I know that look,' said Em. 'And I do *not* want to know.'

Jas laughed. 'Don't worry, I won't inflict that pain on you. You have enough of that from your gran.'

With that exchange they were back to normal.

Jas smiled at Em now, resplendent in her gown.

Teagan leaned to press her shoulder against Jasmine's. 'She looks amazing.'

'She does.'

Teagan sighed. 'I can only hope I look half as good.'

The remark had Jas rolling her eyes. Teagan was a very pretty redhead, and since her move to New South Wales happiness shone from her pores, making her even more attractive. She glowed with good health and that special inner fire that being deeply in love ignited. Certainly Lucas clearly thought she was gorgeous, constantly smiling at her, whispering things, touching her hair and face and hands as if afraid some fairy would wave a wand and make her disappear from his life.

Lucas had met Em and Josh when they floated Teagan's horse Astra to The Falls, where she'd moved, but this was his first visit to her home town and introduction to her other friends, and what everyone noticed—other than Lucas's movie-star looks—was his unadulterated adoration of Teagan. That he'd made her so happy granted him instant approval.

'Any closer to setting a date?' asked Jas.

'Not yet. It's more about where than when. Nearly all my family are here, while Lucas's are mostly in western Sydney.'

'You could always elope.'

'That's been suggested. More than once too.'

'Singing Elvises in Las Vegas?'

Teagan grinned. 'Don't tempt me.'

'It'd be lovely if you were married here,' said Em, catching their conversation. 'But wherever you have it, we'll be there.'

'Even Vegas?'

'You, madam,' teased Jas, 'will be barefoot and pregnant soon and won't be able to go anywhere.'

'I hope so.' Em spread her palms over her flat belly. 'The pregnant bit, not the barefoot.'

'You'll have stunning children,' said Teagan wistfully.

'Oh, right,' scoffed Jas, 'like yours and Lucas's would be ugly.'

Teagan appraised her. 'You'd have good-looking children too, you know. Once we get you married off.'

Jas and Em exchanged a glance. Jas took a hefty swig of champagne. Digby's children by any woman would be gorgeous, but that wasn't a thought-path she wanted to travel. She was going to be hurt enough without indulging in those kinds of fantasies. 'By the time that happens I'll probably be past it. Anyway, I'll be too busy playing doting aunty to your broods.'

It was another twenty minutes before Antje finished her pinning, by which time Jas had scoffed enough champagne to not only feel giggly but a touch lustful too. A few more minutes and they'd be off to meet Digby and the boys at the spa—Em's idea for some fun bridal party bonding and indulgence. Perhaps she and Digby could sneak off somewhere for a massage of their own.

Jas sighed and gave herself another scold, but the wedding and children chatter had embedded a lump of longing in her chest that refused to budge. She wanted Digby so badly it was painful, made worse by the knowledge that there was a limit on how much he could give in return.

Teagan, who these days was teetotal, drove them to the town centre. After parking in Em's car space behind PaperPassion they strolled in the sunshine to the side street where Lush Spa and Beauty was located. The day was suitably glorious, as if in celebration for them, and Jas thought they made a special group as they strode along the footpath, chatting and laughing.

Em was also fizzed on champagne, although much less so than Jas, and greeted her fiancé with a kiss, before turning to smile at a nervous-looking Harry, and finally Digby. It was the first time they'd faced one another since Sunday, and though Jas had tried to broach the subject with Digby, he'd stonewalled every conversation with 'I'm working on it' and a quiet directive to leave it at that.

Jasmine's optimism that this might signal an end to their acrimony was flattened by Digby's cool response to Em. His sister's smile faltered as her joy was punctured by his emotionless stare.

'Dig, please,' whispered Jas. 'Don't spoil things.'

He seemed hurt by the accusation. 'I'm not.'

'You barely smiled.'

He let out a long breath. 'I'm trying. But I'm not going to play happy families just for the sake of it. Not after how she treated you. And Felicity.'

Jas glanced at the others. Teagan was observing them with curiosity, Em and Josh were pretending not to notice their tête–à–tête, while Harry was studying a poster advertising enzyme peels with something akin to terror. 'It's not me you should be worrying about.'

Further conversation was interrupted by the sound of clapped hands demanding attention. Em had recovered from Digby's snub and stood near the counter, smiling again. 'Ready?'

'Dig and I am,' said Josh. 'Harry's not. The big girl. He's terrified he's going to get waxed and lose all his manliness like Samson.'

Harry rolled his eyes. 'At least I've got the testosterone to grow more.'

It was a relief to have the tension eased by the boys' ribbing. Even Digby seemed amused. Jas poked Harry in the ribs. He was so huge she barely came up to his armpit, but despite his powerful size, Harry was a big softie and much adored. 'They'll only wax you if you ask. Stop fretting.'

'I wasn't.'

Jas grinned. 'Sure, you weren't.'

Grace, the salon manager, stepped from the corridor and greeted them. 'Everyone here?' she asked.

Em nodded. 'And looking forward to it.'

'Great. Everything's prepared.' Grace smiled at them in turn. 'Now, girls first.' Three women appeared at the entrance to the corridor that led to the treatment rooms, smiling and professional in their pristine white uniforms. 'Em, you're with Megan. Jas, if you'll go with Sandy? And Teagan, we've paired you with Katie.'

Jas snuck a squeeze of Digby's fingers and was rewarded with a quick squeeze back. It was only a small thing, but the intimacy of it made her momentarily breathless. And she hadn't missed the way he'd placed her first before Felicity, when talking about how Em had treated her. Combined with the champagne in her system, the thought that his feelings might be growing left Jas giddy.

After kissing Josh farewell, Em waved at Harry and Digby and disappeared with her therapist with a call of 'Enjoy!' Throwing Digby a last promise-filled wink, Jas followed her.

Two hours later she emerged to find Digby pacing the shop floor, Harry staring dazedly at nothing, and Josh regarding the corridor as if fearful Em might never reappear. All three held their fists jammed into their pockets.

Bemused, Jas glanced at each of their faces in turn. 'Good massages?'

Josh and Digby returned with a solid 'Yes'. All Harry could manage was a distracted 'Mmm' before drifting back off into ga-ga land.

'Where's Em?' asked Jas.

'Won't be long,' answered Grace from behind her desk. 'She's just getting changed. Did you wish to settle the bill?'

Josh already had his wallet out. 'I'll pay for both Em and me.'

Harry lined up behind him, fidgeting with his own wallet as he stared dopily towards the treatment rooms. Ignoring them both, Digby stepped alongside Jas and quietly asked where she'd left her car.

'At Camrick.'

'Shit.'

She stared at him, wondering what the hell was going on. Then realisation dawned and the urge to giggle rose huge, only to be seared sober by Digby's white-hot gaze. She knew that expression, the fire behind it. Heat pulsed in her groin, along with the need to escape the spa as fast as possible.

Em emerged with Teagan just as Josh finished paying. He regarded his fiancée with an expression almost as blistering as Digby's, before dragging his attention away to Teagan. 'I'll take Em home, if you like.'

'Oh, good. Thanks.' Teagan blushed slightly. 'I should get back to Lucas.' Then she caught Jasmine's eye and winced. 'Sorry, Jas. I'll drop you back to Camrick, of course.'

'I'll take care of Jas,' said Digby.

'I should go too,' said Harry, sounding as though his brain had vacated to another planet.

'Hadn't you better pay?' said Josh.

Now it was Harry's turn to redden. Somewhere during his discombobulation he'd returned his wallet to his pocket. He glanced at the corridor and back at Grace. 'Oh. Right. Sorry.'

With everyone's rides home arranged, Josh fairly hustled Em out the door. As soon as they'd paid, Teagan and Harry bid rapid-fire farewells and scuttled after them, leaving Digby and Jas alone.

Digby passed a credit card to Grace. 'I'll take care of Jasmine's account as well.'

Jas stayed his arm. 'No, I'll look after it.'

He shrugged her off and nodded for Grace to go ahead.

'Digby!'

'You can argue with me later.'

She would too, once they'd dealt with more important matters. That Digby was probably rich enough to buy her a thousand spa sessions without putting a dent in his wealth was irrelevant—Jas could take care of herself.

Digby was parked a short walk away. He crossed the distance with one hand on Jasmine's back, urging her to match his long strides.

It wasn't until they were strapped in the car and Digby had taken a turn south that Jas spoke. 'Not going back to Camrick?'

'No.'

She eyed the speedometer. Digby wasn't speeding but it was obvious from the impatient wrench of his hands around the wheel that he was desperate to. 'What about my car?'

'I'll drive you back later.'

She kept her voice casual, as if unaware what was going on. 'Must have been a hell of a massage.'

Digby threw her a hot glance. 'It was.'

'From the way everyone was acting, all they could think of was getting laid. Except for Harry. Poor thing doesn't have anyone to get laid with.'

'Men have other techniques, you know.'

'Really? Want to show me?'

Digby's eyes raked her breasts and lower, before flicking back to the road. 'Only if you'll show me yours.'

Jasmine's hand slipped between her thighs, her mouth tilted in a smug smile as Digby caught her movement and the car's interior electrified. The power sex gave her over him was heady. 'Now?'

Digby swallowed and inhaled deeply. 'Better not.'

She used her other hand to fondle her breasts; already the nipples were turgid. God, this was turning her on. 'Sure?'

Digby lifted a hand off the wheel and wiped it down his leg, shifting uncomfortably as he did so. 'You're dangerous.'

'Ah, but in a good way.'

'In the best way, but if you keep that up we'll end up in a paddock.'

'I'm not sure I can hang on for that long.'

He slid another look her way as she continued to tease. 'Christ.'

'Don't speed now.'

'Come on, Jas. Fifteen minutes. Even you can wait that long.'

From the way she was feeling, Jas wasn't so sure about that. She rolled onto her hip to face him, arm reaching across to finger circles over the back of his neck. 'What will I get as reward?'

'Promise no more touching yourself?'

She pouted but agreed, only to immediately regret it when Digby spent the remainder of the trip describing exactly what he planned to do, leaving Jas flushed, panting and squirming like a worm.

And wishing she could hold onto this sexy, playful man forever.

CHAPTER
20

True dread didn't set in until the week of the wedding. It crept up on Digby, silent and secretive, and like a nightmare evil twin, gave a vicious pinch when he least expected it.

He'd been, if not happy, then as close to it as he'd been since Felicity died. Jas was driving him crazy in the best possible way. Her unrestrained and unapologetic sexiness was a siren's call to his own desires. He adored her luscious body, the generosity of her lovemaking, her enthusiasm for trying anything, and her giggles when their experiments failed.

But his happiness was due to more than sex. They laughed together, shared food and wine and television and beach walks. Talked about the town, swapped childhood anecdotes, compared their different perspectives of shared memories.

It was when he'd shown her the final design for her garden, laid out properly on a large sheet of cartridge paper, that his sense that Jas was something more than a friend became truly real. He'd taken care with the plans, wanting her to see the potential of the space, the practical beauty it could provide. He filled outlines of the trees and shrubs in watercolours and labelled each with their botanical and common names. Pathways and garden beds were measured out, comfortable seats secreted in leafy bowers. Decking extended the house's rear veranda, creating extra outdoor living space while keeping an all-important view of Oxy's paddock, before stepping down to open lawn. At the beachside end, a pergola and barbecue area were measured out, a trail beyond leading to the dunes.

'I have something for you,' he'd said on Sunday night, hiding the rolled up cartridge paper behind his back. He'd worked on the plans all day in Uncle James's study in Camrick. It was the one room in the mansion he claimed as private, and where he managed his business affairs. Or used to. After meeting Felicity, Digby had lost interest in his holdings. It was only after discovering Mike's duplicity that he'd resumed scrutiny of his investments. Digby's inheritance was extensive and though only part of his wealth was managed by the bank's financial planning arm, in the hands of someone like Mike Boland, even that amount was too much.

Jas had regarded him with one of her expressions. One eyebrow cocked, mouth tilted in one corner. 'I bet you do.'

He'd laughed and leaned in to kiss her. 'Later, babe.'

Using mugs and glasses as weights, he'd unrolled the plans on the kitchen bench, and stood back to let her study them.

Jas peered at the layout and pursed her lips. 'Is this for Camrick?'

'It's for here.'

'Here?' Her frown deepened. 'What? You mean my garden?'

'Yes.' He leaned across her to point out the features. 'See? That's the back of your house. I've removed the rail and extended the veranda into a deck.' He continued to demonstrate, highlighting the garden's ease of maintenance, the entertainment areas, its secret crannies for surprise and privacy. Practical elements like pathways to the garage and relocated clothesline, access to Oxy's paddock.

'... and here I've added a lockable garden gate through to the dunes.' He stared at her. Jasmine's eyes were closed, her face scrunched as though against pain. 'Jas?'

'Oh, Digby.'

Rocked by uncertainly, he'd stiffened. His confidence that she'd love what he'd designed was now somewhere in his socks. Digby began to roll up the paper. 'I was only mucking around.'

Her hand stayed his. He stared at it, afraid. All he'd wanted was to give something back. A thank you for the comfort she'd provided him. It wasn't meant to be a big deal, but from the way she was looking at him it had become one. His heart thudded. In fear. In want. In hope.

'You did this for me?'

He nodded, still unsure.

'Why?'

He covered his nerves with a joke. 'Looked at your garden lately?'

She didn't laugh or smile or do anything except examine his face. 'Have you any idea how amazing you are?'

Digby didn't know what to say. It was too disconcerting. She was looking at him as if he were some miraculous creature that had crawled from the sea and taken up residence in her kitchen. Yet there was something else. As if the tear-salted soil of his grief had been suddenly turned over, exposing the fresh loam beneath, and now the seeds of something green and good were sprouting from it.

They'd spent another hour poring over the plans, Digby soaking up her delight with relief and pride. Then he'd dragged her off to bed, the urge to lose himself inside her big-hearted warmth too great to resist.

The positivity of his feelings had allowed him to enjoy Tuesday-
night dinner at Camrick. On a high, he'd managed to talk politely
with Em about her and Josh's honeymoon to the United Kingdom.
He was even surprised to find himself amused that she seemed far
more excited about that than the wedding itself. Across the table,
Josh had nodded subtle thanks, while later, as Digby waited to dry
the dishes, Adrienne had hugged him tightly. His grandmother
had watched it all with a knowing smile, before retreating to her
balcony to smoke, drink and contemplate the town she considered
her realm.

Afterwards, he'd driven to Admella Beach with eagerness in
his veins, anxious to spend more time with the woman who, he
hoped, was also beginning to feel the change in their relationship.
Her welcome, his fluttery feelings as he kissed her in the hall and,
laughing, all the way to her bedroom made Digby certain he would
make it through the week, that his jealousy and anger were under
control.

Then came the first cruel pinch.

He'd caught up with Harry and Josh late on Monday afternoon
to pick up their suits and enjoy a quiet beer at the Australian Arms.
Theirs were classic dinner suits, with satin shawl lapels and tailored
pleated pants. With the exception of a white shirt, Josh's was all
black, including his bow tie, while Harry's and Digby's were teamed
with navy vests and ties in blue to match to the bridesmaids' dresses.
Harry had poked fun, striking James Bond poses, but on sighting
Josh in his suit Digby had found himself bereft of laughter.

His friend emerged from the change room, shooting his cuffs and
tweaking his tie, a grin splitting his face. Josh strutted, wobbling his
head. 'Bit of a looker, yeah?'

'Not bad,' said Harry. 'As long as you don't count the giant
bonce.'

'No problems, Dig?'

Digby had swallowed the prickly thing in his throat, but it remained jammed. He nodded and quickly re-entered the change room before either of them noticed the sweat forming above his lip and in the hollows beneath his eyes. As he turned to shut the curtain, he caught Josh's eye and lowered his head in shame at the envy burning an acid hole in his gut.

Josh made no comment until they were alone. After one beer, Harry had muttered something about hoping to catch someone on his way home and loped off.

Josh pointed to Digby's glass. 'Another?'

He probably shouldn't but Digby owed Josh an explanation. 'Just a light.'

While he waited he tried to formulate an excuse: a momentary attack of nerves, embarrassment at looking like a penguin. But that was bullshit and Josh would know it.

'You want to tell me what happened back there?' said Josh when he'd placed a beer in front of Digby and settled down.

'I don't know.' Digby palmed his forehead. 'It was weird. For a moment I just felt like I'd been steamrollered.'

Josh considered while he sipped and swallowed. 'Jealousy?'

Though the admission was humiliating, he nodded. 'It's crap, I know.'

'It's four days until the wedding. You going to be over it by then?'

'I'm over it now. It was just a moment.'

Except as the week moved on and the pinches came more frequent and harder, Digby could no longer deny they were simply 'moments'.

The bridal party had another dinner together at Camrick on Wednesday night, this time celebrating the arrival of Teagan's parents, and her glamorous aunt Vanessa with new husband Dom, who'd flown in that day from Sydney. With the weather in the high twenties, Adrienne had arranged a barbecue in the backyard rather than a meal in the cavernous dining room, but that hadn't given Digby respite from his wayward feelings. Nonstop happy wedding chatter had flooded his senses to the point where he'd felt like he was drowning in it.

Aware of Granny B's keen regard, and not wanting to add to Adrienne's excitement, Jas was keeping well away, which left Digby grateful and annoyed at the same time. He needed her stability but was also aware how unfair his feelings were. They'd become so involved he and Jas were practically living together. Yet here he was, sweating and shivering over a dead woman and a milestone event he'd wanted more than anything to share with her.

When he'd been certain no one was looking, Digby had slipped inside the stables and up to the privacy of his apartment until the sick feeling passed, returning twenty minutes later with no one, except Jas and perhaps his beady-eyed gran, any wiser to the turmoil he'd been experiencing.

He was still kidding himself it would be fine when they'd turned up at Levenham's historic Anglican church on Thursday night for the rehearsal, but the moment he entered and saw the aisle and altar and magnificent stained-glass windows, the pinches came fast and vicious.

His skull ached from the thoughts ricocheting inside. The faults in his psyche, the weakness of his manhood. His lack of common decency. He was betraying Felicity by being there, by sleeping with another woman and enjoying it. He was exploiting Jasmine's big warm heart for his own pathetic ends, with no payoff for her. He had no forgiveness in his soul for the sister he was meant to love. He was weak, selfish, and fuelled by jealousy and condemnation.

A stained-glass angel cast her accusing gaze. Even Christ seemed to stare at him in reproof. Digby clenched his jaw. For everyone's sake he had to hold himself together.

'All well, Digby?' asked the minister.

For a long moment Digby stared at the man's face, desperate for any kind of help, before force of will steadied him again. 'As well as can be.'

Reverend Ellis was an astute man, who'd also been witness to Digby's grief at the funeral as well as at Camrick, when he'd been called in by Adrienne for support. His perceptive gaze didn't leave Digby. 'A bittersweet time for you, perhaps?'

Bittersweet barely touched the edges but Digby wasn't about to give himself away. 'I'll get through it.'

'If you need support, even a casual chat, I'm on hand.'

'Thanks. I'll be fine.'

From the way Reverend Ellis watched him for the remainder of the rehearsal, Digby had convinced no one. Not even himself.

Fortunately Harry provided plenty of distraction. Digby was walking behind Josh and Em, focusing on keeping one foot in front of the other and looking everywhere except at the joy-filled couple in front of him. Jasmine's grip was tight on his arm. Like the minister, she'd been observing him with concern and though he'd answered her whispered inquiries with all the strength he could muster, she'd kept encouraging him with smiles and surreptitious touches.

They were halfway down the aisle when Harry attempted to quiz Teagan about what to do about some girl he'd met. Before Felicity, Digby hadn't had the greatest success with women either, but Harry's ineptitude put him in a class of his own.

'You're a woman,' Harry said to Teagan.

'I know this will probably come as a shock to you, Harry, but yes, I am.'

Catching Digby's eye, Jas grinned and tilted her head towards the couple behind as if to say, 'Have a listen to this.'

'What?' asked Harry, clearly flummoxed by Teagan's answer. 'Oh. Sorry. Didn't mean it like that. I mean, you must think like one.'

Jas fell out of step as she listened in, slowing Digby with her.

Teagan's bemused silence was broken by a sulky 'Forget it' from Harry.

'Sorry,' said Teagan, bubbling with suppressed laughter. 'Can't now.'

'Definitely can't,' whispered Jas before calling loudly to Harry over her shoulder. 'Girl problems, Harry?'

Which only brought Em in on the farce. 'Does Harry have girl problems?'

Everyone stopped walking and turned around to face Harry, who was looking even sulkier than he'd sounded.

'Harry,' said Josh, 'suffered a little problem with his beautician at the spa on Friday that he wants to make up for.'

Em's gaze flicked from her fiancé to Harry. 'What problem? They've always been very good at Lush. Gran goes all the time.'

'Nothing,' said Harry, shooting an icy glare at Josh. 'Just forget it.'

Teagan nudged him. 'Come on. Spit it out.'

'No.'

Digby felt a surge of sympathy for the poor bloke. From Josh's unsubtle gibes Digby had already guessed that Harry must have suffered a hard-on during his massage. Unsurprising. They all had, but not everyone had Josh's confidence and Harry seemed genuinely rattled by the incident.

'Is it Maya?' said Jas. 'Because you probably should know she's seeing Dylan Mortenson.'

Harry all but rolled his eyes at this. 'I know that.'

'Then what?' asked Em. Folding her arms, she rested her weight on one hip. 'If there's a problem I need to know. Josh mentioned how impressed you were with Summer so I booked her for Saturday to help with make-up.'

A grin burst over Harry's face. 'You did?'

The church sighed with their ahs. Jas laughed in delight while Harry dropped his head in mortification and contemplated the carpet.

Digby came to his rescue. 'Can this wait? I don't know about you, but I could do with a beer. And Lucas is stuck in the pub by himself.'

At which point Josh hustled them back to the altar for one last run through.

In the pub, Digby let the conversation wash over him as Harry was grilled about Summer Taylor, the girl he'd developed a deep crush on but had zero idea how to ask out. Matters weren't made any easier by Harry previously having bawled Summer out for letting her horse escape onto the road he frequently took into town from the farm. Advice flew around the table before Lucas, who'd been fairly quiet until then, chimed in with a simple, 'Just ask her. She can only say no.'

'Even then it won't be the end of the world,' said Teagan. 'I knocked Lucas back stacks of times before I went anywhere with him.'

Lucas's hand covered Teagan's as he smiled at her. 'Wore her down in the end.'

'Em and I had our moments too,' said Josh, picking up the serious vibe. 'And look where we are.'

Jas planted a friendly kiss on Harry's cheek. 'Cheer up, big boy. You have us on your side now. And thanks to Em booking Summer to do our make-up, we'll have her all to ourselves come Saturday. Hours in which to sing your praises. She won't stand a chance.'

A comment that only left Harry looking more anxious.

'You were quiet tonight,' said Jas, as she poured glasses of wine in the kitchen back at her place.

Digby shrugged. He didn't want to talk about tonight. The thoughts that had pounded his head in the church had subsided but that didn't mean they didn't still exist.

When he didn't answer, she bit her lip and concentrated on pouring.

Digby hunted for an explanation, one that would offer comfort, but could find none. After what happened, he wasn't sure he should even be here. Except he knew himself well enough to realise home would only be worse.

He didn't understand what was happening. For one short period on Sunday he'd felt some sort of closure with Felicity was within reach. Four days later he was sinking back into the mire of his own jealousy and loss.

And from the upset Jas was trying so hard to hide, he was dragging her with him. Digby opened his mouth to tell her that perhaps it was time he went but Jas got in first.

'It's Felicity, isn't it?'

He nodded.

She fiddled with her wineglass. 'I wish I could stop it hurting.'

'You do.'

Mostly. When Digby was alone with Jas the pain faded to nothing, obliterated by her warmth and sexiness. It was the wedding he had no defence against. The chance to say the vows that would have proven to Flick how much he loved her. Instead she'd died without that security in her heart.

Jasmine's head remained down. 'Not enough, I suspect.'

The sight of her lowered head filled Digby with remorse. He held out an arm. 'Come here.'

She folded herself against him and spoke muffled words into his chest. 'I hate seeing you in pain.' A vigorous shake of her head halted his protest. 'Don't deny it. I know you are. We all know it.'

He stroked her silky curls. So much for keeping his feelings hidden.

'I'm trying to make it better but I don't know how.'

'It's not your job, Jas. It's something I can only do myself.'

She pulled away from his chest and rubbed her eyes, her smile forced. 'I know. But do you mind if I hold your hand along the way? That way, if you stumble I'll be there to steady you.'

He didn't deserve this. 'Jas—'

She held up her palm. 'I'm not her. I never will be. I understand that. But I'm still your friend, Dig. Whatever the consequences, I want to stand by you.'

The words had Digby pulling her back against him. Christ, she was something. He buried his nose in her scented hair. 'It might not end well.'

'Can't be any worse than what happened with Mike.'

He laughed despite himself. 'I guess not.'

'Exactly. Now take me to bed. If this really is going to end badly, I want to make the most of you while I can.'

CHAPTER
21

Jas woke on Friday morning and rolled onto her side to stare at the man beside her. Digby was stretched on his back, sheet ruffled down around his hips, his chest rising and falling with every slow sleepy breath.

There was no hurry to rise. In preparation for the wedding Jas had taken another day's annual leave. Em was floating her horse, and another borrowed one for Teagan, to Admella Beach after lunch, and the three planned a leisurely ride together along the bay, like they used to before Teagan moved away. Afterwards, Jas would travel with them to Rocking Horse Hill to spend a girlie night with Teagan and the bride, trading memories, toasting Em, and solving the world's problems.

Until then, she had Digby, her friend turned lover.

But as she stared at his restful features and traced her gaze over his lean body—a body she'd shared in the most intimate way—Jas suddenly realised this was more than friendship, more than sex. Digby had become the man she loved.

And he was going to break her heart.

Stabbed by the realisation, Jas bit her lip. She had to hide this, keep pretending she was fine. It wasn't as if she hadn't been warned. Digby had practically laid out that the relationship was unlikely to survive long term, and last night Jas had had the awful sense that he wanted to end it right then. Only her plea to him to keep leaning on her had kept Digby from withdrawing from her life.

How long she could continue holding him in place, Jas didn't know. Whatever torment Felicity's memory was giving him, it was powerful, and while Jas might have Digby's body, she had only a tiny scrap of his heart. The majority remained with *her*.

'You're staring,' he said, not opening his eyes.

'I am.' She walked fingers up his sternum. 'In case you were unaware, you're a bit of a babe.'

Digby's mouth twitched at the compliment.

Jas skittered her fingers to it, and traced his lips, remembering what that beautiful mouth had done last night. What both their mouths had done. 'I like these. They're smooth and soft and sensitive, but strong too.' Her fingers moved on, following the contours of his cheekbones. 'These are lovely as well.' She traced his eyebrows, avoiding the faint scar on his forehead left from his quarry fall. 'And these are wonderfully expressive. And this,' she skied the straight slope of his nose, 'is very noble looking.'

She continued her slow, seductive exploration, admiring his ears, his Adam's apple, the planes of his shoulders, the density of his biceps and chest muscles. Digby remained unmoving but she could feel and hear his increased breaths.

The lines of hairs on his chest and belly warranted particular attention, with strokes, finger-combs and gentle tugs. She teased his nipples, watching, delighted, as they puckered, feeling her own tighten in response. She slipped her palm over his hip, her voice low. 'I like this spot too, and ...' Her hand slid across to cup his groin. He was hard, the skin of his cock silky, the tip moist. '... I especially like this.'

Jas glanced at his face, expecting amusement but there was none. His jaw was flexed, his mouth a line, and he was swallowing. She shuffled back up the bed and traced the furrows of his forehead, hiding her worry with tenderness. 'I like what's in here.' She cupped his cheek, turning him to her, and carefully kissed his mouth. Her palm slid to his chest to rest over his fast-beating heart, her voice a whisper. 'But it's what's in here that's the most special.'

Suddenly he rolled, plunging her to her back and enveloping her in the human blanket of his body. His arms were folded over her, hugging tightly, his leg hooked around her knee, drawing her into him. His face was jammed in the hollow of her neck. He'd wrapped Jas so thoroughly it was as if he were trying to absorb her. So abrupt had been the change, Jas couldn't tell if he was upset with her or if the attention was due to overwhelming passion.

Jas waited for him to speak but there was nothing. As the cradling continued, she stared at the ceiling, puzzled and a little alarmed. Rolling her over for sex she could understand. She'd been teasing him and he was more than ready, but this?

Gradually, his hold softened. His mouth moved against her neck. Slow kisses teased her throat before curving to her earlobe. The sound of his ragged breath in her ear shot tingles down her spine. Digby kissed his way across her face, each kiss landing in butterfly-soft touchdowns on her eyelids, her nose, her cheeks before drifting to her mouth.

They made love slowly and delicately, as if the moment could break either of them. No words, only shallow breaths and quiet moans, the magic of intimacy. The sadness of their fragility.

When it was over, Jas lay on her side in Digby's spooned embrace, feeling him drift into slumber as she kept her eyes squeezed shut, praying that they'd both make it through the weekend without falling apart.

It was midmorning when they roused again. This time Jas found Digby awake and staring at her with a smile.

'Hey, babe,' he said.

'Hey, good-looking.'

He brushed hair off her forehead. 'Do something for me?'

'What?'

'Never stop being amazing.'

The surprise of his words had Jas falling against him as he'd done with her, and it was another half an hour before they crawled out of bed and into the shower.

Digby watched Jas pack her overnight bag for the stay at Rocking Horse Hill. He watched her in the kitchen, preparing them mugs of tea and Vegemite on toast. He watched her stack dishes in the dishwasher, watched her tidy away the toaster and wipe down the benches. If it weren't for their morning in bed she would have thought he was trying to sear her into his memory, but their intimacy, his words, had given her some hope the relationship would continue. The longer it did, the more chance Jas had of usurping Felicity's hold on him.

After all, a man didn't call a woman amazing for nothing.

It was a glorious day outside. The light northerly that had been blowing the last few days was forecast to continue through the weekend, bringing with it mild conditions and bright skies. Digby relaxed against the bonnet of the car and drew Jas to nestle between his legs, his arms looped around her waist and hands locked loosely in the hollow of her back.

She fingered his collar. 'I wish we could be together tonight.'

'I know, but this is Em's weekend. And Josh's.'

Jas continued to fidget. She didn't like to think of Digby alone in his apartment. Demons lurked there, memories. Her. 'Will you be all right?'

'I'll manage.'

'If you need me, call. I'll come straight away. Em will understand.'

'Jas?'

'What?'

'Stop it.' He pressed his forehead against hers and lifted a single eyebrow. 'Please?'

'I can't help it. I care about you, Dig.' She breathed in. 'A lot.'

Digby pulled back from her, his expression hunted. 'Jas, we talked about this.'

She swallowed. She shouldn't have said anything. 'I know. It's okay, really. Forget it.' She forced a smile and draped her arms around his neck. 'Now hurry up and kiss me goodbye before your sister and Teagan catch us.'

He did but it was different to earlier, although she couldn't quite pinpoint how. Digby was a wonderful kisser, gentle but passionate, as if kissing her really meant something. This was the same, except somehow muted, as though he was holding back. Or, even more troubling, easing his heart out of it.

He smiled and tucked her wayward hair behind her ears for her. 'Enjoy tonight.'

Jas hovered by the car as he settled himself and started the engine. There were so many things she wanted to say but every one of them would risk too much. He was here, still with her, which gave her a chance. And with her heart aching for him the way it did, a chance was better than nothing. One wrong word could destroy that.

He wound down the window and held his hand out to her. Jas took it, playing with his fingers as he stared at the dash. Breathing in, he finally looked at her and Jasmine's heart began to race in fear at the bleakness she glimpsed behind his eyes.

Whatever he was building up to say never emerged.

'I'll see you tomorrow.' Then he squeezed her fingers, and with a tug of his hand broke the connection between them.

Leaving Jas with the heart-sickening impression they might never connect again.

Jas, Em and Teagan were pink cheeked and happily tired by the time they arrived at Rocking Horse Hill. Teagan's mount had been dropped back at its owner's, Lod was brushed down and turned out into his paddock, Em's attention-loving donkeys had been duly attended to by Jas, and the chooks and Chelsea the Indian runner duck were locked safely in their coop. The house was cosy and smelled deliciously of the white chocolate and raspberry blondies Em had made earlier for the next day's morning tea, when Adrienne and Granny B would join them at the hill for make-up and hair styling.

When they were all washed up, Em took three champagne flutes from a cupboard and set them on the bench, then pulled a bottle of sparkling mineral water and another of champagne from the fridge.

As she went to crack open the water, Teagan stayed her hand. 'Half a glass of champagne won't hurt me.'

'Are you sure?'

'Tonight's important, Em. I want to toast you properly. It's not like I'm an alcoholic, and I'll be doing it at the reception anyway.'

'I thought you'd sworn off drinking?' said Jas. Although Jas didn't know the exact details, the past year had been tough on Teagan, culminating in an extended stay in the upmarket health facility that her aunt Vanessa's new husband owned. Since then, as far as Jas knew, Teagan had been teetotal.

'Not completely. I have a drink every now and then.' She smiled a little. 'I can't cope with any more anyway. No tolerance. One glass and I'm practically legless.'

Jas nodded at the bottle. 'Definitely better make it a half measure then.'

Glasses in hand, they settled on stools around the kitchen bench.

Jas held up her flute. 'To friendship and a beautiful bride.'

After they'd sipped, Em smiled at her bridesmaids and sighed happily. 'How many times have we done this?'

'Hundreds,' said Jas. 'Although when we were younger it was with your mum's hot chocolates with those little marshmallows floating on top.'

'Or her homemade lemonade,' said Teagan. 'And cinnamon scrolls. Remember those?'

They did. Cinnamon scrolls and more. It seemed like the kitchen at Rocking Horse Hill had been as much a part of Jasmine's and Teagan's youth as it had been for Em.

Never one to let guests go hungry, Em brought out a plate of nibbles for them to snack on while they reminisced. Dinner was to be simple cold roast marinated chicken and salad, requiring the briefest of preparation. But that was ages away, and the afternoon's ride hadn't come close to running the well of their conversation dry.

Just after six o'clock, Em was standing at the kitchen sink, rinsing their champagne flutes when she caught the sound of a car. 'That had better not be Josh.'

Their visitor turned out to be not Josh but his sister, Sally, who arrived at the sliding door bearing an enormous grin and an equally enormous bouquet of dark red roses.

'A delivery for the beautiful bride,' she announced cheerfully, when Em opened the door. 'From her adoring husband-to-be.' She handed the bouquet over, to cheers and teases from Jas and Teagan.

Laughing, Em buried her nose in the blooms and inhaled. 'They're lovely.' She leaned around the roses to kiss Sally and stood back. 'Thank you. Coming in for a drink?'

'I would but I need to get back to the horrors and I don't want to interrupt your evening. Trust me, tomorrow will be huge. Everyone will want a piece of you, which is nice but exhausting, and won't leave you much talking time with your friends. Best make the most of it tonight. Oh,' she said, pointing at the flowers and winking, 'don't forget to read the card. It might be important.'

As soon as Sally had gone, a flushed Em plucked the small envelope from the bouquet and retreated to the enormous floor-to-ceiling windows overlooking Rocking Horse Hill, leaving Jas and Teagan to roll eyes at one another. Em hurriedly extracted the card and read. Her hand strayed to her chest, her mouth creasing into a smile. She lowered the card and blinked rapidly at the window, before raising the card and reading again.

'Well?' called out Jas. 'What does it say?'

Em slipped the card back into the envelope and tucked it into the pocket of her jeans. 'None of your business.'

Which is exactly how Jas knew she'd react. Em had always been private, especially when it came to matters of the heart.

'Must be good,' said Teagan, taking up the banter. 'You look like the cat that's got the cream.'

'Probably because she is,' said Jas, nodding knowingly. 'Very attractive man, that Josh.'

'He is,' Teagan agreed.

'Lots of muscles.'

'Wears sexy stubble.'

'Plays football.'

'Can lift heavy things.'

'Capable of turning uppity ice-queen Emily Wallace-Jones all squirmy and pink with just a note.'

Em jammed her hands onto her hips. 'Have you two quite finished?'

Jas looked at Teagan. 'Have you?'

'Not really.'

'No, me neither.' At Em's expression Jas broke into laughter. 'What? Aren't we allowed to sing your husband's praises?'

Em lifted her chin. 'I'm not telling you what's on the card.'

Teagan sighed, locked gazes with Jas and shrugged. 'Nothing else for it, we'll have to steal it.'

And with that, the pair leaped off their seats and wrestled Em to the floor, giggling like schoolgirls.

'This,' said Em, struggling to sit up and laughing as hard as her bridesmaids, 'is not how I imagined our dignified evening.'

It was all silly fun. Neither Jas nor Teagan had any intention of stealing the card, but when Em pulled one of her haughty Wallace moves they couldn't help but take her down. It's what they'd been doing for years.

'You can be so like your grandmother sometimes.' Jas grinned at her. 'Which is not always a bad thing.'

'Except when she mentions her lovers,' said Teagan. 'That's not so fun.'

'You don't think,' said Em, regarding them both worriedly, 'she'll try anything with the waiters tomorrow night, do you? The hen's night was bad enough.'

Jas reached out to scratch Muffy, who'd wandered from her basket to see what all the fuss was about. 'She'll probably be too occupied chasing Harry.'

'Who will be too busy mooning over Summer,' said Teagan.

'He's such a sweetheart,' said Em. 'We have to help.'

'And we will,' said Jas. 'We'll have all tomorrow morning to convince this Summer person he's worth a chance.' She nudged and winked at Em. 'No better place than a wedding to get romantic.'

'Speaking of which,' said Teagan, easing up on to one arm. 'What's the story with you and Digby?'

Jas glanced at Em and back to Teagan. 'Is it that obvious?'

'Harry noticed.'

'Harry?' said Jas. If Harry had picked up on them, everyone must know. Her shoulders sagged. This kind of pressure was the last thing either of them wanted. 'Shit.'

'Well? What gives?'

'Nothing.'

Both Em and Teagan raised their eyebrows.

Jas eased to her feet. She needed wine. 'Look, I don't know what it is. Right now it's nothing more than friends with benefits.'

'Jas,' said Em quietly, 'Gran said he hasn't spent a night home in weeks. That's more than friends with benefits.'

But Jas knew how to shut the conversation down. 'So what? I like sex, and Digby just happens to be very, very good at it.'

Em scrunched up her face. 'You did that on purpose.'

It was Jasmine's turn to lift her chin. 'Yes I did. Serves yourself right for being nosy. And if you don't stop, I'll start telling you all about this thing he does in the shower.'

'Dinner time,' said Em, scuttling off to the kitchen, leaving Teagan and Jas to their laughter.

Teagan, however, was made of sterner stuff, trailing Jas to the bathroom when they went to wash their hands before dinner. 'Is it really just sex?'

Jas tried to keep the despair from her voice. 'It has to be.'

'Oh.' Teagan paused in her hand-wiping, her tone gentle with sympathy. 'He still loves her.'

'Yes.'

'I'm sorry.'

'Yeah,' said Jas. 'So am I. But do me a favour? Don't tell Em. I don't want her worrying.'

But Em clearly was worrying. When Jas found herself awake in the early hours, unable to sleep, and wandered out to stare out at the moonlit slopes of Rocking Horse Hill, Em quietly appeared at her side minutes later.

'Thinking about Digby?' she asked.

'Yes. And you.' Jas indicated the hill. 'I'm sorry you won't have the photos you want of us all here, at the hill.' Even for Josh, Digby wouldn't be moved on his self-imposed ban from the place Felicity died, which meant the wedding party photos were to be taken elsewhere.

'It doesn't matter. There'll be ones of Josh and me here.' Em tilted her head and eyed the peak, smiling. Despite the tragedy that had occurred on its slopes, the craggy top of Rocking Horse Hill held special meaning for Em. It was where she and Josh had first fallen in love as teenagers, and found the courage to forgive and love one another again as adults. 'It'll be interesting trying to get up there in my wedding dress.'

'I'm sure your new husband won't mind piggy-backing you.'

Em smiled and then sobered. 'Do you think he'll cope tomorrow?'

Jas didn't need to ask who she meant. 'He says he will.'

'Jas, I know it's not my business, but you and Digby ...' Concern furrowed her brow. 'You love him, don't you?'

Hiding her own apprehension with a smile, Jas squeezed Em's hand. 'Stop fretting about us. Think of tomorrow and all the good things to come afterward. This is the start of your new life. With Josh, the man you've always loved and who's always loved you. You don't want to walk down the aisle yawning, do you? Or, heaven forbid,' she leaned her shoulder against Em's, 'bags under your eyes.'

She laughed softly. 'No.'

'Good. At least we've settled that.' She grabbed Em's shoulders and twirled her to face the hall, giving her a friendly shove. 'Now get to bed or I'll dob on you to your grandmother. Then you'll really have something to worry about.'

CHAPTER

22

Digby jerked awake. His ears were full of pounding blood, his chest painful with the thrash of his heartbeats. He swallowed, trying to clear the coarseness from his throat. Groaning, he rubbed his palms over his face and dragged them together until they sat prayer-like over his lips.

Felicity, huge-eyed and lovely, walking towards him in a wedding dress, the carpet blood-red beneath her feet. She'd been so close, within touching distance. He'd smiled at her with tears in his eyes, fit to burst with happiness that this longed-for day had at last come, and stretched out his hand for her take, only for an avalanche of rock to sweep her away from him.

Digby sat for a while, waiting for his pulse to return to normal. From the window came the faint glow of sunrise. The day was here. He wished it over already.

He was tired, so very tired, the sort of fatigue that penetrated deep into bone and made even the most basic of tasks a Herculean effort. He lay back down but knew there was no point trying for more sleep. His mind was too troubled, his heart too sore.

With a sigh, Digby threw off the doona and padded to the bathroom. The face that stared back at him in the mirror was red-eyed and haggard, like that of an old man. He quickly glanced away and splashed water on his face, hands scraping over the thick stubble of his jaw as he rinsed.

It hadn't helped that yesterday he'd spent the afternoon walking the streets, brooding over Jas and his own screwed-up emotions, followed by an early dinner at a hotel restaurant with his father and not-much-older-than-himself stepmother Paige, along with Digby's two blonde-haired, blue-eyed half-sisters.

Blinded by their resemblance to the children he thought he'd have with Felicity, Digby had struggled to look at them. At seven and nine, they were at that age of sweet cuteness that tugged hearts and made strangers stop and smile. Though it wracked him with guilt, for his own sanity Digby ignored them as much as possible, which left him having to concentrate on the lesser of two evils: his father.

Nothing had changed since his divorce from Adrienne; Henry was still an overconfident schemer. Digby listened politely to his father's concerns about the current government's economic policies and their effect on his export business, about the cost of the girls' private schools, his lightly barbed jokes about Paige's spending habits, and braced himself for the touch-up. It had happened before. With the exception of birthdays and Christmas, Digby and Henry rarely spoke, then every now and again, out of nowhere, Digby would get a phone call that would start off cheerful and over-friendly before descending into a moan about how hard done by his father was. Nothing was ever Henry Jones's fault. Some other unscrupulous person or government was always to blame.

Before he passed away, Uncle James had warned Digby against this kind of pressure, and given him a strategy to fob his father off: the Wallace money was tied up in illiquid investments or under trust, with little available in cash. It was a lie. While a lot of money remained tied up in property and the agroforestry company that had made the family their real fortune, Digby could have sold shares, cashed in investment funds, dug into term investments. He never did though. Beyond paying directly for a few specific items relating to his half-sisters, his father's pleas for money remained unfulfilled.

When it came time to leave the restaurant, his father had followed him out, hand cupped around Digby's elbow like a politician on the hustings.

It had taken all Digby's strength to keep the weariness from his voice. 'I'll pay for dinner, Dad.'

'Thanks, son.' Releasing Digby's elbow, his dad had rocked back on his heels and puffed his lower lip out, then glanced back at his wife and children before leaning conspiratorially towards Digby. 'I've been keeping it from Paige, but things have been a bit tough lately with the dollar the way it is. I love Em, and wouldn't have missed her wedding for the world, but it's cost a bomb to fly us all down here.'

'Yeah, I can imagine. I wish I could help, but ...' Digby shrugged and held his hands out. 'You know how James tied everything up. It's good to see you though. The girls are really growing up.' And before his father could push any further, Digby had slapped Henry's shoulder in farewell and hurried towards reception where he settled not only dinner, but the family's entire stay.

He'd driven home feeling lower and more burdened than ever, wishing only for a quiet night's sleep and the fortitude to do the right thing by the people he cared about most.

Morning found him despairing of both.

Digby trudged out of the bathroom, gathered up an old pair of jeans and a shirt, and began to dress. Maybe if he'd been able to stay in Jasmine's comforting hold he'd have slept, but perhaps not. The way she'd traced her fingers over his body in bed, admiring him, continued to spin in his head. She'd made him feel loved, and for a heady while he'd embraced the idea that if he tried hard enough she could replace Felicity.

But from the moment by the car, when she'd regarded him with yearning and said how much she cared, instead of happiness all he could feel was fear. Fear that he'd let Jas down, that he could never repay her for the solace she'd granted him.

Jas deserved every last drop of love a man could offer. No matter how much he wished things could be different, Digby could only offer her a part of his. The rest belonged to Felicity.

With the day still dawning and nothing else to do Digby drove to the cemetery. He sat on Felicity's grave and watched the sun form a blazing orb in the sky. Everything ached, made worse by the cold granite on which he was seated, but he couldn't bring himself to move. The urge to lie flat across the slab was enormous, but Digby had given that up months ago, once his desolation had past the worst.

The sun rose higher, bringing the wedding closer with it. Digby remained where he was, chained by his memories of Felicity. The brightness of her eyes, the golden length of her hair, the husky softness of her voice, the adoring way she'd looked at him. Her slim, sleek body. Skin that shone pearl-like when wet.

Throat thickening, he stroked the carved letters of her name. 'This should have been us, Flick.' He closed his eyes against the sting of encroaching grief. 'This should have been us.'

On his arrival home, Digby had hoped to sneak up to his apartment for a rest but Samuel caught him in the driveway.

'Come over for lunch,' he said. 'Adrienne's left us a tart and some salad.'

'Thanks but I'm not really hungry.' Digby glanced at the sky. 'I'll have to start getting ready soon anyway.'

'It's only eleven-thirty. You've got hours yet. Plenty of time for some food.' He slapped Digby on the back. 'You can practise your best man speech on me.'

Unable to think of any other excuse to get out of it, he trailed Samuel into the house.

Digby picked at his salad, forked tiny pieces of quiche, sipped juice, and tasted nothing. He was sure it was all delicious but his stomach was too tight and tense. Samuel kept trying to draw him into conversation, making jokes and relating stories from his service club. Finally, when Digby remained uncommunicative, Samuel set down his knife and fork and asked him straight out if he was ready for the day.

'As I can be.'

'Are you sure? If you don't mind me saying, you look like you haven't slept.'

'I'll be all right.'

'If you need—'

Digby held up his hand, his jaw flexed. 'Samuel, I know you're trying to be helpful but just leave it. Please.' He inhaled shakily. 'I won't let Josh down. Or anyone else, okay?'

'Okay.' But Samuel didn't appear convinced.

With good reason. As the minutes ticked by and the ceremony lurched closer, Digby's confidence wavered. He showered and shaved, the latter taking far longer than it should have thanks to the tremor in his hands. If he hadn't had to drive, Digby would have tried a drink. There were out-of-date tranquilisers in the cupboard, prescribed after the accident, that he'd forgotten to toss out. He went as far as taking out the packet and slipping out a sleeve of tablets, before common sense had him shoving them back.

Harry arrived at two, even more nervous than Digby and in a state over what Summer could have learned about him while she was at Rocking Horse Hill doing the girls' make-up. Together they drove to the Sinclairs' to find the groom relaxed and cheerful, and not remotely fazed by the monumental event he was about to participate in.

'I think I hate him,' Harry said at the church when Josh alighted from Digby's car, grinning happily as he shook hands with his two brothers-in-law before ducking inside to chat to Reverend Ellis.

'Yeah,' said Digby, but Josh had never been any different. The bloke was born with balls the size of a bull. It was how he'd originally attracted Em's attention, simply by being one of the few local blokes confident enough to ask her out.

Digby stared up at the pink dolomite church. Built in the late 1850s, it had been the site of every Wallace christening, wedding and funeral since. Felicity had loved it when he brought her for a tour. Digby had been so proud, regaling her with his family history: the story behind the organ—Grandpa Philps's contribution; the structure's magnificent stained-glass windows—great-great-great Grandma Agnes's legacy; the rose garden—Granny B's addition. He'd pointed out the church's unusual crucifix, another donation. And she'd adored every second.

He'd ended the tour at the altar, taking Felicity's hand and walking her down the aisle, beaming lovingly at her as he imagined the day when they'd be treading that same aisle as husband and wife. Except that day had never come. God had snatched Digby's beautiful angel from him and replaced her with a black hole of grief.

He blinked hard and rubbed his mouth. Digby couldn't afford to think of the past, not today, not if he was to hold it together. Yet being here made him feel haunted, as if Felicity's spirit had seeped inside him at the cemetery and curled foetus-like around his heart, clutching his soul covetously to her belly, never to be released.

Josh emerged from the church and wandered over. They were early and the grounds were quiet, but soon guests would begin appearing. Digby, along with all of the wedding party, would be under scrutiny.

Josh studied him for a moment, his mouth pursed. 'Be happy for us, Dig.'

'I am.'

Josh regarded him a little longer and nodded, then looked across at the car park. A sedan was pulling up, another turning in behind it. He tilted his head towards the church door. 'We'd better get into position.'

The wait at the altar was interminable. Digby tried staring at the floor, at the crucifix, at the beamed ceiling, anything to stop himself remembering Felicity, but she refused to leave his head. His palms were moist, his mouth dry. As every minute ticked over he became more and more lightheaded. He wished he had water. Wished he'd eaten properly. Wished he'd downed the tranquilisers after all.

Then fear began to writhe. He was going to let Josh down. Fail his family, fail Jas. Just as he had Felicity. If he'd been a better man she'd still be alive and they'd already have had their own day like this, stood at the same altar, proud and thrilled and passionately in love.

People began to arrive in earnest, bringing the outside warmth with them. The walls vibrated with the echoes of their excited chatter. A hundred scented notes of aftershave and perfume swirled in sickening spirals.

Digby stared at the cross, sweat prickling his upper lip. Despite the Wallace ties with the church he'd never been religious or spiritual.

Science, rationality, nature, ruled his world. God had betrayed him anyway, but in that moment he dragged his faith from the cellar where he'd stashed it and prayed to Jesus and God and whoever else was listening to help him get through this, to be the man he needed to be.

Just one afternoon, that's all he needed. One afternoon of courage and strength, but the fear remained relentless: he wasn't strong enough, he'd never be strong enough. The past had proved it. Felicity died because of him, because he didn't trust her, because he didn't drive fast enough, lunge for her hard enough. He'd even deceived darling, kind-hearted Jas, the woman who'd taken him in when he needed comfort, knowing she'd never receive anything in return. And what had he done? Treated her no better than that shit Mike, snatching all of her goodness, making her care, making her want, and giving nothing back, not even hope.

The world blurred. He began to sway.

Suddenly Harry was looming over him. 'You right there, Dig?'

He swallowed. 'Yeah.' He blinked several times and clenched his fists. He had to do this. 'Yes, I'm right.'

Josh crowded him from the other side, alarm in his voice. 'Dig?'

'I'm okay.'

'If you can't handle it, you'd better say so now.'

Digby's fists were clenched so tight his nails were cutting crescents into his palms. No matter how much he blinked, how much he breathed, the tears of his failure kept stinging. He couldn't allow it. He had to pull himself together for the people he loved. This weakness had gone on long enough.

Staring at the cross, he said another silent prayer before forcing himself to take two long breaths. 'I can handle it.'

Josh glanced at Harry and back at Digby. 'You sure?'

'Yes.' And in that moment Digby did feel sure. He held Josh's gaze. 'I won't let you down. Not after what you did for me.' He swallowed again. 'And her.'

Josh scrutinised him, then smiled and embraced Digby in a brief man-hug. 'You're a good man, Dig.'

Digby wished that were true. It wasn't. But from now on he sure as hell was going to make it so.

CHAPTER
23

One glance at Digby, and Jasmine's good feeling plummeted into dread. His face was pale and clammy looking, his posture tense and rigid. His hands were held in fists at his side, the skin over his knuckles taut. The planes of his handsome face were starker than ever—jawline carved, cheekbones sliced. His gaze was fixed on the cross above the altar, but from the wideness of his eyes it was as if he was focusing on something else. Something inward. A creature devouring him from the inside that was taking every scrap of his strength to fight.

Jas threw an anxious glance at Em, hoping she hadn't noticed. Fortunately Em's attention was narrowed on Josh, and his on hers. The two of them could have been the only people in the church. As Em's father stepped back, Josh took her hands in his. His eyes shone with love and he was smiling softly. He leaned forward to whisper something to her, Em smiling secretly in return as she absorbed the words.

Jas wished she could savour the moment, but all she could think of was Digby and the pain he was clearly suffering. Shuffling closer, she surreptitiously looped her little finger through his in solidarity.

His eyes closed for several seconds, then he opened them and gave her finger a tiny squeeze, before easing his hand free. Her heart sank at the lost contact only to rise when he tilted slightly towards her to whisper, 'You look stunning.'

Jas was so relieved she grinned. 'You don't look too bad yourself.'

Digby let out a self-deprecating chuckle. 'Liar.' He nodded towards Reverend Ellis. 'We're on.'

By the time Em and Josh were declared husband and wife Jas was almost blubbering with tears. Their love was so potent it was if they were shedding love hearts and cupids and horn-blowing angels into the air, although that was probably an illusion from the church's beautiful stained-glass windows. Still, it didn't stop her from feeling stupidly sentimental over the moment. The bride and groom had waited a long time for this day, endured heartache and tragedy. Today they'd made it to bliss.

If Em had looked gorgeous walking up the aisle, marriage made her radiant. She was the most ethereal bride. With her lovely dress and the Wallace family's sapphires sparkling in her ears, matching her blue and white bouquet, the effect was pure understated elegance, and very, very Em.

Jas sniffed and swiped a crooked finger under each eye before glancing sheepishly at Digby. 'Sorry. Bit teary. Can't help it. The way they kept staring at one another.' She sniffed again. 'It was just so romantic.'

To her surprise, he reached an arm around her shoulders and gave her a brief affectionate squeeze. 'You're such a sap, but in the best way.'

Jas sighed and regarded Em and Josh, sniffing again. 'They're so lucky to have found one another.'

'Yeah,' said Digby, his voice hollow. 'They are.'

Jas could have smacked herself for her insensitivity. God knows how bittersweet Digby was feeling in that moment. There was no doubt he was happy for Josh, perhaps he was even happy for Em, but there was no escaping the fact that, if not for Felicity's tragic death, this moment would have been his.

It took forever to leave the church. Everyone wanted a part of Em and Josh's joy and they were crowded by well-wishers. Granny B fairly preened with pride while Adrienne was as teary as Jas. When they finally managed to escape to Levenham Civic Park for photos, it was a relief to be away from the crush.

Summer, who was looking ridiculously pretty in a floral sundress and with her hair in a stylishly loose bun, fussed over her charges, her teasing scolds at the state of their make-up taken with good humour. After a morning of chatter and not very subtle questioning at Rocking Horse Hill, Em, Teagan and Jas had decided Summer was a more than suitable match for Harry. She was smart, sweet, and clearly excellent at her job. Even Granny B had approved.

She laughed when she saw the state of Jasmine's make-up. 'Did you cry your way through the ceremony? You've hardly any mascara left!'

Jas winced. From Summer's dismayed bemusement, things had to be bad. 'I might have bawled a little bit.'

'A bit?' said Teagan.

'Okay, a lot then. But it's not every day you see your best friend married.'

'Our Jas tends to wear her big heart on her sleeve,' said Em, as Summer deftly touched up her face. 'Shocking sook.'

Jas poked her tongue out.

'You have to admit,' said Teagan, waiting her turn, 'that was a pretty emotional moment when Josh kissed you.'

'See,' said Jas, jerking her head at Teagan, 'even the super cynic here got teary.'

'I never said I got teary.'

'You did so!'

Teagan managed to look slightly abashed. 'Only a tiny bit.'

The admission made them all laugh.

'Do you think,' said Summer carefully when she'd moved on to Teagan's face, 'we could get Digby to put some drops in his eyes? They're very red.'

Em regarded Jas, who bit her lip. 'Sure.'

The three men were standing apart; Josh was chatting to the photographer and Harry was gawping dopily at Summer, while Digby was staring at one of the park benches, lost in thought.

Jas went to stand alongside him. 'Remembering that day?'

He nodded. 'Yeah.'

'Funny where things lead. If it weren't for us meeting here you probably wouldn't have started calling round.'

He continued to stare. 'It was the lock on the gate. It bothered me. I couldn't figure out why you'd want to do that.'

'I'm glad things have turned out the way they have.'

He looked at her then, eyes raking her face. 'Are you?'

'Of course. Why wouldn't I be?' She nudged him. 'Think of all the great sex we would have missed if not for this bench.' Jas held up the eye drops Summer had given her. 'Would you mind putting some of this in your eyes? It'll help reduce the redness.'

His mouth twitched unhappily. 'Subtle way of saying I look like shit.'

'Not shit. Just tired.' She paused. 'And sad.'

'Yeah.' He puffed out a breath and smiled at her, then plucked the bottle from her fingers. 'I think I've had enough of being pathetic for one day.'

'You're not pathetic, Dig. Don't for one second ever think that.'

'I am.' He scanned the label and tilted his head back to measure drops into each eye. 'But not anymore.'

With photos to be taken, followed by pre-reception drinks in a marquee at Camrick—during which Harry's clumsy but fervent courtship of Summer provided great entertainment—then on to Levenham's grandest hotel for the reception, Jas didn't have many spare minutes to contemplate what lay behind Digby's statement. Besides, since they'd left the church Digby seemed a lot more together. His best man's speech was heartfelt and exemplary, his gratitude to Josh palpable and his pleasure in welcoming him to the Wallace family sincere. If Jas noticed a faint coolness in the comments directed towards his sister, no one—bar perhaps Granny B and Em—would have picked up on it. The applause was enthusiastic, and Josh's embrace of Digby afterwards moving.

At midnight the bride and groom left the reception in a wave of whoops and applause to walk the short distance to the VIP suite. With the happy couple gone, the remaining guests began to make their departure. Adrienne and Granny B stood at the door, graciously thanking everyone for their attendance. Teagan and Lucas were on the dance floor in a close embrace, moving to their own tune. Harry was standing with his brother Eddie, sucking on a beer and looking distracted, his mind no doubt occupied with planning his next move with Summer.

Only Digby and Jas remained at the head table.

'Will you stay with me tonight?' she asked. Jas had booked a room at the hotel to save a late-night journey back to Admella Beach.

'I should go home.'

She bit her lip. An excess of champagne and fatigue after a long day of excitement had made her emotional. Spending the night alone was too horrible a thought. 'Please? No one will notice.'

He stared at his almost empty beer glass for a long moment, then lifted it and downed the last gulp. 'Okay.'

Jas opened the door to her room and let Digby through, then pressed her back to it, closing it, and waited for him to turn and look at her. She smiled. 'You should dress in a suit more often. It's sexy.'

'You think?'

'Uh huh.' She pushed off the door and sashayed slowly towards him. 'But I think everything about you is sexy.'

'Jas ...'

She pressed a finger to his lips. 'Shh. I know you're tired and I know it hasn't been an easy day for you, but I'm going to make sure it ends very ...' she reached up on tiptoe and replaced her finger with her lips, 'very ...' her mouth brushed his softly, 'well.'

Jas woke to find Digby dressed and perched on one of the room's narrow armchairs, staring at a small gap in the curtains where a vivid morning was filtering in. A slight frown creased his forehead and he was lightly stroking the stubble of his jaw, like a man in the throes of deep contemplation. Or regret.

He must have heard the change in her breathing or the rustle of sheets because he suddenly looked over his shoulder and smiled. 'Good morning, sleepy.'

Jas deliberately stretched, the action dropping the sheet from her breasts, and regarded him with a sultry expression. 'Come back to bed.'

His eyes flicked to her breasts and back to her face. 'We've a brunch to get to.'

'We can be late.'

He lifted an eyebrow.

'What's the time?'

'Nine-thirty.'

'We're not due at the Sinclairs' until eleven. Loads of time.'

Amusement creased Digby's eyes. 'Don't you have to check out?'

'I asked for a late one.' She smiled again. 'Thinking ahead. Now,' she stretched out an arm, 'come back to bed and ravish me.'

'Ravish?'

'Mmm. Ravish. You are, I have discovered, a most excellent ravisher.'

That made him laugh. Digby rose and crossed to sit on the edge of the bed, but instead of playing along he eased the sheet back up over her breasts. 'You're beautiful and tempting, but I need to get home to shower and change.' He tapped her nose. 'You need to do the same.'

Jas sighed. 'So much for my plan for some morning delight.'

'You had plenty last night.'

'I can't help it if I'm greedy. I like having sex with you.'

'I like having sex with you too, but we have things on.'

'Actually,' said Jas, pulling down the sheet again, 'I have nothing on.'

His gaze skimmed her body but failed to linger. He turned serious. 'I have to get going, Jas.'

She sat up. There was a weariness in his tone that rang alarm bells. 'Did I do something wrong?'

'No. You never do anything wrong. It's me. I really need to go.'

'Will you come back? My car's at home. I caught a lift with Em to the hill and then the limos brought us to town. I'll need a lift to the Sinclairs'.'

'Okay.' He glanced at the bedside clock. 'I'll meet you out the front at ten to eleven.'

Digby went to get up but Jas gripped his hand. 'Are you sure there's nothing wrong?'

'Not with you.' He kissed her lightly and walked out, leaving behind a room thick with anxiety.

The feeling remained the entire afternoon, even against the love and laughter that was Em and Josh's first day as husband and wife. For the sake of her friend Jas did her best to hide her growing unease, but Em had known Jas since they were small children—there was no hiding.

'You seem a bit tense.' Em's eyes flicked questioningly to where Digby was chatting with Josh's father.

Jas wasn't going to give her anything. Em and Josh were leaving on their honeymoon early in the morning and Jas didn't want her worrying over this or anything else. 'I'm just tired. It was, as I'm sure you'll recall, a pretty big day yesterday.'

'It was.' Em's gaze switched to Josh and she sighed. 'I can't wait to get away. There's so much I want to see.' She cast excited eyes on Jas. 'Josh has promised to take me to see the Uffington Horse.'

'Nice.' Having spent months scribing and illustrating a hand-bound copy of G.K. Chesterton's epic poem, *The Ballad of the White Horse*, Em had a special affiliation with the ancient chalk carving. 'But you do realise you'll be too busy having sex every which way to take even that in properly.'

'Probably.' Em leaned close, her cheek slightly flushed. 'We're going to try for a honeymoon baby.'

Jas squealed and hugged her, causing everyone to look. Granny B's expression narrowed to laser-like intensity.

'Now look what you've done,' scolded Em, prising Jas off. 'They probably all think I've just told you I'm pregnant.'

'You could be, after last night.' Her eyebrows wiggled. 'Unless you were too knackered to do it, like most brides and grooms are.'

Em gave one of her disdainful chin lifts. 'I'm not responding to that.'

Jas laughed, her own gaze shifting to Digby and memories of the previous evening. He looked casual and cool in pale cotton shorts and leather deck shoes, and a chambray shirt with the sleeves rolled up. Instead of his usual worn Akubra, he was wearing an old-fashioned low-crowned pastoralist's hat, giving him the air of a rich young squatter come to town.

Her chest tightened at the sight. Last night she'd had the pleasure of his lean, excited body, his passionately dreamy kisses, his caring, tender touch. Today she felt like this distant admiration was the only emotion allowed. That morning he'd wanted her. She recognised it in the caress of his gaze, yet for some reason he'd suppressed his desire. Not only suppressed it, but seemed annoyed by it.

As if sensing Jasmine's attention, Digby angled a look towards her. Their eyes connected and he smiled. Jas smiled back. Perhaps she was imagining things and everything really was okay.

'I'm sorry for doubting you two,' said Em.

Jas regarded her in astonishment.

'You were right when you said it was doing you both good. He's a different man.'

'We're both different.'

'You?' She seemed puzzled by that. 'How?'

Jas considered. 'I don't know. All I know is that I was in a hole after Mike, and Digby helped me out of it.'

'You would have made that climb yourself in time, but I'm glad Digby helped you. I hope you and he continue.'

'So do I.'

Jas was still hopeful that would be the case when Digby offered to drive her home late that afternoon, but when he pulled into her drive and sat silent and unmoving, eyes on the distant dunes, her anxiety returned in full.

She touched his thigh. The muscle was rigid. 'Dig?'

He sat for a few seconds longer and pushed the door open. 'Let's go for a walk.'

Digby held her hand as they crossed the rear boundary fence and followed the track through the dunes to the beach. The tide was almost fully out, leaving long sweeps of glistening sand dotted with colourful scraps of seaweed, the occasional cuttlebone and other flotsam. Seagulls hovered and swooped, scavenging for scraps, worms and crabs. The breeze was light, the sun hazy gold. The calm sea sparkled like crystal.

He led her to a sandy dry spot and sat. Jas nestled alongside and searched the immediate surroundings for something to fidget with, finally choosing a half pipi shell. She showed the inside to Digby. 'This one's really purple. Sometimes you find ones with mother of pearl colouring.'

He took it from her, inspected it and handed it back then drew up his knees and draped his forearms on top. 'Jas?'

She swallowed. All weekend she'd feared this might come. She hunted around for something else to distract him with but apart from scraps of desiccated seaweed the sand was annoyingly clean.

'Jas, look at me.'

She did as ordered and wished she hadn't. It was all there: the pity, the determination, the concern. Anger at what he was about to do made her want to throw sand in his face. Except this was Digby, a man whose only fault was to love too much. And Jas had no one to blame but herself for the heartbreak she was facing. The rules had been laid out from the start.

He spoke quietly, almost ashamed. 'I nearly lost it in the church yesterday.'

'No one blames you for that. It was always going to be hard.'

'Maybe. But I should have been stronger. It's not like I didn't have enough time to prepare for it.' He dropped one leg and reached down for a handful of sand. 'It made me realise something.'

Jas felt as though her heart was being dragged out with the tide. She bowed her head, ordering herself to be strong. 'You don't want to do this with me anymore.'

He took a long time to respond. 'It's not you, Jas. It's me. I can't give you what you deserve. I never realised what that meant until yesterday. The way I treat you?' He shook his head. 'All take and no give? It makes me no different to Mike.'

She scrambled to her knees and leaned close, scanning his expression in disbelief. 'What do you mean the way you treat me? Digby, you have been no less than wonderful. As for being like Mike.' She made a disgusted noise. 'You are nothing like him. Nothing!'

'I am. And I don't want that for you.' He stared at her, a plea in his gaze. 'You deserve someone who can give you everything.'

'I have all I need. Great sex, friendship. You even do the dishes without me having to ask.'

He smiled and stroked hair from her face. 'You're so funny. Don't ever change.'

Unable to bring herself to smack his hand away, much as she wanted to, Jas instead snatched up the pipi shell and lobbed it towards the sea. 'Don't fob me off. This is serious.'

'I know.' He let out a sigh. 'Too serious, which is why I'm doing this. Before it gets any worse.'

'This is not worse. What we have is good.'

'It is, but it's also wrong.'

'How can we be wrong, Digby? Tell me that? We were two heartbroken people who found a bit of happiness through friendship and sex. How can that be wrong?'

'Because while you're doing this with me you're not finding someone who deserves you.'

Jas jerked to her feet. She didn't want anyone else. Why couldn't he see that? 'You're being frustrating.' She looked down on him, wanting to yell but her constricted throat wasn't up to it. 'And you're hurting me.'

'I know.' His voice was quiet. 'I'm sorry.'

'Digby, please. I know it's not perfect but I like the way we are. I want ...' She breathed in shakily, warning herself to be careful. For his sake as well as her own. Revealing how she really felt would only make the conversation even more fraught. There was enough guilt flying around as it was. 'I want to keep seeing you.'

He sighed and stood and took her hands. Jas couldn't help her tears. He was breaking her apart.

'I still love her, Jas. I thought it was fading. I wanted it to fade, but yesterday proved it's still there, and that's not fair on you.'

Digby enfolded her against him as she began to bawl in earnest. She dug fingers into his shirt and banged her fist against his chest. 'It doesn't matter. Truly it doesn't.'

'It does. You know it does. Maybe not today but one day it will.' He stroked her hair. 'I want to be a good man, Jas. I want to change, move forward. Be proud of my life again. I can't do that if I'm hurting you.'

'But I'll miss us. Not just the sex, us. You, me, all the silly things.'

'So will I. But it won't all be gone.' He held her away from him, head ducked to look into her lowered eyes. 'We'll still be friends, won't we?'

'Of course.' She sniffed loudly and rubbed her eyes on her arm, then poked him in the chest. 'You're not getting away that easily.'

He smiled and grabbed for her again, squeezing her in a tight embrace. 'I don't know what I would have done without you. If it weren't for you, I'd still be living in darkness. You saved me. Showed me there's a life beyond grief.'

Perhaps that was the truth and she had, but as she knew now, the cost for Jas was her own darkness.

CHAPTER
24

Jas rationed herself to one day of broken-hearted moping.

With Em leaving for her honeymoon in the morning and Teagan on her way back to Sydney, poor, long-suffering Ox was commissioned into service.

On Sunday night, when Jas had finished sobbing all over the horse's sturdy neck, she retreated to the house and ate an entire block of milk chocolate washed down with three glasses of red wine, before throwing herself onto her bed and bawling some more until she finally collapsed into an exhausted sleep.

Monday evening was the same, excluding wine and chocolate but including a cheese toastie that was more cheese than bread. On Tuesday Jas woke to the sparkle and kaleidoscope colours of Em's crystal butterfly catching the bedroom window light, and declared her mourning period over. Time to seize the day, look ahead, and start acting like the independent woman she wanted to be.

It wasn't easy. Without Digby her bed felt lonely and cold, the house too quiet. There was an ache inside her that refused to dull even after a week had passed. If this was how she felt, Jas couldn't even begin to comprehend the pain Digby must feel on a daily basis over the loss of Felicity. That didn't make their break-up any easier to deal with though. Jas might understand his reasoning, even appreciate the nobility of it, but she wanted him back.

As the days drifted Jas found herself surprised by what she missed most with Digby—not sex, but his gentle companionship. Oxy played his stoic role, but his affection was limited to nudges and warm breaths blown into her hair. He couldn't share laughter or tears, or talk about desires and aspirations. He couldn't watch *Doctor Who* and then argue over who was scarier, the Daleks or Cybermen, or which was the best Christmas special. Normally Em would have been Jasmine's sounding board and shoulder to cry on, but she was gallivanting around England, leaving Jas to mine her own spirit for the grit to make it through alone.

To avoid moping, she took to long beach rides, movie watching and early nights reading in bed, but they soon became tiresome. She was bored with her own company, and the lack of productive activity was becoming irritating. After two weeks Jas had had enough and gave herself a solid talking to.

Enough of a life that revolved around men. Mike had already drained almost four hopeless years from it, and though she didn't blame Digby one second for what happened between them, Jas refused to let him or anyone else hijack any more.

Sunday of the second weekend, Jas set herself up at the kitchen table with a pen and pad of notepaper, and made a series of lists: her strengths and weaknesses, her hopes and dreams, all the things she was most passionate about, that she used to measure the quality of her life.

By the time she'd finished cross-matching and refining, Jas had a clear set of goals and an action plan to see her forward. She sat back with her arms crossed and regarded her work with satisfaction. There was a long road ahead but she would do it. For the first time in a long while, she would own her life and what came out of it.

The newlyweds arrived home in mid-December, good-naturedly complaining about the heat after the European cold. Em immediately invited Jas over to catch up on all the news and show off a thousand photos on her laptop.

'You should have seen the Book of Kells, Jas. The workmanship was incredible. And the library at Trinity ...' Em sighed at the memory, eyes alight with wonder.

Jas gave Josh a dry look. 'Thrill-a-minute honeymoon, huh?'

He laughed and regarded Em with amused affection. 'For someone it was.'

'That's what you get for having a book nerd for a wife.'

Em regarded Jas down her nose. 'I did more than look at art and books, you know.'

'Oh,' Jas teased, 'I bet you did.'

'Time for me to leave,' said Josh, leaning across to kiss Em's hair. 'I'd better attack this lawn. Bring me a beer when it's safe to return.'

'Ordering you around already?' Jas tsked when he'd gone.

Em laughed. 'Only in his mind.' She glanced out the big window to where Josh was regarding the lawn borders with his hands on his hips. 'He was so patient when we were away, letting me tour all the galleries and museums.'

'Of course he was. He loves you. Speaking of which, any news?'

Em didn't need a translation. 'No.' She cupped her chin on her palm and sighed. 'And not for want of trying either.'

'It'll happen.'

'No doubt it will.' Em swiped the laptop touchpad, scrolling through random photos of castles, country houses and lush English countryside. 'Josh says I'm being impatient.'

'You've been married, what—a month? Yes, Em, you're being impatient.'

'I know, I know.' She stood and wandered to the kitchen, where she took out coffee mugs and switched on the kettle. 'Anyway, you haven't told me about what's happening with you.'

'Bugger all. Work, rest, not much play.'

Em reached for the teabags. 'Not even with Digby?'

'Digby and I aren't seeing each other anymore.'

Em's arm stilled then dropped. Slowly, she faced Jas and regarded her with a deep frown. She seemed completely pole-axed by the revelation. 'But why ...'

Jas rose from the table to lean against the kitchen bench with her arms folded. 'He didn't think it was fair on me that he still loved Felicity.'

'Oh, Jas, I'm so sorry.'

'Don't be. What we had worked for the time we needed it to. Now we're both moving on.'

Em tilted her head and regarded her with the sort of perceptive look only a best friend could conjure. 'You're being very rational about it.'

'No choice.'

Em's gaze narrowed slightly.

Jas flailed her arms. 'Oh, all right. So I bawled all over Ox for a few days. But then I got over it.' She looked down at her feet for a moment, kicking the heel of her sandal against the toe of its twin. 'Have you any idea how much of my adult life has been dictated by men? Too much. I'm kind of sick of it.'

'You're not going to go all "I hate men" on me, are you?'

'Hardly.' Jas smiled wryly. 'Not in my nature, unfortunately. But I think it's time I thought of myself for a change.'

'Good for you.'

Jas raised an eyebrow. 'I thought you wanted me and Dig to last.'

'I did. But you're forgetting that I've also had to stand by and watch you have your heart broken time and time again by that horrible Mike. I watched you give up on your study, cancel plans, and abandon the people who loved you on the off-chance he might be free. I've watched other decent men left by the wayside because you couldn't stop believing Mike's lies that he'd leave his wife. I never condemned your choices, but it hurt a lot to watch you being treated the way you were. To see you missing out on the love you so deserve. If Digby isn't the one to give you that, then so be it. Find someone who will.'

'Wow.'

Em blushed and busied herself with the tea. 'Sorry. But I really hated your relationship with Mike.'

'You never said.'

'No. Because I know what it's like to make a mistake. We women are good enough at loading guilt on ourselves without having our friends pile it on.'

'Ain't that the truth,' said Jas with a long sigh. 'I'm still angry with myself, and with Mike. He really was a turd, wasn't he?'

'Yes.' Em handed her a steaming mug. 'But he's gone. The future awaits. In the words of Shakespeare, "*It is not in the stars to hold our destiny but in ourselves.*"'

'Quite.' Jas grinned, pressing her mug to Em's in a toast. 'And in the immortal words of the Tenth Doctor, "*Allons-y!*"'

Jas had expected to cross paths with Digby much more than she did but they had an uncanny knack of keeping out of each other's way.

She'd run into him a couple of times since the Sunday he'd called it quits. Once, not long afterwards, when she was still feeling raw, she was hurrying up Levenham's main street to the post office. Digby was inspecting something in a real estate agent's window. It was impossible not to stop; not doing so would have been rude and silly, given they were meant to have parted friends.

After exchanging awkward 'how are yous' Jas found herself staring at him with terrible longing. To make the encounter more painful, it seemed Digby couldn't resist either. Each time they tried to look away both would glance back, locking gazes again, as if neither could stop the pull of the memories they shared together. If Jas hadn't been so desperate to make the post office in her scant lunch hour they'd probably have remained that way. When she finally mumbled an excuse and rushed off, Jas couldn't help a last look over her shoulder, only to find Digby still anchored in place, hands in his pockets, staring after her.

The second time was not long after Em and Josh's return, at Gavin Chalk's property where Summer agisted her horse Binky. The entire wedding gang, including Granny B, who had taken it upon herself to supervise, had been roped in to a working bee to tidy and repair the neglected property. The day was a stinker, in the high thirties, and everyone was baking, but that didn't deter any of them from their tasks. The boys focused on the dilapidated fences while the girls cleared rubbish. Jas volunteered for whipper-snipping, a job that gave her an excellent excuse to block her ears with earmuffs and her face with a guard, and spend all morning far away from Digby.

But it was Digby who came to fetch her for lunch, ordered over by Granny B, who'd been observing them both with pucker-mouthed disapproval since her arrival. Jas wasn't impressed. She was covered in greasy sweat, melting sunscreen, dust, flecks of vegetation and chook poo. Her double application of deodorant was failing, and her hair was disgusting thanks to her sweat-soaked hat. To make matters worse, some of the debris had flown down inside her bra, causing her boobs to itch like crazy. Scratching had left dirty fingerprints all over her front, giving her the appearance she'd been molesting herself.

'You look fed up,' he said.

She'd switched off the motor, dragged off the mask and earmuffs, and was regarding him sulkily. 'I don't think he's touched the garden for years. It's never-ending.' She wiped the sweat from her face with the back of her arm and grimaced at the scrape of dried salt on her skin.

'I can take over after lunch.'

'No. I'll do it.' Jas inspected the area she'd cleared and felt a surge of satisfaction. Then, remembering how awful she looked, she tried to brush past Digby.

He touched her shoulder, bringing her to a standstill. She stared straight ahead, heart thudding horribly, dismayed at what one touch brought alive in her. Wordlessly, he tucked a sweaty hank of hair behind her ear, the movement intimate and wrong, his curled forefinger lingering in the sensitive zone below the lobe.

Jasmine's lips parted. She could feel his gaze zone in on them. The silence prickled.

His hand dropped and he cleared his throat. 'Mum's brought picnic food.' He nodded towards the old stand of shady pines where the others were gathered. 'We'd better hurry or we'll miss out.'

Jas nodded like a wood-brained marionette. 'Yes. Sure. Good idea.' She took off, fists curled, determined not to touch the place his finger had caressed. Determined not to surrender to her heart-pounding want for more of him.

'Jas?'

She slowed but didn't stop walking. 'Mmm?'

'How are you? I mean really?'

She turned to look at him, forcing a smile on her face. 'I'm good. Really. You don't have to worry about me.'

He stared at the sky for a moment before making eye contact again. His silky-lashed gaze was soft and dark and sorrowful. 'I do though. Still.'

'I worry about you too,' she said quietly. 'But we're done, Dig. The way we were, I mean. Don't ...' She breathed in, silently pleading Digby not to make it harder, not to make her fall again when she'd only just learned to stand. 'Just be happy, okay?'

To Jasmine's dismay, barely a week later they accidentally bumped trolleys in the supermarket, leaving her pink with embarrassment. Their last encounter had left her feeling bruised and confused enough, but bumping trolleys in a supermarket was how Digby had met Felicity. After apologising, Jas pretended to be in a rush, quickly scuttling off and leaving half her shopping undone. Oblivious to her melting ice-cream and warming milk, she'd sat in the car with her head on the steering wheel, trying to pull herself together. By the time she'd started the engine and reversed out, Digby was coming out of the supermarket, head down and walking slowly, as if every step required concentration. She was halfway home before she realised he hadn't been carrying anything.

What it meant Jas didn't know, but she refused to dwell. As Em had quoted, it was Jas who controlled her own destiny and she had things to achieve. Everything else could wait.

After working right up until Christmas Eve, Jas spent Christmas with her family on their farm north of town. Her older brother Richard drove over from Melbourne with his raucous young family and her parents' house was filled with the squeals of overexcited children. Jas took the Christmas to New Year gap off work, and spent most of it either mucking around with her nephews and niece on the farm or at Admella Beach, building sandcastles, swimming, and leading a resigned Ox around on horse rides, her niece beaming madly while her parents grumbled about having to suffer another horse-mad member of the family.

The arrival of the New Year set Jas on her action plan. After contacting the university to work out how much credit they would grant for her earlier studies, she re-enrolled in her financial planning course, taking on two subjects. Weeknights found her head down over her laptop, working on assignments and studying for exams, but mostly trying to learn as much as possible about the profession she'd identified as her future career.

Weekends Jas reserved for the outdoors. After obtaining several quotes and poring over designs, she contracted a local builder to restump her house and construct an extended deck. For weeks her home felt like a construction site, but by the end of February the footings were secure and her beautiful new deck finished. All that remained was for autumn to break so she could start work on the garden.

Not being a natural, Jas had long chats with Em over the subject. Bemused by Jasmine's new-found interest in gardening, Em probed at the cause, eventually forcing Jas to reveal Digby's plans.

'I don't want you telling him though,' she ordered, once Em had finished singing the praises of the design.

'Why not? He'd be happy to help.'

'No.' When Em kept protesting Jas held up her hand. 'I need to do this on my own.'

'But you're asking me.'

Jas made a face. 'Best friends don't count.'

'Digby's your friend too, Jas.'

The familiar pang of loss tugged at Jasmine's chest. She stared at the plans, the gift Digby had given her in thanks for her friendship and more. 'That kind of got a little bit messed up.'

Em stroked Jasmine's back in sympathy. 'You miss him.'

'Yes.' She sighed and rolled up the drawing. 'And I'm sure one day in the future we'll be able to talk without it feeling awkward, but for now I'm sticking to my own company.'

Which wasn't quite true. Part of Jasmine's self-reinvention was to rediscover interests that had once made her happy but which she'd let slide during her relationship with Mike. She volunteered to help instruct at the pony club, where she, Em and Teagan had spent many joyous childhood days. Though Jas was nervous at first, it wasn't long before she began to enjoy herself hugely. The children reminded her of herself with their enthusiasm and it was gratifying to see little ones improve under her tutelage.

She also came to the attention of one of the divorced fathers, a local sign-writer who brought his pony-crazy daughter along to the club every fortnight. Simon was friendly, attractive, and adored his little girl. On the occasions his ex-wife turned up to watch they were surprisingly civil to one another, which Jas took as a positive sign about his personality. Not that she brooded too much on him. She wasn't ready to let Simon or anyone else into her new, self-focused world. Not romantically anyway. When he asked her out for a drink she declined, but in such a way that the door was left ajar.

'I'm really busy with study and renovations at the moment, and I've just ...' She flushed with embarrassment. How to describe her and Digby?

'Broken up with someone?'

Jas nodded.

'No worries. It takes a while to get back into things.' Simon stared at his daughter, cantering past on her glossy, round-bellied pony and looking adorably cute. 'Took me well over a year to get back into dating after the divorce. Typical bloke, I never saw it coming.' He grimaced. 'Apparently we rarely do.'

'Oh.' Jas didn't know how to respond to that. A year seemed a long time, then she thought of Digby and his grief and realised a year was nothing when it came to heartbreak. God knows, hers still lingered.

Simon regarded her. 'It was my wife's idea. The divorce, I mean. But if someone doesn't love you ...' He shrugged. 'Shit happens.'

'I'm sorry.'

'Nah, don't be.' He grinned and eyed Jas up and down before winking, causing a thrill of sexual awareness to run through her. 'Sometimes these things happen for a reason.'

Jas managed a half-choked 'mmm' before dashing off to help in one of the showjumping rings where she could work off her libido lifting dislodged jump rails back onto their brackets.

When she related the encounter to Em the following lunchtime at PaperPassion, her friend only laughed. 'You and your sex drive.'

'Tell me about it.' Jas folded her arms on the counter and rested her chin on them. 'He's seriously cute too.'

'So what's stopping you from taking Simon up on his offer? It's only a drink.'

Digby and her stupid pointless feelings for him, that's what, but Jas wasn't about to admit to it. 'No. This is my year. The year I grow up and become an independent woman, beholden to no one.'

'Stop being so hard on yourself. You weren't beholden to anyone before. You were just in love.'

Jas rolled her eyes. 'Yeah, and look at the mess that made.'

CHAPTER
25

If Digby hadn't been aware of how Jas felt about him already, meeting her in the supermarket cemented it. She'd barely mumbled hello before scuttling off, head down and arms braced, weaving her trolley like a Formula One driver through the other shoppers and careening around the aisle out of sight.

For a long time afterward Digby stood in front of the rows of breakfast cereals, lamenting the loss of the beautiful thing he and Jas had briefly shared, oblivious to the complaints of harassed mothers and post-work shoppers. Only a grey-haired man's terse 'Excuse me' had shaken Digby from his stupor. He pushed his trolley up and down another two aisles before realising it was still empty. He gazed around at the normal people going about their normal lives, as Jas had been until she'd spotted him. As he was yet to manage.

That night he'd driven the coast westward for miles, away from Admella Beach, hunting for something, finding nothing.

Having used up every bit of leave he was entitled to, and with no urge to return, Digby resigned from the Department of Primary Industries and the job he'd held since leaving university over a decade before. He refocused on his neglected business holdings, but there was little to do other than monitor and trade the occasional share. Aware his nephew's interests lay elsewhere, his uncle James had made sure Digby's portfolio was well structured and managed—not quite set-and-forget, but as good as.

As the year faded away and January arrived, another feeling rose from the grief and apathy that had afflicted Digby since Felicity's death: boredom.

His time with Jas had at least been exciting, but without her to make him laugh, burn with desire, or even lament his mistakes, there was nothing except his computer games and science journals, his few remaining friendships, Camrick's garden, pointless roaming over the local landscape, and Felicity's grave. In the peak of summer's heat, even that lost its appeal.

'If you're bored, Digby,' said his grandmother one afternoon when she encountered him meandering through the rose garden with a set of secateurs, listlessly dead-heading spent blooms. 'Do something about it.'

He waggled the secateurs. 'I am.'

'No, you're not. You're wandering around like a zombie. If I didn't know you any better I'd think you were on drugs.' She shot him a disgusted look. 'At least Jasmine gave you some life.'

Digby gritted his teeth, and snipped viciously at a stem.

Granny B relented a little and softened her tone. 'I appreciate this has been a difficult period in your life but it's time to move on.'

Another wilting bloom lost its head.

'I don't mean your love life, Digby. Clearly that's beyond you at this point in time, but you cannot waste the rest of your days like a recluse. You're a man with a brain. Do something with it. Find another job, help your community.' Her voice rose to a lead crystal ring as he continued to snip and ignore her. 'Buy a ruddy vineyard, if you want. Just do something with your life!'

Digby jerked his head up. Granny B never swore. It was beneath her.

Her eyes were glittering cold sapphires, her nostrils flared. A thwarted queen on the warpath. 'You have left this family in complete despair. Your mother in particular. If you can't think of anyone else, at least consider her feelings.' With that, Granny B stomped off, snapping her lighter at the end of one of her revolting cigars as she went.

As much as Digby loathed being dictated to, especially by his grandmother, over the following week he found himself galvanised by her speech. It was the mention of a buying a vineyard that did it. Digby had been involved in the district's fledgling industry almost since its inception, either via his Uncle James or through his own work with the department. He'd consulted on everything from irrigation design to the best treatments for downy mildew. Not that he was an expert, but as with most horticultural pursuits, viticulture was something he enjoyed, and the oenology side appealed to his left, science-leaning brain.

A few nights after Granny B's harangue, finding himself bored yet again, Digby fired up his computer and began to search. With each click of the mouse, each scroll through the listings, his sluggish heart beat a little faster. A dream started to form, only in filaments at first as Digby collected and refined his half-formed ideas, until each wisp began to twist and mesh together into a clear design that begged for action.

Three weeks later, one of the land agents he'd been in contact with called. Two hundred and thirty acres to the east of town—twelve acres of which were already under vine and closely fitting the stringent topographical and soil profiles Digby had demanded—had come up for sale. The property was owned by a local pharmacist who was returning to Adelaide due to family commitments, and was keen for a sale.

Digby tried not to get his hopes up. There was bound to be something wrong—bad water supply, zoning restrictions, agronomic issues. He toured the property twice, did more research, had a few confidential chats with former colleagues and winegrowers he'd befriended. With each passing day his dream became sharper, his energy for it stronger. It would be a challenge, but a challenge was what he needed.

On a Friday morning, after spending an hour sitting with Felicity talking about what this development might mean for him, the future he might be able to build, Digby rang the agent and made an offer. After another week's toing and froing, the parties reached an agreement.

'I hear,' said his grandmother during Tuesday-evening family dinner at Camrick, less than a week post-settlement, 'that a certain member of the family has purchased a farm. Care to enlighten us, Digby?'

The entire table stared at him in astonishment.

Digby sighed and set his cutlery down. He'd hoped to savour his secret a while longer without the pressure of his family nagging him about his plans. Given Granny B's spy network, he should have known better. 'I bought Tyndale, John Ashton's place on Foxvale Road.'

He went on to describe it, skipping over most of the detail about the wine-making facilities. As a pharmacist, John Ashton had found that side of the process fascinating and become an enthusiastic hobbyist. The sale had included his very basic but immaculately kept crushing plant, vats, barrels, bottling apparatus and lab. The small young vineyard didn't produce enough tonnage for more equipment. Digby aspired to change that, in time.

Adrienne was ecstatic. 'But that's wonderful, Digby. James would be so proud.'

'There's no house out there, is there?' asked Em, frowning as she tried to recall what she knew of the property.

'No.' That was something else for the future. Maybe.

He caught Josh's eye. His friend hadn't said much but there was no mistaking his approval. After dinner, while the girls and Samuel lingered over coffee, and Granny B disappeared to smoke, Digby and Josh took their beers outside to enjoy the warm evening.

'You kept that quiet,' said Josh. 'Bit like you and Jas.'

'Thought it was better that way.' Digby took a mouthful of beer. 'Have you seen her?'

Josh nodded but didn't elaborate. He was going to force him to ask.

Digby sighed. 'How is she?'

'Good. You could find out for yourself if you bothered to visit her.'

Digby picked at his beer label. 'I don't think she wants to see me.'

'Interesting,' said Josh, then he bent to inspect the mossy leg of a timber garden bench.

Digby waited, but Josh set down his beer and lifted the bench, peering beneath.

'All right. I'll bite. What's so interesting?'

'Bit of rot. I'll take it into the workshop and fit a new leg.'

'That's not what I meant and you know it.'

Josh dropped the bench and retrieved his beer, grinning as he swigged. 'Why should you care whether Jas wants to see you or not? From what Em told me, you're the one who pulled the plug.'

'Just want to make sure she's doing okay.'

'I bet. Nothing to do with you missing her or anything.'

'Piss off.'

But as with his grandmother, the encounter started Digby thinking, and with his first vintage approaching he had plenty of hours alone on the farm to do it in.

The year began to drift towards autumn. Digby spent every day at Tyndale, falling exhausted into bed at night, tired and pleased with each challenge he faced and conquered. Though his first crush was tiny compared to the more established locals, it still enveloped him in excitement and he began to understand how easily people could become obsessed. There was so much at play—from the weather, to the natural flora on the grapes, to balancing fermentation.

Digby's first wine wasn't great. In fact it was pretty damn ordinary, but it didn't matter. He'd get better.

As April arrived, and he stood at the tip of a row of vines, mentally contemplating the winter prune ahead, Digby felt a creeping sensation. One he hadn't expected. It was almost happiness. Almost but not quite, but a far cry from the grief-weakened man he'd once been.

There was strength inside him. Ambition.

He gazed at the gently tumbling hills, at the rows of verdant vines beginning their autumn fade, at the paddocks he'd stocked with Simmental cattle. In the distance rose the monolith of Rocking Horse Hill, and for once the sight of it didn't give rise to sharp emotion. No irrational hatred, no fear, no regret. Only the dull poignancy of dimming sorrow.

It had been more than a week since he'd visited Felicity's grave. Digby had been so distracted it hadn't occurred to him. When inconsistency of supply and the heat of summer had resigned him to cancel his standing order for tulips, he'd continued to take her roses from Camrick. This week, though, he'd somehow forgotten.

The knowledge brought on a surge of guilt but beneath it, like the discovery of his creeping inner happiness, lurked something akin to relief. If he was right, this development signalled the coming of the end of his grieving process, the very process Digby had dismissed as bullshit when his counsellor explained it. No one had ever suffered as he did. Felicity's death had destroyed his soul so thoroughly it would never heal.

Yet it appeared it had, or was at least coming close.

And maybe, just maybe, that meant there was more love out there for him. All he had to do was embrace it.

CHAPTER
26

Jas was pulling clothes off the line in the rapidly darkening evening when she heard the sound of a vehicle crunching its way along her drive. Not that long ago her heart would have soared at the sound, but the days of Digby visiting were well past. She dropped the pegs into their bucket and skirted the deck to check out her visitor.

A white taxi was pulling up at the front of the house. She frowned at it. A taxi? Here? Port Andrews was too tiny to have its own service, which meant it could only have come from Levenham. But who would pay the fare for that?

Not Mike, surely. Jas hadn't had anything to do with him since the ring incident in the park. And it wasn't likely to be anyone else Jas knew. It was nearing winter—the days were short, the weather unpredictable. Antarctic winds whipped across Admella Beach bringing late autumn rains and chilly air. This was the time of year when people began their annual hibernation, venturing out only for necessities and winter sport. After a week of rain, this was the first dry day they'd experienced in a week, but the cold still bit. Jasmine's fingers were tingling from the exposure.

Tucking her hands under her armpits for warmth, she walked towards the idling car, watching the movement behind the windscreen. The driver was turned to whoever was in the back seat, blocking any view of the passenger. Finally the door opened and an extravagant fox-fur hat appeared, followed by a pair haughty eyes.

'Jasmine,' said Granny B, 'I take it you'll be free to return me to Camrick?'

'Um, yes. I suppose.'

'Good.' Granny B's head disappeared back inside the taxi for a moment before she extracted herself fully and shut the door. With a quick salute to Jas the driver put the car in reverse, performed a rapid turn and disappeared back up the drive.

Tossing a length of fox-fur-trimmed wool cape over her shoulder, Granny B dug into the pocket of her leather trousers, pulled out a cigar and lighter and proceeded to light up. When the tip was glowing she took a moment to peer around, before lasering in on Jas and looking her up and down. 'Well, are you going to fetch me a drink?'

So much for niceties.

'Cup of tea?' asked Jas.

'Don't be ridiculous. It's after five.'

'I have some white wine in the fridge. Sauvignon Blanc.'

Granny B sniffed. 'Probably from New Zealand.'

It wasn't but Jas didn't feel up to correcting her. 'It's all I have.'

'I suppose that will have to do then. Honestly, you young folk have no idea about hospitality.'

Jas crossed her arms, tone dripping with false solicitude. Granny B wasn't the only one who could be rude. 'Perhaps if I'd known you were coming I might have had a chance to be prepared.'

'Ah, but where would be the fun in that?' Granny B puffed out a fragrant balloon of smoke and flicked a gloved hand as though addressing a servant. 'Off you go. You and I have matters to discuss and I can't stay all evening. It's far too cold for a woman of my age to be out, does unfortunate things to one's bladder.'

At least she wasn't planning to linger. Jas usually enjoyed Granny B's company but when the old duck was in one of her meddling moods she could test the most patient of people. Much more of the Queen Wallace act and, elderly grandmother or not, Jas would be likely to throttle her.

'There's an outdoor setting on the back deck,' said Jas, deciding Granny B would be far safer outside, where there was less to pry into. 'You can finish your cigar there.'

With the gas heaters she'd bought the area could be quite cosy, and the dry day had prompted Jas to set herself up to study outside for a while, perhaps even eat dinner if the wind remained favourable. Night air tended to sharpen her brain, which was just as well. No matter what Granny B pretended, this wasn't a social visit. This was about Digby. Jas would need every wit about her.

It was, of course, too much to ask for the old lady not to snoop. Jas used her hip to push open the rear screen door and muttered a quiet curse when she saw what Granny B had discovered. Jas had forgotten about Digby's plans. Despite what had happened, they were precious to her and she always had them near. It had become Jasmine's habit to daydream over them whenever she needed a study break.

'Thank you,' said Granny B, accepting the glass and taking a hefty swig before setting her cigar between her teeth. She lifted the plans closer to her good eye and then lowered them again, blinking in surprise. 'This is Digby's work.'

'Yes.'

She scanned the yard then looked back at the drawing a few times, and nodded in approval. 'It's very good.'

'Which is why I'm building it.' Jas took a small sip from her own glass to stop herself from snatching the plans from Granny B's grip. 'Well, sort of. I can't afford a lot of it yet. The deck and this outdoor setting was expensive enough but I have to admit they've been worth every cent. It's like having an extra living room. The pergola and barbecue area will have to wait. I was making some progress on the garden beds but last week's weather put an end to that.'

'A labour of love,' said Granny B, folding the plans and securing them back under the colourful mosaic pot Jas had been using as a paperweight.

Jas narrowed her eyes. 'Something like that.'

'Walk me around. I want to see what you've achieved so far, and what you're going to work on next.'

Jas sighed. 'It's too dark, and you didn't come here to inspect my garden.'

'No, I did not. However, that was before I knew Digby designed this one. Come along. Show me. There's still enough light.'

There wasn't. Nor was there a lot to see. Progress had been slow, fitted in between study, Ox, pony club and work, and Jas didn't have the confidence in what she was doing to operate any faster. All she'd achieved so far was a small ornamental garden bed along the end of the deck, the laying out of stones to indicate future paths, and a clean-up of the rubbish she'd let accumulate near the garage. The next project would be planting out the herb garden. Raised boxes—built under Josh's supervision—were ready for filling with garden mix from the nursery in Levenham, and Em was propagating cuttings in her greenhouse for when Jas was ready to plant out.

Jas stopped by the clothesline to pull the remaining washing off, while Granny B pontificated on plant cultivars and the merits of grafted versus natural rootstocks.

Suddenly she paused. 'You haven't the faintest idea what I'm talking about, do you?'

'Nope.'

The old lady pursed her lips. 'Sounds to me like you need the advice of a horticulturalist.'

'You're not being very subtle,' said Jas, hoisting the basket onto her hip.

'It wasn't my intention to be subtle.' Granny B stared seaward, puffing the last of her cigar. 'Strange taste in men you have, Jasmine.'

Jas laughed. 'Nice way to talk about your grandson.'

'It wasn't Digby I was referring to, actually.' She tossed the stub to the earth and ground it under her heel with gusto. 'Michael Boland.'

The shock had Jas bulging her eyes and almost dropping the basket. 'How ...' Heat flooded her cheeks. She lowered the washing to the ground and hugged herself, shame sitting like a sickness in her stomach and chest. So the old duck knew. The risk of discovery had always existed, Jas had known that for a long time, but the last six months had given hope she was safe. Now she had to face her disgrace head on. At least Granny B was up-front. No poison-pen letters, rotting fish or dog crap for her.

Jas took a couple of fortifying breaths and lifted her chin. 'How did you find out?'

Granny B waved her off. 'Accident mostly. I happened to run into Brenda Morrison a few weeks ago.' She curled her lip in distaste. 'Never liked that woman. Bitter sort. But she's on the hospital auxiliary with Adrienne and one must be polite. We got to talking, as sometimes happens, and the subject of the Bolands came up. Tania is her niece.'

Puzzle pieces began to fall into place.

'Brenda lives here,' whispered Jas, 'in the village.' A few streets back from the esplanade and an easy walk to the beach and across the dunes to Jasmine's house. The sick feeling worsened and Jas hugged herself closer. It must have been her.

'Indeed she does.'

'Hang on,' said Jas, shaking out of her shock and frowning. 'She told you Mike was having an affair with me?'

'Of course not. Brenda's far too proud for that. She did, however, make mention of discord in the Boland household, the fault of which, reading between the lines, she clearly laid at Michael's feet. Not news I like to hear about my financial adviser, in particular after Digby's warning.'

'Digby's warning?'

'Perhaps not an overt warning but I took it as such. A grandson would not ask his grandmother how she'd feel about transferring our business elsewhere without reason—in particular when that would mean breaking a financial relationship of many years' standing. When Adrienne mentioned he'd floated the idea with her as well I knew something was up. Unfortunately, other than going over my statements with extra care, I was too distracted with Emily's wedding to investigate.'

'Until you met with Brenda.'

'Quite.'

Jas shivered. She picked up her basket of washing and carried it to the deck, forcing Granny B to follow. 'So how did you make the connection?'

'It seemed to me that Digby's about-turn coincided rather conveniently with the time you and he began sleeping together.

Then I remembered that you'd once had ambitions to study financial planning. A sly word here and there and I had plenty of evidence of your paths crossing. Couple that with your lack of romantic ties over the years and it all began to fall into place. All I needed was confirmation, so I made an appointment with the bank.' Her nose screwed up. 'Honestly, Jasmine, how could you? I appreciate he possesses a degree of handsomeness but the arrogance alone should be enough to put any smart woman off. Really, you have appalling taste.'

'Something,' Jas said faintly, 'I'm already very aware of.'

'He talked down at me, of course. I let him carry on for while, then interrupted mid sentence, asking straight out if he was having an affair with you.'

Jas made a strangled noise. 'Of course you did.'

'As expected, he spluttered and dithered, but the truth was evident in his pallor. He'd turned such a startling shade of grey at the mention of your name I thought I might have to call for assistance.' Granny B picked up her wineglass and drank, wincing at the taste and declaring it hideous, although that didn't prevent her from taking another sip.

'Did you want water?' God knows Jas needed some. Anything to wash the sourness from her mouth.

'Not at present.'

'So what did Mike do?'

'Threatened me with defamation and some other nonsense. At which point I told him to go right ahead. The Wallace coffers are deep, as he is well aware, and I'm sure his wife would appreciate being dragged into a court case regarding her husband's infidelity. I let him bluster for a while then suggested that perhaps it was best if he considered a transfer back to Adelaide. If he so wished, I would be generous enough to put a good word in for him with my friend

Alistair Greschke, who just so happens to be on the board. Imagine my pleasure to discover last week that Michael had acted on my suggestion.'

'Mike's gone?'

She cast Jasmine a triumphant look. 'Of course. What other choice did he have?'

None at all. Between Digby and Granny B, Mike would have known his end had come. He might be scum of the highest order, but he wasn't a complete fool.

Unlike her.

Jas slumped into a chair and put her head in her hands, wishing her visitor away so she could tend the wounds of her heart in privacy. Admittedly, the chance of Jas and Digby getting back together had been remote, but with Granny B's revelation even that was gone. While the truth was far more complex, Jas had shown herself to be deeply morally flawed—not someone Granny B would like to see with her grandson, especially after Felicity, and the scheming old lady had an excellent track record of getting her way.

Granny B continued to speak as if Jas was still involved in the conversation. 'The new chap's rather dishy. Refrains from all the salesman's jargon Michael was so fond of. A bit academic. More an accountant type. Lovely partner. A shame he's gay but one doesn't judge these things. Not when one's own son was homosexual. Which leads me back to Digby, who is, as you are well aware, not homosexual.'

Jas sighed and stood. 'It's cold and getting late. I should take you home.'

'I'm quite fine here, thank you. Your heaters are proving more than adequate.' Granny B studied her from over the rim of her wineglass. 'Sit back down.'

She rubbed her forehead in exasperation. 'Granny B, please.'

'No. I haven't finished.'

'I don't want to talk about him.'

'Well, I do. So sit.'

Jas thought about arguing further and decided she didn't have the energy. Besides, the quicker Granny B finished issuing her directive for Jas to stay away from Digby the quicker Jas could deliver her back to Camrick and end the ordeal.

'He's doing well,' said Granny B, once more carrying on the conversation as though the interruption had never happened. 'Purchasing Tyndale was the best move for him. He'll make a fine success of it, too. His uncle James was an appalling wine snob but there was never any questioning his expertise, some of which he passed on to Digby.'

'I'm glad for him.'

Granny B regarded the dregs of her glass before pushing it away, folding her hands across her stomach and settling her sharp gaze on Jas. 'He needs a friend, Jasmine. Someone who understands him. For a while you were it and the relationship made him better, even happy at times. That probably had more to do with sex than anything else, but whatever you two shared, it changed him. I'd very much like to see him like that again.'

Anguish flooded Jas. 'He's unhappy?'

'I wouldn't describe it as unhappy, more lonely.' She pointed a polished nail at Jas. 'You could change that.'

That Digby might be lonely was heartbreaking, but asking Jas to remedy the situation was too much. She leaped up. 'I need to take these clothes inside before they get damp.'

'Stay where you are, young lady.'

Jas ignored her, snatching up the basket, her head crowded with worry for Digby. Worry she had to let go of, if only for her own wellbeing.

For an elderly person, Granny B could move fast when needed. Furry cape billowing, she blocked Jasmine's path and folded a gloved hand around her arm. 'He needs you.'

Jas jerked free and tried to push past but Granny B stepped in her way. Exasperated, she let the basket fall and jammed her hands to her hips. 'Why would you want me near him? I had an affair with a married man, remember? Hardly a suitable match for your grandson.'

Unperturbed, Granny B tilted her head. 'How long have I known you?'

Thrown by the question, Jas answered. 'Since I was six.'

'Exactly.'

She blinked.

'Jasmine, I have watched you grow from childhood into the adult you are today. Your affair with Michael was ill-advised, yes, but I do not believe it reflects the person you truly are. Your loyalty to my grandchildren has been proven many times over, from your years of friendship with Emily through to your compassion for Digby when he needed someone to turn to.' Granny B let that thought settle. 'I want Digby happy, and it's clear to me now that he can be so with you.'

'I can't.'

The wise old lady scanned her face. 'Because you fell in love with him.'

Jas nodded miserably. 'It'll hurt too much to go back.'

'You're likely correct.' Granny B smiled and spread her arms. 'But what is life if not a series of chances? Take yours, Jasmine. You might even find the odds are in your favour.'

CHAPTER
27

'I happened to venture down to Admella Beach yesterday evening,' announced Granny B in the kitchen where the Wallace family had gathered for Tuesday-night dinner.

Dinner had just been served, and the table was aromatic with the scent of Adrienne's famous minestrone and freshly baked sourdough bread. The atmosphere was relaxed and convivial. Granny B couldn't have timed her statement more perfectly.

Digby quickly placed his glass down and exchanged a wary glance with Josh. Adrienne, Samuel and Em were swapping questioning looks. Granny B hadn't driven a car in years, which meant she'd either caught a taxi or had organised a lift with someone, but who? From the puzzled exchanges, clearly it wasn't any of them.

'Called in to see young Jasmine,' Granny B continued, dabbing a napkin to the corners of her mouth. 'She's looking well.'

Josh asked the question everyone wanted the answer to. 'How did you get down there?'

'Caught a taxi. How else? Jasmine kindly delivered me home.'

Digby picked up his spoon and swirled it though his soup. He'd been at Camrick yesterday evening, working in the office on irrigation plans for the vineyard extension. Samuel had a service club dinner, and Adrienne was at a function. The only person he'd heard come inside was Granny B. Jas must have dropped his grandmother off and left immediately, without popping in to say hello.

'Had quite a chat. Marvellous job she's done on her garden.'

At the mention of the garden, Digby cast a questioning look at Em, who refused to meet his eye.

'It's going to be wonderful when it's finished, although that will be some time away. Jasmine mentioned the new rear deck was rather expensive and stretched her finances. Worth it though. Excellent view across to the dunes and back towards Port Andrews.' Granny B indulged in a sip of wine and smiled innocently at Digby. 'She's going to work on the herb garden next.'

Jas was building his garden. She had to be. The deck, the herb garden. They were all part of his design. The idea both thrilled Digby and made him tense. He wanted to see what she'd done but that would mean calling in on her, and there were a whole lot of reasons why that was a bad idea.

'Why the visit to Jas?' asked Em. 'You've never bothered before.'

Granny B picked up her spoon and waved it airily. 'Oh, no real reason. It's been some time since I saw her, that's all. Thought I'd better check up, make sure she's taking care of herself.' She smiled as if daring them to trip her up on the lie.

'Actually,' said Adrienne, addressing Em, 'we haven't seen much of her lately, have we? She used to pop round quite often. I hope everything's all right.'

'She's just busy, Mum. Lots on.'

'So I hear,' said Granny B, not finished with her tormenting. Digby was only too aware that the entire conversation was directed at him but that didn't stop his ears straining to catch every word. 'A regular volunteer at pony club now. Apparently, she's even met a decent chap there. Jasmine is training his daughter.'

Digby reached for his glass of wine. A decent chap? Like who? He glared at Em and Josh over the rim of his glass. They'd kept that to themselves.

Em caught his look and stammered. 'I don't think—'

'Keeps asking her out,' Granny B bulldozed on. 'Won't take no for an answer. Owns that signwriting business on Chute Street. Thought I'd poke my nose in for a look this morning. He seemed quite personable, not to mention rather handsome.'

'Sounds like a stalker,' snapped Digby, then, realising he'd reacted exactly how his grandmother wanted, stared at his bowl.

'Don't be mean-spirited, Digby. It's nothing like that. He's keen, that's all. As you'd expect with an attractive girl like Jasmine. Besides, the man has a young daughter and a business to run, I doubt he has time for stalking.' She turned to Em. 'It'd do Jasmine good to find someone, what with you and Teagan now settled down. There's never any joy in playing gooseberry.'

'I don't think she has any plans in that direction.' Em's voice was faint with discomfort. 'She has too much else she wants to achieve.'

'Perhaps,' said Granny B, before blithely changing the subject to her latest skirmish with wowser Councillor Herriott.

Digby couldn't escape fast enough after dinner. The unrestrained scrutiny of his meddling grandmother was bad enough, but thanks to his snarky stalker comment his mother kept throwing him curious looks too. Josh had taken him briefly aside and promised to catch up over a beer later in the week before escorting a grim-faced Em out.

Crossing the path from the house to the stables, Digby couldn't help looking south. A full moon lit the sky, casting the road and tree-lined park opposite in silvery light. He folded his arms against the cold, kicking at stones as he brooded. So Jas had built the deck. Perhaps she was sitting out there, watching the heavens, moonlight dancing over her curls and shining on her pretty blue eyes, thinking of … that other bloke, the handsome one with the business and the daughter? A stone went flying so high and hard it pinged off the tray of his new ute.

'Let it go,' he muttered, except he couldn't.

Digby scratched his head, agitation burning. He glanced up at the blank windows of the stables and felt the jaws of his loneliness clamp around him. He shook his head. It was over. He should leave her be. The garden was his gift and Jas was building it. That should be enough.

'Shit,' he said, and strode to fetch his car keys.

The engine purred as he headed west out of town, retracing the route he drove in the days when his grief and anger over Felicity forced him from the hollowness of his apartment. When he used to race his demons and her ghost on the empty back roads.

Tonight he didn't need to race. All he wanted was to drive for a while, let the hypnotic span of the disappearing bitumen settle his heart and calm his wayward thoughts. At the windmill farm, he steered left to travel through the quiet grazing country, passing the marker where once he would have wound down the windows, accelerated to madness, and prayed for the furious rush of air to sweep his tortured mind clean.

Funny how that misery no longer existed inside him. When the flood of anguish and fear had left him trembling in the church, Digby had been convinced recovery would never come. Yet it had, creeping so carefully he hadn't noticed.

No question he still loved Felicity, but it was an abstract feeling now. His love used to be a tangible thing. Something alive inside him that he could hear beating, that sighed and throbbed in her presence, and later bled and howled with ear-splitting intensity, such was the wrack of pain from her death.

Being with Jas had somehow changed that. She'd calmed him with sex and laughter and caring and protectiveness. Healed him smile by smile, kiss by kiss, touch by touch. And, fool that he was, he'd cruelly pushed her away, as if what she'd done didn't matter.

As he'd explained to her on the beach, that made him not much better than that shit Mike, stringing Jas along while he was still tied to someone else. Only someone as callous as Mike would think he could walk back into her life with acceptance.

The coast road appeared. Digby braked at the stop sign but made no move to turn. Instead, he wound down the driver's window and let the salt-tainted air fill the car. In front of him the Southern Ocean swept over sand and churned over rocks and reefs. A low wind shivered the dune grasses and bent the leaves of the boobialla scrub. No different from the last time he'd driven here. Except then he hadn't known what he wanted. Now he did.

Minutes passed as Digby continued to stare and breathe and think through his indecision. Every scent, every sound, every sight reminded him of Jas and the happiness he'd found at Admella Beach. Finally, he took his foot off the brake and turned the car left. He would simply drive past, check out the house from the road and continue on. No harm done to either of them, but his curiosity satisfied.

Digby crawled through Port Andrews. The village was normal, locked up inside and sleepy, yet Digby's heart wouldn't stop hammering.

On the outskirts, where the speed limit rose, he kept his foot relaxed. He cruised, then slowed further as Jasmine's white house appeared. Digby leaned forward to squint through the windows as her property came and went. The angle was wrong to see the back yard in any detail, the night too heavy, even with the moon.

Lights flashed behind as a car sped up from the rear, forcing Digby to accelerate. Jasmine's house disappeared behind as the road veered to follow the inlets and points of the wider sweeping bay. If Digby followed it far enough he'd hit the river and the road north. Another turn and he'd be on the main highway leading into Levenham. Away from Jas.

It was for the best. It had to be.

So why did he feel so crap?

His headlights caught a sandy side road on the right, one of the many beach access tracks carved by surfers and fishermen over the years. He steered into it, the Mercedes bumping its belly along the ruts. With the car behind well past and the road clear, Digby reversed back out onto the bitumen and swung the wheel towards Port Andrews again.

A few minutes, that was all. A moment to say hello, ask how she was. Act like the friends she'd promised they'd always be.

Lame, but what else did he have?

It was after eight and the kitchen was the only room lit when Digby pulled up at the front of Jasmine's house. He stared at it for a moment, sick with nerves, wishing he'd kept driving and not given in to his stupid urge, but it was too late to turn around. If she'd seen his car she'd know he'd driven in and been too gutless to face her. If she hadn't, she at least would have heard its engine, and fleeing would risk leaving her with the fear that her harasser was up to her old tricks.

Digby opened the car door and stepped out, standing momentarily confused. Instead of the expected sound of breakers and swishing tide, music drifted towards him. It was old rock music, a half-forgotten hit song from his teenage years. A song that Em and Jas had played ad nauseam at Rocking Horse Hill until even Adrienne had cracked.

Smiling, he shut the car door and followed the noise.

Jas was lounging on a colourfully cushioned teak chair under the blasting warmth of two tall gas patio heaters, eyes closed, ugg-booted feet up on the table and crossed at the ankles. A set of portable speakers were perched near her waggling toes, her phone feeding into it nearby. She was singing softly under her breath, a hardcover book splayed open on her belly like an exhausted moth.

Digby lingered at the edge of the house, afraid to disturb her indulgent relaxation. There was no way of announcing his presence without frightening her, yet his feet refused to turn around.

He called to her softly. 'Jas?' Lost in her song, she didn't hear. He took a few steps closer, raising his voice a little. 'Jas?'

She jerked up, sending the book tumbling. Her feet slid off the table, hands braced on the chair arms in alarm.

'Jas, it's me. Digby.'

Her palm flew to her chest as though to keep her panicked heart inside. 'Dig.' Her voice was breathy and fast. 'Bloody hell. You scared the daylights out of me.'

'Sorry, I thought you would have heard the car.'

'No.' She rubbed her chest then her mouth. 'I was daydreaming.'

He smiled. 'You were singing.'

'I love this song.'

'Yeah, I remember.' Shoving his hands into his pockets, he regarded the yard. The low-watt floodlight illuminating the deck wasn't powerful enough to extend beyond its edge, but the night was moonlit enough to determine faint stone trails. Outlines of pathways through what would one day be the bowers and shady hideaways of her garden.

Leaning over the side of her chair, Jas picked up the fallen book and laid it on the table, then adjusted the speaker volume downward. The song gave way to another, a recently released love ballad Digby had heard multiple times on the shed radio at the farm. After a few bars, Jas reduced the volume even further.

She sat back with her hands rested on the arms of the chair. No hello kiss, no invitation to join her, only cool regard. 'I'm guessing your grandmother told you about her visit.'

Digby scratched at his jaw. 'She said you were working on a garden.'

'I am. Yours.'

'I thought it might be.' He surveyed the stained timber deck. 'This looks good.'

'Thanks.' She tilted her head. 'Why don't you come on up?'

He took the steps and stood awkwardly.

'Take a seat.' She pointed to a chair opposite, not alongside. 'Can I get you anything?'

Digby shook his head. 'I wasn't planning to stay long. I just wanted to say hi, see what you've done.'

'Not much so far. If the weather stays like this I'll plant the herb garden out on the weekend. After that, I'm not sure. Depends on time and finances.'

Digby stroked the sawn edge of the teak table. Already weathering was causing it to silver in places. He should buy some linseed oil. Give it a protective coat before winter fully arrived. He dropped his hand. There'd be none of that. This was a one-off visit, as Jas was making abundantly clear.

'Gran said you're busy with pony club these days.'

'And study.' She fingered the cover of the book for a moment and pushed it towards him.

He read the title: *Taxation Strategies in Financial Planning*. He glanced at Jas and picked it up, flicking through the pages, noting the underlined passages and margins filled with her generous, loopy handwriting. A horrible thick feeling of fear rose inside Digby, along with something else he could only identify as intense pride.

'I've already completed half the course,' she said. 'Seems a waste not to finish.'

Digby returned the book to the table. For a long while he didn't know what to say. She'd moved on and was chasing the goals mothballed after Mike. He should be happy for her. And he was, yet the fear wouldn't fade. Would her new career take her away from Levenham? From him?

'You're doing well.'

Jas shrugged and stared at the stars. 'I'm getting there. What about you? How's life as a vigneron treating you?'

'Okay. I managed to make it through my first vintage unscathed. Not that there was a lot to harvest with budburst being so heavily frost affected.'

'Did you crush it into wine?'

'Yeah, but it's pretty undrinkable. Uncle James is probably rolling in his grave.'

They shared a smile and quickly looked askance. Digby kept sweeping the yard, wishing he could see it properly. Night sounds and Jasmine's music covered their lack of conversation—the whisper of the wind-teased coastal scrub, the eternal swoosh of the ocean, the occasional cry of a hunting bird.

It should have been peaceful, amiable, but their extended silence soon became noticeable. Digby had a million things he wanted to ask yet nothing to say, and Jas seemed in no hurry to talk. He patted his palms on the arms of his chair several times, then gave a final push upright. She wasn't going to ask him back again or for help.

'I'd better leave you to it,' he said.

Jas at least accompanied him to the car, which was more than he expected, but with every step the feeling he was walking away from a chance of something special tugged at his temples. He kept glancing at her, hunting for a sign of the friendship she'd promised, but Jasmine's expression remained as coolly inscrutable as when he'd arrived.

He opened the car door and stood drumming fingers on the frame as he had on the chair only minutes before.

Jas observed him a moment before squinting at the house and back to him. 'It was good to see you, Dig.'

'And you.' He hesitated, then leaned down to kiss her cheek. The feel of her skin, the scent of her, was like a surge of opiate in his veins. Gritting against it, he forced himself not to let his lips linger and instead put his feelings into his gaze. 'I'm proud of you, Jas.'

'Most of it's thanks to you. If you hadn't started calling in, I'd probably still be mooning over Mike. And locking my gate.' Her gaze softened. 'You caught her, didn't you? Brenda Morrison, the woman behind all the harassment. You made her stop.'

Digby glanced at the village lights. 'You didn't deserve what she was doing.'

'Thank you for that.' She paused and scuffed an ugg boot. 'For taking care of me.'

'I could have done better.'

The softness faded and she crossed one arm over herself to rub her shoulder, her 'Yes, you could have' lingering unsaid but loud.

Cursing his stupidity and suppressing the urge to hold her, Digby indicated the car. Time to get out of here before he screwed things up any further. 'We both have work tomorrow.'

'We do.'

Another silence fell. Jas stared at her feet, Digby at the empty driver's seat. Then it seemed like they were both talking at once.

'Jas—'

'Dig—'

They shared a shy smile.

Digby indicated towards Jas. 'You first.'

'It wasn't anything.' She scraped her teeth over her bottom lip and rubbed her shoulder some more. 'I just thought perhaps you'd like to check out the garden in daylight one day.'

The relief made him want to cheer. 'I would. Maybe over the weekend sometime?'

'Sure. I have work Saturday morning but I'll be home in the afternoon. Sunday I'll be at pony club.'

Digby tried not to let his jealousy show at the mention of pony club. 'Okay, good. I'll call in later in the afternoon, when I've finished at the farm.'

'I'll look forward to it.'

Digby swung into the car, closed the door and started the engine. With a wave he put the car into gear, only to stop when Jas tapped on the window.

'You didn't tell me what you were going to say,' she said when he'd lowered the window.

'Nothing important.'

'You sure?'

He glanced at the house, at the friendly glow from her kitchen, at her. To hell with his pride. He wanted her, and being bashful about it wouldn't get him anywhere. 'I miss our friendship, Jas.' He looked at her squarely. 'I know I probably don't deserve it but I'd like it back.'

For a few seconds she held eye contact before switching focus to the front gate. Her lips were rolled together, the protective arm over her chest tight. 'Would this friendship be with or without benefits?'

Digby considered a lie and abandoned it. Yeah, he wanted to sleep with Jas again, but right now, as long as it meant seeing her he'd take anything she had to give. 'Whatever you want.'

'That,' said Jas, dropping her arm, 'is something I've yet to figure out.'

CHAPTER
28

Digby took a swig of beer and placed it back on the mat, staring at the few mouthfuls remaining as he rotated the glass with his fingers. Finally he sighed and looked at Josh. 'I need to visit the hill.'

Josh lifted his eyebrow slightly then nodded slowly. 'Okay. Whenever you're ready.'

Digby gave the glass a full rotation before answering. It was late on Sunday afternoon. He should have been at Tyndale. Where he wanted to be was at Admella Beach but it was one of Jasmine's fortnightly pony club rally days where she was no doubt laughing with that Simon the sign-writer bloke. Like she hardly did with him these days.

It had been a month since he'd started seeing Jas again. If you could call it that. Though she was thawing, their relationship was nothing like it had been. Digby helped her with the garden, lugging materials, digging holes and turning compost, showing her how to tend the young plants, what diseases to watch out for. Jas was thankful and full of praise for his expertise, but that was all. Any time Digby even hinted at getting close, her expression would shut down and she'd make some excuse to escape.

He didn't know what he'd expected from their resumed relationship but it wasn't this.

Digby looked up from his glass. 'How about now?'

'Em's home.'

'Doesn't matter.' He downed the last of his beer and picked up his keys. 'It's time I did this.'

The journey out to the turnoff proved uneventful. Leading the way in his ute, Josh drove slowly, as if giving Digby a chance to change his mind. He needn't have bothered. Digby's problems with the main road had ended the night he'd driven Mike to Levenham from Admella Beach—another change in himself he had Jas to thank for. But when Josh's brake lights lit up as he slowed for Bradley Road, Digby's stomach lurched and he wondered if he was truly ready to face the last and worst of his weaknesses.

He gripped the wheel and indicated. He was ready. His pointless hatred and broken relationship with Em had gone on too long. Rocking Horse Hill wasn't evil, it didn't wish him or anyone else ill. It was an eroded extinct volcano that his family had once managed and quarried without incident until the land was forcibly annexed by the government back in the eighties. If anyone was to blame for the quarry's collapse it was bureaucracy.

Still, he took the gravel surface slowly and kept his eyes averted from the menacing form that was the jagged volcanic vent marking the T-intersection of Bradley and Stanislaus Roads.

Josh was leaning on the passenger door of his ute with his arms and ankles crossed when Digby pulled up alongside. Digby alighted, pausing a moment to take in the western slope rising steeply above him. The crater's sharp craggy rim was alight with the falling sun. Digby tried not to imagine the rocky edge as teeth.

'You sure you're up for this?' asked Josh.

He wasn't sure of anything but Digby nodded anyway. 'Yeah.'

'You want me to come along?'

'No. Thanks.' He glanced at Josh and caught his brother-in-law's concern. Understandable given the landslide that had crashed through their lives, the consequences of which they were still dealing with over eighteen months later. And might always continue to. 'I'll be all right.'

Josh looked unconvinced but nodded. 'Whatever you do, don't go past the stabilisers. That last dump of rain's weakened the edge again. The rest of the path is safe enough.' This time it was Josh's turn to glance at the slope and the dark scar that was the quarry. 'As safe as it can be.'

'I won't.' Digby gripped Josh's shoulder, the touch more to reassure himself than Josh, and with a last squeeze let go.

Snatching a wool beanie from the back seat, Digby tugged it on and trudged up to the hill paddock gate without looking back. Cattle lows drifted on the air. A hawk released an eerie cry. From a further paddock one of Em's donkeys wheezed a hee-haw before falling silent. Pausing at the gate he searched for Em's horse and found him grazing in the far reaches of the road paddock. With the animals elsewhere, Digby swung the gate open and left it that way, and with a leaden tread began his pilgrimage to the place where he'd lost the woman he'd loved, and almost lost his own life.

An old wooden stile allowed easy access over the boundary fence and onto what was State Heritage land. He climbed over and stood for a moment, taking in air before walking on. For years this had been Em's favourite route up the hill, and though flanked by tall grass and weeds, a worn trail still existed. Wet grass flicked his legs and soaked his jeans but Digby barely noticed; his gaze was fixed ahead on the ugly stabilisers spiking the slope like giant knives.

He was nearing the quarry when the tall grass disappeared abruptly. Someone had cleared a small opening and wilted vegetation blanketed the space. Digby stopped and frowned at it, then his heart began to stutter. On the far side, just in front of the spikes and the quarry lip, like Eden at the border of Hell, lay a carpet of carefully tended blue and white pansies.

Felicity's colours: blue eyes, angel white.

He stepped closer, his breathing hoarsening, then staggered and dropped to one knee as he saw the stone and realised what this was: a memorial, for Flick. One he had no idea existed.

And it was beautiful.

Emotion threatened to undo him. Digby bent his head and dug the heel of his palm into his forehead as his throat choked and his eyes stung. After several heaved breaths, when he was sure his painfully thudding heart could take it, he looked up to absorb the scene properly.

Felicity's commemorative marker was simple: a large, unpolished piece of blue dolomite with a single planed face, onto which a small brass plaque had been attached. The engraving was equally simple—just Felicity's name and the date of her death. What made it extraordinary was the location.

The rock was positioned near the quarry edge, a breath in front of the ugly steel spikes. Viewed from standing height it appeared safe, but from his knees the collapsed slope gave the illusion that the dolomite teetered at the edge of a void.

Digby stayed on his knee for a long time. Finally he stood and gazed across the landscape, thinking about Felicity, about his sister, about the mistakes they'd all made. So many. So very, very many. If not for the sounds of someone making their way up the hill, he probably would have stayed lost in reverie until dark.

The footfalls stopped a short distance behind him.

'You did this?' asked Digby, not turning around.

'Yes.'

'Why?'

'Because I lost her too, Dig,' said Em, moving parallel but a careful arm span away. 'Because we failed her. Because she should have been part of this family.' Her voice turned husky with emotion. 'Because you loved her.'

Digby had no response to that.

'I keep getting notices to clear the site. The management committee say the flowers don't fit in with their revegetation plan, not being native. I toss the notices in the bin. If they want it gone they can dig it up it themselves. They won't though, not after all the finger-pointing that went on. Even if they did I'd replant. There are tulip and iris bulbs below the pansies, for the spring.' Em's voice dropped to almost a whisper. 'She liked tulips.'

Digby tilted his head back and stared at the bleak winter-grey sky, blinking hard. What a fool he'd been. 'There's so much I wish I could take back.'

'Same here.'

For a while they stood in silence, buffeted by the frigid wind.

'Dig ...'

He swallowed, wishing the roughness in his throat would ease. They needed to talk this through, but it had been so long and Digby had been so wrong, and seeing this place, what she'd done, made everything hurt again.

Em's words came quiet and careful, her watchfulness a weight on his skin. 'Josh said that the thing that cuts you most is that you think she died believing you didn't love her. But she did know. She knew it more than any of us.'

Digby shook his head. If she'd known, she'd be with him, living and breathing and loving, and not some fucking rock in the ground.

'It's why she let go.'

He regarded her with disbelief and anger. Her hands were cupped together and anguish twisted her face. He quickly looked away. He didn't want to fight, not about this, not here.

'Dig, she sacrificed herself for you. Surely you know that.'

He didn't. He didn't know anything except the crush in his chest and the lack of air in his lungs as the memory of that night bore down on him. The groaning, trembling earth. The wind. Muffy's barks. Felicity's huge eyes as the light of her faith in him flickered and went out.

Em stepped closer, urgency lifting her voice. 'Think about it. The ground was heaving, about to give way any moment. She knew you had no chance of reaching her but would try anyway. From Josh's yells she knew I was safe, that he had me. She could see the cracks deepening in the quarry wall and knew it was only seconds before it collapsed. Felicity had to let go. Right then. Any longer and she would have taken us all with her.'

He could barely breathe. None of this sounded right. 'No. I could have saved her. All she had to do was swing towards me. One lunge. Just one.'

'There wasn't time. She didn't have the chance and neither did you. She didn't want you dying for her, Dig. She wanted you to live.'

He nearly hadn't. When the edge gave way and she plummeted, momentum carried him too. Somehow he'd survived that plunge and it was only through Josh dragging him to safety that he'd lived through the second collapse.

The idea that she'd let go to save him refused to sit straight in his brain. He rubbed his forehead hard. 'It's because of the fight we had, isn't it? I doubted her and it broke her. But it wasn't like that. I told her and told her. If she had hurt Gran then we'd work it out. It wouldn't have mattered what she'd done, I'd have still loved her.'

'I think she thought it was too late,' said Em sadly. 'I think she believed that no matter what you said, how you supported her, things would never truly be the same again.'

Digby was barely controlling his grief. 'I would have made them right.'

'I know you would have. We all would have, but Felicity's background meant she had no experience of kindness without strings. So she did what she thought was best for you.'

'I didn't care about me. I only cared about her.' He blinked and a tear leaked from his eye. 'I screwed up so bad, Em.'

'We all did,' she replied in a voice sodden with tears. 'Me more than anyone.'

Digby stared at the grey pit of the quarry and felt the truth settle over him. What happened to Felicity was a collision of fate and human error. Every one of them, including Felicity herself, shouldered some of the blame for her death, but in the end it had been her choice to turn her face to his and smile, before loosening her grip and snapping the last fragile thread of hope they had in her survival.

Em touched his arm. 'I'll leave you.' She took a few steps and stopped again. 'She wanted you to live, Dig. That's why she let go. Because she loved you and wanted you to live. That was her gift to you. Please don't throw it away.'

'Yeah,' he said, breathing shuddery breaths. 'Yeah.' He coughed and rubbed his wet cheeks and mouth. 'I've seen enough.' He indicated the memorial. 'Thank you.'

She stared at the plaque. 'I wish I could do more.'

'So do I,' said Digby.

And this time he would. For her. In honour of the sacrifice she'd made.

When they'd crossed back on to Wallace land, Digby placed one hand on Em's shoulder. Startled, she glanced at him and gave a hesitant smile. It was the most companionable he'd been with her for a long time, even before Felicity's death. Today they'd found a kind of peace between them.

He glanced back to the quarry and its flash of blue and white and felt a strange wash of closure.

Peace in his own heart too.

CHAPTER
29

'It's hard work trying to get pregnant,' Em complained, making Jas laugh.

'Sure it is.' Jas pointed to Em's sliding glass door and the garden beyond where Josh was hefting a plank of timber onto a couple of sawhorses. The man was strong, capable, and stupid with love for his wife. And he'd begun building her a new greenhouse without her even asking. 'Yes, I'm sure sex with Josh is a terrible chore.'

Em plucked a sultana from the fruitcake batter she was mixing and threw it at Jas. She dodged the missile with another laugh and bent to pick it from the floor before it could be forgotten and trodden into the slate.

'All right, so it's not that bad. But it's been months. I'm so desperate I've turned into one of those women who take their temperature and measure their cervical mucus to check how ripe they are, for God's sake. I even do it in the shop. Last Wednesday everything matched so perfectly I phoned Josh straight away and ordered him over.' A pink flush spread across her cheeks at the memory. 'I had to lock the door and put the "Back in five minutes" sign up.'

'Five minutes? Now that's a quickie and a half.' At the sight of her friend's crestfallen expression, Jas stopped teasing. With her study and pony club commitments, and endless tooling in the garden, she hadn't spent much quality time with Em lately. Now Jas wished she'd scrounged the time. For all her stoicism there was no hiding Em's low spirits. 'It'll happen. You're both young, healthy and mad for each other. It hasn't been that long.'

'It has. We're closing in on eight months. That's a long time when you're the wrong side of thirty and I'm not getting any younger.' She sighed and resumed her mixing. 'Mum said it took her a year to get pregnant. Gran reckons she fell on her wedding night.'

'Knowing your grandmother, that's probably because she crammed a year's worth of sex into one night.'

Em screwed up her nose. 'Not something I want to contemplate.' She dragged a buttered and papered cake tin close to the bowl and began spooning mix into it. 'What about your love life? Still set on celibacy?'

'Sure am.' Although the truth was it was getting harder and harder. Jas missed sex—the silly messy fun of it, the intimacy and pleasure. But most of all she missed the comforting care of a relationship.

Digby tempted her more than she could say, and several times in the garden, in the kitchen over coffee, or on the clear days when they'd carried sandwiches down to Admella Beach to watch the ocean, she'd come close to giving in. Then Jas would remember that it wasn't her that Digby really wanted, and how far she'd come in her own journey. Sex with Digby was fun, which would be fine if she could separate her emotions from the pleasure, but she couldn't. One broken heart a year was enough.

'What about Simon?'

Jas sighed and toyed with the sultana she'd picked up, avoiding Em's gaze. The more time she'd spent with Simon, the more he'd proved to be kind, good-humoured, and a loving father. And his attraction towards her hadn't waned.

'I went out for a drink with him after work the other night.'

Em stopped spooning. 'You did?'

Jas nodded, still not looking at her.

'And?'

'He's nice but ...' She shrugged and held out her hands. 'You know.'

'No, I don't.'

'I'm not really interested.'

Em frowned. 'Then why go out with him in the first place?'

'I don't know. Because he asked me so many times I couldn't say no anymore?'

Except that wasn't even close to the truth. She'd done it to test how free her heart was but all it had proven was that, as appealing as Simon was, Digby still gripped it tight.

'He sounds a good man, Jas,' said Em, sliding the cake tin into the oven.

'He is.'

'But he's not Digby.'

Jas stared at the mutilated sultana. What was there to say? Of course Simon wasn't Digby, no one could be, but what was the point in lamenting the fact?

The sultana disappeared as Em began wiping down the bench. 'He visits often now.'

Jas looked up at the change of subject. 'Who visits?'

'Digby.'

Her mouth dropped. 'What? Here?'

Em ceased her wiping. 'He never told you, did he? He promised me he would. I didn't mention it because it was such a big step for him. I thought he'd want to tell you in his own way. Because you were once ...' She hesitated. 'Close.'

Jas shook her head. 'He never said a word.' They never discussed intimacies like that. Not anymore. Jas had made sure of it. Intimacies led to places she wasn't ready to go. 'He goes to visit the quarry, doesn't he? For her.'

'Yes. I think he's still trying to make sense of it. The way he lost her.'

'Do you think he ever will?'

'In time.' She glanced out to where Josh was working. 'Josh swears he already has, but I don't know.' Her voice trailed off as her gaze drifted upward, to the hill.

Jas knew the question Em was asking herself because she was silently asking the same. 'So why keep coming?'

Em's gaze returned to Jas and she smiled. 'I suppose you could ask the same of his visits to Admella Beach.'

'Vested interests.' At Em's frown she clarified. 'His garden. He wants to make sure I don't stuff it up.'

'Or maybe it's you.'

Jas wished she still had her sultana so she could throw it. 'It's not like that. We're friends.'

'Which you were before, and look what happened.' She clasped Jasmine's wrist and gave it a little shake. 'You want him, Jas, and I think he wants you. Perhaps it's just a matter of one of you making the first move.'

'Then what? I fall in love all over again and for what? Nothing. A bit of sex, someone to watch re-runs of *Doctor Who* with, a few laughs and no love because his heart still belongs to *her*.' With the last word she jabbed her finger towards the hill. 'It'd be Mike all over again.'

'Digby isn't Mike.'

'No. He's something far worse.'

'Digby? Worse than Mike? I know he's my brother and I'm biased, but come on.'

Jas said nothing.

'Jas?' Em braced her forearms on the bench and leaned forward to peer at her. 'You can't be serious. Can you?'

'It's the truth, Em. I can't go back, not with Dig, no matter how much I want to.'

'But why?'

Jas rubbed her fingers over her eyes. She felt tired now. Tired and worn down and discouraged. 'Isn't it obvious? Because he comes here to see her. I bet he still visits her grave all the time too. And I don't blame him for still loving her, truly I don't, but I can't risk it. I've come too far.'

'Oh, Jas, those things are just his way of working through his loss.'

'Yeah, and that's good. I'm glad and I hope he finds the peace and happiness he's looking for.' She flared her hand over her chest. 'But I need peace and happiness too, and I can't do it with someone whose heart belongs to someone else. Mike was bad enough, but Digby has a power over me Mike never had.'

'He wouldn't hurt you. You know he wouldn't.'

'Em,' said Jas, holding her friend's gaze, 'he already has.'

Which was why when she arrived home, Jas was dismayed to find Digby's farm ute parked alongside the garage and the man himself at Oxy's fence, giving the horse a thorough head scratch.

'I wasn't expecting you,' she said, wandering over with her hands shoved into the pockets of her parka.

Digby shrugged and continued to dig his fingers into the space between Oxy's ears. The horse's eyes were drooped in ecstasy at the attention. 'Finished at the farm so I thought I'd drop by.'

Jas nodded and scanned the sky. Low grey clouds were chasing one another, bellies fat and dark. Rain was coming. 'I have an assignment due in a week. I wasn't planning to work in the garden.'

Digby dropped his hands, suddenly awkward. 'Right.' He rubbed the back of his neck and surveyed the yard. 'Next week then?'

'If you want.'

He pursed his mouth. 'Something the matter?' He tried a smile. 'Other than me turning up unannounced.'

Jas sighed. She did not want to be having this conversation, not on the heels of what she'd just learned from Em. For a while she'd been careful with her hope that, over the long term, she might feel safe enough to make the transition from friendship into something serious. Digby seemed to be giving plenty of signals he was ready but now it was clear the attraction was garden-variety sexual tension. Exciting and fun until some poor sucker got hurt.

And as before, that poor sucker would be her.

'No. It's just me,' said Jas. 'Too much to do.'

'Know the feeling.' Digby regarded his feet for a moment. 'I like being with you, Jas. Home is ...' He lifted and hand and dropped it. 'I don't mean to be a bother. I'll leave you to it.' He gave Oxy's head a final rub and began walking away, only to stop and pull a plastic bag from his coat pocket. 'I nearly forgot.' He walked back and handed it to her. 'I saw this and thought of you.'

The bag contained a DVD, the latest *Doctor Who Christmas Special*, complete with bonus material. Jas would have bought it already, but with the money she'd been spending on renovations and the garden she'd had to curtail treats like this. It wouldn't look good for a future financial adviser to be behind on her mortgage.

She stroked the cover, feeling stupidly emotional. 'Thank you.'

'Maybe we can watch it some time. When you're not studying.'

'That'd be good.' Jas slid the DVD back into the bag and smiled.

'Maybe,' he said, and cleared his throat when the word came out husky, 'some other day when you have a free hour or two, you'd also like to check out Tyndale?'

Jas sucked in a deep breath. 'Sure. How does next Saturday afternoon suit?'

Saturday was one of Jasmine's rostered mornings at the building society. With Digby's farm in the opposite direction to Admella Beach, she didn't bother returning home to change, lobbing up at Tyndale still dressed in her skirt, blouse and heels, and full make-up. Not exactly suitable attire for touring a farm, but there was a change of clothes in the boot, and having stripped in the back of horse floats and behind screens made from draped horse rugs on plenty of occasions on the show-horse circuit, a farm shed posed no fears.

Digby—looking old-school agricultural in a pair of work jeans, long leather pull-on boots, battered oilskin coat and Akubra hat— regarded her outfit with apprehension.

Jas poked her tongue out at him. 'Don't fret. I brought something more suitable. I just need somewhere to change.'

'Follow me.'

He led her into the large blue steel shed close to where she'd parked. The massive roller doors were open, exposing bays filled with neatly arranged farm equipment and what she assumed was stainless steel wine-making paraphernalia, along with a bright green tractor.

The last bay of the shed was blocked off with unpainted particleboard sheeting, which held two separate doors. Digby pushed open the first and stood aside for Jas to peek inside. 'This is the lab.'

The room was small, perhaps three by three metres, with a white bench and built-in cupboards running around two walls upon which sat important-looking electronic machines, glass vials, and other scientific apparatus.

'What's all that for?'

'Testing sugars, alcohol, pH, that kind of thing. There's a fair bit of chemistry involved in making wine.'

'And you know what you're doing?'

'Not really. But I'm learning.' Digby walked to the next door and pushed it open. 'Lunch room.' He pointed to another door at the rear. 'Loo and bathroom through there. I'll leave you to it.'

When Jas emerged she found Digby leaning against his ute, staring at some red and white cattle grazing near the road.

'They look healthy.'

'Yeah. Ashton didn't run much stock so there's plenty of feed.' He straightened and looked her up and down. 'That's better. You look like you now.'

'I looked like me before.'

'Sorry. I'm just used to you ... you know.' Digby reddened slightly as he realised the hole he was digging himself into, and Jas suddenly cottoned on that he was nervous, which was weird. 'Come on. Time to see the important bit.'

The vineyard was behind the shed, on a sheltered slope running down to a small, sweetly meandering creek. The vines were dormant, their leafless canes pruned and tied to tightly strung trellis wires in orderly arrangements. To the right, a stretch of land had been ripped into vertical lines and spiked with new trellising and garlanded with lengths of poly pipe. Beyond the creek, where the land undulated into the distance like a green ocean, ancient manna gums formed majestic patterns with their gnarly branches and old sheep trails formed dark doodles against the verdant pasture. The region around Levenham had always been known for its bucolic beauty, but this was something else.

'It's stunning,' said Jas at the breathtaking view. 'Like something out of a fairy tale.'

'You like it?'

'I'm not sure "like" is the right word.' She smiled. 'You must be so proud.'

'I am.' Digby sucked in a breath as he surveyed his realm. Pleasure, maybe even satisfaction, lit his handsome face. 'I should have done this a long time ago.'

'I guess you weren't in the right headspace for it.'

'No.' He held eye contact. 'But I am now.'

For a long moment Jas couldn't drag her eyes from his. The connection shot her pulse racing. There was meaning in his words, in the heat of his gaze. She recalled Em's contention that Josh said Digby had come to terms with losing Felicity, and felt a surge of hope. Then his attention dropped to her mouth and in that single movement the connection faltered. Jas blinked and studied a curving vine, rubbing her upper arm. So he wanted to sleep with her? That was hardly new. She wanted to sleep with him too but that didn't mean it was wise.

She indicated the newly ripped area. 'What are you putting in there?'

'Chardonnay. I've already started.' Seemingly as eager as Jas to escape that awkward interlude, Digby strode towards it and ducked down a row. He gestured to a series of vines that looked not much more than dead sticks. 'Did these yesterday.'

Jas screwed her nose up. 'Are you sure they're alive?'

'Don't be fooled by their looks.' He crouched down in front of one of the vines and pointed out a series of small lumps. 'These are the dormant buds. That's where the new growth will come from in the spring. As the shoots develop, I'll train the most vigorous up the trellis.'

She did a quick mental calculation, multiplying rows by the number of vines, while Digby pulled out a weed and tossed it aside. 'It sounds like a lot of work.'

'It is, which is why I'm starting off small.' Digby straightened and dusted his hands on his jacket. 'I don't expect to make anything off the vines for a while. Fortunately the rest of the place is productive enough to earn its keep.'

He trailed towards the creek, chatting about his plans as he walked—the trial plot he intended to establish of lesser known varieties he thought might do well in the location, but that no one else had tested; cutting-edge viticultural techniques he wanted to implement; the oenology course he was considering.

With each elaboration Digby's confidence seemed to grow. There was passion in his voice. Spirit.

His enthusiasm increased as he drove Jas around the remainder of Tyndale. He pointed out paddocks he intended to renovate, areas he wanted to fence off for native plant regeneration, sites for a couple of new dams. When they'd covered most of the property he took her to a crest near the northern boundary where the view stretched wide and magnificent, and shyly admitted that this was where he'd like to build a home.

'That's a long way in the future though.'

'Why wait?' asked Jas. Clearly he loved Tyndale, and it wasn't as if he couldn't afford to build.

'Too much of a distraction. I want to concentrate on getting everything else right first.' He stared towards Rocking Horse Hill, a dark peak in the distance. 'I guess it'd be lonely too.' Digby glanced at her and quirked his mouth. 'Camrick has its moments but at least there's always someone around.'

'And your mum's cooking.'

'That, too.'

They shared a smile and again Jas felt the stirring of feelings she was trying her damnedest to keep suppressed. This Digby, with his strange mix of confidence, sheepishness and passion, was confusing her. She found it disturbing that he'd chosen a property where the hill could be seen so easily. Before her chat with Em, Jas had imagined he'd want to be far away from that hated memory. Now it was a distant but ever-present reminder.

Accident or deliberate homage? Jas desperately hoped the former, but bitter experience suggested the latter.

An opinion that would take more than a farm tour and *Doctor Who* DVD to change.

Digby took a sip of tea and squinted across Jasmine's garden. There was still an enormous amount to do: pavers and edging, plants to fill gaps in the understorey and add colour, the pond he'd decided would look good near the pergola. What was here made him proud though. Not of himself, but of Jas.

Pride wasn't the only emotion in his heart these days. Something far bigger and life-changing had lodged there. Something he'd never expected to feel again. Not with this intensity, but it was there. More incredibly, as he worked and laughed and enjoyed his too-short time with Jas, it kept growing. Now the feeling was so dominant every second spent with her risked it bursting out and ruining their resurrected friendship.

He slid a look sideways. Jas was perched alongside him on the edge of the timber deck, feet dangling, their denim-clad thighs and jacket sleeves almost touching. She was gazing fondly at Ox, who was resting near his fence, eyes droopy with slumber and bottom lip hanging like a sulky child. Jas's skin was pink from the morning's exertion, one cheek marked with a stripe of potting mix from the ornamental grasses they'd planted out earlier around the new pergola edge. Thanks to the sea breeze, her ponytail had developed even springier curls. The band holding it had loosened and tendrils had escaped to dance around her face. In the midday sun her eyes were deeply blue.

He'd once loved a woman with eyes even bluer, but that was before, in the time when he was different.

In the time when he was lost.

Jas blew a kiss at Oxy and slid forward to stand up, but Digby snagged the end of her fleece jacket. 'Sit for a while.'

She tossed him an amused look. Not that long ago she wouldn't have granted him even that, but in the weeks since Jasmine's visit to Tyndale something had changed. She'd softened towards him, become friendlier. 'Too much to do, as you pointed out on your arrival.'

He had. He'd come straight to Admella Beach from the vineyard where he'd spent the early morning seeding a specially formulated pasture mix between the rows of his new chardonnay vines. His mind should have been on his task, on schedules and expansion plans. Instead, as he steered the narrow tractor and seeder, all he could think of was Jas.

She was enjoying morning tea when he arrived. Coffee and a fat slice of carrot cake she'd bought from a CWA fundraising stall, savouring its delights with her unique brand of gusto. There were crumbs on her lips and she'd continued to make moaning noises with each bite in an attempt to tease him into joining her in a slice. Digby couldn't have eaten if he was starving. His stomach was too knotted at the sight of her mouth and half-closed eyes, and the memory of the sounds she used to make when they were lovers.

To cover up he'd faked impatience, muttering something about seedlings drying out and striding off to begin planting the border. Anything to get away, because another moment longer watching her eat and months of careful control would have been destroyed.

Now it was lunch time, and sexual tension had given away to something else—a need for a different kind of intimacy.

'Work can wait,' he said, even as his head warned he was treading dangerously. His heart though, wanted to linger with her.

Jas studied him for a moment, then placed her mug aside and eased onto her back, holding her hand to her brow to shade out the sun. 'This weather won't last.'

Digby turned onto his hip and propped on his elbow so he could observe her. Every night he seemed to dream of Jas. He knew her face, her body, yet come daytime each glance, each new angle, seemed to provide a fresh way to captivate him. 'Probably not, which is why we should make the most of it while we can.'

She rolled her head to the side. 'By not working?'

'Nothing wrong with a bit of relaxation.'

She twisted her bottom lip and blew sideways to shift a curl that had fallen on her cheek. Without thinking, Digby reached to stroke it out of the way, the tips of his fingers stalling on the silk of her hair and the satin surface of her skin. Her eyes widened before she quickly covered her surprise. Realising he'd crossed a boundary, Digby withdrew and sat up, but he could feel her gaze on his back.

They were friends. No benefits unless she decided. That was their tacit agreement. He had no right to that degree of closeness. But not sharing any at all with her was driving him insane.

His own mug was beside him, the tea cold. Digby rose and tossed it onto a garden bed. When he turned around, Jas was still lying down, hand back shading her eyes so he couldn't read them. Her jacket was open and the stretch of her arm had lifted her T-shirt up her belly, exposing a pale sliver of skin. Digby found himself staring like a teenager, fingers twitching.

'Dig?'

He blinked and forced himself to look at her face.

'What are you doing?' Jasmine's voice was soft, with a husky edge that made his groin tighten even further.

'Nothing. Waiting for you.' He regarded the mound of crushed stone they were meant to be shovelling, then lifted his face to the sky. 'You were right. We should get on with it.'

'What happened to relaxing?'

Her, that's what happened. Jas and her pale belly and blue eyes and sexy smile and husky voice that punched want into his chest. And elsewhere.

Which was the truth, but not an answer he could say out loud. He reached out his hand for hers. 'Come on, lazybones.'

'Lazybones? I'm not the one who wanted to stay flopping about.' She allowed him to pull her up and swatted him in the chest. 'Good thing I need the cheap labour or I'd have you fired for cheek.'

'You wouldn't dare.'

Her look turned sly. 'Wouldn't I?'

She was being playful, like she used to be when they were lovers, when moments like this usually led to sex. Digby tried to keep his breath even but his blood was rushing into places it shouldn't and he couldn't stop staring at her mouth. The subtle fragrance of her soap, overlaid with the earthy tones of sweat, soil and plants, curled around his senses, making it worse. He should step away now, while he could still stuff his secret desire back out of sight, but the thought of having sex with her again fogged his reason.

The hungry caw of a hovering seagull broke his thoughts. Digby took a quick step backward and shoved his fists into his pockets to ease his discomfort and camouflage what was happening in his jeans.

'You want your path laid or not?'

Her teasing smile and glittering eyes dimmed. 'Of course I do.' She gathered up the mugs and walked straight-backed to the house, wretchedness falling over Digby as he watched her go.

The screen door banged closed. He kept staring, rolling over in his mind the rapid change in her demeanour. What it might have meant.

Could she have wanted him to make a move?

It seemed unlikely. She had things going on, a life to rebuild. Perhaps, God help him, even the prospect of a relationship with that Simon, the one everyone promised was a decent bloke and would be a good match for Jas. Digby's jaw tightened. He stared at the house. Midday sun pounded his head. He needed his hat. He needed escape. He needed something, anything other than the thought he could lose her.

Digby had already lost once. He wasn't about to lose again.

He leaped up onto the deck and strode across to the screen door, swinging it open. The hall was empty. Jas was probably still rinsing the mugs in the kitchen. He hurried towards the front of the house only to stop when he glimpsed movement in her bedroom.

Jas was sitting on the edge of her bed, her face turned from the door, but he could tell from the way she was hastily swiping her cheeks that she'd been crying.

Digby stood in the doorway. He wanted to go to her but fear of getting it wrong had him anchored.

She sniffed, but kept her face averted. 'Aren't you meant to be shovelling?'

'I came to find you.'

'I'll be out in a minute.'

He took two steps into the room, willing her to look at him. She gave her cheeks a last brush and began smoothing the doona. Three strokes, four, five, until barely a wrinkle remained. As though aware another would only draw even more attention, she straightened. Digby took another step closer. One more and he'd be within touching distance.

She spoke stiffly to the window. 'You get started. I won't be long.'

'Jas?'

'It's okay. I just need a moment.'

'Why?'

The noise she made was a strange cross between a sob and a laugh. 'Because I'm an idiot, that's why.'

'You're not.' The next step brought him close enough to place his palm on her upper arm and slide it down to take her hand. 'You're beautiful and funny and clever and kind.'

Her fingers curled around his. He could hear the pull of her ragged breaths. Digby took another step so he could see her face. Her eyes were closed, her mouth too. There was a pained rigidity to her expression as though she was holding the threads of herself together.

He raised her hand and pressed the back of it to his lips. Her eyelids fluttered open. Jas stared at their joined hands, then at him, as a tiny furrow formed between her brows. Her voice was barely a whisper. 'What are you doing?'

'Taking the chance I should have never let pass the first time round.'

Her mouth opened and quickly closed. The furrow deepened. She tugged her hand free from his and gripped her elbow. 'The first time round wasn't anything more than a way for us to lick our wounds, Dig. You know that.'

'Doesn't mean it didn't matter.'

Biting her lip, she stared hard at the window, elbow gripped even tighter, arm wedged across her belly like a shield.

'Jas?'

She shook her head, loosening a teardrop. He reached to gather it with his finger and rested his palm against her cheek. Her skin was hot, her mouth trembling. 'Please look at me.'

It was a few seconds before she complied, infinitely long seconds in which each heartbeat seemed to thud and vibrate in a noise too loud for the moment.

'Jas, do you think ...' Digby faltered, suddenly afraid, but aware if he didn't take this chance it mightn't come again. That she'd snatch away even the little he had of her because he'd broken the rules they'd set. He cleared his throat, desperate to get this right. 'You and me ...'

'Do you still love Felicity?'

'Yes. No.' He winced. That hadn't come out the way he wanted. 'I'll always love her, Jas. I won't ever be able to stop that. But if you're asking whether I've finally moved on, then the answer's yes. I'm ready. For us. If you still feel the same as before, and want there to be an us.'

She didn't say anything.

Digby swallowed. 'Do you?'

'How do you know? That you're ready, I mean?'

He knew because he loved her, and if there was one emotion he knew intimately it was that.

'I just do. I can feel it. When I'm around you ... I want you, Jas. Have done for ages.'

Jas made a dismissive noise. 'That's just sex.'

The weariness of her tone made his heart clench. 'No. It's more than that.'

She shook her head.

'It's the truth.' He cradled her face with both hands, desperation thickening his voice. 'I'm ready. For everything.'

'Everything?'

'Yes.'

Jas stared at him and Digby thought for a moment he had her, but her quiet words indicated otherwise. 'I want to believe you, I really do. But you hurt me.'

'I know and I can't tell you how sorry I am for that.' He stroked her cheeks with his thumbs. 'I promise you, this is real. How I feel about you. About us. It's big, Jas.'

She didn't speak for a long moment, but her gaze was intense on his and there were two tiny wrinkles between her brows. Then her face relaxed and with it rose his hope. 'You mean it?'

Digby nodded. 'Yeah, I mean it.'

Slowly, she began to smile.

'So,' he said, smiling in return, his heart floating somewhere in space. 'You and me?'

'Okay.'

'Just okay?'

A grin burst across Jasmine's face. 'All right then, yes.' Then her lips were on his and she was breathing yes after yes into his mouth as if she couldn't say it enough.

Laughing and kissing, they tumbled onto the bed, both talking at once. Stupid, nonsense things that were as perfect as they were silly. Why it took so long. How close they'd each been to forcing the issue. How dumb they were for pretending they were happy with only friendship. Their fears that it would never happen. Their elation at finding each other again. The relief of feeling each other's touch.

Jasmine's shirt and bra were on the floor, Digby's hand on the corner of exposed flesh where her unbuttoned jeans had been pushed down, when he paused to hover above her. He absorbed her look, the pinking of her skin, the hooding of her eyes, the swell of her mouth. Her nipples were turgid, her ribcage rising and falling rapidly with her excited breathing.

'Christ, I missed this,' he said.

She arched towards him, her own gaze sweeping his chest and downward. Wanton, sexy. The way he loved her. 'Me, too.'

The feeling in his heart turned thick as he realised how intense his feelings were, how close he'd come to letting her slip from him. 'I don't want to hide us this time. You and me, as a couple. We play this for real. No keeping us secret.'

She smiled and curled her hand around his neck, whispering as she drew him close. 'Try to stop me.'

CHAPTER
31

Though the sky was dotted with clouds and a light southerly had risen, flapping shirts and disturbing hats, spring was at last making itself known across the south-east. In a sheltered, fragrant bower of Em's abundant garden at Rocking Horse Hill, where Jas stood watching Digby return from his pilgrimage, it could have been blissful summer.

If not for a last layer of uncertainty.

Goosebumps skittered along her skin as she stepped back into the breeze. Em broke from her conversation with Josh's sister Sally to move alongside and join Jas.

Josh and Em had invited close friends and family out to Rocking Horse Hill for a barbecue. To celebrate spring, so the story went, but they weren't fooling anyone. There was news afoot and the mood was jubilant, despite the breeze.

Josh's nephews and nieces were wearing off lunch by playing kick-to-kick with their fathers in the grassy area between the house and the donkeys' paddock. Adrienne and Josh's mum Michelle, both green fingers and excellent cooks, were wandering around Em's verdant vegetable patch, comparing notes. Samuel, Tom and Josh were holding an animated discussion about the forthcoming local football grand final, while Harry and Summer were strolling around the orchard, hand in hand. Over near the drinks table, Granny B was holding court with the remaining guests.

Half an hour earlier, Digby had asked if Jas minded him visiting the quarry for a while. What else could she do but swallow her selfish hurt and say it was fine? That horrible dark place was where Felicity had died. Who was she to tread on his need to visit there?

'He looks happy,' said Em.

From the way Digby was moving, unhurried and relaxed, it seemed true. 'I hope he is.'

Em's gaze was probing. 'And you?'

Jas smiled. 'I'm kicking along pretty well.'

More than well, as long as she discounted the twinges of self-doubt and worry that attacked her whenever Digby visited the quarry memorial or Felicity's grave. Perhaps it would always be this way, sharing half of him with a dead woman. He'd promised he was over her and she had to believe it was true, but the uncertainty remained.

Em took a sip from the glass of water she was holding. 'You didn't look it for a moment.'

'Must have been wind. I blame those lamb and burghul patties your mum made.'

Em laughed. 'You're such a terrible liar.' She sobered again, focus back on Digby as he neared the stables. 'I know it's hard but don't blame him for wanting to talk to her.'

'I don't.' She never had. Communication with Felicity was part of his life, part of his grief, and deserving of respect because it came from the deepest and purest of love.

Josh called out for Em. 'Oh,' she said, checking behind, 'I'm wanted.' Em touched Jasmine's arm. 'Look after Digby for me. This might hurt.'

Jas followed Em's progress as she made her way through the gathering to her husband. Their embrace was immediate, eyes glittery with smug love. She turned back to Digby, now walking towards her. Jas held out her hand, grateful when he took it without hesitation. Higher up the volcano's cone, where the quarry's maw acted as a wind tunnel, the wind would have been biting. His hand was cool but his smile was warm. Even so, Jas searched his face, checking what memories lay there, how close they were to the surface. But Digby appeared fine—flush-cheeked from the southerly but his normal self.

'Wrap around me,' she said.

The warmth of his chest settled against her back. His arms enveloped her shoulders, crossing over in front of her. Digby nuzzled his cold nose against her neck and she felt the width of his grin against her collarbone as she tried to jerk away. He gripped tighter, thawing his skin against hers.

Jasmine's chest swelled. The urge to utter the words neither had said grew inside her. Jas kept her mouth shut and waited for it to pass, as it had on so many other occasions. Now was not the time, not after he'd been to see Felicity.

'You're all soft and cosy,' Digby breathed into her ear.

'And you're cold. Fortunately I'm hot enough for both of us.'

'Don't I know it.' With the words he snuck in a tickle of her left breast, shooting tingles into Jasmine's groin.

'Do you mind?'

'No. Can we go? I've had enough and I want you alone.'

Jas laughed. 'So what else is new? You'll just have to wait.' She twisted in his arms, expecting to find playfulness. What she discovered was a serious intensity that made her stomach sink. Despite the tickle it wasn't sex he was after, which could only mean he wanted to talk. Avoiding his eyes, she toyed with the buttons of his jumper. 'You were gone a long time.'

He shrugged.

She kept fiddling. He was in a mood she didn't understand, and if Em and Josh announced what she suspected they were going to, Jas wasn't sure how he'd take it. 'Was it ...'

Was it what? Good? Cathartic? Heartbreaking?

'It was the same as usual.'

Jas wished she had the courage to ask what the 'usual' was. Fear at what he might answer kept her from prying, it was part of the pact she'd made with herself to keep looking forward instead of back. For this to work it was what they both needed to do.

His attention drifted and he grimaced. 'Trouble coming.'

Jas turned around. Granny B was heading their way, tumbler of Scotch in one hand, Muffy at her heels. Her outfit was what Jas could only describe as French sailor chic: red and white striped top, navy trousers, tailored cropped jacket, also in red, and a jauntily angled navy beret.

'Come to tell us your yacht's leaving?' Digby asked.

'Don't be ill-mannered, Digby.' Although she said it without rancour. Watching them the entire time, she took a long slurp of Scotch, rolled it round her mouth and swallowed. 'A pity the wind has come up.'

Jas exchanged a glance with Digby. Granny B was making small talk, which typically meant she was up to something. Both tilted their heads to the side.

Granny B flapped a hand. 'Oh, do stop that. You look like a pair of owls.'

'What do you want, Gran?'

The old lady gave a disdainful sniff. 'Can't a grandmother talk to her grandson and his girlfriend?'

'Of course you can,' said Jas. 'Once you tell us what you're up to.'

'Who says I'm up to anything?'

Jas lifted an eyebrow.

Granny B huffed. 'If you must know, I enjoyed an excellent lunch with Barry McLintoff on Tuesday.'

Which was hardly news. Granny B and the mayor managed to fit in lunch most weeks. If it weren't for the that fact that Barry was only ten years or so younger than his lunch companion, Jas might suspect they were indulging in an affair. A man in his late sixties was unlikely to fit Granny B's penchant for fit young toy boys.

'You should be very proud of me, Digby.'

'I should?'

'Indeed. After much negotiation, I,' she pronounced the word with a haughty lift of her chin and all the grandeur of an empress, 'have finally secured a wine festival for our town.'

Jas let out a whoop. 'You sly old duck. How the hell did you manage that?'

Granny B's eyes twinkled. 'Let's just say I used my charms.'

A groan rumbled through Digby but Jas could only laugh at Granny B's audacity. Maybe Barry McLintoff was fit enough after all. She leaned across to kiss her on the cheek. 'Well done.'

'It was rather.' She held out the other powdery cheek to her grandson. 'Congratulations are in order, Digby.'

He dutifully obliged with a peck. 'Good work. So when's the big event?'

'The weekend ending Art Week, to encourage visitors already here to linger. Of course the long-term goal is to hold it separately over a few days, but one must crawl before one gallops.' She poked Digby with a scarlet fingernail. 'You'll be able to offer your first vintage. Speaking of which, have you decided on a name for your label yet?'

'As a matter of fact I have.'

Both Jas and Granny B regarded him with astonishment.

'Since when?' asked Jas.

He shrugged. 'About half an hour ago.'

The sinking feeling returned to Jasmine's stomach. He would name it after *her*. From the stiffening in Granny B's shoulders, she held the same fear.

As if to fortify herself against unpleasantness, Granny B downed the final finger of Scotch. 'Well, spit it out.'

For some reason Digby looked at Jas when he spoke. 'Gratia.'

Granny B harrumphed. Jas simply stared.

She could guess what it meant: some sort of derivation of thanks. The question was where the thanks were directed. He'd decided on the name at the quarry, yet his gaze was intense on hers.

'It's ...' Jas tried to come up with something appropriate, and failed. 'Nice?'

The corner of Digby's mouth twitched and he bent as though to elaborate, but Josh began clanging the back of a knife against a beer bottle, calling for attention. 'I'll explain later.'

Everyone turned towards the verandah, where Josh and Em had perched themselves. Feet shuffled, hands twitched, and excitement buzzed in the air like bees. Adrienne was wringing her hands, already on the verge of tears. From the way she was biting her bottom lip and blinking, Josh's mum Michelle wasn't far behind.

Jas checked on Digby. He smiled and gently stroked a crooked finger down her cheek, letting her know he was ready and okay. She covered her hand over his and squeezed.

'Thanks, everyone, for coming today,' said Josh. 'From the way you're all staring at us I guess you've figured out what we're going to announce. So to put you out of your misery, yes, Em's pregnant. The baby's due in February.' He squeezed his wife against his side. 'Poor Em's in for a long summer.'

If Digby had reacted in any way negatively, Jas missed it. As soon as the announcement was out, he was applauding and cheering with the rest of them.

'Did you know?' Jas asked, as they waited behind Josh's two sisters to offer their congratulations to the ecstatic couple.

'I guessed.'

'From Em?'

He shook his head. 'Josh. He's been strutting around like a rooster lately. I figured the reason had to be a baby.'

'She wanted this with Josh so badly,' said Jas, suddenly feeling teary. It was all so romantic. Em and Josh falling in love at a young age, breaking up and then finding each other again. Now, after months of trying, they were going to complete their family. 'I'm so thrilled for them.'

'I am too. Josh deserves this.' He paused before adding a quiet, 'They both do.'

Champagne appeared. Toasts were made. Advice on pregnancy and parenthood flowed. Desserts were brought out—pavlova from Michelle's kitchen, some sort of complicated layered chocolate and hazelnut torte from Adrienne's. Em managed to trump them both with an icing-slathered white chocolate mud-cake, cheekily pink on one side and blue on the other, along with the proclamation that no one, not even the parents, would know the baby's sex until it was born.

'If she was conceived here,' declared Granny B, strutting past, this time with a flute of champagne, 'she'll be a girl.' She nodded towards the volcano. 'It knows how to bring them on.'

'Do you think she's right?' asked Jas, after Granny B had moved away from the food and guests to indulge in a celebratory cigar.

Digby's arms were around her chest again, keeping her warm. Soon the sun would fall past the house, plunging them into shadow. Then the cold would settle in properly and they'd either have to move inside or leave. As happy as she was for Em and Josh, Jas wanted the latter.

'Hard to say. She has a fifty-fifty chance.'

'Look at you two,' said Michelle Sinclair, beaming at them. 'So in love.' She sighed deeply and turned to regard her son and daughter-in-law. 'I'm going to spoil that child very badly.'

'You and Mum both,' said Digby.

'It's what grandparents are for.' On cue, one of Josh's nephews hurtled around the side of the house, footy under one arm and wailing, his red-faced elder brother hot in pursuit. Casting them a wry smile, Michelle hurried to referee.

Jas continued to watch the sunbeams strike the garden like a blessing. Her heart was beating hard from Michelle's comment. It was the first time anyone had ever mentioned the L word. There'd been plenty of comments about how good she and Digby looked together, how pleased they were to see them happy, but no one dared to use the term love. Perhaps, like her, they feared his true heart still belonged to Felicity.

'Jas?' His voice was husky and barely above a whisper.

She closed her eyes. 'Yes?'

'Are we?'

The pound in her chest escalated. Jas swallowed. If she said yes and he said no there'd be no hiding her despair. Knowing her rampant emotions, she'd probably burst into noisy sobs and ruin everyone's day. 'Are we what?'

'What Michelle said.'

She squeezed her eyes even tighter shut. To tell the truth or not? Jas sucked in two more breaths and opened her eyes. It was time.

'Yes. I mean, I am. I can't speak for you.' She winced at how dumb that sounded. This was meant to be a profound moment. The time when she revealed her heart. Instead she sounded as if what it held was embarrassing.

'Yeah, you can.'

She could?

'I don't understand.'

Digby gently placed his hands on her shoulders and eased her round to face him. 'It's true. I love you.'

Glancing at the hill was almost reflex. 'But ...' She bit her lip.

'Look at me. Not there. At me.' He grabbed her hand and held it against his chest. 'There's only you in here.'

She sniffed but it was too late. 'I'm going to bawl.'

'I thought you might, which is why I wanted to take you home earlier so I could tell you there, but Michelle beat me to it.' He bent close, a smile in his voice. 'Can you hang on? My grandmother's watching.'

She sniffed harder and made a noise that was half-laugh, half-sob. 'Of course she is.' Gathering all her strength, Jas wiped her watery eyes. 'She thinks this is all her doing. You'd better take me home before she comes over to gloat.'

'No goodbyes?'

'Not unless you want to.' Em would understand. Josh too. Granny B would have to lump it.

'Nope.'

Digby steered her away from the gathering. At the end of the path, Jas chanced a glance back. Granny B was holding her champagne glass up in salute. Behind her, Em had her hands folded in front of her mouth as if in prayer. Josh had one hand on her shoulder and was grinning. Every one of them held an expression filled with delight. Though they might not have heard Digby and Jasmine's conversation, clearly they'd caught the meaning of the moment.

Jas grinned in return and leaned into the wonderful solidity of Digby's body.

'So what does it mean?' she asked from the passenger seat as Digby negotiated the road to Admella Beach. 'The wine label.'

'Gratia?'

'Yes.'

'It's Latin for thanks. Thanks from me to you. For all you are, for all you've done.'

Jasmine's jaw hung. 'But I thought ...' Her throat closed over. Prickles itched her eyes. Not good. After so far managing to hold it together she was going to bawl, which would be fine if she cried delicately but Jas never did anything delicately.

Digby glanced at her. 'You thought it was for Felicity?'

'You were up the hill when you came up with it.'

'I was, and the whole time I was thinking about you. How amazing you are. How crazy I am about you.'

'Really?'

'Really. You brought me out of darkness, Jas. I thought I was broken forever. That I'd never be able to love anyone again. I was angry and empty and had no hope, then you came along with your *Doctor Who* and sympathy and things began to change. Everything became that little bit brighter. You made me smile again. Reminded me what it was like to be with someone who cared.'

'I did more than care, Dig. I fell in love with you.'

He frowned a little. 'Christ, I'm sorry. I knew you felt strongly but I didn't realise that.'

Jas shrugged. 'I didn't want to pressure you.'

'It's a wonder you didn't hate me after the beach.'

'Believe me, I had moments when I wanted to but I couldn't. You weren't leaving me to be mean, you were leaving because you thought it was right.'

'I was wrong.'

She had thought so too, for a long time, but time had given Jas perspective.

'No. If you hadn't left neither of us would have discovered our own strengths. We needed that break.'

'Maybe.' He thought on it for a moment. 'I suppose if I hadn't been so bored and missed you so much I wouldn't have bought Tyndale.'

'And I wouldn't have reassessed what I wanted. So it worked.'

He glanced from the road to her. 'Doesn't take away the fact I hurt you.'

'That's okay. I survived. Just don't do it again.'

'I won't. That's a promise.'

A promise. After almost four years of them with Mike she should have been cynical about its worth, but this was Digby. A man who'd cared so much about her he'd forsaken his own comfort so Jas might find happiness. His promise was worth everything. *He* was worth everything.

'Thank you.' Utterly inadequate, but her brain was full of dopamine and God knows how many other hormones let loose by her love-drunk body, and it was all she could think of to say.

Digby winked at her. The gesture was so sexy her stomach lurched before bolting heat to her groin. 'You can thank me properly when we get home.'

This was firmer ground. Jas rolled her eyes and pretended exasperation. 'There you go, thinking about sex again.'

'Yeah, right. Like you don't think about sex all the time.'

'Only with you. And I think about other things too.'

'Like love?' There was hesitation in his voice. Neither of them was used to the step they'd taken, but it would come. Their love was a topic Jas intended to explore in great detail.

'There's been quite a bit of that.'

He reached for her hand and gripped it. 'The way it should be. You, me, no one else. Just us and what's in our hearts.'

Jas smiled and leaned back against the seat, fingers entwined with Digby's, his smile as content as hers.

Absolutely the way it should be.

ACKNOWLEDGEMENTS

I had such a wonderful time writing this book and was thrilled to finally get Digby and Jasmine's story down, but stories never reach shelves without a lot of people helping along the way. My special thanks to agent Clare Forster of Curtis Brown and the clever team at Harlequin Australia, including but not limited to Sue Brockhoff, Rachael Donovan, Annabel Blay and editor Di Blacklock. I've enjoyed working with you enormously. To Harlequin's clever cover designers, THANK YOU! You exceeded even my dreams with this cover, and may have created a few new ones with it too. Beautiful work.

Also huge thanks to my special writing buddies who keep me sane and are always up for a laugh, a whinge, or a glass or two of fizz. Extra mention must go to Rachael Johns for being such a great support and always being available at the end of an email, text or phone.

Most of all to Jim. My rock. All heroes should be modelled on you.

Turn over for a sneak peek.

The Country Girl

by

CATHRYN HEIN

OUT January 2018

Chapter 1

There were locals who claimed Fortune had always gazed favourably on Castlereagh Road. Perhaps that was true, back in the day—the long-lost good times before Fortune's ugly cousin Tragedy crawled in and tore a family's heart apart.

For Patrick Lawson, those people couldn't have been more wrong. Castlereagh Road was where despair battled hope in a war where victory for one was as unthinkable as the other was impossible.

Some days he never felt like this. Some days Patrick imagined he was happy. That the two-kilometre drive from his parents' farm to Springbank was the same as it had been eight years ago, when he was seventeen and he and Maddy had first fallen in love. That she'd greet him in the yard like she always did, grinning the smile that made his heart feel proud and possessive, and other parts of him hunger.

Some days he deluded himself that the world was okay, and the joyful life he'd mapped out could still happen. Then a day like today would rise up and kick him so hard it was like it was *his* body shattered beyond repair. *His* brain wiped of its human beauty.

It was the horse that set him off. Again. Hanging over the post and rail fence with his dark brown eyes and snip of white on his nose, and stupid twitching ears constantly moving as if guided by intelligence. Khan spotted the ute and tossed his head and flared his nostrils in happy greeting, and for one blinding moment all Patrick wanted to do was smash his foot on the accelerator and drive as fast at the fence as the engine would allow.

Instead he kept a steady pace down the drive while sweat beaded his brow and his grip turned slippery, and he pretended not to notice as Khan followed his progress at a lively trot and then broke into a canter and veered away from the rail, racing, racing, like Maddy would now never do.

It took Patrick a good few minutes under the blast of the car's aircon to set himself right. He never liked for Grant and Nicola to see him when he was like this. They had enough to cope with as it was without the burden of his anger. And he sure as hell never wanted Maddy to sense it.

He got out and slammed the door shut and glanced at the paddock. Khan had cantered away to the far end, below the slope and out of sight. Patrick hoped he rotted there.

There was music playing, drifting through the screen door. He could hear Nicola singing softly, probably preparing dinner. Patrick wondered why the familiarity of it didn't soothe him.

'Hey,' he said, knocking on the jamb and entering.

Nicola looked up from the spuds she was peeling. 'Oh, Patrick. Hi.' She smiled. 'Sorry for the singing. I thought you were Grant. He's due back from town any minute.' She nodded towards the radio. 'You can turn that down now.'

'And spoil your fun? I'll leave it.' He paused. 'How is she?'

Nicola's smile slipped a fraction as it always did when talking about her daughter. 'Oh, not too bad.'

Which meant not too good. Patrick glanced at the doorway that led to the living-dining area, now converted to Maddy's day room. He could only see the edge of the bed. Nicola must have wheeled Maddy to the French doors so she could look out.

'Need me to do anything?'

'No. Grant helped me bath her earlier. You go on in.'

He nodded, stepped towards the door and took a breath. No matter that he did this every day, he still needed that pause. He was a man stuck in a loop of disbelief, as though each night erased the truth and each afternoon he had to face it again for the first time.

A heartbeat was all it took, a fortifying half-breath and then he could stride in, smiling the love he still felt. That he'd promised he'd always feel.

'Hey, babe.' Patrick kissed her hello, closing his eyes and letting the soft skin of her cheek caress his own as he breathed her in. Maddy smelled of the body wash Nicola favoured, and the massage oil she used for the muscle-stretching exercises.

He moved back a little, searching Maddy's eyes for a hint of recognition, anything, but they remained unfocused. In the early days Patrick used to fret that she might be blind but the doctors assured him she wasn't. The blankness was simply a symptom of her minimally conscious state, plus there were moments when Maddy definitely recognised her parents. Followed by really shitty times when she would notice Khan through the window and make a movement that could have been anything, but Nicola swore was Maddy reaching.

Something she never did for him.

Spotting a crust of dried saliva, Patrick automatically snatched up a wipe and cleaned it away, then caressed her hair and moved across to the bookshelf. A velvet box sat in one corner. He picked it up and took out the ring, and shifted back to gently unhook her curled left wrist and hand, and slide it on her ring finger.

He sat with her hand cupped in his, the diamond sparkling in the afternoon sun, and began to talk.

'First of the weaner sales today. Prices were strong. Most of them northern buyers. They've had good rains up there and are looking to restock, plus the export market's picking up. About time. Things have been pretty crook.'

He paused and stared out the French doors at the view of the patio and garden, and paddocks beyond. Grant and Nicola had been graziers once, before the accident. In the past they would have been with Patrick and his dad at the saleyards on a day like this, assessing the lots, watching the auctioneers in action, nodding in approval at the rally in prices, but most of Springbank had been sold, leaving only a few hundred acres around the house. Patrick's dad had bought the 600 acres that bordered their own property, Wiruna, along the southern side, and the rest had gone to the McDayles.

'You would have enjoyed it, Mad. Everyone upbeat.' He returned his gaze to her, amazed at how she could look the same yet so different. The accident had left her once-fit body twisted and wilted, despite regular physical therapy. The golden tones of her skin had faded long ago, leaving it almost translucent.

Her face remained beautiful but also heartbreakingly wrong. The nose he used to plant affectionate pecks on was still straight and fine, her cheekbones high. Nicola kept Maddy's dark eyebrows as precisely shaped as they'd always been, and the thick lashes surrounding her chocolate brown eyes remained long and still fluttered against him in butterfly kisses when he pressed close. Her hair was clean and silky but was now kept shorter for practical reasons. No thick pony tail to give teasing tugs.

His darling Maddy, and yet not.

The mouth he'd kissed so often moved involuntarily in yawns and contortions. Her eyes rolled. Frowns appeared and disappeared at random. There was no speech, only incoherent vocalisations. Sounds unlike anything Patrick had ever heard, like something in agony. He hated them. They made his gut clench in fear for her, that she was trapped and hurting and calling for help.

Nicola believed she understood every nuance of voice and movement. That Maddy was communicating to her with what she had left. Grant humoured his wife but in secret had revealed to Patrick that he thought it was only wishful thinking. The doctors were certain that the slow transition from coma to vegetative state to minimal consciousness had progressed as far as possible given the severity of Maddy's brain injury. But hope was a living thing, and every real or imagined sign of improvement brought with it the idea that the experts could be wrong. That one day those who loved her would have her back.

'I heard a bit of news today.'

He rubbed his thumb over the diamond of her engagement ring. The ring that had taken him four long months to save for. The ring that he'd slid on her finger while bended on one knee like a cartoon Prince Charming as she'd nodded over and over, and half-sobbed, half-laughed above him.

Patrick studied Maddy's expression and saw nothing. His fingers tightened. Maybe he shouldn't tell her. Maybe there were some things she didn't need to know.

But he'd made a pact from the start that he wouldn't keep secrets. That their lives and those of their families and friends would remain as talked about and dissected as they'd always been. This was news he would have told her before. No matter how bittersweet, he'd tell her now.

'Clipper finally found the balls to ask Bec to marry him. She said yes. Wedding's going to be in November apparently. They want …' He inhaled deeply as his throat seemed to fill with gravel. 'They want to start a family straight away. Clip reckons he's wast—'

Patrick got up, breathing and blinking hard. He shoved his hands into his pockets and faced the doors, away from Maddy, ordering himself to pull his shit together. He peered at the sky, feigning interest in the weather while he tried to swallow the painful thickness from his throat.

A keening noise sounded behind him. Patrick closed his eyes and pressed his forehead against the glass, wanting to smash it through. It was Maddy making one of her sounds. Nothing more. Yet the keen kept coming. To his heart it was like a wail.

He forced himself to turn around and felt like he'd been sledgehammered. Maddy's mouth was curled and her eyes were scrunched shut. It wasn't an unusual contortion but today it was different. Today, sliding from the corner of her right eye, was a tear.

'Patrick?'

Nicola was at the doorway, tea towel in hand. He stared at her with his mouth open as Maddy continued to keen.

Frowning, she stepped into the room. 'Patrick, what's the matter?'

He stared back at Maddy.

Nicola walked briskly to her daughter's side and inspected her face. The worried expression softened as she gently brushed Maddy's fringe aside. 'It's okay, honey. Dinner's not far away.' She smiled at Patrick. 'Her stomach's probably hurting. She was in a mood and didn't eat much at lunch. I'll bring her bowl in a minute.'

But Patrick knew better. It wasn't hunger, it was grief and anger at the unfairness of life. The same emotions boiling up in him. Except in his case he didn't want to just shed a tear, he wanted to wreck things, destroy, the same way Maddy's life had been destroyed, the way Nicola's and Grant's had. The way his own had.

He didn't look at Nicola as he shoved past. His thoughts were elsewhere, on the rifle Grant kept. The gun safe and ammunition.

Patrick had been coming to Springbank his entire life: as a typical farm-kid neighbour, as a teenager in love, and as a man. He knew pretty much where everything was kept. Most of all he knew where the keys to the gun safe were stored.

'Patrick?'

Nicola's startled voice carried up the hall but he ignored it. He rummaged in the office drawer and plucked out the keys. Minutes later he had the rifle and bullets.

When he turned back into the hall Nicola was there. She took in the gun, her eyes turning enormous.

'What are you doing?'

He shook his head and pushed past her.

'Patrick?'

He kept walking.

'Patrick!'

The kitchen screen door opened with a squeal and banged shut behind him.

'Oh, God. Oh, God. Grant! *Grant!*'

The outside air struck Patrick's face, cooling the tears there. Unaware he'd even been crying, he swiped at them as he marched. Grant must have come home. Patrick had to hurry now, before the older man stopped him.

Khan was back grazing near the fence. He whickered when he spotted Patrick and immediately wandered over to hang his head over the top rail.

'Good boy,' crooned Patrick, holding his hand out and stroking the horse's forehead. He rubbed, sniffing back tears, hating even touching the animal but needing it calm for what he was about to do. Satisfied, he stood back to aim the rifle.

The horse stayed still in anticipation of more attention.

Patrick's teeth were clenched, his breathing ragged. One squeeze, one gentle little squeeze, and the thing he hated most would be gone. He breathed in and sighted, honing in on an imaginary crossing of diagonal lines drawn between Khan's eyes and ears.

More tears slithered, bringing with them another noise. It was a few heartbeats before he realised it was coming from his own mouth. A kind of inhuman rasp.

He swallowed it away, shoved the butt harder against his shoulder and tightened his grip on the forestock. Khan blinked, the skin above his eyes wrinkling as if in confusion.

One squeeze. Just one.

Footsteps approached. Grant stood alongside him. Patrick kept focus on the wavering barrel, trying to hold it steady. He wasn't a cruel man. This wasn't about suffering. This was about eliminating the reminder of everything that had gone wrong. A bullet in the right place would ensure that.

Patrick sniffed and blinked, and braced his legs harder. Slowly he drew in a breath and began to move his finger.

A worn hand rested on the barrel. 'Don't, son.'

'I have to.'

'You don't.'

Patrick shook his head but he eased back on the trigger. He couldn't fire with Grant this close.

'It wasn't his fault. It wasn't anyone's.'

But it was. It was absolutely the horse's fault. Maddy hadn't done this to herself.

'Pat, it won't change anything.'

'I just want to go back. To the way it was.'

'I know, son. We all do.'

There was no pressure on the barrel, just the weight of Grant's hand, but it felt like the sky pushing against him. Patrick clenched his jaw. He needed to do this. Why couldn't Grant see that?

'Don't kill the thing she loves.'

'I hate it.'

'I know. But shooting Khan won't help you and it'll only hurt Maddy. You don't want that.'

The barrel dropped, Patrick's head with it. He would never hurt Maddy. Never. He let out a sob as the older man took the rifle from his hands and placed it on the ground. Then Grant's arms were around him and his choked voice was promising Patrick that the pain would pass. It was just a moment. They all had them now and then.

'It'll be all right, son,' said Grant, patting his back one last time and letting go.

'Yeah.' Patrick rubbed his hand across his mouth, wiping his tears as he went. 'Yeah.'

But they were words he was finding harder and harder to believe.

talk about it

Let's talk about books.

Join the conversation:

 on facebook.com/harlequinaustralia

 on Twitter @harlequinaus

www.harlequinbooks.com.au

If you love reading and want to know about our
authors and titles, then let's talk about it.